I would like to take this long-overdue opportunity to thank Diane Pearson, the President of the Romantic Novelists' Association, for first introducing me to my wonderful agent, Judith Murdoch – and I only hope Judith feels the same way, after enduring my sense of humour for several years.

TRISHA ASHLEY

A Winter's Tale

avon

AVON

A division of HarperCollins*Publishers*
1 London Bridge Street
London SE1 9GF
www.harpercollins.co.uk

This Paperback Edition 2017

6

First published in Great Britain by
HarperCollins*Publishers* 2008

This edition published by HarperCollins*Publishers* in 2017

A catalogue record for this book is
available from the British Library

ISBN-13: 978-0-00-819179-5

Typeset in Minion by Palimpsest Book Production Ltd, Falkirk, Stirlingshire

Printed and bound by CPI Group (UK) Ltd, Croydon, CR0 4YY

MIX
Paper from
responsible sources
FSC™ C007454

For Margaret James, a friend for all seasons.

Prologue: The Dream

*Mother, what did you foretell, when you held my hand
so tightly and wept, then said that the future could not
be altered and I must go to the manor of Wynter's End
in your stead?*

From the journal of Alys Bezzard, 1580

No house as ancient as Winter's End was ever entirely silent:
even at eight years old, Sophy Winter knew that. Crouched
on the floor of the gallery, she felt like Jonah sitting in the
belly of the whale, surrounded by creaks and sighing,
feeling, rather than hearing, the heavy heartbeat of a distant
long-case clock and the sharply flatulent rattling of the
water pipes.

She peered through the wooden banisters, down into the
depths of the stone-flagged Great Hall where her grandfather's King Charles spaniels lay in a tangled, snoring,
comatose heap on a rag rug before the log fire.

Nothing stirred in the darker shadows beyond. Satisfied,
she ran to the end of the gallery and climbed onto a curved
stair rail that seemed to have been designed for little fingers
to grip; then, clinging on for dear life, she slid with an exhil-
arating, rushing *swoosh!* of cold air, right to the bottom.

Slowing down was always tricky. Fetching up with a
thump against a newel post bearing a carved cherub's head,

1

she lost her grip and would have fallen off, had she not been caught and rather roughly set on her feet.

In the ensuing silence, a moth-eaten stag's head dropped off the wall and landed with a clatter, glassy eyes vacantly staring at the intricately plastered ceiling.

Sophy looked up and her impish, round-cheeked face, framed in dark curls, not unlike the carved cherub's behind her, became instantly serious. Grandfather didn't like her to use the front stairs, let alone slide down the banisters. In fact, Grandfather didn't seem to *like* her at all, and it was somehow Mummy's fault – and where *was* Mummy? If Sophy hadn't been sitting on the gallery floor watching for her for so long, she wouldn't have been tempted to slide down the banisters in the first place.

Grandfather stared back at her, ferocious bushy brows drawn together over a formidable nose and an arrested expression in his eyes. 'A Pharamond, that's who *your* father was,' he said slowly, 'from over Middlemoss way. Why didn't I see that before? But which one . . . ?'

Nervously Sophy began slowly to back away, ready to make a run for the safety of the kitchen wing.

'Hebe!' he shouted suddenly, making Sophy jump and all the spaniels start awake and rush over, yapping.

'What are you bellowing for? You sound like a cross between the Last Trump and a cow in labour,' Great-Aunt Hebe snapped, appearing suddenly round the carved screen. Her fine, pale, red-gold hair stood out around her head in a flossy halo and she brandished a large wooden spoon that dripped a glutinous splat onto the flagged floor. One of the spaniels licked it tentatively: you never knew quite what Hebe was cooking up.

Sophy gave a little nervous giggle – Grandfather *was* loud enough to wake the dead slumbering in the grave-yard, and since that was her least favourite of Aunt Hebe's biblical bedtime stories she found the idea slightly worrying . . .

'Aunt Hebe,' she said urgently, running to her and grabbing a handful of slightly tacky cotton apron, 'the dead people won't climb out and walk round the graveyard in their bones, will they?'

'No, they'll all wait for the end of the world,' Hebe said. 'It was just a figure of speech.'

She looked over her head at her brother. 'What's up?'

'The child was sliding down the banisters again.'

'Well, she *is* a child. You did it, I did it, Ottie did it . . . we all did it! Now, let me get back to my stillroom. Come on, Sophy, you can give me a hand.'

'Wait,' he said. 'Take a look at her and tell me which family round here has black, curly hair? I don't know why I didn't realise it before: she's a Pharamond.'

'What, from the Mosses?' Hebe held Sophy away and stared at her. 'What nonsense! There's been the occasional dark-haired Winters ever since Alys Blezzard married into the family in the sixteenth century – and anyway, all the Pharamonds *I've* ever met have had dark blue eyes, not hazel, and narrow, aquiline noses. If anything, Sophy's nose turns up.'

'She's got the look,' he insisted.

'I don't think so – and does it matter anyway?'

'Of course it bloody matters! They're all mad as hatters in Middlemoss!'

'Sophy isn't mad.'

'Oh, no? What about her imaginary playmate?'

Aunt Hebe shrugged. 'Lots of children have invisible friends.'

'Alys isn't *always* invisible,' Sophy said in a small voice, but Grandfather didn't seem to hear her.

'I'm sure I'm right,' he said, 'and why wouldn't Susan say

3

who the father was, unless he was a married man? God knows where she's been the last few days, but if she doesn't mend her ways, she'll find herself out on her ear.'

At this inopportune moment Susan Winter slid in through the great oak door, setting down a colourful carpetbag on the floor; tall, fair, slender and pretty in a long, floaty dress with little bells that chimed softly as she moved, smelling of sandalwood and patchouli. Like a fairy, Sophy always thought, not a dark little hobgoblin like herself.

'So you're back, then? Where have you been?' Grandfather demanded, switching that fierce gaze to a new victim. 'And, more to the point, *who* have you been with? Another married man?'

Susan, who had been smiling vaguely at the group, her blue eyes unfocused, flinched and took a step backwards. 'W-what do you mean? Some friends took me to the Reading Festival to see Genesis, that's all, Daddy!'

'Friends! I know the riffraff you call friends! Layabouts and hippie scum! I'm telling you, Susan, I won't tolerate any more of your loose behaviour, so if you want me to house you and your bas—'

'*Not* in front of the child!' protested Hebe, and Sophy was suddenly snatched off her feet and carried away through the baize-lined door to the kitchen wing. It slammed behind them, cutting off the escalating sound of shouting and weeping.

'What's Mummy done now?' Sophy asked, as she was set back down again. 'Is it my fault, for making Grandfather angry? Aunt Hebe, what has Mummy—'

'Quickly!' Aunt Hebe said, flapping her apron and shooing her through the kitchen past Mrs Lark, like a reluctant hen into the coop.

The cook, who was single-mindedly pounding steaks with a sort of knobbly wooden mallet, looked up long enough to remark, 'Bile pills, that's what *he'll* be needing, before the night's out,' before resuming her assault.

'Deadly nightshade, more like,' muttered Aunt Hebe. 'Come on, Sophy, into the stillroom – I've got rose conserve on the stove, and I don't want it spoiled. And you should know by now that your grandfather is all bark and no bite.'

Although Aunt Hebe was tall and rangy and not at all cosy, she always smelled of roses, which was safe and somehow comforting, unlike Mummy's patchouli, which made Sophy feel excited but vaguely unsettled, much like Mummy herself did.

And after Mummy took her away late that night, leaving behind Winter's End, Aunt Hebe, the little dogs, and everything loved and familiar, she always did find the scent of roses a comfort in an alien world, long after she had forgotten the reason why.

Chapter One: There Must Be an Angel

*Despite my fears I found Wynter's End most delightfully
situated above a river, with terraces of sweet-scented
knots. Sir Ralph was greatly pleased to see mee – but
not so the mistress. Mary Wynter is Sir Ralph's second
wife and I perceived from the moment she set eyes on
mee that she was mine extreame enemy, though I know
not why unless she hateth every woman of less years
than herself.*

From the journal of Alys Blezzard, 1580

No matter how many times I dreamed of the terrible day
that culminated in my mother taking me away from Winter's
End for ever, I still woke up with my face wet with tears
and a sense of anguish – *and* guilt.

Was the final argument that precipitated our flight *my*
fault for provoking Grandfather once too often? I had been
a mischievous child, always getting into trouble.

My mind groped desperately after the disappearing echoes
of once-familiar voices, the last lingering fragrance of Gallica
roses ... but as always they slipped away, leaving me with
only the fragmented memories of my early childhood to take
out and examine, one by one, like faded treasures.

Since my grandfather's brief visit earlier this year
everything had been stirred up again and old wounds had

reopened. But surely it shouldn't still hurt so much. It was so long ago, that settled time before my mother and I, cast out of Eden, had moved around the country from squat to travellers' van to commune. Eventually, like random jetsam, we'd washed up at a remote little Scottish commune, where we'd run out of road. And then later my poor feckless mother had *literally* run out of road . . . but as Marlowe said, that was in another country: and besides, the wench is dead.

Dead and gone.

It was still dark and I reached for the bedside lamp, only to find that it wasn't there. Then, with a sickening jolt under the ribcage, I remembered that it was already packed away – and why.

I had to pad across the cold, bare floorboards to switch on the ceiling light before climbing back into bed. The white candlewick coverlet, with its raised diamond pattern and central flower motifs, suddenly reminded me of the intricately moulded plaster ceilings of Winter's End. Strange that I hadn't thought of that before, but perhaps, subconsciously, that had been why I bought it.

Yet I barely ever allowed myself to think of Winter's End – not with my conscious mind, anyway – for that was the past, with the door forever shut, and the present had to be dealt with.

And what a present! That day I would be moving out of the tied cottage where Lucy and I had lived for over twenty years, because my elderly employer recently suffered a bad fall and the consequence was that my job had come to an abrupt end.

At first I thought everything would work out fine, especially when Lady Betty's nephew arrived to look after things until she recovered enough to come home. Conor was a chubby, balding man who always reminded me of an amiable frog, though unfortunately he turned out to be a complete toad.

On previous visits to Blackwalls he had seemed fond of Lady Betty and otherwise entirely harmless (apart from a slight tendency to invade my personal space and squeeze my arm with his plump white fingers, while telling me how grateful he was to me for looking after his aunt). That opinion lasted right up to the point where he got power of attorney and had poor Lady Betty, confused but weakly protesting, whipped straight from the hospital to an expensive retirement home. Personally, I don't see that keeping fourteen cats, and telling visitors to your stately ruin that you are the reincarnation of Ramses the First, is anything *like* enough reason to be declared incompetent to manage your affairs. She'd managed them perfectly well for years, with a little assistance from her faithful staff, and she *never* wore the headdress and robe in public.

I think Conor's betrayal was a much greater shock to her than the fall, which I told him straight the day I found out about it – and then he had the gall to come round to the cottage that very evening, well tanked up, to try to exercise some kind of medieval droit de seigneur, insinuating that keeping my home and my job depended entirely on how 'friendly' I was.

I had an instinctive knee-jerk reaction and droited his seigneur until his eyes watered. Pity Lady Betty hadn't been able to do the same, once he had charmed and weaselled the 'temporary' power of attorney out of her and showed his true colours.

The upshot was that Conor gave me immediate notice and put my cottage and other assets up for sale – and of course without a job I couldn't get a mortgage to buy it myself. In any case, I couldn't match the price the people buying it as a weekend cottage were prepared to pay. Let's face it, I couldn't even raise the deposit.

When my husband, Rory, did his vanishing trick and left me holding the baby over twenty years ago, I took the job of Lady Betty's general factotum and moved to a remote little Northumbrian village with Lucy, mainly because it offered a cottage as well as a small salary. There weren't many applicants, or I don't suppose I would have got the job at my age and with a small child, despite having had lots of relevant experience working for the mistress of a small Scottish castle ever since I left school.

But the minute we arrived at the village I knew it was *meant* to be, because I recognised the place. My mad mother and I (and her man of the moment) had once set up home in our vans in a lay-by just outside it, and for several days no one had tried to move us on. That was exceptional, since normally we seemed to be as welcome as a bad smell.

So you see, serendipity brought us here, and Lady Betty loved children and was quite happy for me to fit my work around Lucy's needs. But my pay wasn't huge, so I'd staggered from one financial crisis to another over the years, with never quite enough money to make ends meet, juggling bills and later helping Lucy out at university when her student loan and part-time job weren't quite enough.

If only the interest wasn't so high on that small loan I took out . . . and if only I hadn't had to increase it further still to cover nearly two thousand pounds of vet's bills for poor Daisy! And all in vain, though of course I had had to *try* because she was Lucy's dog too, and we both loved her. And if only I hadn't economised the month before she got ill by letting her pet insurance lapse, it would have been perfectly all right.

If only . . .

Why did everything have to go pear-shaped at once? My

life was like a volcano: it lay dormant for long enough to let me think it was acquiescent, and then suddenly tossed out hot rocks.

My mother would have said, 'Accept your karma and go with the flow, darling,' but just look where doing that got her. She flowed over the Atlantic, over California and down a rather steep canyon. And then, since she still had her old passport, they returned her to Winter's End for burial: a toss of the dice and right down the snake to where you started out, though perhaps not in quite the same pristine condition.

But it was not in my nature to be miserable for long, and soon fingers of silvery sunlight began to gleam around the edges of the black cloud of despondency. I knew something good was coming, even if not precisely what, because I have a touch of the second sight from my witch ancestor, Alys Blezzard.

And after all, there were hours yet before I had to hand over the keys of Spiggs Cottage to strangers and always, *always* in the past something had happened to avert calamity at the last minute ... though perhaps calamity had never been on such a grand, overwhelming scale before. I mean, I'd put down roots here at last, shallow and tentative though they might be, and it was the only home Lucy had ever known. I'd been so determined that Lucy would have the secure and settled upbringing I hadn't had myself once Mum had torn me away from Winter's End.

I sat up, hugging my knees. It wasn't too late to save the cottage – the contract wouldn't be exchanged until later that morning. There was still time for the cavalry to come riding over the hill to rescue me, bugles blowing and flags flying, just as they always had.

I was filled with a sudden glow of unfounded optimism. Getting up, I sprayed on a liberal, fortifying blast of

Penhaligon's Elisabethan Rose perfume (the only extravagance in my life, unless you counted Lucy), pulled on a red jumper and jeans that clung to my abundant curves, and ruthlessly dragged a hairbrush through wildly curling dark hair.

Then I went to make coffee and await the arrival of the postman. The last post . . .

No, I wouldn't think like that! The postman would bring *good* news – a reprieve. Maybe I'd won the lottery (despite never buying a ticket) or the Pools. Or perhaps Conor had metamorphosed overnight from a cockroach into a human being and, repentant, he would refuse to sell the cottage and instead beg me to stay there rent free for ever (no droit de seigneur included).

My best friend, Anya, who believes our guardian angels watch over us twenty-four seven, would say that she heard the hushing whisper of mine's wings as she (or should that be *it*?) rushed to the rescue.

I only hoped my very own Personal Celestial Being wouldn't collide on the doorstep with the cavalry or there would be feathers everywhere.

Chapter Two: Distant Connections

I applied all the cures and simples my mother taught mee so well, and young Thomas Wynter's suffering is much alleviated, though it is clear to mee that he will not make old bones.

From the journal of Alys Blezzard, 1580

I'd been so *positive* I could hear those hoofbeats and the *swoosh!* of angel's wings coming to the rescue – but either I was mistaken or they took a wrong turn, for Spiggs Cottage was lost to me.

I couldn't understand it . . . and even several days later, I still couldn't quite believe it. My life had gone full circle so that I'd have to start all over again, twenty years older but still with no money, qualifications or assets other than a vintage Volkswagen camper van with about twice the world's circumference on the clock, inherited, by rather permanent default, from my mother.

Lucy and I had always used it to travel about with friends in the holidays, but it began to look as though I would have to live in it again permanently, until someone in the village came to the rescue with the offer of a big static caravan for the winter.

Though grateful for any temporary roof over my head, there was nothing quite so freezing as a caravan out of season. The cold pierced from all directions, like living in an ice cube. I wouldn't have been surprised to find a shivering polar bear at the door asking to be let out.

But at least it was a roof over my head until the site reopened in March, and it was far larger than either the van or the cottage. This was just as well, since the materials for the little round silk and satin crazy-patchwork cushions I made and sold mail order took up quite a bit of space.

My cushions, each feather-stitched patch embroidered and embellished, were *very* upmarket. Luckily the buyers couldn't see the raggle-taggle gypsy making them, or the charity shops and jumble sales where I bought the old clothes to cut up for pieces!

I blew on my frozen fingers and read over the letter I had written, breaking the news that we were homeless to Lucy, so very far away teaching English in Japan.

Darling Lucy,

My job at Blackwalls has finished rather suddenly. Poor Lady Betty was making a good recovery from her fall, but her nephew got power of attorney and took charge of things, with disastrous results. Do you remember Conor? You said when you met him once that he was a slimy little creep, and you were quite right – he has put Lady Betty into a home and now seems to be selling up the whole estate.

In fact, he's sold our cottage already, but though it was sad to leave it I am ready to have a change of scene and a new job. Meanwhile, Dana – you remember her from the Pleasurefields camping site? – is letting me live in one of her static caravans rent free, which is very kind of her. I'm making a special cushion as a thank-you.

Don't worry, I packed up everything in your room very carefully, and the contents of the cottage are stored in the next-door caravan. I can stay until they open up again in March, but I don't suppose I will be here very long. There are one or two nice-looking jobs advertised in *The Lady* magazine, with accommodation included, so I've written off with my totally impressive CV. You can't say I haven't had a lifetime's experience of looking after ancestral piles, even if I've only ever really been a glorified cleaner-cum-tour guide.

I'll let you know when I hear anything and hope to have a lovely new home for you to come back to when you return.

Love, Mum xxx

Who was I fooling? Lucy would be on the phone to me two minutes after she got the letter . . . which was why, I suppose, I was taking the cowardly way out and posting her the news.

I hoped, by the time she got hold of me, to have a new job and a new life lined up somewhere else. The applications lay on the table, ready to post except for stamps – and then I suddenly remembered it was the post office's half-day and the clock was hurtling towards twelve.

Leaping up, I dragged on my jacket and flung open the door – then teetered perilously on the brink, gazing down into a pair of eyes of a truly celestial blue, but even colder than the caravan. Missing my footing entirely, I fell down the two metal steps into the surprised arms of an angry angel.

Maybe Anya was right after all, I thought, as he fielded me neatly – except that angels are presumably asexual, while this one was undoubtedly male, even if his short, ruffled hair was of corniest gold. He smelled heavenly too, *and* expensive. I think it was the same aftershave that Conor used, at about a million pounds a molecule, but it smelled *so* much better on my visitor.

He set me back on my feet, stared down at me in a puzzled sort of way, then said, 'I'm looking for Sophy Winter – I was told she was staying here.'

'She is – you've found her.'

'*You're* Sophy Winter?'

'Well, I was last time I checked in the mirror,' I said tartly.

'But you can't be! You don't look like—' he began, then broke off to give me a comprehensive once-over, checking off my minus points on some mental list: dark hair – check; hazel eyes – check; unfashionably generous hourglass figure – check; supermarket jeans and jumble-sale jumper – check. Number of Winter attributes scored: nil.

'Right . . .' he said doubtfully, 'then you must have been expecting me. I'm your cousin, Jack – Jack Lewis.'

'But I haven't got any cousins,' I protested. I certainly didn't recall any . . . and surely even my mother would have mentioned them if I had.

'I'm a very *distant* cousin and since I didn't go to live at Winter's End until shortly after you and your mother had left, you wouldn't remember me. But I'm sure you've heard of me?'

'No I haven't,' I began – and then the full import of what he had just said sank in, shaking me to the core. I exclaimed incredulously, 'What do you mean, *you* lived at Winter's End?'

I'd always imagined Winter's End and Grandfather and the twin aunts and the little dogs and *everything* just going on for ever, like a scene securely enclosed in a snowglobe. Even if I could never get back into that closed world again, at least I had been able to take it out and give it a shake occasionally . . . But now it seemed that this stranger had almost immediately taken my place there!

He misread my amazement as suspicious disbelief and flushed crossly. 'If you must know, my mother was your grandfather's cousin and we lived in New Zealand. She died when I was five, and when my father remarried I was sent back home.'

'Oh,' I said uncertainly, because despite his hair not having the true red-gold Winter tint he *did* have a look of my mother, now I came to consider it – or how she would have looked in a rage, if she'd ever had one. While 'feckless' and 'stoned' would have been the two words that summed my mother up best, she was good-natured to the point where it was a serious handicap in life. 'But why are you here? And why did you think I would be expecting you?'

I must have sounded as genuinely bewildered as I felt for the anger in his eyes slowly thawed and was replaced by something like speculation. 'You mean you don't know anything about me? And you haven't heard the news yet?'

'No! And what news?'

'That William Winter is dead, for a start,' he said bluntly.

'Grandfather's *dead*?' Things seemed to blur dizzily around me and I sank down onto the top step of the caravan.

'Dead for months. And while I, as the last male descendant of the Winters, get the title, I don't suppose you will be surprised to learn that he left Winter's End and everything else to *you*.'

My vision cleared and I looked up to see that he was eyeing me narrowly.

'W-Winter's End? *Me*? You're mad or . . . or there's some mistake!' I stammered. 'He's only seen me once since we left, and he didn't seem to like me any more then than he did when I was a little girl!'

'*Once*?' It must have been obvious that I was telling the truth, for his expression slowly altered to a rueful smile of singular and quite dazzling charm, exuding such warmth that, despite my state of numb shock, I found myself returning it.

'Sorry, I seem to have got hold of the wrong end of the stick. I've made all the wrong assumptions! What on earth

17

must you think of me? Look, let's start again, shall we?' He took my hands and pulled me to my feet. 'Sophy, I'm *delighted* to meet you at last!'

Then, enfolding me in his arms, he kissed me on each cheek before taking my hands again and stepping back to look at me with what appeared to be genuine admiration.

But do not think I was entirely inactive during this embrace – no, I was actively inert and acquiescent. I hadn't had my hands on such a gorgeous man within living memory, even one with a dodgy temper who had just told me things I didn't want to hear – *and* some I couldn't believe.

You try dating in a small village, while juggling a low-paid and exhausting job and turning your hobby into a little business on the side, all under the critical and jealous eyes of your daughter. None of my potential suitors had made it past first base. If I actually managed to find a babysitter and got out of the house with a man, you could bet your bottom dollar Lucy would be running a high fever or throwing out interesting symptoms before I reached the end of the street.

And I hadn't had much more luck since she went off to university. All the men in my age bracket seemed to be looking for skinny young blondes. That, or they had a serious impediment they forgot to mention, like a wife.

So now, enfolded in softest cashmere and anaesthetised by Amouage Gold Pour Homme, if I had any conscious thought at all it was along the lines of, Yes! Bring it on!

Ten minutes later we were sitting in my icebox of a caravan drinking coffee and talking like old friends.

'So you see,' Jack was explaining, 'we didn't even know old William had found you until the will was read. He'd tried and failed to discover where you and your mother were in the past, of course. Then when your mother ...' he searched for a tactful phrase, 'when your mother was brought

18

home, he tried again to trace you – but on the wrong side of the Atlantic, since we assumed you would have been in America with her. After that we thought he'd given up, until we discovered he'd secretly left you Winter's End and,' he shrugged and smiled charmingly, 'we thought *you* must have finally got in touch with *him* and managed to persuade him into leaving you everything.'

'No, he traced me through an advert for cushions I put in a magazine, and a few months ago he simply turned up out of the blue. And although it was lovely to know he'd never stopped trying to find me, I don't know why he bothered, because he spent most of the time lecturing me about where I'd gone wrong in life and which decisions I could have made better. He'd hired a private eye to dig into my past, so he even knew things I'd forgotten. He didn't look much different from how I remembered him, either . . . except he seemed frailer and his hair was white, of course.'

I looked back at my early memories of him: a tall figure with the Winter pale red-gold hair, bright blue eyes and the beard of a biblical prophet. (The only one of those attributes I don't regret not inheriting is the beard.)

'So that's the only time you saw him?' Jack asked, accepting another refill but declining anything to eat. I'd laid out before him everything I had in the way of refreshments – two cherry-topped coconut pyramids and a carob-covered rice cake – but going by his expression, I don't think he recognised them as food.

I took the rice cake myself, the pyramids, crumbly and sticky, being a bit hard to eat neatly in company. 'Yes, he just turned up one afternoon on my one day off – but of course the private eye would have told him when I'd be in. Lucy was home and she is *so* defensive that she and Grandfather spent most of the time trying to score points off each other.' I shuddered. 'They actually seemed to enjoy it, but

I hate arguments and fights. He didn't suggest we visit Winter's End, either – he said it was too late and would just stir things up.'

At the time that had hurt and I had wondered why he had gone to the trouble of finding us at all, but then he had added that he wasn't in the best of health and had just wanted to assure himself that we were all right.

Which we were, of course – totally penniless, but all right.

'Who's Lucy?' Jack asked.

'My daughter. She's twenty-two, and out in Japan teaching English for a year . . . at least, I hope it's only a year, because I miss her terribly.' I cupped my hands around my own mug and stared down into it. 'But you did say that Grand-father left me Winter's End, didn't you? I didn't imagine that? Only I'm sure you *can't* be right because – I mean – why on earth would he? It's too incredible to be true! And in any case, surely I would have been told about it by now if he had?'

'You haven't, because the solicitor had strict instructions from my uncle to wait until the estate was settled before contacting you – or telling the family where you were. He knew there would be a fuss because, you see, I was brought up expecting to take on Winter's End as the next *legitimate* heir . . . even if you turned up again, which of course you didn't. But it wasn't entailed on the next male descendant, so he was free to leave the estate to who he liked.'

'So, why did he do it?' I asked, ignoring this slur on my birth.

'My uncle and I didn't see eye to eye about some things: he just couldn't understand modern business methods, for a start. And he'd been draining the money that should have gone to keep the house in good repair into his garden restoration schemes instead, but when I remonstrated with him, he flew right off the handle.'

20

'So when the will was read you naturally assumed I'd schemed to get him to leave Winter's End to me?'

'Yes – sorry about that! But you can understand how I felt, can't you? The old man must have been senile to do such a thing – I love the place and I'd grown up believing it would one day be mine, that's what made me so unreasonably angry. As soon as I managed to find out where you lived I thought I'd come up here and make you an offer for Winter's End, but temper got the better of me!'

'Make me an offer?' I'd started to be convinced I was in some strange dream and would wake up again any minute. 'You mean, you want me to *sell* Winter's End to you?'

'Yes, just that. I could challenge the will because William was clearly unhinged when he wrote it – but this way seems more civilised.' He leaned forward and took my hand in his, looking down into my eyes in a way that made the caravan seem suddenly very much warmer. 'Listen, Sophy, it's the only practical thing you *can* do, because I'm afraid you've inherited a total white elephant and all the liabilities that go with it. Winter's End is falling down and has been for years, because of all the income being diverted into the garden restoration. He even took out a bank loan against the house to fund the final stages. It's got wet rot, dry rot, woodworm . . . you name it, and it's got it. And there aren't even any major assets you could sell off. There was one decent painting, a Stubbs, but William arranged for it to go to the nation in lieu of death duties.'

Despite the mesmerising effect his nearness and those devastating blue eyes were having on me, it occurred to me that Grandfather seemed to have had it all worked out – not the actions of a senile man.

'But *you* still want Winter's End?' I asked him curiously.

'Yes, it's my family home, after all, where I was brought up . . . I love it. And I'm a property developer, a very

21

successful one, so I know what needs to be done and I can afford to do it.'

'I understand. I was just starting to feel the same way about my cottage, even though it didn't belong to me.'

He looked seriously at me, his eyes frank and earnest: 'Please let me buy it back, Sophy! I'll even pay well over the market value – how about that? It can't mean anything to you, can it, since you left it when you were a small child? And I don't suppose you could afford the upkeep, anyway.'

I said slowly, 'No, I – no, how *can* it mean anything to me? I was eight when I last saw it.'

'*Liar!*' said a voice in my head – Alys's voice, tenuous and far away, as if speaking down a very bad telephone line, but instantly familiar to me even after all these years.

Alys, are you back again?

But if she was, she was now silent. Maybe my subconscious had simply ascribed her voice to my innermost thoughts? For of course I did long for Winter's End – but the Winter's End of my childhood, before Jack took my place and everything changed – and there was no way back to that.

'You could come and visit whenever you liked anyway,' he offered, with another one of those glorious smiles. 'We're family, aren't we? And now I've found you, I've no intention of letting you get away again!'

I sighed and shook my head. 'You know, it's *so* ironic! I was waiting for an angel to come to the rescue – but now it's too late. Only a week ago I'd have jumped at the chance without a second thought, because I could have bought my cottage and not had to move out.'

He looked puzzled, so I explained what had happened, and then he suggested I could still make the new owners of the cottage an offer they couldn't refuse.

'I could, but they are rich City types who've bought it for a holiday home and I don't think they would be likely to sell it even at more than its value. They're busy ripping out every original feature and tossing the cottage's entrails into a skip, so all the things I loved about it have already gone. If there is one thing my early life has taught me, it's that when everything changes, you move on – and you can never go back and expect things to be the same.'

Not even at Winter's End, except in my dreams . . .

'But you could buy somewhere new?' he suggested. 'I expect you've got friends here?'

'Not really. I know a lot of people but I've only got one *real* friend, from way back, and she tends to move around a lot.'

In fact, she moved around permanently; but Anya, with her dreadlocked red hair and her home made from an old ambulance, was probably a world away from the sort of people my cousin Jack knew.

'Well, now you've got me,' he said, giving my hand another squeeze and then letting it go. 'Whatever you decide, we'll always be friends as well as distant cousins, I hope. But I know, when you have thought it over, you'll realise that the right thing to do is to sell Winter's End to me, to keep it in the family.'

'I expect so, but – well, none of this seems real at all yet. I need time to think – and hear the news officially from a solicitor, too, before it sinks in properly and I start to believe it!'

'You will. Hobbs is the family solicitor, though he is semi-retired, and he said he was going to call in and see you personally on his way up to Scotland. I expect he's hard on my heels. Oh, by the way,' he added casually, 'I promised Aunt Hebe that I'd ask you if you had the book, and if you have, take it back with me.'

'The . . . *book*?' I stared at him blankly while the clanging of alarm bells sounded in my head. 'Do you mean that

23

Victorian children's book of gruesome stories from the Bible that Aunt Hebe used to read to me? I did take that away with me – still got it, in fact, though I didn't inflict it on Lucy. It used to give me nightmares, but I was horribly fascinated by it!'

'No, she meant Alys Blezzard's household book, a little, really ancient notebook of recipes. It's a priceless bit of family history, and it's been missing since your mother ran off. They just sort of assumed she took it with her.'

I shook my head. 'No, sorry. Mum told me all about Alys – she liked the idea that she was descended from a family notorious for witchcraft – but she never mentioned any book.'

'Are you *sure* it wasn't among her things?' he pressed me. 'It's quite an heirloom, so Hebe's always been upset that it's missing.'

'She didn't leave a lot of possessions behind when she went to America, so I'd have noticed something like that.'

'And she wouldn't have taken it with her?'

'No, I'm sure she didn't. I helped her decide what to take and did the packing. We had to buy a suitcase especially, because we didn't think her old carpetbag would stand up to aeroplane baggage handlers.'

'Then Aunt Hebe *will* be disappointed!' He stood and pulled out a slim gold case from his pocket. 'Look, I'll have to be off now, but here's my card – ring me when you've seen Hobbs and had a think about my offer. Selling Winter's End is the only sensible option, you know . . . and remember, whatever *anyone* says, I love the place and only want the best for it.'

'OK,' I said, slightly puzzled, and he put his arm around me and gave me a squeeze. He seemed a very hands-on kind of person, when he wasn't miffed. But I understood how he felt about Winter's End because I, too, had loved my little cottage.

'And at least you have inherited something I, a mere female, can't – the title,' I pointed out. 'Sir Jack!'

'Very true. And of course there *is* a long family tradition of intermarriage in the family, especially when a girl is the heiress . . . much like now, I suppose,' he said, with a teasing smile. 'Keeps the title and the property together.'

'I – yes, I suppose it does,' I agreed, slightly taken aback.

'Oh, Sir Jack, this is so sudden!' he said in a mock-modest falsetto, and I laughed.

'But seriously, Sophy, I don't intend letting you go out of my life five minutes after I've found you, whatever you decide,' he said, and kissed me again before he left, this time in a less than cousinly way. But that's OK – he *is* something less than a cousin, after all.

After he'd gone everything seemed a bit leached of colour and lifeless, including me. I drank about a gallon of Rescue Remedy, then went out to the VW and fetched a wooden box from the ingenious special hiding place that one of my mother's friends had made for it (and her stash) long ago.

It was rectangular, quite deep and surprisingly heavy, and when I opened the lid the delicious aroma of ancient books wafted out. I should know that smell, I've dusted libraries full of them in my time. Anyway, I adore books. That's where I acquired most of my education. The scent of old leather bindings promised escape into another, comforting world, much as the scent of roses once reassured me that Winter's End still existed just as I left it.

Carefully I lifted out *A Little Child's Warning: A Treasury of Bible Stories* with its faded gilt edges and the cover depiction of a small child praying, eyes cast up to heaven, but my icy hands fumbled and almost dropped the book.

A positive cascade of pressed roses fell out, with the papery whispering of old ghosts.

Chapter Three: Diamond Cut

They have given mee a chamber in the solar to be near Thomas. I spend much time there – or in the stillroom, which is sadly neglected, Lady Wynter having no interest in those arts in which it should be her pride to be accomplished. I walk in the gardens when I can spare the time and pick herbs. The plants I need that grow wild in the woods and pastures are harder to obtain and some must be picked by the light of the moon . . . To slip out here unseen is difficult.

From the journal of Alys Blezzard, 1580

'Anya!' I said, when I finally managed to reach her. 'My guardian angel is a golden Lucifer – diabolically handsome and slightly sulphurous round the edges. He's hot – and I think I'm in love!'

'How do you know?' she said, sounding as if she was standing in a metal oil drum (which she might have been – you never know with Anya).

'That I'm in love?'

'No, that your guardian angel is a Lucifer.'

'Oh – because he visited me yesterday,' I said. 'He's sort of a cousin – a very distant cousin.' Then I told her all about my grandfather's death, my inheritance – and Jack's offer.

'And he was furious when he first turned up, because he

26

thought I'd somehow managed to brainwash Grandfather into leaving Winter's End to me. Once he realised I hadn't he was really, really nice.'

'I bet he was,' she said, sounding unconvinced. 'But after all you've told me about your childhood at Winter's End and how you feel about the place, I can't understand why you don't sound delirious with pleasure.'

'Well, for one thing I'm still stunned and wondering why on earth Grandfather did it; and for another, it isn't the Winter's End I remember, because it's clear that Jack took my place soon after I left,' I said slowly. 'Apparently the house is really run down and there is a big outstanding bank loan against it too, which Grandfather took out to pay for his garden restoration.'

'What were you expecting, a Shangri-La that always stayed the same?'

'It *did* always stay the same, in my imagination – and part of me thinks it's better left like that, and I should never try to go back there.'

'Well, they always say, be careful what you wish for,' Anya said breezily, 'but actually, I always thought the only reason you started working in stately homes was because you were trying to recreate a bit of what you once had – and just think how useful all that experience will be now! Doesn't the thought of doing such a major clean-up get your juices flowing?'

She knows me only too well.

'I wish *my* angels would conjure something up like that, Sophy. I'm getting a bit tired of wandering around now,' she confessed to my surprise, because she has been on the road since she was eighteen and left the commune. We did this sort of role-reversal thing. When I arrived at the commune I was tired of moving about and just wanted to settle down, while she was fed up with the whole thing and attracted to the kind of life I'd had with Mum.

'I think when Guy gets a job I might settle somewhere near him,' she added thoughtfully. 'He's got lots of interviews.'

'I'm not surprised; he got a first-class degree.'

Guy is Anya's son, a year younger than Lucy, and was always bright – and very determined. When he was eleven he insisted on staying with his grandmother in Scotland during the school terms and got grade A *everything*.

'How is Lucy doing?' Anya asked.

'She seems fine, but I wish she wasn't so far away. And some man keeps pestering her, which I find worrying. She says he seems fascinated by her being so tall and blonde. There have been a couple of cases of British women being stalked and even murdered in Japan.'

'But Lucy is very sensible, Sophy. I'm sure she wouldn't put herself at risk.'

'Perhaps not, but if I *did* sell Winter's End to Jack, she could come home and I would be able to pay off her student loan and buy a cottage somewhere. Then maybe we could start up a business together and—'

'Don't you do anything hasty,' she warned me, 'especially with this relative of yours. He doesn't sound like any kind of angel to me, but he *does* sound the kind of clever, tricky, devious man you always seem to go for.'

'I don't know what you mean by "always". I can count on one hand the number of men I've been out with since Rory left me,' I said with dignity and some modesty, leaving one or two of my brief encounters with absolute no-hopers out of the reckoning. 'And I can't imagine what I've said to make you think that about Jack! He's a really genuine, lovely person – and what's more, he's *family*. Anyway, I can't do anything at all until the solicitor turns up. I'm still trying to take it all in, but I'm worried that Grandfather might have changed his will on impulse after arguing with Jack about spending too much on the garden, and then died

28

before he could change it back. It *does* seem unfair that he should leave the house to me. Anya—'

There was a plaintive bleeping. 'Blow – my phone's almost dead,' she said, and was cut off.

My belated rescue turned out to be a very belt-and-braces affair, for next day the cavalry, in the sober and suited form of the family solicitor, turned up too.

You see, I knew good things were on the way. My second sight was just a bit dodgy about *when*.

Mr Hobbs said he had already written to tell me he was coming to see me today 'on a matter to my advantage', but of course I haven't had the heart to go back to Spiggs Cottage and collect my mail since I left. The new owners are probably putting it straight into the skip, anyway.

Any more strange men visiting my caravan and, as far as the village is concerned, I might as well hang a red lamp over the door, even if this one looked so old and desiccated that strong winds could have blown him away. I've learned the hard way that a divorced woman is always seen as a sexual predator, after everyone else's menfolk (which is why, I suppose, I haven't made many friends here and hardly ever get asked to dinner parties).

But I invited Mr Hobbs in, and he was surprised to find I already knew of the legacy, until I told him about Jack's visit and his offer to buy Winter's End. Then, over tea and rather overdone rock cakes (the caravan stove is a bit temperamental), I asked him if he knew exactly *why* my grandfather hadn't left the estate to Jack.

'After all, he was the obvious heir, wasn't he, even if they had had one or two disagreements? It does seem unfair.'

'He had his reasons,' he said cagily. I suppose it was only natural that he should side with my grandfather – they were of an age and had probably been friends. 'Jack is the only son of his cousin Louisa, now deceased, and was born in New Zealand. When his father remarried he was sent back here to school, about a year after you and your mother left . . . and of course he spent the holidays at Winter's End and looked on it as his home. He is divorced with no children – another disappointment to your grandfather – and has a house in London. You know he is a property developer?'

'He did mention that. Presumably a successful one, if he could afford to buy me out?'

'Yes indeed: one cannot say that he hasn't risen by his own endeavours. His father purchased a small house for him to live in when he was at Oxford, and then later he renovated it and sold it at a profit and bought two more on the proceeds . . . and so it went on. I suppose his enterprise is quite remarkable. *Nowadays* he specialises in buying large period properties cheaply and converting them into extremely upmarket and expensive apartments,' he added meaningfully.

I stared at him. 'But surely you don't think he would do that to Winter's End? He said he loved the place and wanted to restore it to its former glory – and he seemed so sincere.'

'I am sure he did: his sincerity must be one of his greatest business assets,' Mr Hobbs said drily. 'And of course he *has* restored the houses he has purchased, which might otherwise have fallen into irreversible decay. They were all, like Winter's End, within an easy commuting distance of thriving major cities.'

'Oh,' I said, digesting this. 'But in the case of Winter's End, that could be just a coincidence?'

'Of course, that may be so. However, in his eagerness to persuade you to sell your inheritance, he may have been perhaps a little *selective* in the information he imparted to you. For instance, did he touch upon the various responsibilities that come with the legacy?'

'I . . . no, *what* responsibilities?'

'Apart from your grandfather charging you to complete a garden restoration scheme that has, in my opinion – and I have to say in all fairness, Jack's – nearly brought the house to ruin, the livelihoods of several people working for the Winter's End estate depends on your decision. You might also want to consider that Winter's End has been your Great-Aunt Hebe's home for all her life, though she does, of course, have some means of her own, as does her twin sister, Ottilie, who resides for part of the year in the coach house.'

I felt responsibility settle round my shoulders like a lead cape. 'But I know nothing about managing an estate! How could I possibly take it on?'

'But you *do* have relevant experience in looking after old properties, Ms Winter. Sir William thought you were just what Winter's End needed.'

'He did? But I've no experience of running one, only doing the donkey work and passing on orders to the other staff. And do call me Sophy – I have a feeling we are likely to see a lot of each other.'

His face broke into a smile like a rather jolly tortoise. 'Or one of my sons – I am semi-retired, you know, though I like to keep my brain active by retaining one or two clients. But to get back to business, Sophy, Winter's End is not a large house, although the gardens are extensive and take quite some keeping up, especially the yew maze and all the box hedges and topiary. Do you remember the spiral maze?'

I nodded. 'At the front of the house.' I felt a sudden pang for the small, mischievous Sophy who used to run through it with Grandfather's pack of miniature spaniels chasing after her, yapping madly – and who would then usually have to go back and rescue one or two of them who had got lost among the labyrinthine turns. 'It was quite low, wasn't it? Most tall adults would be able to see over the top of the hedges.'

'That's right, and all those curves and rounded edges take a good deal of clipping. Then there is a considerable area of woodland on the opposite side of the valley to the house and one tenanted farm. Are you interested in gardening at all?'

'I had enough of mulching and digging in all weathers when I lived in the Scottish commune to cure me of wanting to be a hands-on gardener, but I do love the frivolity of gardens made just to *look* at.'

'Quite,' he said. 'And Sir William told me that you have considerable expertise in caring for old houses and their contents from your previous employment, do you not?'

'Oh, yes, I left school at sixteen and my first job was in a Scottish castle. The Mistress saw to it that I learned the correct way to clean it and all the valuable things it contained.'

'The *Mistress*?'

'That's how she liked to be addressed by her staff,' I explained, 'which I was, until I ran off and married her cousin Rory. Then after I had Lucy I got the job here at Blackwalls with Lady Betty, keeping everything clean and in good repair, passing on her orders to the other staff, taking guided tours around the house on open days, being her PA . . . you name it, I did it. Lady Betty didn't pay me a lot, but she was very kind to me and Lucy, and I was fond of her.'

I touched the little gold, enamel and crystal bee brooch I wore. 'She gave me this as a keepsake when I visited her in the hospital, because she said she had a premonition she wasn't going to see Blackwalls again. And she was quite right, because once she signed the power of attorney, her nephew had her moved to an upmarket old people's home and she just lost the will to live. The last time I visited her she didn't really recognise me.'

I fished a tissue out of the box and blew my nose, while Mr Hobbs looked away tactfully.

'After he had been up here to see you, your grandfather said, and I quote his very words, "It seems to me the women of the family have always run things behind the scenes here at Winter's End, so one might as well take over as head of the family and have done with it." He thought you would make a better job of it than Jack ever would, especially with Lucy to help you. Yes . . .' he added thoughtfully, 'he was particularly taken with your daughter.'

'He *was*? But they quarrelled the whole time he was here!'

'He said she had the typical Winter temperament, allied with an almost masculine sense of business.'

'Well, I suppose he meant that as a compliment,' I conceded. 'She *is* very bossy and argumentative, though it's called assertiveness these days, and she did business studies and English at university.'

'Those would be considerable assets in running the estate. Sir William also said that, although so unlike your mother in character, in appearance Lucy reminded him very much of how Susan had been at the same age.'

'Yes, she's tall, slender and has that lovely red-gold hair – nothing like me. I don't look like a Winter at all. Even Jack, who is only a cousin several times removed, looks more like a Winter than I do!'

'Oh, there are the occasional darker Winters,' he assured me. 'Sir William told me that he was deeply sorry that he had not seen you grow up, but I believe he *would* have discovered your whereabouts much earlier had your mother not changed her name to all intents and purposes, to –' he looked down at his papers – 'Sukie Starchild.'

'I know. Dreadful, isn't it? She wanted to call me Skye, but I stuck to Sophy. I did have to use the surname Starchild on the few occasions when we stayed somewhere long enough for me to go to school, though, so Grandfather couldn't find us. She *said* she was afraid I would be taken away from her, but I often wondered if there was something else making her so paranoid about it.'

'There was,' Mr Hobbs said. 'Sir William did tell Susan that he would cut off her allowance and have her declared an unfit mother if she didn't change her ways, but those were merely empty threats that he had no intention of carrying out, for he often said things in temper that he afterwards regretted.'

'But my mother obviously believed he meant them that time?'

'That is so, but when she left she also took with her a diamond necklace that was not actually hers to dispose of – a family heirloom, in fact. He circulated its description, so he would have been notified if it came up for sale, but when it didn't he assumed it had been broken up and the stones recut.'

'I *wondered* how she bought the van in the first place!' I exclaimed. 'And she did have some very dodgy friends when I was very small and we were living in squats in London.'

'Sir William assumed she would return when the money ran out, so by the time he realised she wasn't going to, and began to try to trace you both, you had vanished.'

'She was terrified of him finding her, and I suppose that explains why – but she never could stand anger and loud voices; she was such a gentle person.'

'He never quite gave up hope that you would both be found, Sophy – and then, of course, he discovered that your mother had died in an accident. You know that her body was repatriated, and is buried in the family plot in the Sticklepond graveyard?'

I nodded. 'Though I didn't find out until much later what had happened.'

'Your grandfather assumed you had been in America with her, so that is where he searched again for you, without result.'

'No, I was fourteen by then, and I'd had enough of travelling. I didn't like my mother's new boyfriend much, either, so I didn't want to go to California with them. We'd been living in a commune in Scotland and my best friend's mother offered to look after me if I stayed, so I did until I got a live-in job at the castle, when I was sixteen.'

'And stayed lost until someone pointed out the unusual name "Sophy Winter" in a magazine advert,' Mr Hobbs said, 'when, on making enquiries, Sir William discovered that you were indeed his granddaughter.'

'Yes, I reverted to my real name after my mother died. I always felt ridiculous as a Starchild – *so* old hippie. And I didn't change my name when I married Lucy's father, I just stayed a Winter. I was only married for five minutes anyway.'

Actually, that was a slight exaggeration: it was five weeks, just long enough for me to fall pregnant and for commitment-phobe Rory to get such cold feet that he went away to find himself. So far as I know, he's still looking.

'Yes, that did worry your grandfather a little – but at least you *had* got married.'

'Unlike my mother?'

He ignored that, smoothing out the papers in front of him with a dry, wrinkled finger. 'You have no contact with your former husband?'

'No, none. He was a cousin of the owner of the castle I was working in, a diver working on the oilrigs – you know, six weeks on, six off. He was ten years older than me, but we fell in love and married in Gretna Green – very romantic – and then settled down in a rented cottage. Then he supposedly went off back to work and instead vanished.'

I had waited and waited for him, sure he would come

back, until I finally realised that he'd taken everything he valued with him and never meant to return at all. With hindsight I could see that I had been the one in love with the idea of marriage and domesticity, the family I yearned for, and he had simply gone along with it in a moment of madness, or frustrated lust, or . . . something.

'And that is the last you saw of him?' Mr Hobbs prompted gently. 'He never contacted you again?'

'No, though I'm sure his family knew where he was. But they wouldn't have anything to do with me, of course, because they were horrified when he married the help. I've heard that he has been working abroad ever since, and I divorced him eventually. There hasn't been anyone serious in my life since then. I don't need anyone really; I've usually got a dog.'

'Quite,' he said, though looking slightly perplexed. 'That does, however, simplify matters. I would most earnestly advise you *not* to consider selling the property at this juncture, and certainly not without visiting it first. Indeed, they are all expecting you to take over the reins as soon as possible.'

'*All?*' I said, startled. 'How many people are we actually talking about here?'

'Well, your twin great-aunts – though of course they were provided for under the terms of your great-grandfather's will. Ottilie leases the coach house, which she converted into a studio with living accommodation soon after your mother left. You *do* remember her?'

'Yes, though I saw much less of her than Aunt Hebe. She didn't come to Winter's End much when I lived there – isn't she a sculptor?'

'Indeed, a very well-known one. She made something of a misalliance in her brother's eyes when she was in her forties by marrying his last head gardener, though I believe

Sir William was more grieved at the thought of losing his right-hand man than at the marriage itself. But as it transpired he did not, since Rufus Greenwood was as passionate about restoring the Winter's End gardens as he was himself. He stayed on and Ottilie had the old coach house converted so she could divide her time between her husband at Winter's End and her studio in Cornwall. Still does, though she is now widowed.'

'So, who else is there? I remember a cook-housekeeper . . .'

'Yes, Mrs Lark and her husband, Jonah, are the only live-in staff now. There are three gardeners – four, if you include the head gardener . . .' He ruffled the papers a little, seemed about to say something, and then thought better of it. 'Ye-es. There is a daily cleaner . . . and Mr Yatton, the estate manager, who like myself is semi-retired, but he comes in most mornings to the office in the solar tower.'

'Four gardeners and only one cleaner? For a place that size?' I exclaimed, amazed, because if there is one thing I do know about, it is the upkeep of old houses.

'At first a cleaning firm was brought in occasionally, but I don't think that has happened for three or four years now.'

'A specialist firm? One used to dealing with the contents of historic buildings?' I asked hopefully.

'No, a local agency called Dolly Mops. They are very thorough – my wife uses them.'

I winced, thinking of all the damage a well-meaning but untrained cleaner might have inflicted on the fabric and contents of Winter's End.

'Then, of course, there are the Friends,' Mr Hobbs added.

'The . . . friends?'

'The Friends of Winter's End, a local group of history enthusiasts, who volunteer to come in on the summer opening days to sell tickets, and look after those rooms open to the public – the Great Hall and gallery. The house and gardens are open two afternoons a week, from May to the end of August.'

'I understand from Jack that the house is in very poor condition and there isn't enough money to restore it. Is that so?'

'While it is true that your grandfather diverted most of his income into renovating the gardens, he did not touch the capital, which is securely invested – though of course, no investments bring the returns they used to, and an old house like Winter's End needs a considerable amount of keeping up. And unfortunately, he took out a bank loan when he started to restore the maze and the terraces, secured against the property, which is a drain on the estate.'

'Jack mentioned that. How big a bank loan?' I asked hesitantly. I wasn't sure I really wanted to know.

'I believe there is still twenty thousand pounds outstanding.'

'Good heavens!'

'Yes, indeed – it is all *quite* a responsibility.'

The 'r' word again – and although I had pretty well run Blackwalls for Lady Betty, having the ultimate responsibility for my own stately pile was still a scary prospect. On the other hand, the thought of having a whole neglected house to put right sort of appealed . . . OK, I admit it, it drew me like a magnet, especially if this time the house I would be working in would actually be *mine*!

But I now had two rather differing views of my inheritance to compare – three, if you counted the letter from my grandfather that Mr Hobbs now handed to me, though actually it was more of a brief note scrawled in thin, spidery writing, urging me to complete the garden restoration project – his 'Memorial to Posterity' as he put it. It was abundantly clear that I needed to see Winter's End for myself before deciding what to do, and the sooner the better: I would be upping sticks and decamping to rural west Lancashire as soon as I could get my act together.

Besides, I was beginning to feel a strong, almost fearful tug of attraction, as though some connecting umbilical cord stretched almost to invisibility had suddenly twitched, reminding me of its existence.

Mr Hobbs must have drawn his own conclusions from the expression on my face, for he seemed to relax and, with a satisfied smile, said, 'So, I may inform the family that you will be arriving shortly?' He looked around at the cluttered caravan. 'It would seem you do not have a home or employment to keep you here.'

'Very true,' I agreed. 'No, there is nothing to keep me here – so I'll go to Winter's End and then make my own mind up what will be the best thing to do.'

'Spoken like a Winter,' he said approvingly.

'Yes, but Jack might not be pleased about it,' I said, suddenly remembering my handsome cousin's existence (be still my beating heart!). 'He told me that he'd decided, before he met me, that if I wouldn't sell Winter's End back to him he would challenge the will. If he has a strong case, is there really any point in my going to Winter's End?'

'Oh, that's an empty threat, my dear,' Mr Hobbs assured me. 'Your grandfather was perfectly *compos mentis* when he made the will: only look at the way he left instructions for everything to be settled before you were informed of your inheritance, so you could step right in and pick up the reins. I am sure Jack has already taken legal advice and been told the same thing.'

He stood up and began to gather his papers back into his briefcase, declining my offer of more tea and rock cakes with every sign of polite revulsion. There's no accounting for tastes.

Chapter Four: The Moving Mollusc

Now Thomas is somewhat recovered it is pleasant to have such a sweet-natured companion little older than myself, for he is not yet twenty. We play at Glecko in the evenings, or I read to him. In truth, I read better than hee, for my mother's father was a great scholar and taught her well, and in turn she has taught mee. Other skills she had from her own mother, and though some may whisper of black arts, she does only good, not ill.

From the journal of Alys Blezzard, 1580

When Mr Hobbs had gone I tore up the letter to Lucy, which was still lying unposted on the table and, blowing the expense, phoned her.

I was then under orders to give her every minute detail from the moment I got to Winter's End, and not make *any* major decisions without consulting her. She also, like Anya, said Jack sounded clever, devious but attractive – just my type, in fact – and I was not to promise him *anything* until she got home and OK'd it.

I didn't know why either of them should jump to conclusions about poor Jack like that – nor did I know why my daughter turned out to be such a bossy little cow. She even tried to organise my life for me, just as I did for my own feckless mother, only with much less justification . . .

'Great-Grandfather left Winter's End to *you*, not Jack,' she said, 'so there must be a reason. The least you owe him is to go back and look at the place.'

'Yes, I know, and I feel quite differently about him now that I know he never really gave up looking for your granny and me. And Mr Hobbs said he took quite a shine to you, Lucy, and thought you would be great for Winter's End.'

'Well, I rather liked *him*, too,' she said, then, changing the subject, enquired in a bored voice that didn't fool me in the least, 'How is Anya? And I suppose Guy has sent me all kinds of messages?'

'Actually, no, he hasn't, though Anya was asking after you. He's on the road with her at the moment, now he's finished his degree, but he's job-hunting.'

'I suppose that accounts for why he hasn't emailed me for ages,' she said, sounding a bit miffed, 'though there *are* internet cafés.'

'I expect he's been busy and he will catch up with you later. Anyway, you always said he emailed too much and he should get a life,' I pointed out mildly.

'Well, he's such a nerdy little geek – but he's still one of my oldest friends.'

'You haven't actually seen him for a couple of years, Lucy – you were both always off doing things in the university holidays whenever Anya and I met up. But take it from me, he doesn't look remotely like a nerdy little geek any more. He's all grown up.'

'I'll believe that when I see it,' she said.

I only wished she could see it right then, and all my maternal urges were telling me to send her some cash and tell her to get on the next plane home . . . except that I hadn't got any money, of course. But Jack had, and I was sure if I accepted his offer to buy Winter's End he would advance some to me straight away, when he knew what it was for.

But I simply couldn't rush into a decision that would affect many more lives than mine, even though I realised that if I was mad enough to take on Winter's End I would still have the same money problems I'd always had, only on a much, *much* grander scale.

It took me a while to think what to say to Jack, but in the end I only got his answering service. I left my mobile number and a message telling him that, now I had spoken to the solicitor and read my grandfather's letter, I felt a responsibility to at least *go* to Winter's End and see how things were for myself, and I hoped he would understand.

But if he did, he didn't tell me so . . . unless that was the series of phantom text messages on my phone? I usually manage to delete them before reading them. They just slip through my fingers and vanish.

I have a disease called Technological Ineptitude; I'm some kind of throwback to the Stone Age, but I'm not proud of it.

I managed to lose three more text messages before Jack got the idea and phoned me instead. He has a voice like melted Swiss milk chocolate – smooth, rich and creamy; my knees went quite weak. He was so sweet too, and said he quite understood.

'That's such a relief. I thought you might be cross!' I blurted out, and he laughed.

'Now, why should I be cross? In fact, I'll come down myself and show you what needs urgently doing to the house, and I'm quite sure that when you've seen the scale of the problems – not to mention the sheer costs of running a place like that, and paying back the bank loan – you'll be more than happy to let me buy it. After all, it will still be your family home, where you will always be sure of a welcome, but without all the expense and hassle of trying to keep it from falling into a ruin,' he pointed out reasonably. 'You'd be in a win/win situation.'

'I expect you're right,' I said, feeling a warm glow at the thought of being part of the extended family again. Since he was being so nice about it, I asked, 'Do you think it would be OK if I had our belongings sent down there to store? Only, whatever happens I don't think I will be coming back here to live, and it will be easier to pack them up now.'

'Of course – there's loads of room. Give Hebe a ring and tell her when your stuff is arriving – unless you've already spoken to her?'

'No, I will do, of course, but I am feeling a bit nervous about it. I don't know why, because she was always very kind to me, in her way.'

'Oh, old Hebe's all right – you give her a ring,' he said cheerfully, then added, his voice going deeper and sort of furry, 'I'm *really* looking forward to seeing you again, Sophy! I haven't been able to stop thinking about you since we met,' and my insides turned to a mass of quivering jelly. I was rather looking forward to seeing him again too.

Our meagre possessions, including a few small bits of good furniture culled from local auctions or given to me by Lady Betty, were dispatched to Winter's End as a part-load with a furniture removal firm. I just don't seem to accumulate things like most people do, except books, which I buy second-hand like other people buy sweets. I keep my absolute favourites in a little shelf unit built into the camper van because, deep down, I think I'm always expecting to move on. In fact, I keep *all* my treasures in the van.

I didn't know what Aunt Hebe would do with our stuff when it arrived; when I nervously rang her to warn her of its imminent appearance, I suggested she stack it all in an outhouse somewhere for me to sort out.

'Oh, I expect Jonah will find somewhere,' she said vaguely.

'You don't mind my coming back to Winter's End, do you, Aunt Hebe?'

'Not at all, for how else can things be settled satisfactorily? And I'm sure we're very *happy* to welcome you back to the fold, Sophy,' she added, in a voice that suggested that she was anything but, 'though of course I always thought Winter's End would go to Jack, and it's very hard on the poor boy—'

Then she broke off and said again that I would be very welcome, but it was clear that as far as she was concerned, my advent was a very mixed blessing.

When I spoke about Lucy, I feared my own voice had the very same doting tone in it as Aunt Hebe's when she uttered Jack's name: bewitched, besotted and bewildered. But that didn't stop me feeling slightly jealous. I had always thought that she was fond of me, in her way, yet evidently my absence had been more than compensated for by Jack's arrival, the cuckoo who'd taken my place in both the nest and her affections.

When I finally managed to see Lady Betty before I left for Lancashire, it was clear that she had all but forgotten me too.

I had been to the stiff and starchy care home once before, and the same white-overalled woman was on the reception desk. She asked me for my name and then checked a list while I undid my coat. It was hot in there and smelled of air freshener and surgical spirit.

'I'm afraid you are not on the list of permitted visitors,' she said, pursing her lips, 'though you have been before, haven't you? I recognise that funny little brooch you're wearing.'

'My bee?' I said, taken aback but thinking fast. 'Yes, it is unusual, isn't it? Lady Betty gave it to me – and I won't be on the list of visitors because I'm just an employee. Mr Conor Darfield asked me to bring in a few things that she wanted.' I lifted the carrier bag to show her.

'Oh, right,' she said, 'perhaps if you leave—' She broke off as an elderly gentleman, who had been shuffling about the foyer in a desultory sort of way, suddenly made a determined, if hobbling, sprint for the front door.

'No, no, Colonel Browne, come back!' she called – but too late, he'd gone. 'Oh, blow – I'd better catch him before he vanishes,' she said distractedly, lifting up the flap in the counter and coming out.

'That's all right,' I assured her, sincerely hoping the poor colonel made it to wherever he was going, 'I know where Lady Betty's room is – I'll just pop up.' I don't know if she heard me because she was off in pursuit, but I seized the opportunity to run upstairs.

I tapped gently on the door of Lady Betty's room before going in, finding her in bed. As soon as I saw her I realised that this would be our last goodbye, for she seemed suddenly to have grown smaller, as if she was already shrinking away into death, and there was no recognition in her clouded eyes.

I sat quietly with her for ten minutes, feeding her bits of ratafia biscuits and sips of whisky and water from the supplies I had smuggled in (both of which she had always loved), and she took them with greedy eagerness, opening her mouth like a baby bird. She seemed to become slightly more alert then, and I talked to her, trying to raise some spark of recognition, but there was only one brief moment when her eyes focused on my face and she said my name and smiled. Then she closed her eyes and to all intents and purposes went to sleep.

I left the remainder of the biscuits in the bedside cabinet, but took the whisky bottle away with me. I had a feeling that anything remotely pleasurable would be banned in this sterile place.

The receptionist, looking distracted, was on the phone and only acknowledged my departure with a wave of the hand. 'Yes,' she was saying, 'he's gone again. Must have had a taxi waiting outside – and God knows which pub he's gone to this time . . .'

I only hoped the colonel had a good time before they caught up with him.

The exterior of the VW was painted in time-faded psychedelic flowers, just as it was when my mother drove it, but I had made the interior over to my own tastes. Now, it was more like an old-fashioned gypsy caravan than a camper – deep, glowing colours, brightened with lace and patchwork and painted tables, ingenious shelves and cupboards, all sparklingly clean and smelling of roses.

There was a place in it for every item that was essential to me, so I felt as reassured as a snail in its shell once I was driving down to Lancashire, even though I was nervous about actually *arriving*.

But after all, if I got cold feet, I could always just get in my van and vanish again, couldn't I? Though come to think of it, that's what my mother always did, and that's really not a pattern I want to repeat.

It's a long way from Northumberland to west Lancashire, especially when you don't drive at much more than forty miles an hour, and since my heater wasn't working very well my fingers were frozen to the wheel most of the time. But the autumn colours were very pretty coming over the Pennines, and I noticed that, as I dropped back down towards Brough, all the bushes were covered with scarlet berries – supposed to be a sure sign of a hard winter to follow.

I made one overnight stop soon after that, near a village with a wonderful bakery, and then set out early next morning on the final leg.

It was just as well that Mr Hobbs had given me directions to Winter's End, for I was lost as soon as I took the Ormskirk turn off the motorway and then drove into a maze of small, hedged lanes. And although as I reached the large village of Sticklepond everything looked vaguely familiar (except that the general shop had turned into a Spar and the village school into a house), I don't think I would have easily found the right narrow road leading off the green.

I paused to consult the Post-it note I'd attached to the dashboard: 'Half a mile up Neat's Bank take the first right turn into a private road, by the white sign to Winter's End. Fifty yards along it, you will see a car park on your left and the main entrance gates to your right . . .'

The tarmacked road had a ridge of grass growing up the middle and the walls seemed to be closing in on me. Surely they couldn't get coaches up there?

I slowed right down and, sure enough, here was the sign and an arrow – but set back into a sort of clipped niche in the hedge so as to be almost invisible unless you were opposite it. I'd overshot a bit, so I reversed slightly and started to turn – then slammed the brakes on to avoid the tall man who leaped athletically down from the bank right in front of me and then stood there, blocking my way.

The engine stalled, and while we stared at each other through the windscreen a bird dropped a long series of sweet, high notes like smooth pebbles into the pool of silence.

The tall man had eyes the cool green of good jade, deeply set in a bony, tanned face with a cleft chin, a straight nose and an uncompromising mouth. His floppy, raven-black hair looked as if he'd impatiently pushed it straight back from his face with both hands and his brows were drawn together in a fierce scowl.

If he wasn't exactly handsome he was certainly striking, and I had a nagging feeling that I'd seen him somewhere before . . . *especially* that scowl. A warning dream perhaps, half-forgotten?

Since he showed no sign of moving I reluctantly wound down the side window and, leaning out, said politely, 'Excuse me, do you think you could let me past?'

'No way,' he said belligerently, folding his arms across a broad chest clad in disintegrating layers of jumpers, each hole showing a tantalising glimpse of the other strata beneath. 'And you can go right back and tell the rest of them that they're not welcome here. This is private property.'

'The rest of them? Who?' I asked, tearing my eyes away from counting woolly layers with some difficulty.

'The other New-Age travellers. I've had trouble with your kind before, setting up camp on land I'd cleared for a knot and making an unholy mess.'

A *knot*? Wasn't he a bit big to be a Boy Scout?

'Look,' I said patiently, 'I'm not a New-Age traveller and—'

'Pull the other one, it's got bells on,' he said rudely. 'You're not welcome here, so if you're trying to scout out a good spot for the others you'd better turn right around. Tell them the car park's locked up for the winter and patrolled by dogs, and if they come up the drive they'll be run off!'

'Now see here!' I said, losing patience, 'I don't know who you are, but I've had a long journey and I'm too tired for all of this. My name is Sophy Winter and—'

'*What!*'

He took an impetuous stride forward and I started

48

nervously, banging my head on the top of the window frame. 'Sophy Winter and—'

'Good God!' he interrupted, staring at me in something like horror, then added unexpectedly, in his deep voice with its once-familiar Lancashire accent, 'Blessed are the New-Age travellers, for they shall inherit the earth!'

'I'm *not* a New-Age traveller,' I began crossly. 'I keep telling you and—'

But he still wasn't listening. With a last, muttered, 'Behold, the end is nigh!' he strode off without a backward look. I know, because I watched him in the wing mirror. His jeans-clad rear view was quite pleasant for a scoutmaster, but I still hoped he'd get knotted.

Chapter Five: Pleached Walks

Today to my great grief and sorrow came the news of my mother's death and the babe with her. But I already knew the very moment of her passing: it was as if all my mother's arts flew to mee on the moment of her quitting this earth and my eyes were opened to a terrible pre-knowledge of destiny that moved like dark shadows around mee, step for step.

From the journal of Alys Blezzard, 1580

Slightly shaken, I restarted the engine and crawled up the lane between grassy banks and sad, autumnal brown hedges, feeling that this first encounter did not bode well. I only hoped he wasn't tying knots anywhere close by . . .

And then it occurred to me that since he looked a bit son-of-the-soil, he could even be one of my inherited three gardeners, though maybe not. Greeting his future employer like that was hardly the way to achieving lasting job security.

A wide, gated and padlocked opening on the left declared itself to be Winter's End visitors' car park, well and truly shut for the winter. Opposite was a matched pair of sandstone lodges linked by an arched chamber set with a weathered shield, carved with a crest that looked exactly like a whippet with a black pudding in its mouth. An immaculate half-moon of turf in front of each had been bordered with box hedging torturously clipped to form the words 'WINTER'S' on one side, and 'END' on the other – a strangely municipal and time-consuming labour of love that contrasted strangely with the once-splendid iron gates. For goodness' sake! Had they never heard of wire wool and Cure-rust?

The gates were open, but, in their present state, looked more like the jaws of a trap than a welcome. I turned cautiously between them onto a drive that ran through a dark tunnel of trees, slowing to wait for my eyes to adjust after the bright autumnal sunshine.

This was a lucky move, as it turned out, because a large grey horse was advancing to meet me – if you can call it an advance when it was going backwards rather fast. I stamped on the brakes for the second time in five minutes, and the creature briefly slammed its fat rump into the front of my van before whirling round, snorting down two red, foam-flecked nostrils, its eyes wildly rolling. The rider, almost unseated, was clinging on like a monkey.

Two thoughts about the matter crossed my punch-drunk mind from opposite directions and collided in the middle. One was that the woman seemed to have no control over her mount whatsoever; and the second (rather regretfully), was that *I* would never look so good in riding clothes: too big, too curvy, too *bouncy*.

Imagine Helen of Troy in tight cream breeches and a velvet hat.

She spared me a fleeting glance from curiously light brown eyes and called, 'Sorry about that!' very casually, considering there was probably a horse's-bottom-shaped dent in the front of the VW. Then, with some inelegant flapping of the reins, she urged her mount off down the road at a clattering trot.

'Idiotic creatures, horses,' said a voice in my ear, and I jumped again. 'Saw me dressed in white and ran off – though it's a holy colour, I always wear it to go to church and I'm off to do the flowers later. But she was a Christopher before she married, and none of them ride well. I suppose she thought Jack was here – though you never know, because she's never been what you might call fussy where men are concerned.'

I might have tried to explore this interesting statement further had I not had other things on my mind, for I would have known my great-aunt Hebe instantly anywhere: tall, bony, aquiline of nose like a slightly fuzzy Edith Sitwell, with her shock of fine hair, now white rather than red-gold, partially secured into a high knot with a chiffon scrunchie.

If I *hadn't* recognised her I would probably have been running after the horse, due to the polar-bear-crossed-with-Miss-Havisham style of her apparel. A floating, ivory-coloured, crystal- and sequin-dotted chiffon dress, layered for warmth with a yellowing fake-fur coat and fluffy scarves, and worn over white wellington boots of the sort only usually seen in hospitals and clinics, made for a striking ensemble.

There was a lump in my throat. 'Hello, Aunt Hebe,' I said, slightly unsteadily.

She regarded me severely, then leaned in through the still-open window and kissed me, though the silver pentacle and golden cross that hung around her neck on separate chains swung forward and bashed me on the nose first. Evidently Aunt Hebe still liked to hedge her bets, a family tradition.

'You're late! We expected you over an hour ago, so I thought I would walk down and see if there was any sign of you. I'd better get in.' She opened the passenger door and, clambering up with some difficulty, arranged her skirts. The familiar scent of crushed rose petals came in with her, and I felt eight again . . .

'Off you go,' she said briskly, and I realised I'd been staring at her, waiting for some sign that my return held real meaning for her. Maybe I hadn't quite expected bunting, banners and a fatted calf, but a little more than a peck on the cheek and a ticking off – but then, there had never been much in the way of maternal softness about Aunt Hebe.

Obediently I moved off again up the dark driveway – and then nearly went off the road as something beat a sudden tattoo on the roof. It was definitely one surprise too many in a very eventful day.

'Nuts,' said Aunt Hebe, unfazed.

'Right . . .' I said uncertainly, my heart still racing away at twice the normal speed. 'There certainly are!'

She gave me a sharp, sideways look and I managed to get a grip on myself. 'I didn't know I was expected any particular time, Aunt Hebe. In fact, I nearly stopped to get something for lunch in the village. I've been thinking about Pimblett's hot pies all the way down here – didn't Mum sometimes buy me one on the way home from school?'

'I dare say, but lunch is being prepared for you up at the manor,' she said reprovingly, 'and I believe it *is* hotpot pies. Everyone is waiting to meet you first, though.'

'*Everyone?*' I echoed, then added, perhaps too eagerly, 'Is Jack here already?'

She gave me another sidelong glance. 'Jack sent his apologies, but business matters prevent him from welcoming you home until the weekend. He's probably putting it off, for he'll find it difficult, seeing someone else in his place – but there, what's done is done, and the obvious solution is in his own hands.'

I supposed she knew all about his offer to buy Winter's End and there was no question about where Aunt Hebe's loyalties lay.

'You've turned out not too badly, considering,' she added, turning her beaky head to study me.

'Thanks.'

'Though you appear to have no dress sense. Jeans are *so* unflattering on women of a certain age.'

'I don't know, they hold me in where I need holding in, like a twenty-first-century corset. Exactly *who* did you say was waiting to meet me?'

'*Everyone*,' she repeated as we came out of the darkness under the trees. 'Everyone that matters, anyway.'

And there was the house sitting in a puddle of autumn sunshine, the light dully glittering off the mullioned windows, a shabbily organic hotchpotch of black and white Tudor and local red sandstone, with the finger of an ancient tower poking triumphantly upwards above the rest.

It looked as if it had grown there, like some exotic fungus – but a ripe fungus on the point of decaying back into the earth it had sprung from. Before the porch a distant double row of miscellaneous figures waited, like the guard of honour at a low-budget wedding and, as if on cue, a small, fluffy pewter cloud let loose a confetti of snowflakes.

'Oh, yes – I see them now,' I croaked nervously, crunching slowly up the gravel. To my left stretched the curving, billowing shapes of yew that formed the maze, the gilded roof of the little pagoda in the centre visible in the distance. My feet would know the way to it blindfold . . .

'The maze has been extended at *huge* expense back to the dimensions of the old plan, and the pagoda regilded, since your time,' Aunt Hebe informed me, so maybe I *wouldn't* find my way into it so easily – and I suspect a lot of the bank loan went on restoring it.

'Most of the rest of the garden has been extensively restored, too, since you were last here. It became quite a *mania* with William.'

Everything in the garden looked pleached, parterred, bosketted and pruned to within an inch of its life. A mere glance showed me that there were still abundant examples of all four garden features here, but the immaculately manicured grounds only served to make the house look the more neglected, like a dull, dirty jewel in an ornate and polished setting.

I circled my incongruous vehicle left around a convoluted pattern of box hedges and little trees clipped into spirals, and the fountain at its heart sprinkled me with silver drops like a benediction as I came to a halt.

We climbed out to a thin scatter of applause and a voice quavering out: 'Hurrah!'

Hebe rearranged her collection of white angora scarves around her neck and, taking me by the elbow, drew me forward and began making introductions.

'You remember Mrs Lark, our cook – Beulah Johnson as was? And her husband, Jonah?'

'Welcome back, love,' Mrs Lark said, her twinkling eyes set in a broad, good-humoured face so stippled with brown freckles she looked like a deeply wrinkled Russet apple. 'Me and Jonah are glad to see you home again.'

'That's right,' Jonah agreed, baring his three remaining teeth in a wide grin. He had mutton-chop whiskers and looked like a friendly water vole.

'I certainly do remember you, Mrs Lark!' I said, basking in the genuine warmth of their welcome. 'You used to make me gingerbread men with currant eyes.'

'Fancy remembering that, after all this time! Well, I'll make some for your tea this very day – and some sticky ginger parkin too, that you used to love.'

Hebe urged me onwards by means of a small push between the shoulder blades. 'This is Grace from the village, our daily cleaner.'

'But no heavy stuff, me knees won't take it no more,' piped Grace reedily, who indeed looked even more steeped in the depths of antiquity than Mrs Lark, and was about the size of the average elf.

'And Derek, the under-gardener, and Bob and Hal . . .' Aunt Hebe said more briskly, towing me onwards before I could register any more than that Derek was a morose-looking man whose ears stuck out like old-fashioned car indicators, Bob was the one wearing a battered felt hat with a pink plastic daisy in the band, and Hal's large front teeth had a gap between them you could drive a bus through.

Aunt Hebe made a tut-tutting noise. '*No* sign of Seth. I expect he forgot all about it.'

'Who's Seth?' I said, irrationally feeling faintly aggrieved that one unknown man was missing from my royal reception committee.

'Seth Greenwood, the . . . well, I suppose he's the head gardener. But he's a bit of a law unto himself.'

'Oh, right!' I said, comprehending, because head gardeners *could* be tricky. They often seemed to think they owned the garden and did it their way regardless of what the owners wanted. Though according to Mr Hobbs, in this case he and my grandfather had been two minds with but one single thought.

'My sister, Ottilie, *married* the last head gardener,' Hebe started, in a tone that made it clear that she had committed a major *faux pas*, 'and so Seth—' She broke off and added curtly, 'Here *is* Ottie.'

A tall figure in jeans and a chambray shirt over a polo-necked jumper strode round the corner of the house, smoking a long, thin cheroot. This she flicked into a bed of late-flowering pansies and then embraced me vigorously, thumping me on the back. 'Glad to have you back, Sophy: you should have come sooner.'

'Thank you, Aunt Ottie,' I said, coughing slightly. Even now, in her eighties, Ottie seemed to be twice as alive as her twin; she crackled with energy.

'Just call me Ottie, everyone does. Clear off, you lot,' she said to the staff. 'You've only come out of curiosity and you've all got jobs to get to.'

'That's a fine way to talk,' Mrs Lark said good-humouredly, 'but I do need to see to my split pea and ham soup for tonight's dinner. There'll be lunch in the breakfast room in fifteen minutes.'

'I'll see you later,' Ottie said, 'settle in. Tell that vacant sister of mine to show you your room. You don't want to be hanging about out here in the cold.'

'Perhaps you would like to follow me?' Hebe said without looking at her, and it became obvious that my aunts were not speaking to each other. 'I expect my sister wants to get back to making mud pies in the coach house.'

'I'm just finishing the last figure in a major sculptural commission,' Ottie said pointedly. 'You must come and see it before it goes to be cast, Sophy.'

Then her eyes caught sight of something behind me and opened wide in surprise. 'Look, it's *Charlie!*'

Turning, I found the final resident of Winter's End on the top step, staring at me with slightly bulging eyes set in a pansy-shaped face – one of those tiny, black and white spaniels that you see so often in old paintings.

'Oh, of course, Grandfather always had several King Charles spaniels, didn't he? Though *this* can't be one of the ones I remember.'

'No, this is the last one my brother had. He's only five, and— Good heavens!' Aunt Hebe exclaimed, as Charlie descended the steps slightly shakily and bustled up to me in the manner of all small spaniels, tail rotating like a propeller.

He skirmished around me, whining, until I sank down and stroked him. Then he attempted to climb into my lap and I fell over backwards onto the gravel, laughing, while he tried to lick my face. Finally I got up with him in my arms.

'Well!' Hebe said, sounding surprisingly disapproving. 'He's been pining after William for *weeks*, but he certainly seems to have taken to you!'

'Poor old Charlie,' I said, holding him close. He felt like little more than skin and bone, and smelled like a dirty old carpet. I didn't think anyone could have brushed him since my grandfather died and, like the house, he was in serious need of some TLC.

'My sister is a sentimentalist and would probably have preferred him to howl on the grave permanently, like Greyfriars Bobby,' Ottie said with a grin, then walked off, her shirttails flapping and the black bootlace that held back her long grey hair starting to slide off.

'Perhaps you would like to go to your room before lunch?' Hebe suggested.

Everyone else had vanished. Still carrying Charlie, I lugged my carpetbag out of the van with one hand, then followed Hebe through the door from the porch and round a huge, heavy carved screen into a cavernous hall paved with worn stone.

She crossed it without pause and began slowly to ascend the curved staircase towards the balustraded gallery – but I had come to a stop in the middle of the floor under a sky of intricate plasterwork, overwhelmed by a flood of emotion. Suddenly I was fused to the house, wired in: I was Sophy at eight and at the same time Sophy at considerably more than thirty-eight ... But I was back where I belonged and the house was happy about it, for there was a space in the pattern of Winter's End that only I could fill.

It was an acutely Tara moment: the years when I had been away were gone with the wind. This was *my* house, *my* place on God's good earth, and nothing would ever tear me from it again. I knew I would do anything – *anything* – to keep it.

I had thought I was a piece of insignificant flotsam swept along on the tide of life, but now suddenly I saw that everything I had learned, every single experience that had gone into moulding me, had been leading up to my return.

I was transfixed, translated, transformed ... trans-*anything* except, ever again, transient.

Tomorrow might be another day, but it certainly wouldn't be the one that saw me signing away my inheritance.

Jack was out of luck.

Chapter Six: Unravelled

Father still hath not sent for mee, nor any word, so I asked leave to return home. But Thomas Wynter hath suddenly set his heart on marrying mee, despite his family's opposition – and mine, for I feel for him as though he were a brother, no more than that. They do not like the match, yet he is Sir Ralph's onlie child and he will denie him nothing . . .

From the journal of Alys Blezzard, 1580

I did a slow turn, arms spread wide to embrace the house, letting my long-suppressed memories of Winter's End rise to the surface at last like slow, iridescent bubbles.

The Great Hall and the cross passage, which was partly hidden by the enormous carved wooden screen, separated the family part of the house from the service wing, the area I seemed to recall best. Over there was the door to the kitchen with its huge black Aga, Mrs Lark's domain and the source of comfort, warmth and treats. Then came the stillroom, where Aunt Hebe held sway, brewing up potions and lotions, and receiving mysterious late visitors to the side door for whispered, urgent consultations. Beyond that again, a maze of stone-flagged, utilitarian rooms and the cellar steps.

Here in the hall there was no longer a fire in the cavernous hearth, only cold grey embers, but ancient cast-iron radiators were dotted about as though dropped randomly into place and a hollow, metallic clunking indicated that they were working, a fact that wasn't immediately obvious from the chill air. A powerful energy ran up from the soles of my feet to the crown of my head, filling me to the brim with a life force compounded of the vital essence of Winter's End and of my ancestors who had loved it before me – the alleged witch, Alys Blezzard, among them.

From the dark shadows behind me I heard the once-familiar echo of her light, serious young voice whispering, '*Welcome – welcome home, at last!*'

'There you are,' I murmured.

'*Of course – I never left.*'

'I missed you, Alys.'

Aunt Hebe's face, an elderly Juliet, appeared like a waning moon over the balustrade high above and she called, slightly querulously, 'Aren't you coming, Sophy?'

'Yes, of course!' I came back to earth with a start, and ran up the stairs to the gallery with Charlie, who had been sitting watching me, at my heels.

She looked at him with disfavour. 'The dogs have *never* been allowed upstairs.'

'But he's so sad and lonely at the moment, Aunt Hebe. I'd really like to keep him with me.'

'You can do as you wish, of course – for the present. *Fill* the house with dogs if you want to, though I expect Grace will complain about the hairs.'

'I think one dog will do to be going on with, and he won't shed so much hair once I have given him a good brushing.' That was an experience neither of us was going to enjoy, because currently he was just one big tangled knot and a pair of bright eyes.

Following her through a door at the back of the gallery I found myself in the Long Room, which was exactly what it said on the packet – a narrow, wooden-floored chamber running from one wing to the other, jutting out at the back of the house above the terraced gardens.

The wooden shutters were all partly closed over diamond-paned windows yellowed with grime, so that we walked in a soupy half-light past paintings so dirty it was hard to tell the subject matter. Even so, I noticed that nothing above shoulder height had been cleaned within living memory, and cobwebs formed tattered silk drapery across the ceiling. Some of them brushed Aunt Hebe's head, but she seemed oblivious.

Lower down everything had been given a rough once-over, the legs of the furniture showing evidence of repeated violent batterings with a Hoover nozzle.

'Grace surely can't be the *only* cleaner?' I said, itching to get my hands on a duster. 'It must be too much for one person to cope with, especially since she's getting on a bit.'

'She does what she can, and my brother occasionally got a team in from an agency to give the place a good spring clean until a couple of years ago, when he said it had got too expensive. The Friends of Winter's dust the Great Hall and the minstrels' gallery when we open to the public. Those are the only parts of the house the visitors are allowed into, you know. It's mainly the gardens they come to see.'

Clearly she'd never considered lifting a duster herself, and the house was *desperate* for some TLC. Poor tiny, ancient Grace could never hope to manage it all herself, for while the house was not some enormous mansion, it was low and rambling, with lots of panelling and wooden floors and ups and downs.

I was yearning to make a start on it . . . but maybe five minutes after I arrived wouldn't be tactful. With an effort I managed to restrain myself, thinking it was ironic that I had spent all my life learning the art of cleaning other people's stately piles, not knowing those skills would one day be necessary to transform my own. Again, I had that strange sense of fitting into some preordained pattern, the vital bit of missing jigsaw.

They say everyone has some skill or talent and mine just happens to be cleaning. Not romantic or exciting, perhaps, but there it is – and exactly what was needed here. Now a missionary fervour was invading my heart, filling me with the longing to convert the dirt.

As we walked along I noticed lighter patches on the walls where pictures had been removed – perhaps when Grandfather was searching for something to pay death duties with. How odd to think of him here, planning the implications of his impending death on the Inland Revenue, making sure everything was settled before I was even told he had gone.

'Are the missing paintings still away being cleaned and valued?' I asked.

'No, they have been returned. They're stacked in the Blue Bedroom waiting to be rehung.'

At the end we turned left past a suit of armour made for a short, fat gentleman and went through a door into the West Wing, down two steps, round a corner, and up one step to a passage.

'This is the Blue Bedroom,' Hebe said, indicating a door, 'then my room and a bathroom. The Red Bedroom will be Jack's when he arrives. Of course, he should have had my brother's room, only,' she added resentfully, walking on and throwing open another door, 'Ottie *insisted* that you should have it.'

'But really, I don't mind at all if Jack has Grandfather's room,' I protested. (Especially if Grandfather actually died there!) 'I thought perhaps my old room on the nursery floor . . .'

My voice petered out: someone had lit an incongruous little gas heater in the magnificent fireplace and the red glow reflected off a great mahogany bed covered with the kind of jewel-coloured crazy patchwork that I make myself. The curtains were of the same soft, faded gold velvet as the bed hangings and, like the Long Room, the oriole windows jutted out over the terraces at the rear of the house, with a distant glimpse of the river at the bottom and the wood across the valley.

'What a lovely room! You know, I don't think I ever came in here when I was a child,' I said, pulling back the drapes. Below were laid out the intricate, lacy shapes of terraced knot gardens, though the lowest level looked to be still very much a work in progress.

'I'm so happy to be back, Aunt Hebe!' I said spontaneously, turning to smile at her. 'I haven't forgotten how kind you always were to me, telling me bedtime bible stories and giving me rose fondants when I hurt myself.'

She softened slightly. 'Couldn't have you growing up a *complete* heathen. We missed you when Susan took you away, but we thought she'd be back again eventually, when the money ran out. And of course you were only a *girl*. It would have been different if you had been a boy.'

'Sorry about that,' I said drily, though her casual dismissal hurt.

'My brother hoped that Susan would come to her senses and get married, and there would be more children – a son,' she added, rubbing it in. But I'd already got the message: to Aunt Hebe, girls didn't count, and illegitimate girls counted even less.

'But then my cousin Louisa died and eventually Jack was sent back to school in England, and spent all his holidays here.'

'Well, I'm sure that made everything right as rain, then,' I said sourly. I mean, I liked Jack, but much more of this kind of thing and I would start to go off him rapidly.

'It should have done, but I'm afraid Jack was a disappointment to my brother. Their characters were just too dissimilar, though Jack did try, by taking an interest in the architecture of the house and the family history. Then

William somehow got the idea that Jack was thinking of marrying Melinda Seldon – or Christopher, as she has been calling herself again since her husband died. But if he *had* been, which I personally very much doubt, he gave it up once William made it clear he disapproved of the match. He never liked her, though of course she's very wealthy now and, goodness knows, Winter's End could do with a rich heiress marrying into the family.'

'Was she the blonde woman on the grey horse that ran into my car?' I asked, thinking rather despondently that the equestrian Helen of Troy and Jack would have made a wonderful couple – but also that Jack hadn't seemed the kind of man who would meekly give up the woman he loved just to please his grandfather.

'Yes, that was Melinda. She was widowed last year and moved back here to live with her mother, who is one of my oldest friends. Naturally, she and Jack saw a lot of each other. For one thing, they have lots of friends in common, but also he had entered into a business arrangement with her to develop the property she inherited from her late husband.'

'She is very beautiful,' I said wistfully.

'She is, but also a great flirt – as a girl she played all the local boys off against each other quite shamelessly – but if Jack was tempted after she was widowed, then I expect he thought better of it, even before William mentioned the matter. He had already made one misalliance, you see, soon after he left university – a short-lived affair.'

'So was mine, though in my case it was my husband's family who thought he'd made a misalliance.'

'Oh no, dear, nobody marrying a Winter could possibly think that,' Aunt Hebe assured me – but then, she had never met the Mistress.

'Things did seem to improve between Jack and William until they had that last ghastly argument . . .' She shuddered.

'Oh? What was that about, Aunt Hebe?'

'Jack had long wanted William to transfer ownership of Winter's End to him, to try and avoid death duties, but he wouldn't hear of it. This time Jack told his uncle that if he didn't divert some of his income into keeping the house standing, he would have nothing but a garden to inherit anyway.'

'Well, goodness knows, he was right about the house. Another couple of years of neglect and possibly it would have passed the point of no return.'

'Yes, but my brother took it badly and told Jack he shouldn't count his chickens before they hatched. And then, to top it all, he'd heard about one of Jack's business deals – such a *clever* boy – and accused him of only wanting to get his hands on Winter's End so he could turn it into an apartment block. I told him he was being absurd, because Jack wouldn't dream of doing anything of the kind to his ancestral home.'

'No, I'm sure he wouldn't,' I agreed.

She smiled approvingly. 'I'm sure my brother would have seen sense if he hadn't suddenly discovered where *you* were and made that disastrous will. I can't think what got into him.'

'Sickening for you and Jack,' I agreed, fascinated despite myself by this one-viewpoint argument, because it had obviously never occurred to either of them that I had any kind of right to inherit Winter's End.

'Yes – you do understand, don't you? William didn't even tell us he had found you, so the will came as a complete shock. And although Mr Hobbs says he was in his right mind and the will can't be challenged, he can't have been, really.'

'He seemed to be all there with his cough drops when I met him,' I assured her. 'He spent most of his visit arguing with Lucy and it perked him up no end.'

'Lucy?'

'My daughter.'

'Oh, yes, I'd forgotten.' Clearly, yet another girl was not

of great interest. 'Didn't Jack say she was working abroad somewhere?'

'Japan – teaching English, but only for a year to make some money. The wages are good, and they run up such huge debts these days with the student loans, don't they?'

'Jack didn't. In fact, that's when he started his property renovation business.'

With an effort I refrained from remarking that Lucy had not had a rich parent to buy her a house when she went to university.

'So you see,' Aunt Hebe said insistently, turning her finely lined, hawk-nosed profile towards me, 'Winter's End should have been Jack's. You *do* see that, don't you? But he says he is going to buy it from you, so everything will be right again.'

'He *did* offer to buy it when he visited me in Northumberland,' I agreed, and again that overwhelming burst of feeling for Winter's End ran through my veins like liquid fire, 'but of course I hadn't seen it then. I – I didn't realise . . .'

'No, I suppose you barely remember it. It can't mean to you what it means to Jack.'

'Until I got here I only had a few random memories . . . and dreams. I used to dream about Winter's End,' I said. 'But from the moment I stepped into the house it felt like . . . like *home*.'

She was looking at me sharply now, seeing a little of what I felt in my face. 'Of course – and it is your home. Dear Jack said that you would always be welcome to visit Winter's End. We're very happy to have you back in the family circle again.'

'That's very kind of you, Aunt Hebe,' I said, then took a deep breath and added, 'but actually . . . well, I think it is going to be the other way around. *Jack* will always be welcome to visit Winter's End, but I'm not parting with it, even to him!'

Her mouth dropped open. 'But Jack said you *would* – he's had the documents drawn up and everything – and now I have explained it all to you, you *must* see that it is Jack's by right!'

'No, it's not – it's mine. Grandfather trusted me to look after Winter's End and his dependants, and that's what I'm going to do. The house *needs* me. I'm sorry if Jack is disappointed, but that is my final decision. Here I am, and here I'll stay – whatever it takes!'

She stared at me. 'You looked just like my brother when you said that! Strange, for you are so dark you could be a changeling in the family. But you are quite attractive, in your way,' she added in a non-sequitur, 'and possibly not too old to give Winter's End an heir.'

'I already have – Lucy,' I pointed out, 'and I wasn't planning to have any more.'

She shrugged off Lucy and changed tack. 'Jack is coming down this weekend. He is *very* handsome, isn't he?'

To my annoyance I felt myself grow pink. 'Very.'

'And very persuasive,' she added, and smiled slightly acidly. 'I am sure you will soon see sense once he has explained things to you in person. He sent you the bouquet over there, by the way, with a very nice message.'

One of those arrangements of out-of-season, sterile-looking blooms in an incongruously modern vase filled with what looked like (and possibly was) frogspawn, stood on a side table, a white card propped up against it: but shouldn't my message have been sealed in a little envelope?

'We won't discuss it any more at the moment, because I am sure things will work out for the best in the end,' Aunt Hebe said, seemingly more to herself than to me. 'Right will prevail, one way or the other.'

I could see which way her mind was now heading – and whose rights she was concerned about – but I no longer knew quite what to think of Jack. For one thing, I'd like to know if my grandfather's suspicions were correct and something had been going on between him and this Melinda Christopher, who would be a rather hard act to follow . . . I was just about to try a bit of delicate – or indelicate – probing on the matter, when I saw that Aunt Hebe was staring fixedly at the shabby carpetbag I'd dumped on the bed.

'Wasn't that your mother's?'

'Yes. She had very few possessions because she was always travelling about, and she tended to give her stuff away. But this she hung on to.'

'But the book – Alys Blezzard's household book – Jack said you hadn't got it? You don't think your mother would have given *that* away or . . . or lost it? We assumed, when we discovered that it was missing, that she took it with her.'

I looked directly, and slightly accusingly, at her. 'Mum did tell me about Alys Blezzard's book, and that the original was kept locked away. But just how did Jack know about it? I thought it was supposed to be a secret, passed down only through the women of the family?'

She shifted a little, guiltily evading my gaze. 'Oh, Jack thinks it's only an old book of household hints and recipes – which it *is*, really. He's terribly interested in anything to do with the history of Winter's End – and anyway, it isn't *truly* secret because copies of the recipes have been passed on by generations of Winter women, especially daughters leaving to get married – but not all of it, of course, just the useful bits. We always assumed your mother took it with her, but I suppose she could simply have hidden it somewhere before she left.'

'If you thought she took it, you probably haven't had a real search for it. I expect it'll turn up,' I suggested, noticing for the first time that Charlie had managed to scramble on the bed and now had his head inside the carpetbag.

So *that's* where I had put the Eccles cakes.

Chapter Seven: Cold Embers

Father hath ridden over and hastily closed with the bargain, not seeking my wishes in the matter, though it is contrary to my will. I hear rumours that he too is to wed again, not a month after my mother and the babe departed this life . . .

From the journal of Alys Blezzard, 1580

After she had gone I let Charlie finish the Eccles cake, since he clearly needed feeding up – but on the floor, not the ancient and quite beautiful patchwork quilt.

It obviously refreshed him, because afterwards he started to chase invisible mice around the room, energetically leaping and pouncing.

There was an antiquated little bathroom through what looked like a cupboard door in the panelling, but I had little time to do more than splash my face with tepid water and shove my snarled hair behind my ears before I heard someone beat merry hell out of a gong, down in the depths of the house.

'Now, where do you think lunch is?' I asked Charlie, who wagged his tail but showed no sign of guiding me there, though he did follow me out when I called him.

I retraced my steps to the minstrels' gallery and luckily spotted Jonah crossing the Great Hall. He was wearing a stiff brown linen apron and staggering under the weight of a huge tray, on which reposed several covered serving dishes and a large squeezy bottle of scarlet ketchup.

Quickly I ran downstairs and followed him through the door into the West Wing and then into the breakfast room.

'*There* you are,' said Aunt Hebe, a spooky figure in the Stygian gloom. 'We always eat in here when it is just family – so much cosier and more convenient than the dining room, I always think.'

While I wouldn't have called a room that was a ten-minute hike from the kitchens convenient, I supposed it was all relative. Once my eyes had adjusted to the darkness I did have vague recollections of the room, with its sturdy Victorian table, carved wooden fire surround and the faded hearth rug on which Charlie immediately curled, in front of the dead grate. But if only someone had taken the trouble to wipe the grime of years from the windows, things would have looked a lot better.

Or maybe they would have looked worse? For, while there was some evidence of a little low-level duster activity, the wainscoting and furniture didn't exactly gleam with beeswax and love, and whole colonies of spiders seemed to have taken up residence in the dirty chandelier. Did no one in this house ever look up?

The table had been reduced to a cosy ten feet or so in length by removing several leaves, which were stacked against the wall. Two places had been set.

Hebe indicated that I should sit at the head of the table. 'William's chair, of course, and though it should be Jack's place now, since my poor misguided brother made it perfectly clear that *you* were to be the head of the household, so be it – until poor dear Jack can take his rightful place.'

Jonah, who had been clattering things about on a side table, now plonked a warm plate down in front of each of us. Then, removing tarnished silver covers from the serving dishes with a flourish, he handed round two pastry-crusted hotpot pies, some mushy peas and a generous helping of pickled red cabbage.

'You've forgotten the water,' Aunt Hebe reminded him.

'I've only got one pair of hands, missis, haven't I?' he grumbled, adding cloudy tumblers and a large jug of dubious-looking fluid to the table. Then he stood back and said benevolently, 'There you are, then – and your semolina pud's on the hotplate yonder when you're ready for it, with the blackcurrant jam.'

'Thank you, Jonah.'

'Yes, thank you,' I echoed, looking down at my plate, on which the violent red of the pickled cabbage had begun to seep its vinegary way into the green of the mushy peas. I put out my hand for my napkin, then hesitated, for it had been crisply folded into the shape of a white waterlily and it seemed a shame to open it.

Jonah leaned over my shoulder and poked it with one not altogether pristine finger. 'Nice, ain't it? It'd be easier with paper serviettes, though, like they have at the evening class down at the village hall. It'll be swans next week.'

'Will it? Won't the necks be difficult?'

'*Thank* you, Jonah,' Aunt Hebe said again with slightly more emphasis, before he could reply, and he ambled off, grinning. Charlie hauled himself up and followed him, and I hoped Mrs Lark would give him something to eat. I was so starving I'd rather not share my hotpot pie, and I didn't think he would fancy mushy peas or pickled cabbage.

Mind you, my last dog ate orange peel, so you just never know.

'We generally find our own lunch and tea in the kitchen, but Mrs Lark wanted to give you something hot today. Though there is usually soup –' she looked around as if surprised at its absence – 'and we just have fruit for dessert.

But today there's semolina, which is apparently your favourite pudding.'

'It might have been once . . . I can't remember.' I hoped Mrs Lark wasn't going to feed me exclusively on the type of nursery diet I ate as a child. My tastes have changed a little over the years.

Mind you, when I stirred a generous dollop of home-made blackcurrant jam into my semolina and it went a strange purple-grey colour, it did all sort of come back to me why I had liked it – stodgy puds are nearly as comforting as chocolate.

When we had finished, and Jonah had brought coffee in mismatched cups and saucers, Aunt Hebe said that she would give me a brief tour of the house. 'Just enough to remind you of the layout, for I am sure you will want a more detailed survey as soon as you have time,' she said shrewdly.

She was quite right, I was already mentally compiling a mammoth shopping list of cleaning materials, some of them only obtainable from specialist suppliers. It was lucky I already knew a good one, called Stately Solutions, wasn't it? Serendipity again, you see.

'After that, I am afraid I must go out, she said, glancing down at the watch pinned to her cardigan. 'I am closely involved in the work of the Church, and it is my turn to do the flowers.'

She fingered the heavy chased gold cross that swung against her bony chest – and I remembered I had seen the small silver pentacle on its chain around her neck earlier that day, the two symbols in incongruous proximity. Perhaps they summed up the conflicting sides of her heritage – the old religion hidden against her skin, the new for outward show?

With the brisk, detached air of a tour guide running late (which of course I recognised, having been one), she took me round the major rooms of the house. 'Dining room, drawing room, morning room, library, cloakroom . . . Mr Yatton's office is here, in the solar tower, and of course at Winter's End he is always called the steward, rather than estate manager.'

'Like on a cruise ship?'

'I know nothing of cruise ships: the appellation is a tradition here,' she said dampeningly.

This part of the house was only vaguely familiar, for my allotted domain as a child had been the nursery, kitchen wing and garden. Stumbling after her through such a warren of dark passages that I half-expected a giant rabbit to bound around the corner at any minute, I thought that each room seemed dingier and more neglected than the last. But I suppose once the sun vanished and the day started to fade it was bound to look worse, especially since the lights weren't switched on.

'This is Lady Anne's parlour.' She cracked open a door a few measly inches, then prepared to shut it again.

'Lady Anne? You don't mean Alys Blezzard's daughter, do you?' I asked, sticking my head under her arm and peering round the door into a small chamber, whose furnishings and decoration, like that of the rest of the house, were an eclectic mix of several centuries.

'Yes, did Susan tell you about her? This was her favourite room and, so it is said, her mother's before her. She was the heiress, of course, and married a cousin, so she remained Anne Winter and stayed on at Winter's End. Over there in the alcove is the wooden coffer that Alys Blezzard's household book was always kept in. We discovered both the book and key had vanished soon after your mother left, and so drew the obvious conclusion . . . but then, being the elder of us, Ottie had charge of the key after your grandmother died, and she is so careless, even with important things.'

The box was about two feet long and perhaps thirteen or fourteen inches high, with two narrow bands of carved flowers and foliage to the front. The sturdy strap-work hinges and lock plate were of decorative pierced metal.

'It's quite plain, isn't it?' I said, feeling slightly disappointed. 'Somehow I expected it to be more ornate – and bigger.'

'This one is a *very* unusual design for the late sixteenth century,' she corrected me, with a look of severe disapproval. 'Not only is the inside heavily carved instead of the outside, it also has a drop front and is fitted out with compartments. Family legend has it that Alys Blezzard's husband, Thomas, gave it to her as a bridal gift, since he was afraid that she might be suspected of witchcraft if she left her book and some of the ingredients she used to make her various charms and potions lying around.'

'So she really *was* a witch?'

'Only a white witch – little more than what we today would call a herbalist,' Aunt Hebe said defensively, and her long bony fingers curled around her gold cross.

I turned back to the box. 'So, how did you know the book was missing, if you hadn't got the key, Aunt Hebe?'

'The box was lighter, and nothing moved inside it when it was tilted.'

'Of course – though if it had been one of those huge heavy affairs with a complicated locking mechanism, which I thought it would be, I don't suppose you would have known it had gone.'

'Actually, there *is* one of those in the estate office, full of old family papers, which I expect Mr Yatton will show you, if you are interested. That's where my brother discovered the original plans for both the terrace gardens and the maze, rolled up in a bundle of later documents. Smaller boxes like this one were probably intended to keep precious things like spices under lock and key originally, but Alys locked away her mother's household book instead.'

'Which became known as Alys Blezzard's book – even though she was really Alys Winter after she married Thomas?'

'Yes. When she received the book after her mother's death,

75

she continued to add to it, as women did then, often passing them on for several generations. But at the front she still signed herself as Alys Blezzard, so I don't think she ever really considered herself to be a Winter. She was the last of that particular branch of the Blezzards too; her father married three times, but had no more children.'

Like a curse, I thought, shivering. I noticed that Charlie was looking fixedly at a point behind me, his tail wagging, but when I turned there was nobody there – or nobody visible.

'I keep having the feeling that there's someone standing right behind me, Aunt Hebe. Is the house haunted? I mean, apart from Alys.'

'Oh, yes. When you were a little girl you called your imaginary friend Alys – I had forgotten. And you were quite convinced that she talked to you! But of course she *does* haunt the house, because of her tragically early death, and there are several other ghosts including the robed figure of a man from about the same time. They say the family was hiding a Catholic priest who was taking gold back to the Continent, to further the work of the Church, but he was betrayed and is still searching for his treasure.'

'You'd think if he hid it he would know where it was, wouldn't you?'

'Well, yes, I suppose so, though each generation has made major alterations to Winter's End so he might be a trifle confused. There are several other legends too, for of course there had been a dwelling on this site for many centuries before Winter's End was built. If you are interested in such things, there is a book in the library called *Hidden Hoards of the North-West* . . . unless Jack still has it. He's been fascinated by the idea of hidden treasure since he was a little boy,' she added indulgently, 'and I had to read to him from that book at bedtime every night.'

That caused me another unworthy pang of jealousy. 'You

used to read to *me* from a scary Victorian book of bible stories, Aunt Hebe!'

'But you were an ungodly child,' she said severely, 'born of sin.'

I didn't think I had been particularly wayward, just mischievous, but I let it go. 'Have *you* seen any of the ghosts?'

'I thought I saw a Saxon in the garden once, at dusk, looking for the hoard he had hidden before a battle. But it was probably just one of the gardeners.'

The windows of Lady Anne's parlour looked out over the terraces at the back of the house and were curtained in a predominantly coral-coloured William Morris fabric. The walls above the inevitable dark wainscoting had been painted the same shade, and coral tones softly echoed in the faded, but still beautiful, carpet.

I felt as though the room was casting an aura of welcome around me and I could see myself sitting there in the evening, piecing together my crazy cushions. 'Aunt Hebe, would you mind if I used this room? It's lovely, and I'll need somewhere to make my patchwork.'

'I can't say I ever much cared for sitting in here,' she said, looking slightly surprised, 'and though Mother was a skilled needlewoman and used to embroider beautifully, she did it in the drawing room after dinner. The firescreen in the study is her work.'

'I'll look out for it. Where do *you* like to sit in the evening, Aunt Hebe?'

'Sometimes one place, sometimes another . . .' she said vaguely, like an elderly Titania – which indeed, she resembled. 'Though I often work in the stillroom until late, or go out – I am on several village committees. There is a TV in the library, but I also have one in my room, for William and I tended to live *very* separate lives.'

'We didn't have a TV in the commune and I've never really felt the need for one since, but we always had a radio when I worked at Lady Betty's. I like to listen to Radio 4 when I'm sewing. You can't really watch something and sew properly, can you?'

'I don't know, I've never tried.' She looked at her watch and then shooed me out along a tapestry-hung passage and up some spiral stairs. The door at the top opened between my bedroom and the arch leading to the upper level of the tower, which was a complete surprise – I'd noticed it, but thought it was another cupboard.

'I don't remember these stairs at all!'

'That is because you were not allowed to use them. William insisted you were confined to the nursery and the kitchens, though we were forever finding you sliding down the Great Hall banisters. There are the stairs to the attic nursery floor over there, which you will recall, so we won't bother going up – the rest of the roof space is now entirely given up to storage. I keep the door to that side locked, otherwise Grace sneaks off up there and smokes.'

She turned on her white, wellington-booted heel and sped off, appearing to be losing interest in the tour fast. 'You know this bedroom floor already,' she tossed over her shoulder. 'There are six bedrooms – eight if you include the nursery suite – but the Rose Room is never used.'

I fell down some ill-lit steps and bumped into her round the corner as she came to an abrupt stop.

'Turn left and you enter the Long Room again, at the end of which is the door to the East Wing where there are further bedchambers, the Larks' living quarters, and the backstairs to the kitchens. This one takes us onto the landing, of course, commonly called the minstrels' gallery, and, since it projects over the hall, I expect they did sometimes have musicians there when they were entertaining. When Ottie and I were girls we had parties with dancing in the Great Hall, and the band sat up here and played.'

That must have been quite a sight – the tall, slim, blue-eyed Miss Winters, their red-gold hair floating as they danced the night away with their dinner-jacketed partners . . .

'What sort of music did you dance to?' I asked curiously, and would have loved to have known if she had a favourite partner too, had she been in the mood for reminiscence, but the past clearly held no fascination for Aunt Hebe. Ignoring my question as though I had never asked it, she carried on with her tour. 'The Great Hall and the solar are much older than the rest of the house, but the Winters were forever knocking bits down and rebuilding them. You can see from the blocked fireplace halfway up the wall that the hall was once single storey with rooms over it, and then the height was increased and the ceiling plastered, leaving only the minstrels' gallery.'

She clomped off and I could feel the gallery floorboards bouncing under my feet. 'Most of the lesser family portraits are hung here, and on open days the visitors can come up. We lock the door at the end, but the family can still reach either wing of the house by way of the Long Room if they wish, without meeting a member of the public.'

'It's very dark; you can hardly make the portraits out. Does anyone actually want to come up here?'

'Oh, yes, for Shakespeare is rumoured to have visited Winter's End, and if so presumably would have stood on this very spot – if he came at all. But show me an old manor house in this part of Lancashire where he *isn't* supposed to have been!'

'Really?' I said, interested. 'I didn't know that.'

She shrugged bony shoulders impatiently. 'There is a theory that he spent the Lost Years here in Lancashire, in the employment of various local families, especially the

Hoghtons – and he is supposed to have a particular connection with Rufford Old Hall, near Ormskirk, which is now, of course, a National Trust property. There is a book about it in the library, I believe.'

'Really? I'll look for it later, along with that hidden treasures one.'

It was beginning to look as if I would have plenty of bedtime reading for the foreseeable future!

Aunt Hebe was losing interest in Shakespeare. 'One of the volunteer stewards, the Friends of Winter's End, stands at either end of the gallery, and they have a fund of anecdotes concerning his apocryphal visit and stories about Alys Blezzard. That portrait in the middle is supposed to be her, but it is some dreadful affair painted by a jobbing artist, from the look of it, more used to depicting prize bulls and sheep.'

'Hard to tell,' I agreed, peering at it. 'It looks as if it has been dipped in Brown Windsor soup. In fact, most of the paintings I've seen seem in want of a cleaning.'

'Only a few in the Long Room were cleaned when your grandfather was searching for something to pay the death duties with. But once they found the Stubbs, that sufficed.'

She started to descend the stairs, but I paused and ran my hand over the curved banister, remembering the small Sophy who used to climb up onto it, clinging on for dear life as she swooshed down . . .

The Great Hall looked dark and yawningly empty below me, but not half as big as I recalled – *nothing* was: The house, which had seemed so huge in my childhood memories, had in reality shrunk to quite modest proportions, though it would still be a worryingly monumental task to restore it to its former glory.

'Do you ever light the fire now?' I asked, joining her at the bottom of the stairs.

'The fire?' She turned to look at it, as if, by magic, flames would appear. 'We always used to – but I suppose no one has given the orders since William died.'

She pointed at a stack of screens against one wall. 'On open days all these are set out into a display of the history of the house, the supposed Shakespeare connection – and Alys Blezzard's story, of course. You know the legend is she was distantly related through her mother to the Nutters, who were known witches?'

'Yes, Mum told me all about that. She said Alys really *was* a witch.'

'Yes ... Susan was always a fanciful child,' Aunt Hebe said dismissively. 'A knowledge of simple herbs and their curative effects does not mean one is versed in the black arts and in league with the devil.' She pulled out the corner of a screen: 'This one is the history of Winter's End and the Winter family. Then there is the story of how the original Elizabethan plans for the terrace were discovered and the restoration begun – and about the missing part for the lower terrace.'

'Missing?'

'Yes, torn off and not anywhere to be found. William and Seth were still arguing about what *might* have been on the lower terrace right up until the end. Indeed, the arguments kept William's spirits up amazingly.'

'Seth?'

'The head gardener – so called.'

'Oh, yes, I'd forgotten, though his name's pretty apt for a gardener, isn't it? Sort of *Cold Comfort Farm*. I only hope there isn't something nasty in the woodshed.'

'Only wood,' she said seriously, 'and spiders – did you mean spiders? I am not fond of them myself, but freshly gathered cobwebs make an excellent poultice for wounds.'

The tour ended in the kitchen, where Mrs Lark was sitting

in a rocking chair in front of the Aga knitting, with the radio on. Charlie lay in a position of blissful abandon on a rag rug at her feet. His stomach, as round as if he'd swallowed a small football, rose and fell to his stertorous breathing.

Aunt Hebe again consulted the watch attached to her flat bosom by a bow-shaped golden brooch. 'Time to go – but before I do, I will be happy to pass you these.'

And she literally *did* pass me the most enormous bunch of keys, some of them museum pieces in their own right. 'But Aunt Hebe, I can't take these from you!' I protested.

'There is no reason why not, for this bunch is mainly symbolic. We hardly ever lock anything away – except the Book, when we had it, and a fat lot of good that did us. Indeed, I have no idea what half of the keys are for, and in any case I was only ever nominal housekeeper, for Mrs Lark does it all. No, my business is the walled garden – which that Seth Greenwood is forbidden to touch! I grow practically all the fruit and vegetables for the house and I have bees and chickens. And of course, the stillroom through there is for my use only. You may look at both,' she added grandly, 'but not poke and pry and stick your fingers into what doesn't concern you!'

'Yes, Aunt Hebe,' I said meekly, hearing the echo of the same words in the voice of an eight-year-old, curious to know what her witchy ancient relative was cooking up.

'I expect Mrs Lark will show you her apartment herself, though perhaps after your long journey you might wish to put off any further inspections of your *realm* until another day,' she said slightly acidly, and departed back through the swinging, baize-lined door to the hall.

She left a snail trail of silver sequins behind her: she must have caught a loose thread on something.

Chapter Eight: Sovereign Remedies

Sir Ralph asked mee whether I was of the Old Religion and I said I was. I swore to it, and he was well pleased. I know them to be Catholics like Father, despite their outward show of compliance to the new faith; they do not know that the old religion I swore to is not the same as theirs . . .

From the journal of Alys Blezzard, 1581

Mrs Lark said, 'Don't you worry about her – she never took any interest in the housekeeping, but she's kept us in fruit and vegetables for years – and honey, chickens and eggs too. Now, do you want me to show you our rooms? Up the backstairs, they are.'

'I would – but not today, if you don't mind, Mrs Lark. So much needs doing that I think I need to go round in daylight with a notebook and write down a list of priorities,' I said, though actually, what I really wanted to do was run about the house shrieking, 'It's mine, mine – all mine!' at the top of my lungs, now that Aunt Hebe was no longer there to depress my pretensions.

'The whole house is falling to pieces and that filthy I'm ashamed of it,' Mrs Lark said forthrightly. 'I clean my own rooms, but though poor Grace does her best with the rest of it all, it's too much for her. And I do the cooking and ordering, but further than that I don't go – not at my time of life.'

'Of course not. You shouldn't have to do anything else. It isn't your job.'

'That's right,' she agreed, less defensively. 'My Jonah, he's butler, valet, handyman – whatever's wanted – though he started out as groom when Mr William used to hunt. But he's a man, so he doesn't notice what wants doing, never has – you have to tell him.'

That explained the lack of a fire in the Great Hall then: it was merely that no one had thought to give the orders! I mooted the point.

'I'll tell him when he comes in,' she said. 'September to March it's always kept lit, because it takes the chill off the whole place.'

'What do we usually burn?'

'Logs. The gardeners cut and stack them in the old stables – there's always plenty. Ecologically sustainable,' she added conscientiously, 'from our own woodland.'

'Oh, good,' I said. 'How often does Grace come in?'

'Weekday mornings generally, unless there's a party or visitors. She does the beds and towels Wednesdays and Fridays – they go to the laundry, though there's a machine out through the back, if you want it. Grace does any other washing as required, and the ironing. Other than that, when she's vacuumed through and done the kitchen floor and the bathrooms, she's no time for anything else. In fact, I reckon it's all getting a bit much for her; she's not as fast as she used to be.'

'I think it's amazing she does so much!'

'She's not as old as she looks. I keep telling her all them cigarettes she smokes make her look like a living mummy and wheeze like a piano accordion. I've never smoked and we're the same age, but *I've* got the complexion and figure I had at thirty to show for it.'

84

Leaving Mrs Lark knitting and Charlie sleeping, I took a quick look at the stillroom, Aunt Hebe's domain, where racks and bunches of anonymous vegetation hung everywhere and the scent of attar of roses and rush matting vied with other, stranger, odours.

A small table with a chair each side stood near the side door to the shrubbery: Aunt Hebe's consulting desk for furtive evening customers?

Gingerly (and guiltily!) opening a cupboard, I found myself nose to nose with a row of glass-stoppered jars and bottles, all bearing labels written in a spiky black gothic hand: 'ORRIS ROOT', 'HOLY WATER (Lourdes)', 'FULLER'S EARTH,' 'POWDERED GINGER', 'GROUND BARN OWL BONES (Roadkill 1996)'.

Ground owl bones?

'LIQUORICE EXTRACT', 'POWDERED AMBERGRIS', 'DRIED BAT WINGS'.

I shut the door hastily, deciding not to open any more cupboards – then immediately did, thinking it was the way out. This one contained shelf after shelf of much smaller bottles and jars with fancier labels. Pinned to the inside of the door was a hand-written price list. 'Number 2 Essence: A sovereign remedy for restoring the joys of marriage,' I read, 'Two pounds fifty.'

After all these years without even a word from Rory, it would take more than an essence to restore *my* marriage! The next remedy was clearly aimed at all those exhausted wives with priapic elderly husbands, pepped up on Viagra: 'Number 5 Essence: The tired wife's friend. Two drops in any liquid given to the husband near bedtime will ensure an unbroken night's rest. (Do not exceed dose.) Three pounds.'

It looked like Aunt Hebe had gone into production on a large scale.

I popped my head back through the kitchen door. 'Mrs Lark, do Aunt Hebe's remedies actually work?'

She looked up. 'Well, no one's ever asked for their money back to my knowledge.' She cast on a couple more stitches and added, 'Or died from them, either.'

'That's a relief,' I said, and went back to my tour, though I hesitated before opening any more doors. But luckily the next one merely gave on to a passage with the narrow backstairs going up from it and the cellar entrance. There was a warren of rooms beyond it, many of them unused except for storage (one of them was stacked practically floor to ceiling with what looked like empty florist's boxes), but this area looked very familiar to me. I had been allowed to play here and to ride my red tricycle up and down the flagged floors. How I'd loved that trike! The chipped skirting boards were probably my doing.

Feeling nostalgic I wandered on until I came to another passage, across which a fairly new-looking door had been installed. It was unlocked and when I passed through I saw that it had a sign on the other side saying: 'PRIVATE! NO ADMITTANCE BEYOND THIS POINT.'

Here, by removing the door between two rooms and throwing out a little glassed-in conservatory overlooking the top terrace at the back of the house, a tearoom of kinds had been created. There was a counter topped with a glass food display cabinet adorned with dust and dead flies, and a collection of mismatched pine tables and chairs, varnished to the deep orange shade of a cheap instant suntan.

It all looked terribly half-hearted and uninviting, though perhaps in summer when they opened they gussied the place up a bit with bright tablecloths and flowers.

The visitors' loos were off the further room and a brief glance told me were of Victorian servants' quality, though

I suppose at the time it was the height of luxury for the staff to have indoor toilets at all.

I retraced my steps to the warm kitchen, where Mrs Lark ceased knitting long enough to look up and smile at me. Charlie didn't appear to have moved an inch since I left.

'Did you remember your way around, lovey? You played out there all the time when the weather was bad, making dens out of old cardboard cartons, or riding that little trike of yours, though in the summer you were always outside. You used to run round and round the maze like a mad thing, with your granddad's spaniels all chasing after you, barking their heads off.'

'It's all coming back to me – I remembered my way around this wing perfectly, despite a few changes. What are all those empty boxes in one of the rooms for?'

'Mistletoe. Winter's End is noted for it. But I don't suppose you remember the mistletoe harvests before Christmas, when the gardeners gather it and it's packed off to London?'

I shook my head.

'Perhaps you were kept away, for the berries are poisonous. The boxes used to be stored in a shed, but the mice got at them.'

'I suppose they would,' I agreed. 'The tearoom is a bit rough and ready, isn't it? And the toilet is inadequate, I should have thought, especially if there's a coach party.'

'It was the staff toilet until Sir William put in that nice cloakroom under the backstairs, and the teashop used to be the laundry and brewhouse. But we don't need a laundry now we've got the utility room, and the only brewing is what Miss Hebe does next door, and better not to ask about most of *that*,' she said darkly.

'Definitely not,' I agreed. 'When we're open, who does the teas?'

'The Friends serve them, but I cook the pastries and scones.'

'That must make a lot of work for you?'

'I like to do a big bake, and Grace comes in extra and cuts the sandwiches, but we don't get so many visitors.'

'I'm surprised you get any, because there isn't much of the house open to see, is there?'

'No, but they come for the garden mostly. It's a picture in summer, though Seth says the terraces are still a work in progress. Gardening clubs and so on – they like to keep coming year after year to see how it's going on.'

'Surely it must be nearly finished by now? They've been at it for years, from what Mr Hobbs was saying!'

'Oh, yes, I think there's only the bottom terrace to do, though it seems to me they spend as much time maintaining the garden as they did making the thing in the first place – all these grown men snipping and clipping! Miss Hebe seems able to manage the whole walled garden on her own, apart from getting one of the gardeners to do the heavy digging, or clean out the hens, which makes Seth mad. He thinks of nothing but his blessed restoration scheme and your granddad was just the same.'

'I'll look round the garden as soon as I've got the chance, but it sounds as if it's had enough time and money expended on it and getting the house back in good order will be what's important now. Things are going to change.'

'I'm glad to hear it. When we heard how Sir William had left things, we did wonder if you would come back or just sell the place.'

'I wondered too, at first, but once I'd seen Winter's End again I knew I was back for good,' I said firmly, though somewhere inside I was quaking at the thought of explaining that to Jack . . .

Charlie gave a sudden snort and opened his eyes, then

got to his feet and ambled over, tail wagging. I bent down to stroke his matted head. 'Do you know where Charlie's brushes are?'

'The cleaning room, two doors down the passage on the left. I doubt you'll get a brush through that mess, though, but I'll tell Jonah to give it a go, shall I?'

'No, I think you might be right about not being able to get a brush through it. He'll have to be clipped, and I'd say from the way he's walking that his claws need cutting too. He can't have been getting out and about enough to wear them down, while he's been moping. In fact,' I decided, 'what I *really* need is a dog grooming parlour!'

'Milly's Mutt-Mobile,' Mrs Lark said.

'What?'

'Jonah's sister's husband's brother's girl. She has a mobile dog parlour. Shall I ring her?'

'Oh, *would* you? Ask her if she could come up and do something with Charlie as soon as she has time.'

'I'll be glad to. I feel that bad for neglecting the poor little thing, though I kept trying to coax him to eat, and Miss Hebe tried one or two of her potions on him. But he's just had a huge dinner now, so he's on the mend.'

Yes . . . Aunt Hebe's household-book-derived potions.

'Mrs Lark,' I said, sitting on the wooden settle facing her, 'I expect you know about Alys Blezzard's book, don't you?'

'Oh, yes, there've always been copies of what you might call the *everyday* recipes in circulation, and they were used in the kitchens here, but of course not nowadays . . . though come to think of it, I do still use the one for medlar cheese. Your aunt got her recipes for the lotions and potions and stuff she brews up from the original, though they're not Christian to my way of thinking, because it's well known that Alys Blezzard and her mother were both witches. Lots of people locally, they come up here of nights and buy

89

them. I use the rose face cream and hand cream myself,' she added reluctantly. 'There's no harm in *them*.'

'My mother always said Alys was a witch. She liked to think she took after her, brewing up charms and spells, but she didn't really. It was just a pose.'

'Alys Blezzard was distantly related to the Nutters through her mother, and *they* were witches,' Mrs Lark said. 'Some of them were burned for it, I think, a lot later. Alys was took – betrayed by the family, some say.'

'Took?'

'Gaoled her for questioning, but she died before they could do anything. Just as well, though Seth says she probably wouldn't have been burned as a witch back then; the burnings was later. But ducking would likely have been just as fatal, especially in the wintertime, if they got carried away.'

I shivered. 'What a horrible thought! And didn't they sometimes tie suspected witches up and throw them in the water, and if they sank they were innocent, but if they floated they were guilty? They had no chance, did they?'

'Before she died Alys entrusted the book to a servant, to give to her daughter when she was old enough,' she said, with a bright-eyed look at me. 'I overheard Miss Hebe saying so to Jack – and that it was full of treasures. Alys had said so herself on the flyleaf.'

'She told *Jack* that!' I exclaimed, because Mum had definitely led me to understand that the ancient, handwritten book with all its recipes, was some great and precious secret handed down only to the women of the family – and if there was one thing certain, it was that Jack wasn't one of those.

'Of course, that was enough to get him going, seeing the way he's been treasure-hunt mad from a little lad – and he turned the place upside down looking for the book in case your mum hadn't taken it after all.'

'But the treasures are just the recipes!'

She shrugged her plump shoulders. 'Miss Hebe couldn't even remember properly what Alys had written in the book because it was Ottie that had charge of the key to the box, and she'd rarely let her look at it. And when Ottie found out she'd told Jack, she was right mad! They haven't spoken since – but then they were forever falling out, so that's nothing new. When Ottie married the gardener they didn't speak for five years, Hebe was that disgusted – only it was probably all down to jealousy because he was a fine figure of a man, though she'd never of married him herself, of course.'

'You know, I *thought* they weren't speaking. But how did Ottie find out that Hebe had talked to Jack about it in the first place?'

'Because he tried pumping her about the book and got a right flea in his ear for his trouble. Ottie told him straight it was nothing to do with *him*.'

'That explains a lot. I was surprised Jack knew about the book at all, when he came up to see me in Northumberland, but I can see now that of course its existence was bound to be generally known about within the family and copies of some of the recipes in circulation. But Aunt Ottie was right – the rest is no business of Jack's.'

I got up. 'I think I'll just bring the rest of my bags in, then move the van round the back. It lowers the tone of the place, standing out there.'

'You can park it in the courtyard or the barn, if you like,' she said. 'Leave your bags in the hall and Jonah will take them up for you. Your other stuff that came, we stored it in the attic nearest your old nursery. You remember where that is?'

'Yes, Aunt Hebe showed me, but more and more is coming back to me anyway.'

'Your mother's things that were returned with her, they're all in her old room – the Rose Bedroom. Mr William wouldn't let us change a thing in there after you both ran off. It's just the same as the day she left and it's never been used for visitors.'

This was unexpected of Grandfather, and rather touching. And I'd never given a thought to what had happened to any of the luggage Mum took to America with her – but of course it would have been returned to Winter's End.

'I expect you'll want to go down to the graveyard in a day or two, pay your respects,' Mrs Lark suggested. 'It's got a nice stone angel – looks a bit like your mum did the last time I saw her. Mr William had fresh flowers sent down every week.'

'Yes, I'll do that,' I said, getting up. 'Thank you, Mrs Lark.'

'Come back for a bit of tea later, if you want. If I'm not here, there's parkin and gingerbread men I made special – they're over there cooling on the rack.'

I ate one right there, hot and bendy though it was, and then, with Charlie still following me like a small shadow, I brought in the rest of my bags and piled them at the bottom of the staircase. Then I drove round the back, past the tower and through an arch into a flagged courtyard. A pair of doors opened onto a barn that already contained a battered sports car that I somehow knew was Ottie's, and the Volvo estate that had been Grandfather's. But there was still plenty of room, so I put the van in there and then walked out into the yard again.

One side of the courtyard was formed by the old coach house, now transformed into a home and studio in which, through a large glazed door standing ajar, despite the cold wind, I could see Aunt Ottie standing motionless in front of some monstrous shape, smoking a cheroot, her back to me.

I pushed open the door and went in. Without turning, she said: 'Well, Sophy, what do you think?'

Chapter Nine: Lost in Translation

Tomorrow I will be married. Fond though I am of Thomas, to embrace him will be to embrace death itself – yet there is no escape. I look to the future and see only dark shadows closing in on mee.

I asked one bride gift only – that my mother's maid, Joan, be sent for, since my father hath turned her off, and this boon was granted to mee. Though seemingly a simple creature, she is of our old ways and was devoted to my mother. She brought with her my mother's household book, which I mean to continue with, and some other things I have hid to be safe.

From the journal of Alys Blezzard, 1581

I wasn't surprised that Ottie knew who was there without turning round, because I can often do that myself. I think it's a Winter thing – like the way I frequently have a flash of foreknowledge that something good or bad is heading in my direction. That was partly why I didn't go to America with my mother, though it turned out that the dark shadows were gathering for her, not me.

I examined what looked like a cross between a cow and a giant bat, the clay seemingly slapped on over the armature with a giant paddle, and said cautiously, 'It's a very interesting interpretation.'

I mean, what do *I* know of modern sculpture? My knowledge of art comes from dusting several miles of old pictures in a freezing Scottish loch-side castle, or Lady Betty's collection of pseudo-antique Egyptian relics; and if I never see another washy watercolour of Highland cattle, or crumbling alabaster Canopic jar, it won't cause me any grief whatsoever.

'Interpretation of what, exactly?' Ottie enquired with interest.

'I have absolutely no idea,' I confessed, and she laughed.

'Good – I hate humbug.' She regarded her monstrous creation with complacency. 'It's called *Folded: 25* and it's the final one for an installation in Swindon. This could be the most exciting thing that's ever happened to the place.'

She turned her bright blue eyes on me and asked, 'Settling in all right?'

'Yes, thanks. I've just unloaded the van and put it in the barn, and Aunt Hebe gave me a quick tour of the house to remind me of the layout, before she had to go down to the church. Aunt Ottie . . .'

'Just call me Ottie, everyone does.'

'Ottie,' I said firmly, since she had seemingly lost interest in me again and gone back to contemplating her sculpture through a haze of sweet blue smoke, 'Aunt Hebe appears to have told Jack all about Alys Blezzard's book and now he thinks it might hold a clue to finding a hidden treasure.'

That regained her attention. 'My sister's a fool – always was, always will be. She said she thought he ought to know, since there were no female Winters left after us. But of course there were – you! And I knew you would come back one day, because I've got a dose of the family second sight, while Hebe just inherited the skills to whip up potions and charms.' She looked at me sharply. 'You're like me, I think?'

'A bit. Not so much second sight as more of a vague sense of good or bad coming my way – either as a light on

94

the horizon and my spirits lifting, or dark shadows closing in on me.'

'Hmm,' she said. 'You'll probably get a stronger dose when I've popped my clogs. That's what happened to *me* when my grandmother died. I suppose it's only the Winter tendency to marry second or third cousins that has kept it so strong in the family all these centuries.'

I remembered Jack's joke about that and also, guiltily, that he was still entirely unaware of my transition from reluctant heiress to Homecoming Queen. I had an uncomfortable suspicion that 'consort' wasn't in his vocabulary . . .

Ottie ground the stub of her cheroot out under the heel of her boot. 'That Hebe's daft as a brush, wittering on about things she knows very well she shouldn't, and putting ideas into Jack's head. Not that there aren't enough twisty little cunning ideas in there already,' she warned, with a sharp look at me.

'Is that why you and Hebe aren't speaking to each other?'

'Partly. I suppose Susan told *you* all about the book?'

'Yes, and everything that *her* mother told her, but she thought you knew more than she did.'

'William's wife was giddy, like Susan – sweet, but no substance to her – and she died young. It put me in a bit of a dilemma, to be frank, though I had great hopes of you. Did you ever see that series on TV, *Buffy the Vampire Slayer*?' she added, with disconcerting abruptness. '"Into every generation a vampire slayer is born"?'

'No, we never had a TV. And where do vampires come in?' I asked uneasily.

'They don't – but into each generation or so of Winter women is born one to be trusted to keep Alys Blezzard's secrets safe, and pass them on to the next, like an endless game of tag down the centuries. There have been Regency belles, disapproving Victorian misses and twenties flappers,

but they've all kept the faith. I'm the Buffy for *my* generation – but there seems to have been a slight glitch with the
next two. However,' she added more cheerfully, 'since I also
had a bit of the magic about me, I knew it would all come
right in the end! You're here, and here to stay, aren't you?'

'Well . . . yes – but I have absolutely no idea how I'm
going to manage it!'

'You'll find a way,' she said confidently.

I would have to. Losing Winter's End again simply wasn't
an option. I went back to what Ottie had been saying. 'So
Mum *was* right and you do know something more – and
maybe Alys's references to treasures mean more than *I*
thought, too?'

'The book is itself a rare treasure – a household manū-
script of that age, written by a woman,' she said evasively.
'There have always been copies of the more useful, everyday
recipes circulating within the family, but when Hebe showed
an interest in the more esoteric side, I let her go through
the original book to look for others – more fool me! Now
she's blabbed about things she had no right to, and Jack's
been creeping about searching the place like something out
of a Secret Seven novel, looking for buried gold. Seth found
him using a metal detector in the grounds just after William
died and threatened to wrap it round his neck if he caught
him digging holes in the beds again. Then I told him he
needed the permission of the owner to do it anyway, which
made him even more furious, of course.'

'I suppose it would, since apparently he's been brought
up to think himself the heir all these years,' I pointed out.
'It's a difficult situation for him. But I can't understand why
Hebe told Jack in the first place.'

'She doted on the child from the moment he came back
from New Zealand and spoiled him to death, so I suppose
it was on the cards that she would tell him everything she

knew eventually. But goodness knows why, because he isn't showing any sign of getting married again, so there's no wife to take the secret on to the next generation.'

'Oh? I saw Melinda Christopher this morning as I was arriving – her horse tried to sit on my car. Aunt Hebe said Grandfather thought she and Jack seemed to be getting close when she first moved back here, until he showed that he disapproved.'

Ottie thought that one over. 'I don't think so. They are just old friends and move in the same circles. But she's a rich widow, so now William isn't here to put his oar in, perhaps Jack will see her in a different light. He's always found money powerfully attractive. He and Melinda have got *that* in common.'

I returned to our original subject with an effort. 'I still don't see why Aunt Hebe had to tell Jack anything.'

'Nor me. She just said she thought he ought to know, now he was the last of the Winters.'

'Only the last of the *male* Winters, and he's not actually a Winter at all unless he takes the name by deed poll, is he? Still, all he seems to know is that Alys mentions secret treasures on the flyleaf of the original book.'

'That's right, and luckily she couldn't even remember the exact wording of that. In fact, there's only me who knows *everything* now – custodian of the family secrets, as you might say.' She paused. 'When I realised Hebe had blabbed, though, it did make me wonder if *I* should confide in someone, too. Especially someone who could keep an eye on Jack's treasure-hunting when I wasn't here.'

She looked at me and away again. 'You see, I knew you were going to come back, and since the key and the book vanished when your mother did, I assumed you had them. I mean, you *have* got them, haven't you? It would be terrible if the book was lost for ever!'

I ignored that, staring at her, aghast. 'Ottie, are you saying that *you* told someone else the family secrets too?'

'Well, I'm no spring chicken any more,' she replied defensively. 'I knew you would return, but not *when*. What if you came back too late? So I told someone I trusted exactly what Hebe had told Jack, and left a letter with the solicitor to be given to you when you turned up, telling you the rest.'

'Ottie, *who* did you tell?'

There was the sound of heavy, rapidly approaching footsteps, and then a tall, broad-shouldered shape blotted out the light. 'Ma?' a familiar deep, Lancashire-accented voice demanded. 'Ma, are you there? I think old William must have been off his head! He's only gone and left the place to a spaced-out New-Age traveller and she—'

He stopped dead when he suddenly saw me and his mouth closed like a trap. Charlie, who had been sitting on my feet, got up and wagged his tail. That dog has no discrimination whatsoever.

I turned incredulously to Ottie. '*Ma?*'

She looked self-conscious. 'Yes, this is my stepson and your head gardener, Seth Greenwood. Have you met?'

'*Your* stepson is *my* so-called head gardener?'

'Yes.' She looked away and fiddled with a metal modelling tool while I put two and two together fast: 'Don't tell me your tit-for-tat retaliation for Hebe's indiscretion was to tell *him*?' I jerked a finger at the gardener, who glowered at me. 'At least Jack was *family*!'

'Well, so is Seth – by marriage. And at least he can be trusted to do what is best for Winter's End, while Jack's just out to line his pockets in any way he can,' she said defensively. 'If he'd inherited, the place would have been converted into some kind of upmarket apartment block and slapped on the market five minutes after probate was granted.'

'I think you are wrong – and I don't know why you're

so against Jack. He seems to me to care deeply about Winter's End! But that's beside the point, because *neither* of them should know anything about it at all.'

'Someone needs to keep an eye on Jack, Sophy, you take it from me – and I'm not always here.'

'But now *I* will always be here.'

'Yes, and Jack's going to be pressing you to show him the book the minute he realises you have it, after all – which you do, don't you?' she asked again, slightly anxiously.

'If I have, then it is mine by right – and in any case, I refuse to discuss it any further in front of *him*. Or, in fact, at all! I think you and Hebe have both betrayed a sacred trust.'

I turned and for the first time spoke directly to Seth, who was lounging in the doorway with his arms folded across a broad expanse of holey jumper and an evil look in his green eyes, like a villainous but worryingly attractive character in a B movie. That elusive memory stirred again . . .

'Just bear in mind, Seth Greenwood, that I am not about to have my property searched by you, or anyone else, for a treasure that doesn't exist. If you want to keep your job, and Jack wants to keep his visiting rights, then you'd both better consider that!'

He straightened up suddenly and said furiously, 'Now just you look here—'

But Ottie broke into a great peal of laughter, drowning him out. 'That's it, Sophy, you tell him straight!'

'I will,' I said, 'especially now I've remembered where I met your stepson before!'

'Not a happy meeting?' she asked interestedly.

'No!'

'I *thought* I recognised that van,' he said coolly, making it clear that *I* certainly wasn't memorable enough to stick in his mind. 'Didn't I move you and your New-Age traveller friends on a couple of years ago, over near Rivington?'

'You certainly *tried* to move us on, even after we'd explained that we'd had to stop because Sandy's baby was coming early.'

'I'd heard that sort of story before.' He rubbed his straight nose and then added grudgingly, 'Though that time it turned out to be true, I admit. You know, I thought women in childbirth only screamed like that in films.'

'Sandy believed in letting out the pain.'

'She did that all right. They could hear her up at the house.'

'That's a gross exaggeration. And we left as soon as we could, didn't we, without doing any damage?'

'No, you didn't – you made a mess of the ground I'd had cleared for a knot garden.'

From the way he said 'knot garden' you would think we had desecrated a sacred site, but it gave me the opening to hit him where it hurt.

'Well, bear in mind that now Winter's End is mine I can invite *hordes* of New-Age travellers to camp here any time I want to,' I said nastily and out I marched, though I wasn't entirely convinced that Seth was going to move aside and let me through until the very last minute.

He towered over me and out of the corner of my eye I noticed that his mouth was twitching, which was probably either temper or a nervous tic. After his remarks earlier in the day I sincerely hoped he hadn't got religious mania too.

Mrs Lark consoled me in the kitchen with tea and very gingery parkin. She also confirmed my suspicion that my aunts had immediately divided into two opposing camps once Jack had arrived and then Ottie married Seth's father, the new head gardener.

'Jack looked like an angel, but he was mischievous, and Seth always ended up getting the blame for his pranks until Ottie stepped in. He was a stoical little boy and I don't suppose

100

he would have said anything, but she said she wouldn't stand by and see him being punished for things he hadn't done.'

'No, I don't suppose she would,' I agreed, digesting this new insight into what had gone on during my absence from Winter's End. Maybe if I had remained there it would have been *me* who would have got all the blame, bottom of the pecking order?

Mrs Lark suggested I should go and change for dinner, but she didn't say into what – a giant moth, maybe? If I carried on eating at the current rate I'd certainly be changing into something bigger, but not necessarily better, though I did take the hint and put on a long plum-coloured crinkle-cotton skirt and flat Chinese silk slippers.

When I went down I found Ottie and Hebe studiously ignoring each other in the drawing room, both looking defensive and sheepish. Ottie was still in clay-smeared jeans, though she had removed the outsize man's plaid lumberjack shirt she had been wearing in the studio as an overall. Hebe, abandoning her whites, was arrayed in a long, dark green velvet dress that was bald on both elbows and the seat.

'There you are,' Aunt Hebe said. 'I've poured you a glass of sherry. My sister seemed to think you wouldn't like it, but then, she has very depraved tastes. It comes of living as a bohemian for most of her life and only pleasing herself.'

I took the glass, though actually Ottie was right and I don't really like it much.

'In fact, I don't know why my sister is here at all,' Hebe added. 'Perhaps you ought to ask her.'

'William liked the family together for dinner,' Ottie said. 'I always come over when I'm home, unless I'm working late. Then Mrs Lark sends it over. Saves cooking for just me too. Do you mind, Sophy?'

'Not at all. In fact, I like it, but I'd like it even more if you two would speak to each other! I'll find it very wearing being a sort of conversational conduit, and so far as I can see, you have both betrayed a trust, so the honours – or dishonours – are even.'

'Huh!' said Ottie, and she and Hebe exchanged wary sideways glances from identical bright blue eyes.

Then Jonah beat the gong and we trooped into the breakfast parlour. Dinner was the split pea and ham soup that Mrs Lark had mentioned earlier, giant Yorkshire puddings filled with roast beef, carrots, peas and gravy, and apple tart and cream, washed down with a glass of red wine from a dusty bottle. The room began to slowly waver like something seen through bull's-eye glass: it had been a very long and tiring day.

We had coffee in the library, and then Ottie left for the coach house and Hebe vanished upstairs. Jonah, when he came in for the tray, said she was addicted to soaps, which she recorded on video and watched in the privacy of her own room, my grandfather having been scathing about them.

By then I was really fit for nothing except the long, satiated sleep of the python that ate the goat – and if this sort of food appeared in front of me every day, I thought, my waist would vanish and my figure would not even resemble an extreme hour glass, but a fishing float.

'I'm going to my room too, Jonah,' I said, yawning hugely. 'I'm so tired I'm starting to feel as if I'm underwater with my ears about to pop. It's been a long and eventful day.'

'If you want a nightcap, it's in the drinks cabinet over there,' he offered.

'That *would* finish me off!'

'Breakfast's at eight, Miss Sophy.'

'Just call me Sophy,' I said, getting up wearily. I'd noticed that Mrs Lark, as befitted her important position as cook, was always addressed as such, and everyone called my aunt Miss Hebe, but other than that there was precious little formality between the family and staff, which suited me.

102

'I'm more used to being the hired help than the lady of the manor, Jonah, and, goodness knows, you've known me since I was a little girl. I remember you leading me round on one of Grandfather's hunters!'

'Kingpin, that was – a gentle giant. It was a sad day when Sir William sold up the horses, but there, his hip was giving him the gyp, so he had to do it.'

His words were starting to come and go . . . as was the room. 'Well, good night, Jonah,' I managed, then added, remembering, 'Oh, and could you light the fire in the Great Hall tomorrow morning and every morning after that?'

'Yes, Mrs Lark's already said you wanted it lit. The logs are ready and I'll put a match to it first thing tomorrow. And she says to tell you Milly from the dog parlour will be here right after breakfast to sort Charlie out.'

'Oh, good,' I said, thinking that it was odd, but strangely pleasant, to have people do things for me for a change, rather than the other way round! Charlie, his days of looking and smelling like a small unwashed rag rug so nearly at an end, heaved himself up from in front of the fire and followed me out, but showed no signs of coming upstairs. 'Where does Charlie usually sleep?'

'In the kitchen. The Aga stays warm all night and Mrs Lark's got a nice bone for him, she's that pleased to see him eating again. I'll let him out first, though, before I lock up.'

I think even Charlie's limited vocabulary included the word 'bone' – or maybe he just felt that everything was back to normal again, for he followed Jonah off across the hall without another glance back, tail waving hopefully.

I have vague recollections of shedding my clothes, dragging on a nightdress and climbing into the big mahogany bed, where I sank deep into feathers and unconsciousness.

I didn't need to dream about Winter's End any more – I was there.

103

Chapter Ten: Clipped Edges

Lady Wynter taunts mee much, saying how is it that I can read and write so well, yet it is well known that my mother's family was lowborn and tainted with rumours of witchcraft? I return soft answers – that my mother's father was a scholar and she in turn taught mee everything she knows – such cures and salves as anyone versed in such things might know. She is curious about this little book, but I keep it about my person.

From the journal of Alys Blezzard, 1581

There was a chill in my bedroom next morning that the small gas fire and one lukewarm radiator did little to dispel. I showered hastily under an antique contraption over the claw-footed bath and then went downstairs to the Great Hall – to find it quite transformed!

My instructions to Jonah had been obeyed and now a log fire blazed and crackled on the wide hearth, throwing out a fierce heat that made the huge, dark and dusty chamber almost cosy. Heat rises, so over the next few days my arctic bedroom and the upper regions of the house might, with a bit of luck, begin to thaw out.

Reluctantly tearing myself away from the fire I headed for the breakfast parlour, where I half-expected what I found – a lavish spread of cooked dishes on hotplates, including (as though Mrs Lark had purposely chosen all the foods starting with 'k') kippers, kidneys and kedgeree, plus a line of Tupperware boxes of cereals, a bowl of prunes and a jug of orange juice.

I don't usually eat a cooked breakfast, but of course any resistance was useless once I'd smelled the bacon.

'That's the way,' Jonah said approvingly, coming in with a fresh pot of coffee while I was demolishing an indecently large plateful. 'You're a grand, strapping lass, not one of these skinny Minnies with stick arms and bosoms like two fried—'

'*Thank* you, Jonah,' Aunt Hebe said firmly, looking up from a well-thumbed garden catalogue, 'we have got everything we want now.'

She was dressed today in workman-like brown corduroy trousers and a green-patterned Liberty lawn shirt under a quilted gilet, and was breakfasting frugally on toast and a poached egg.

'I normally just have porridge or cereal,' I said, 'but it was too tempting to resist, all laid out there.'

'Yes, you must watch your figure,' she said, looking at me thoughtfully. 'Most men these days, Jack included, seem to prefer the svelte woman, like Melinda Christopher.'

'I've seen bigger stick insects than Melinda Christopher,' I retorted, hurt. 'I'm not overweight, I just naturally have big boobs and wide hips. My waist measurement is quite small.'

'You are not at all a typical Winter – it is such a pity.'

'Neither was Alys Blezzard, if that painting upstairs is a true portrait. But I would much rather not have so much temptation at breakfast. I'm sure there's enough food here for at least ten hearty eaters – and I don't know about you, but I wouldn't eat kidneys any time of day, and though I love both kedgeree and kippers, *not* first thing in the morning.'

'William liked a good choice – and anyway, Jack is partial to a full English breakfast. Men are, aren't they?'

'I can't remember, it's too long since I lived with one. But Jack's not here all the time and when he is, I don't suppose he would find having just bacon and eggs too much of a hardship, would he? Do we really need all the rest of it?'

'Perhaps you had better discuss it with him when he comes down at the weekend?'

'Perhaps,' I agreed, refraining from saying that it wasn't actually going to be any of his business now. I *must* stop being such a coward and break the news to him that I'm not going to sell Winter's End (even if I still have only the vaguest of ideas on how to generate enough income to keep it), or Hebe will get in first. In any case, since I hoped he would still consider Winter's End his home and help me to get it back on its feet again, it might be tactful at least to make a show of asking his advice occasionally!

But I made a mental note to do something about the lavish catering because there must be such a lot of waste, though I expect some of it goes into Charlie, now he is eating again. He had greeted me effusively when I came downstairs, but was currently shadowing Jonah, who now popped his head through the door to tell me that Milly had arrived and wanted to know what she was to do with Charlie.

'And Mr Yatton is in the office,' he said, with a jerk of the head in the direction of the solar tower, 'but no hurry, Mrs Lark always gives him a bacon and egg bap and a cup of coffee to keep his strength up. His sister, Effie, does for him at home, and she doesn't let him have anything like that – rabbit food he gets, there.'

Milly, a fresh-faced girl in jeans and jumper, was waiting in the Great Hall with an unsuspecting Charlie, who looked like a giant, unappetising furball. 'What,' she said, looking at him slightly despairingly, 'would you like me to do with him?'

'I think the only thing you *can* do is clip his coat short, then give him a bath. And I'm sure his toenails are too long, because he hasn't been having walks, so could you do those, too?'

'OK – and had you better buy him a coat until his fur gets longer again? Only he'll be cold when he's out, otherwise.'

'Yes, I suppose I had, you're right.'

'I've got some in the van, nice red tartan ones, with matching leads and doggy-doo holders.'

'Er – lovely,' I said weakly, 'could you put it on the bill?'

She took the unsuspecting victim out to her van while I went off to the estate office.

Mr Yatton, my steward, was small, slight and handsome, with silvery hair and a finely lined face – and, at a guess, the wrong side of seventy. To my huge relief he seemed to handle all the financial side of running the house and estate, right down to paying the staff wages, balancing the books and sorting out the accountant. He had the whole thing literally at his fingertips for, apart from the office desktop computer, he had a laptop of his own and a plethora of electronic gadgets, and so was not so much a silver surfer as a silver technobabe.

'I am here weekday mornings and Sir William used to come in at some point every day to discuss matters, give any orders, sign cheques . . . that sort of thing. That is his desk,' he indicated an oak roll-top, 'now yours. Though you may, of course, prefer the computer desk?'

'No – I mean, I do email and so on, but I don't use the computer much.'

Mr Yatton, looking quite as shocked as if I'd admitted to being illiterate, discoursed enthusiastically about the advantages of the computing age for fully ten minutes, before recalling the true reason for our meeting and proceeding to outline for me the complicated financial affairs of Winter's End.

He was very patient, considering how hard I find it to grasp financial details, but I *longed* for Lucy, who had the sort of brain that could make sense of all this *and* think it was fun, like Mr Yatton.

The annual outgoings were of nightmare proportions and ranged from those I had expected, like the staff wages and fuel bills for heating the house, to things that had never even crossed my mind, like Public Liability Insurance . . . and that bank loan. How could I have forgotten about that even for one second?

It was scary to try to take in everything at once, but eventually I began to see a kind of pattern emerging. 'So, basically you are saying that before Grandfather took out that bank loan, there was just about enough income coming in from various sources, including investments, to keep Winter's End in a reasonable state of repair – except that for many years the lion's share of it has been diverted into the escalating cost of restoring and maintaining the gardens?'

'Yes, in a nutshell, though of course costs rise and income may fluctuate,' he pointed out. 'The bank loan was spent entirely on the garden – large yew trees to extend the maze to its original size did not come cheaply – and the repayments are now a heavy drain on the estate on top of all the other expenses.'

'Oh God!' I said, closing my eyes briefly. 'Well, given all that, and with four gardeners but only one cleaner, the house was bound to deteriorate to the point where there's a huge amount of work to do to get it back into good order. I only hope it's structurally sound, because there's no contingency fund in these figures, is there?'

'No, I am afraid not, though one of the other paintings

Sir William had cleaned proved to be a Herring – a horse painting, though not, of course, in the same league as the Stubbs. He put it to one side.'

'I'll look for it later. I don't really want to sell off more heirlooms than I absolutely have to, though clearing that bank loan has to be a priority. But on the other hand, it would be pointless doing that if the house then fell down about my ears, wouldn't it? Jack seems to think Winter's End needs a lot of expensive repair work.'

'Oh, I should doubt that very much,' he exclaimed, shocked. 'Sir William may have been, if I may say so, blinkered by his fanatical ambition to fully restore the gardens to their previous glory, but he would not have let the fabric of the house disintegrate to that extent.'

'Let's hope you're right; it will make things so much easier. Did you know I'd spent my working life in stately homes, Mr Yatton? I expect I know as much about the best way to clean a marble floor, or get the dust out of a carved overmantel, as any professionally trained conservator, though applying those techniques here will be a bit like shutting the stable door after the horse has bolted. I'm going to do my best to conserve what's left, but to do that I'll need help – and without increasing the staffing bills.'

'Do I deduce, therefore, that you will be reducing the garden staff and increasing the indoor?' he guessed intelligently.

'Not *exactly*, because I couldn't possibly fire any of the people working for Winter's End. They all seem to have been here for years and years! But obviously I can't afford to take on more until I find a way of drastically increasing the revenue, so –' I sat back – 'it looks like I will just have to reallocate some of the gardeners to help around the house when needed, won't I?'

'I suppose that would be the logical solution,' he agreed after a moment, 'but of course Seth won't be pleased, with the garden restoration scheme finally being so close to completion. The last stage is the lower terrace, for which the original plan is missing. We found most of it in that chest over there, mixed up with all sorts of papers, though the bottom had been ripped off. But even when finished, the gardens will take quite a bit of maintenance.'

'But not so much in the winter.'

'No, there is that, though of course a lot of woodland maintenance takes place then, and there is the mistletoe harvest.'

'Exactly how much do I pay Seth Greenwood for his services?' I asked curiously, realising I hadn't seen any mention of his salary among all the figures.

'Nothing at all, though he lives in the lodge rent free. Sir William treated him as one of the family, since he is also your great-aunt Ottilie's stepson. Seth agreed to come back and oversee the remainder of the restoration after his father died, as nominal head gardener, with the proviso that he was free to do his own work whenever he pleased.'

'His own work being . . . ?'

'Designing and restoring knot gardens and parterres – that is his speciality, you know. He writes books and articles, too. Indeed, he is also the author of the little pamphlet on the history of Winter's End that we sell on open days.'

'He's a man of many talents,' I said, curiously put out to find I was getting his services for free. 'Renaissance Man, in fact!'

'Sir William was very fond of him and treated him almost like a son – though, of course, he couldn't have left him Winter's End, since there was no relationship other than through marriage.'

'*And* there was Jack, the obvious heir,' I pointed out, wondering if Jack had felt jealous that Seth had claimed his rightful place in Grandfather's affections, just as *he* had claimed mine in Hebe's? This nest had had two rival cuckoos jostling for position . . .

'Er – yes, though he never really entered into your grandfather's passion for gardening. Are you fond of gardening, Sophy?'

'I love walking in gardens, or sitting in one with a drink in my hand; but I had enough of grubbing about in the soil in all weathers when I lived in a commune in Scotland.'

I contemplated the knotty problem that was Seth Greenwood, and concluded that there wasn't really any way I could get rid of him if he was working for nothing *and* Ottie's stepson – though of course, he might leave in high dudgeon when I radically cut the garden budget . . .

'I do intend completing the restoration, but perhaps not as quickly as my grandfather would have liked, since the house must take priority now. And to fund anything that needs more than simple hard work and elbow grease, I'll need to increase the revenue from Winter's End in some way.'

'The woodland is already well managed and the tenancy terms for Brockbank Farm are very fair,' Mr Yatton said doubtfully.

'Yes, I expect they are, but I was thinking more about increasing *visitor* numbers. Opening Winter's End to the public seems to have been a bit half-hearted and I'm sure there must be lots of opportunity there to generate income.'

'Sir William hated opening the house at all, though the family side was shut off and so quite unaffected by the visitors. But certainly you *could* open for more days, if you wished.'

'I'll give it some serious thought and perhaps, meanwhile, I should harden my heart, sell the Herring and use the money to renovate the visitor facilities? We could enhance our existing assets, like having Alys Blezzard's portrait cleaned and making more of the witchcraft angle, and the legend that Shakespeare might have visited Winter's End could be turned into a major draw too . . . Bigged-up, as they say.'

I was starting to feel hopeful and enthused – washed over by one of those golden glows of unfoundedly optimistic second sight. 'We could have a shop as well as a better tearoom, and sell all kinds of merchandise.'

He looked dubious. 'Sir William hated anything commercial.'

'Commerce is what kept a roof on the last house I worked in, *and* the Scottish castle where I was before that. I know what visitors want,' I said confidently. In fact, in the past I'd frequently wondered why half of them even bothered going round the buildings at all, and didn't just have lunch and then buy souvenirs.

He had been scribbling onto a notepad while we had been talking and now came to a halt and looked up. 'So, your initial idea is to redirect most of what income there is away from the garden and into restoring the house. Then, secondly, to generate new income from increased visitor numbers. Any work needing to be carried out to enhance visitor attractions is to be funded in the first instance by the sale of the Herring painting.'

'Yes . . . that's it so far. That way we should be able to keep repaying the loan and still have some profit left over. I haven't really had much time to work on the finer details, because until I got here I thought I would probably sell the estate to Jack.'

'Oh, no, that wasn't at all what Sir William intended,' he said, looking shocked. 'He expected you to take on the running of the estate and thought that your daughter, Lucy, had a good head for business and perhaps could replace me when I retire.'

I stared at him. 'He did? But he only met her once!'

'Sir William was extremely good at summing up character and – excuse me! – from the sound of it, their encounter seemed to have been a case of like meeting like.'

I cast my mind back to Grandfather's visit and had to concede that he was right. 'They clashed, but they did both seem to enjoy it. And I am sure she will be invaluable in running Winter's End, though she's in Japan at the moment, you know, teaching English on a year's contract. I'd like to get her home, because she's being stalked and there have been all those horrible cases in the newspapers lately.'

'You could send for her now, if you are worried,' he suggested.

'No I can't, because for one thing I'd have to buy her a plane ticket, which would be horrendously expensive, and for another, she's dead stubborn and took this job to try and pay off some of her student loan debts, so I'd have to have something to offer her.'

'If you explain to her that you need her help, then give me her email address so I can start sending her figures, spreadsheets, and an outline of what I do, she may well become so involved and interested that she will agree to come back early,' he suggested craftily.

'You know, Mr Yatton, you may just be right? You're a genius!' I kissed him, which made him go slightly pink and flustered.

Then Jonah came in with coffee and butterfly sponge cakes, after which, fortified, Mr Yatton took me off in an ancient Land Rover to meet the tenant farmer, bumping down the back drive behind the coach house, past a slightly neglected tennis court.

He dropped me off at the door a couple of hours later, by which time I was exhausted, my head buzzing. *He* seemed enlivened, if anything, by the whole thing and clattered off

113

with a cheery wave, saying he had to go and collect his sister, Effie, since it was the Sticklepond teadance club tonight down at the village hall and they were dining at the pub first.

'Tell Miss Hebe that she must save me a jive,' he said, on departing.

A *jive*?

Charlie, looking faintly aggrieved, was sitting on the doorstep, a vision of short black and white fur and lurid tartan coat, a small bone-shaped device under his chin holding, I discovered, a couple of matching red doggy bags. Very tasteful. He kept shaking his head, so it seemed to be annoying him – but then, King Charles spaniels don't have a lot of chin. Perhaps it would be better clipped to his lead, instead?

'Milly said poor Charlie's claws were so long they were going into his pads,' Mrs Lark told me when I went into the kitchen. 'She's going to pop out and give him a going-over once a month, if you like.'

'Yes, I think she'd better,' I agreed, though here was yet another expense.

'Do you want a sandwich? You've missed your lunch and it's gone teatime. I've just made one for Miss Hebe and taken it through into the stillroom. She's been in the garden all day, and if you don't remind her to eat or put it in front of her she'd be no wider than a piece of knotted string.'

'Is she in there now?' I asked, looking at the closed door.

'Yes, brewing something heathenish up for a customer – I didn't ask what. Now, about that sandwich?'

'Oh, no, thanks,' I said with a shudder. 'I've just been out to the tenanted farm, and I'm full of strong tea, fruitcake and Lancashire Crumbly.'

I took Charlie out for a quick walk down the drive and back in the wintry late afternoon gloom, then took his coat off and hung it up in the kitchen with his lead. I left Mrs Lark feeding him and went upstairs to change.

I'd left my mobile behind and there were two voicemail messages: one from Anya, asking how the bloated plutocrat was feeling today, and the other in Jack's smoothly spine-tingling tones, saying he hoped I'd liked my flowers, and he looked forward to seeing me on Saturday.

So, Aunt Hebe hadn't told him about my decision to keep Winter's End yet? Maybe she thought that I would change my mind when I realised the enormity of the task – or that Jack, when he arrived, would change it for me? Or even that restoring Winter's End would quickly become a joint venture.

I did keep imagining what it would be like if Jack accepted my decision with good grace and then helped me restore Winter's End. It was going to be enjoyable, but also very hard work, and it would be fun to share that with someone else . . .

I still had the phone in my hand when it rang, making me jump, but this time it was Lucy.

'Hi, Mum.'

'That was good timing, darling. I've just come in from spending the most exhausting day, being given a crash course in estate management! I thought I had the estate manager for that – or steward, as Mr Yatton calls himself – but I suppose I ought to try and get my head round it, if only to understand how much I've got – or not got – to keep the place running. That bank loan is *crippling* and since we've only just repaid the interest and started on the capital, there would be nothing to be gained by paying it off early even if we could . . .' I tailed off. 'But, Lucy, just wait until you see Winter's End! I only hope you love it as much as I do.'

'Actually, Mum, I already have.'

'Have what?' I said, puzzled.

'Seen Winter's End. After Great-Grandfather visited us I was curious. You'd always made Winter's End sound like some lost Eden, the Shangri-La of Lancashire, so I thought I'd have a look.'

'But no one has mentioned—'

'No one *knew*,' she interrupted. 'You always said I had the Winter colouring, so I disguised myself with a beanie hat and dark shades and just came on an open day. I saw Great-Grandfather on one of the lower terraces, talking to a gardener, but he didn't see me. He looked ill – much frailer than when he visited us.'

'You could have told me.'

'I thought it might upset you. You always said you could never go back, though I didn't see why not.'

'Because my mother always said—' I stopped. Susan had said a lot of things, not always the exact truth – more an embellished retelling of old stories that grew and changed in time. But somehow her fear of going back to Winter's End had infected me, so that even long after she had died and I was an adult with my own child, it had never occurred to me to return.

Perhaps it was partly because I had loved it so much and felt secure there that I feared to go back and find it all changed. I didn't want the memories tarnished by reality. Just as well too – I'd have been devastated to find Jack had taken my place in Hebe's affections, and Seth in Ottie's and Grandfather's. Not that I think I had ever featured much in either of the latter's, since Ottie was the most unmaternal woman I had ever met and Grandfather had seemed at the time to regard me merely as an irritating blot on the family escutcheon.

'What did you think of it, Lucy?'

'Well, I only saw the gardens and the Great Hall, really,

though the maze was . . . well, amazing! The house looked pretty shabby and the catering facilities were tea and buns in this sort of outhouse at the back. But it . . . I don't know, as soon as I started up the drive I knew it was one of those magic spots that seem to be in a time warp of their own. Do you know what I mean? Like when we took the van up to the Roman fort at Vindolanda, that was a magical place too. You felt you'd stepped out of time.'

'That's interesting, because I feel the same way, and I just *can't* let Winter's End go. Mind you, I can't really afford to keep it, either, because the house has been terribly neglected. All the money for its upkeep has been poured into the gardens and no one even took an interest in keeping the place properly clean. It's disgustingly dirty!'

'Oh, Mum!' Lucy sighed. 'Handing you a big neglected house of your own is like the best present ever! What have you cleaned so far?'

'Only the dog. There's a little spaniel called Charlie, and he was all matted and dirty. But I didn't do it myself – he was beyond that. I had someone come out to clip and bath him and do his toenails.'

'Bet you are dying to get on with sorting everything out, though?'

'Yes, I am, but I had to have this session with Mr Yatton, today first – and apparently the solicitor, the accountant and even my personal bank accounts manager are going to visit me too, in the next few days. I wish you were here, Lucy. You are so much better at business and figures and stuff than me.'

'I should be; that's what I did my degree in.'

'Yes, and amazingly enough, Grandfather seems to have sussed that out. He suggested to Mr Yatton that you could learn to be the steward when you came back, and take over from him when he retires. I don't know how you feel about

117

that? If you like the idea, Mr Yatton said he could start sending you figures and spreadsheets (whatever they are) by email right now. I gave him your address. Is that OK?'

'He emails?'

'The estate office has a computer, but he has a swish laptop too – he's a silver surfer.'

'Cool.'

'So, what do you think? He said he could teach you quite a lot of it by email.'

'Why not? He can send me the figures over and keep me up to date, and I can discuss it with you, or send him emails to show to you – and we'll see how it goes when I get back. But it would be a job, wouldn't it?'

'Yes, a proper job – though the salary might not be huge, to start with. But if we can keep Winter's End going, then one day it will be yours.'

'That's a really, really odd thought . . . though Winter's End sort of got to me, and I keep thinking about it . . .' She added more briskly, 'Don't do anything sudden without asking me first, especially involving men. You know you always go for the wrong sort.'

'I don't! In fact, I've hardly had a chance to go for *any* sort, and it's not my fault that when I started dating again only the dregs of humanity were left over.'

'Jack sounds to me like the wrong sort, or why wouldn't Great-Grandfather have left Winter's End to him? Bet he's a snake in the grass. Don't be too trusting.'

'He is not a snake in the grass and I am not too—'

'I'll have to go. Love you lots. Byee . . .'

I stared at the phone, feeling aggrieved. Lucy had managed to get rid of the few boyfriends I had acquired while she was growing up, and by the time she left for university the pool of available men in my age group had shrunk to a very dubious puddle. I washed and changed, then flaked out on the bed until Jonah beat the gong for another gargantuan dinner, which Hebe, after her day spent in the garden and stillroom, fell on with huge gusto. She ate Ottie's share too, since she was in Manchester at the opening of someone's exhibition. How can she put away so much food and stay so thin?

She was wearing a forties-style dance dress and her hair in a roll with a butterfly hairpin, and after dinner left me to my solitary coffee and went off to the dance.

I spent a happy and productive couple of hours in the cleaning room, checking off and reorganising the supplies, and adding to my shopping list.

I had a feeling that it might take some time to teach Grace new ways of doing things – if it was possible at all. But then, I could just confine her activities to the floors, the bathrooms, changing the beds and doing the laundry, where she couldn't really do that much more damage.

Charlie got bored watching me after a while and vanished, and on my way to bed I found him fast asleep and blissfully snoring in his basket next to the Aga.

Chapter Eleven: O Mother, Where Art Thou?

Thomas in his great kindness has given mee a wooden coffer such as I have never seen before, carved prettily inside and out, and fitted with ingenious drawers and compartments. There is a sturdy lock – he says he fears for mee, and I should keep my secrets therein and the key close.

From the journal of Alys Blezzard, 1581

Breakfast was, if possible, even more indecently lavish than the day before. Recalling Mr Yatton's final words of advice, which had been to the effect that I should take control straight away and start as I meant to go on, I decided to make my very first economy. It might save my figure, as well as some money.

'Aunt Hebe, you know when I said yesterday that cooking this much food was such a huge waste?' I began cautiously, gesturing to the hotplates groaning under the weight of enough calories to keep an entire rugby team happy. 'Well, I've decided to ask Mrs Lark not to do it any more.'

She looked up from her toast, which she was consuming while reading a new gardening magazine that had been left by her plate, presumably by Jonah. 'But I always eat a full cooked breakfast on Sundays, Sophy, and I like a poached egg most days too – and occasionally a bit of bacon.'

'That's fine, then – we can still have bacon and eggs every day, but the full monty just on Sundays, as a special treat.'

'Jack won't like that in the least,' she protested, shaking her head. 'He often brings friends for the weekend too, and they all have good appetites.'

'I'm quite sure Jack will have the good manners to be happy with whatever he's offered – as will his friends. We simply can't afford to go on wasting food on this scale, and it would make less work for Mrs Lark.'

'But she's the *cook* – that's what she *does*.' Aunt Hebe looked at me blankly.

'Yes, and she does it very well too,' I said patiently, 'but she's no spring chicken, is she? Cutting down her workload wouldn't hurt.'

'I suppose you will make what changes you like, Sophy, but I think you are unwise to start without consulting Jack, for you may well find yourself having to put things right back again to how they were before.'

I mentally counted up to ten. 'Of course, I'll always be glad to hear any of Jack's suggestions, Aunt Hebe, and I will always value his advice. But this is only the first of many economies and changes I'll have to make if I'm to turn Winter's End back into the beautiful place it used to be, rather than the shabby, neglected creature it is now.'

'That is a very odd way of putting it! You make it sound as though the house were alive.'

'It is, to me.'

She looked at me strangely, then put down the magazine, drained her cup of tea, and rose to her feet. 'Well, I must get off to feed the hens – but I warn you, any changes to my walled garden will be done over my dead body!'

'Of course, Aunt Hebe – I wouldn't dream of it. But I'm

going to tour the grounds later and I hope you'll at least show me the walled garden and the hens?'

'Certainly,' she said grandly. 'What are you going to do this morning?'

I indicated the embroidered fabric bag slung over the back of my chair. 'Mr Yatton gave me a big notebook and I'm going to go round the house again, this time writing down what needs to be done in order of urgency, and adding to my shopping list. I did a stock-check of the cleaning room last night, while you were out.'

'Oh? Perhaps you should just get the agency in for a sort of late spring clean,' she suggested vaguely. 'What were they called? Ah, yes – Dolly Mops.'

'I'll see,' I said tactfully, because I hated to think of the damage a domestic cleaning agency had already unwittingly wreaked on Winter's End, not to mention Grace's casual attentions over the years.

'Jonah,' I said, as he came into the room and started loading a vast brass tray with crockery and unused dishes of hot food, 'I'm going around the gardens this afternoon – could you send word to Seth Greenwood? Tell him he can come with me himself if he wants to, or delegate it to one of the other gardeners. About two o'clock.'

'I'll do that,' he said, and I followed him back into the kitchen, where I proposed the revolutionary idea of reducing the number and style of breakfast dishes to Mrs Lark.

She looked even more incredulous than Aunt Hebe. 'But we've *always* done it like that!'

'I know, but times change and no one is eating most of it, so it's such a waste.'

'As to that, I make sure Mr Yatton has something in his stomach to start the day with, other than the rabbit food his sister gives him, and then what's not eaten in the kitchen, Jonah makes into swill for the pigs out at the back of the courtyard. All our bacon and ham comes from pigs reared at Winter's End.'

I resolved to avoid the pigsty since I didn't want to meet my future breakfasts face to face. 'It's a pity to cook lovely food just for the pigs, Mrs Lark, but of course you can still cook bacon and eggs every day – just not the kippers, kedgeree, kidneys and all the rest of it.'

'I *suppose* so,' she reluctantly conceded, 'and you'll still want all the trimmings, of course, like tomatoes and mushrooms. Then, on Sundays, you can have a *proper* breakfast.' The thought of pulling out the culinary stops at least once a week seemed to cheer her. 'We could have an extra high tea every day too, to make up!'

'I'm trying to make less work for you, not more,' I protested.

'Now, Sophy love, you've got to keep your strength up – and so has Miss Hebe, what with all the work she does in her garden.'

We seemed to have reached an impasse, so I gave up the battle at this point and changed the subject. 'Mrs Lark, I wanted to ask you a favour.'

'Ask away.'

'I thought I'd invite all the indoor and outdoor staff – that sounds terribly grand, but you know what I mean – to a meeting in the Great Hall on Saturday morning at about ten, to tell them my plans for the future of Winter's End. I should think everyone has been in limbo long enough, wondering what's going to happen. I wondered if you could provide refreshments? Tea and coffee and biscuits, or something?'

'You leave it to me – and do you want me to make sure everyone knows? The Friends too, they had better be there.'

'Friends?' I said, absently.

'Friends of Winter's End.'

123

'Oh yes, I'd forgotten all about them and they are going to be a really important part of my plans!'

'There are about a dozen Friends, but I only need to tell one and then it's like in that film *Village of the Damned*.'

'Film?' I said, baffled.

'Yes, you tell one of them and then they *all* know. Faster than the speed of gossip – uncanny it is, sometimes. Mr Yatton's sister, Effie's, one.'

'I'll bear that in mind, Mrs Lark.'

'All the gardeners pop into my kitchen during the day for a bite of cake to have with their tea, so I can spread the word then. Grace's here now. She's just washed all Charlie's bedding – said since he was so clean, his blankets ought to be too.'

'That was kind of her.'

'Loves dogs, does Grace. Charlie's in the laundry room with her now; he took his bone.'

So that accounted for his vanishing act after breakfast.

'This meeting . . . some of the gardeners said Mr Jack seemed to assume he would still be running the place, the last time he was down,' she suggested. 'He told them Winter's End would be too much for you to run, so you'd sell the place to him. But I said, "No, that can't be right – Miss Sophy's here to stay."'

'Yes I am, and I want Winter's End to be clean, beautiful and whole again, just the way I remember it. It seems to have gone to the dogs since Mum and I left.'

'Sir William threw himself into his plans for the garden even more when your mother took you away,' she agreed, 'to distract himself, I suppose, until you came back – which he was convinced you would, at first.' She sighed. 'Oh, well, it's all water under the bridge now, isn't it?'

'Yes, and now we will all have to pull together to save Winter's End, which will mean some big changes. That can be hard when people are set in their ways.'

I took the notebook and a pen out of my bag. 'I might as well start making my list of things to make, mend and order. I'll do the rest of the house first and then come back to this wing. Perhaps you wouldn't mind just giving me a glimpse of your rooms then?'

'Certainly.'

'And if there's anything, either in the kitchens or your rooms, that you'd like changing or replacing, note it down for me, would you?'

'I'll do that,' she agreed. 'The weekly shopping list is pinned to the inside of that cupboard door there, and Grace puts any cleaning stuff that we're running out of on it.'

'Good. I did an inventory of the cleaning room last night, so I'll add a few everyday things to that, but I'll also have to order some specialist products. Luckily I know a good supplier. Stately Solutions will have everything that I need.'

The entertainment of watching his bedding go round must have palled, for Charlie nudged open the door and came in carrying the remains of a large bone, which he tenderly deposited in his basket. From the smell that wafted in with him, Jonah was boiling up pigswill out at the back somewhere.

'I think we'll have a nice jam roly-poly pudding to follow the salmon and Duchesse potatoes tonight,' Mrs Lark said, absently thumbing through a battered notebook – she appeared to have her own household book. 'Cream or custard?'

'Custard,' I said decidedly, and went out with Charlie at my heels.

All this comforting stodge was lovely in the winter, but I had a feeling that by spring I'd have started to long for a good salad and a big bowl of fresh fruit – and goodness knew what would have happened to my figure by then!

*   *   *

125

I'd written three pages of notes before I even got out of the Great Hall.

It had always been the heart of the house, the room where everyone's paths crossed repeatedly in a complex minuet of daily living, and now the fire once again glowed in the vast hearth it was much more welcoming.

It was also the place where Alys Blezzard seemed to be most with me – and where I felt positively wired in to Winter's End itself. Standing in the middle of the Great Hall was like recharging my batteries, and filled me with energy and the unfounded golden glow of optimism that reassured me that everything would turn out all right . . . in the end.

There *were* a few shadows drifting like dark smoke in the corners of my consciousness – but then, what life doesn't have its share of shadows?

I looked around me, noticing for the first time that the lime mortar between the stones of the hall floor needed attention and the old rag rug in front of the fire was now so grey and stiff with dirt that it blended into the colour of the floor. I would bet good money on Grace mopping it over every time she washed the floor in here – probably with bleach in her bucket too! But we could try soaking it in mild soap and warm water and see what happened.

The stuffed stag's head on the wall looked ghastly. It was not only balding, but had lost an eye. I guiltily remembered the last time I slid down the banisters and knocked it off – perhaps that had loosened it?

Jonah, coming through the West Wing door with a tray of crockery, said, 'Your grandfather got that head at a sale. A great one for buying junk at auctions, he used to be, before he got so caught up in the gardening. The eye's in that bowl of potpourri on the mantelpiece.'

'Thanks, Jonah,' I said, glad he'd told me before I'd looked in the pot. An eye staring back at me from the dried rose petals would have been a bit of a shock.

'If you like, I can Superglue it back in.'

'Yes, please – and give the head a good brushing while you're at it, will you? I'll try and find something nicer to replace it with later on, when I've got time.'

'I'll do that,' he said, going off whistling.

Half the candle light bulbs in the wheel-shaped holder suspended from the ceiling were dead when I flicked the switch, as were those in the wall lights – muscular naked bronze arms holding out what looked like frosted glass whirly ice-cream cornets.

Humming the tune to the Cornetto ice-cream advert, I slowly turned, taking everything in. The tops of the windows were draped with spider-spun silk, and most of the assorted chairs, settles and benches that furnished the room looked dull and unpolished, except for the tops, where the application of countless bottoms over the centuries had rubbed them up to a fine gloss.

Grace must have gone up the backstairs, because there was a zooming noise from the dimly lit minstrels' gallery way above me, and I could just see the top of her head as she pushed the Hoover to and fro. Then it stopped, and she started working backwards down the stairs with a dustpan and brush.

A hand-held vacuum cleaner would be easier for that, and I made a memo to unpack mine from its box in the attic – if I could remember which one I'd put it in. On the end of the growing list at the back of the notebook I added foam tubing to pad the end of the vacuum cleaner hose, which would stop any more chips being knocked out of the furniture.

Going into the family wing, I popped my head in the steward's office to say good morning to Mr Yatton and tell him what I was up to today, and where he could find me if he wanted me.

'Very good – and Lucy and I have made contact already,' he said. 'I emailed some figures, and she sent me a list of very pertinent questions right back.'

I could imagine – she would shortly be running his affairs much as she tries to do mine. A mobile phone like a thin silvery clam played a snatch of waltz music and, as he picked it up, I smiled at him and returned to my inventory.

In the passage abutting the solar tower a cupboard had been cut into the wall, which was now filled with dull silver and the sad, cracked relics of several valuable tea services. Mum had told me that there had once been an emergency trapdoor exit down into it from the priest's hole above, but after Alys Blezzard's death the family had forsworn the Catholic faith and the priest's hole had fallen into disuse. I couldn't see any trace of it in the cupboard ceiling, but it was pretty dark in there.

The library was quite cosy and, since presumably William had used it a lot, relatively clean and tidy. Even the books, including many very ancient gardening tomes behind glass, looked as if they had been dusted within living memory, and all the lights worked. There was a billiard table at one end, a small TV and video, and a wind-up gramophone with a stack of old 78s in cardboard covers next to it, all humorous monologues.

The top one was 'Albert and the Lion'. I put it on and wound the handle and, as the crackling monologue played, I tried to square this evidence of my grandfather's sense of humour with what I remembered of him. It wasn't easy. After a while I gave up and carried on with my survey.

Like the library, the drawing room was in reasonably good order, though the chairs and sofas were still wearing grubby summer chintz covers, which should have long since been taken off and washed. I wondered if there was a winter set, too? Grace or Mrs Lark would probably know.

Aunt Hebe had staked a claim to a comfortable chair and Berlin-work footstool, next to a table loaded with gardening magazines and catalogues, plus an overflowing bundle of knitting that was the rather snotty green of mushy peas. I sincerely hoped it was intended as a gift for Jack and not some kind of welcome-home present for me.

Not, so far, that there had been much evidence from Aunt Hebe of any real pleasure in my return . . .

The dining room was grandly dingy, with a splendid chandelier that tinkled in the draught from the door, and I noted the threadbare but rather beautiful rug that would have to be professionally cleaned, if I could ever afford it. Goodness knows what state the tapestries hanging in the corridors were in. It was probably just as well that it was too dark to see, and at least the gloom meant they had been protected from much light damage.

I'd left the room I most longed to look at, Lady Anne's parlour, until last . . . and strictly speaking, of course, that should be Lady Winter's parlour, though it doesn't sound quite so cosy.

It was strange that although it was a lovely light room with a door on to the terrace, if felt unused, unloved and neglected.

The dark, dull panelling that covered the lower half of the walls looked seventeenth century, but at some point the plaster above had been painted a deep, coral colour. The shade was echoed in the pattern of the curtains that hung at the windows and over the door to the terrace, and though they were a little faded they had been well lined.

'*Alys Blezzard scratched her initials on the windowpane in the little parlour at the back of the house, in the left-hand corner, and so did her daughter,*' I could hear my mother's voice saying in my head. And when I pulled aside the drapes and looked, there they were, a tangible link to the past – the faint spidery tracery of '*AB*' and '*AW*'.

Maybe I would add '*SW*', for this would now be Sophy's parlour, somewhere I could sit and sew my crazy patchwork and dream. There was even a needlework table, a Victorian pedestal affair with clawed feet like a lion ... which for some odd reason made me think of the head gardener. It wouldn't surprise me if he had big clawed feet inside those sturdy boots and maybe he even turned into a big black cat – something pantherish – when the moon was full?

I shook off this rather disturbing image and turned to the alcove where the ancient wooden coffer in which Alys had kept her secrets stood. I had got over my first disappointment at its outward plainness now and could see that it was a thing of beauty in itself – as was the key, which Mum gave to me as a gift on my fourteenth birthday, just before she made her final, fatal trip. Why hadn't I known the dark omens were gathering for her, not me? And, even if I had warned her, would she have listened?

Shaking off old memories I looked thoughtfully at the box and then at a substantial cupboard built into one corner of the room, with glazed upper doors. If I moved a rather funereal arrangement of wax flowers under a dome of glass and some dubious Egyptian funerary ushabti up a shelf, I thought the box would fit on the lower one. An extra line of defence for Alys's secrets – if they were returned home.

Did they really need defending? Was Jack that keen to find clues to some treasure that, if it ever existed, would have been long discovered and gone? But even if he was, I was certain he wouldn't go to such extreme lengths as breaking open an antique and valuable box to get at the book ... or would he? I had now heard so many opinions of Jack, his character and intentions that I wasn't sure what to believe any more.

But then, how could I possibly doubt the sincerity I'd heard in his voice when he told me how much he loved Winter's End and how pleased he was to meet me at last? I wasn't looking forward in the least to telling him that I wasn't going to sell the place to him, after all, and dashing all his hopes.

I couldn't find a key that fitted the cupboard on my ring, until I thought to open the door below and discovered it hanging inside on a small brass cup hook. I moved everything up a shelf, then slipped out of the door to the terrace (locked, but this time there was a key on the ring) and round the house to my secret cache in the van, returning with the weight of the fabric bag dragging at my shoulder.

I lifted the chest onto the bergère sofa and managed to undo the lock and hasp. Inside, it was as Aunt Hebe had described, completely carved with flowers and foliage and smelling faintly spicy, fitted out with little drawers and compartments. There seemed to be nothing in there, apart from the powdery residue of what might once have been dried herbs until, in a space behind a false drawer front, I discovered a strange polished stone with a hole in it and a rotting velvet bag full of small yellowed bits of bone or ivory scratched with symbols that I thought might be runes. Whatever they were, clearly they had once held some kind of magical significance.

There was a rectangular central compartment that had room and to spare for the little book of bible stories I placed in it – one of my childhood treasures safely returned, at least, even if not the one the box was intended for . . .

'*Alys?*' I looked up, searching the dark corners but seeing nothing, and it occurred to me that perhaps, now I was an adult, I never would. For a moment I wondered if she ever really existed, except in my imagination . . . until, as I locked the chest away behind the glazed cupboard doors, I caught sight of her dim reflection in the dingy glass before she slowly dissolved into the shadows. I could have *sworn* she winked at me.

I left the little room guarding its secrets and went up the stairs that wound round the solar tower. The upper storey had once been a bedchamber, with the ex-priest's hole converted to a powdering closet, but it was now an empty and long-neglected schoolroom. I suppose my aunts must have been taught there, but I went to the village infants' school.

I took a quick, guilty look into Aunt Hebe's bedroom, which was cluttered and cosy, with a sort of kitchen corner by the sink where she could brew cocoa or whatever her favoured bedtime drink was, a La-Z-Boy chair and a giant TV screen. I didn't linger there but wandered through the rest of the bedrooms, including the one where the cleaned pictures were stacked, finding little that a good clean wouldn't fix.

I came at last to more familiar territory – the bedroom that had once been my mother's. I remembered the wallpaper with its plethora of pink roses and the brass four-poster bed, fit for a princess. The frilled muslin curtains were pulled back to reveal a French poodle nightdress case, its topknot tied with red satin ribbon, reclining on the glazed pink chintz eiderdown. It was all the same – and yet, in the cruel light of day, a faded and dusty travesty of how I remembered it.

In one corner of the room lay a battered suitcase, the one we had bought specially for her trip to America. The locks were broken and it had been tied up with twine, which now lay loosened and unknotted around it, and a trapped and limp cotton flounce stuck out of the side of the case like a dead thing.

Suddenly I felt angry: whoever had searched my mother's possessions should have put it all back again neatly. Who could it have been? Grandfather, searching for traces of his lost daughter? Hebe, perhaps, or even Jack, looking for the book?

A handbag rested against the case, but there wasn't much in there, except a wallet containing a picture of me as an awkward teenager with an unfortunate hairstyle, a few dollars, and a dried-out rose-pink lipstick.

In the wardrobe, long cheesecloth dresses swayed like old ghosts and the familiar disturbing scent of patchouli still lingered, reaching out to invade the room.

I hastily closed the door and left. It might be touching that my grandfather had ordered that my mother's room should remain as it was when she ran away, but this was *not* how I wanted to remember her. The room needed exorcising of the past, but for now it could wait.

And so could visiting her grave. She wasn't in either of those places, but with me. For, oddly enough, I had begun to feel closer to my strangely elusive mother once she was dead than I had ever been when she was alive.

Chapter Twelve: Foxed

I have taken over the preparation of household remedies and simples and of the making of preserves, fruits and sweetmeats, Lady Wynter having little interest in such things, other than the lotion of roses that I made to clear her complexion. Sir Ralph is in thrall to his young wife, despite her barrenness, yet he continues in gratitude to mee that his only son and heir still lives.

From the journal of Alys Blezzard, 1581

Upstairs, under the eaves, the old nursery lay cold and neglected and the narrow sleigh bed was stripped and dustsheeted. I stood looking down at it, remembering the last time I had slept there . . .

It had been the night we left Winter's End, and Alys had woken me in the small hours, shaking her head sorrowfully before fading away at the first faint sound of my mother's tiptoeing steps.

I'd had time to snatch the book of bible stories from under my pillow, but very little else before I was whisked away . . .

All the familiar playthings and books had been put away in the cupboards, along with some I didn't recognise, which must have been Jack's. He seemed to have had a penchant for weapons of mass destruction.

I unlocked the door to the rest of the attic space and found a light switch, but the warren of disused rooms stretching ahead was only patchily lit, a depressingly cluttered vista of anonymous shrouded shapes. I could see why they kept the door locked, though, because if Grace did smoke up there, it would be a major fire hazard.

My own and Lucy's belongings were stacked in one corner of the first room. A quick look through the others didn't reveal anything terribly ominous, like daylight shining through missing tiles, or pools of water on the floorboards, which was a relief. But a better examination would have to wait for when someone (probably me) had swept away all the hanging cobwebs and their occupants. I was sure there would be woodworm, too – what old house doesn't have woodworm? – though I knew that few actually fall down from it.

Sorting the attics would be a huge task, but also a sort of treasure hunt too, for goodness knows what I might find! I would save it as a treat for when I had the rest of the house clean and tidy.

Locking the attic door behind me, I went back down and took a look at the minor family portraits hanging in the gloom of the minstrels' gallery, including that supposed to be Alys, then checked out the Long Room. You could see the light patches on the wall where the paintings that were stacked in the Blue Bedroom and the Stubbs had once hung, but I didn't think any of the other pictures and engravings that were left looked to be of any great value – though if they were, at least the very dirty windows had served to keep most of the sunlight out of the room. I added blinds to my list, but until that could be managed the shutters ought to be completely closed in here when the light was full on the back of the house to prevent any further fading. The furnishings were a mix of chairs in various periods, a love seat and two glass-topped curio tables, containing an assortment of items, including a couple of rather amateur miniatures, a porcelain snuffbox, three carved whale teeth, a bit of netsuke carving and a glass perfume bottle shaped like the Eiffel Tower.

Flanking the door at the far end were two horrid plinths of reddish mottled stone, looking like cheap salami. On one was a marble bust of a hawk-nosed man wearing a lace collar and with his hair in a shoulder-length bob, and on the other reposed a gruesomely detailed small hand carved in alabaster, probably Victorian. I had watched an old black-and-white horror film in the servants' sitting room at Blackwalls once, about someone's chopped-off hand that had run about strangling people, all on its own. I wished now that I hadn't, and I was just wondering which dark corner of the house I could banish the hand to, when Mrs Lark suddenly popped her curly grey head out of the door to the East Wing.

'Thought I heard you! Do you want to come through now and take a peek at our rooms?'

The Larks' suite was immaculately clean, but very shabby, and seemed to have been furnished with old cast-offs from the main house, though a personal touch was supplied by hundreds of cat figurines in every possible pose, and an awful lot of crocheted tablemats.

'Are you a cat lover, Mrs Lark? I don't remember seeing one in the house.'

'I am that! But Sir William couldn't stand them, so we've never had one at Winter's End,' she said sadly.

'Really? Well, *I've* no objection, except that I'm not keen on them in kitchens, walking around on the worktops and table. Would you like to get one?' I asked, and her face lit up.

'Oh, I'd *love* to, Sophy, if you're sure you don't mind? I'll make sure it doesn't go anywhere it shouldn't.'

'That's OK then. I like cats, I'm just more of a dog person, myself.'

'I'll get Jonah to take me to the animal rescue centre and pick out a nice kitten as soon as I've got a minute,' she said happily, and then showed me through the rest of their little flatlet, which included a rather Spartan bathroom.

'So, is there anything that you would like that you haven't got?' I asked.

'A shower over the bath and one of them heated towel rails,' she suggested hopefully.

I made a note of it. 'I'll have them installed as soon as I can afford it. Anything else? Painting and decorating, perhaps?'

'That would be lovely. Jonah put all the wallpaper up himself, but that's years ago now.'

'If you'd like to choose the paint and paper, and let me know, we should be able to get on and have that done quite quickly.'

'I'll do that. I've seen some nice wallpaper in *Good House-keeping* magazine that would look lovely in the bedroom – big pink chrysanthemums. I'll go and see if I can find it.'

'It sounds lovely,' I said, though to be honest, while I could picture rosy, freckled Mrs Lark in such a flowery bower of a bedroom, Jonah, who resembled nothing so much as an amiable rodent, would look quite incongruous. Leaving her searching, I went down the backstairs, meeting Grace on her way up again.

'We're nearly out of Harpic,' she said, by way of greeting. 'I'll be making Mr Jack's bed up now, ready for Saturday.'

'Thanks, Grace,' I said and, feeling the now-familiar *frisson* of nerves, guilt and excitement run through me at the thought of seeing Jack again, carried on down the stairs.

At the bottom I paused, then decided to leave the teashop area for another day. Nor did I need to bother much at this point with the rest of the rooms downstairs in the East Wing, though I did glance in the cellars. They were dry and whitewashed (though in need of a new coat), with the boiler ticking away in one, and another filled with half-empty wine racks and shelves of dusty bottles.

In the kitchen Aunt Hebe had just come in and was washing her earthy hands at the sink, and she asked me, slightly acidly, how my inventory was progressing.

'Fine. Mostly the place is just in need of a really good clean through,' I replied, adding Harpic to the huge list in the notebook while I remembered. 'I can't wait to start!'

'Then your zeal is admirable and should be encouraged, to which end I will give you a big jar of my own beeswax polish. A little goes a long way, with a bit of elbow grease. I'll put some out on the cleaning-room table. Oh, and I've just seen Seth,' she added, in tones that led me to believe she had not enjoyed the encounter. 'He says he is coming at two to show you round the garden.'

I wiped a grubby hand across my face and glanced at the clock, amazed at the time. 'I'd better have a quick wash, then, and have something to eat before he does.'

But just as I reached my room Anya phoned, and by the time I'd updated her on what was happening, washed off the outer layer of filth and returned to the kitchen, Seth was already sitting there, wolfing down ham sandwiches from a platter in the middle of the table.

He seemed to be arguing with Aunt Hebe, for she was saying tartly, '*William* never minded if I took one of the gardeners off for a couple of hours to clean out the hens or do some heavy lifting and digging, and I'm sure dear Jack would have no objection.'

Mrs Lark smiled at me and placed an empty plate opposite Seth, so I sat and helped myself to a sandwich. It was good thick ham, with English mustard that made my eyes water slightly, just the way I like it.

'I wouldn't mind either, if you told me *when* you wanted them and didn't just hijack them when they are doing something else!' Seth snapped. 'We're in the middle of filling in the lily pond on the bottom terrace and Derek's about to start rebuilding the collapsed retaining wall, and we need to get on with it while the weather is good.'

I put in my four penn'orth. 'Losing one of the gardeners for an hour or so occasionally isn't going to cause the whole thing to grind to a halt, is it?'

'That's perfectly true,' Aunt Hebe said, looking at me with approval.

'In fact . . .' I took another bite, chewed and swallowed, feeling Seth's green eyes resting on me coldly, 'in fact, we are all going to have to work as one team from now on, and multitask – as you will find out if you come to the meeting in the Great Hall the day after tomorrow.'

He pushed his plate away and leaned back, folding his arms. 'I see. The old order changeth . . .'

'Yes . . . this meeting, Sophy,' Aunt Hebe said doubtfully, 'shouldn't you wait until Jack arrives and get his approval, before you make any changes?'

'There's no time to waste and I've already had the benefit of the solicitor's advice and then Mr Yatton's – *and* Lucy's.'

'Lucy?' Seth questioned.

'My daughter,' I said shortly, because I was getting tired of having to explain who she was, though that certainly wouldn't be a problem once she got here and made her presence felt. 'She's in Japan, but Mr Yatton has been emailing her. She has much more of a head for figures than I have and she's amazingly practical. I'm hoping she'll come home soon.'

'Sir William told me about her, after he'd been up to see

you,' Mrs Lark chipped in unexpectedly. 'He said she'd turned out just the way he'd hoped Jack would and it was wasted on a girl. But then, he was a bit of a mis . . . what's the word?'

'Misogynist?' I suggested, though what she had just told me had made me think more kindly of Grandfather.

'That's the one.'

'You mean, you knew my brother had found Sophy and you never mentioned it to me?' demanded Aunt Hebe, gazing at her with acute disapproval.

'Sir William told me in confidence, Miss Hebe. Some of us don't go blabbing about things we shouldn't to them as shouldn't know!'

Aunt Hebe coloured slightly.

'It sounds to me as if Winter's End is going to suffer from an overdose of managing women,' Seth said gloomily, so maybe *he* was another misogynist.

Draining the contents of a giant blue and white striped china mug, Seth rose to his feet – and I had forgotten quite how tall he was until he was towering over me. 'If you want to see the gardens in the daylight, we'd better get going right now.'

'OK, I'll get a coat,' I said, quelling an irrational urge to challenge everything he said, just for the hell of it. Apart from trying to throw me off the premises when I first arrived, aiding and abetting Grandfather to spend money he couldn't afford on the garden and knowing more about Alys Blezzard's book than he should, nothing was actually *his* fault, was it?

'Do you want to come, Charlie?' I asked. 'Walkies?' But he was now lying on the braided mat in front of the Aga and didn't stir apart from thumping his tail a couple of times, so I left him there.

Outside there was an icy wind blowing that Seth, clad

in what looked like the same multi-holed layers of old jumpers as before, didn't seem to feel. He waited impatiently while I wrapped my scarf around my neck and fastened up my duffel coat, before shoving my hands in my pockets in lieu of gloves.

'We'll start at the front and work round,' he said, as we stood in the entrance porch. 'We have one seventeenth-century engraving of the front garden, when it was set out pretty much as you see it now, though we had to replant part of the maze that had been grassed over, and also restored some of the parterres. The hedging has changed. The maze was hornbeam originally, but now it's yew, and most of the parterres and knots are edged in box – it's longer-lived and easier to manage.'

I followed him down the steps, lingering to look through a clipped arch of variegated holly. 'What's through here? I looks a bit bare.'

'It's the new rose garden – still a work in progress. Do you want me to show you the way round the maze?'

'No, I used to play in there all the time when I was a little girl and I remember the trick of it, which is probably the same even now it is much bigger. I'll find my own way later.'

'Right,' he said shortly, giving me the impression that he wouldn't care if I got lost in there and never found my way out, and off he strode. I trotted after him down gravelled paths between intricately shaped box-edged parterres, sometimes with trees clipped into cones, balls or pyramids at the corners or centres, until finally he halted at a wicket gate set in a long yew hedge that billowed like a satiated green python.

'On open days, this is as far as the public can come. We put a "No Entry" sign on the gate, and ropes across the other paths. Through here is the wilderness and the fern grotto, which I expect you remember? This is a later part of the garden, of course, but Sir William liked it as it was.'

'And the dogs' graveyard is somewhere over here, isn't it?'

'Yes.' He opened the gate for me and then was off again.

We finally came out of the wilderness onto the rear drive behind the coach house, within smelling distance of the pigsty. I was glad to stop for a minute, and catch my breath.

'Over there's the tennis court,' he said. 'Another complete waste of time, in my opinion, taking the gardeners off their work to mow the grass and paint lines, especially since it's only ever used when Jack brings his friends down for the weekends in summer.'

'*You* don't play tennis?'

'No, I already get enough hot, sweaty exercise.'

My mind was suddenly and disconcertingly full of rather wild and earthy speculation, some of which must have shown on my face, because he explained, after a pause, 'Gardening.'

'Of course . . .' I said, my cheeks burning. 'I've never played tennis, but I do enjoy a game of croquet,' I babbled, hastening to change the subject. 'Lady Betty – my last employer – taught me. She swung a mean mallet when she'd had a gin or two.'

'It would be a lot easier to maintain a croquet lawn than a tennis court,' he hinted.

'I expect it would – and look nicer too. We could have a neat, low trellis fence around it, instead of this tattered netting . . . and perhaps a little gazebo in the corner to keep the hoops and stuff in. And a rose growing up it . . . what kind of rose?'

'A Falstaff – dark crimson, with a lovely scent.'

I had an enticing vision of cold drinks set out in the shade, the thunk of mallets on wooden balls and the smell of new-mown grass and roses – though goodness knew when I thought I'd have time for all that, with so much to be done!

Seth was looking at me with a glimmer of approval that would probably wither on the vine as soon as he'd heard what I had to say on Saturday. 'Come along,' he said, and led me into the walled garden that was Hebe's domain, though there was no sign of her.

Again, I remembered it quite clearly from my childhood – full of roses and herbs, fruit bushes, hens, beehives and lean-to greenhouses. Aunt Hebe's hard work out here made us pretty well self-sufficient in fruit, vegetables, eggs, honey and chickens. It was no longer a surprise that she hadn't taken the housekeeping in hand, too!

'I have the greenhouses abutting the other side of the wall,' Seth said as we emerged, 'and the nursery garden. There's a big wooden building where we keep the tools and the gardeners brew tea and eat their lunch. There's a phone extension there, so you can ring down from the estate office in the house if you want one of us for anything. Behind that is the old orchard. Most of the apple trees bear little fruit, but they are valuable for the mistletoe that grows on them. Do you know about that?'

'Yes, Mrs Lark told me about it.'

'It grows wild in the woods too, mainly on the oaks, and the sale of it is increasingly lucrative, in season.'

He didn't offer to show me, but instead walked around the solar tower to the terraces at the back of the house. 'On visitors' days those trellis dividers are pulled out to block off the top terrace to the left of the cross-passage door, so visitors can't look in the windows of the family wing.'

He came to a halt and surveyed the three descending terraces proudly. 'This is what I *really* wanted you to see – the restoration of the knot gardens to the original sixteenth-century design and planting, a very early scheme

– though as I said, we are mainly using box edging, since it's easier. We're on to the lower one now, the last phase. We found all but that part of the plan, so your grandfather and I were trying to come up with a scheme that would be in keeping with the rest.'

I looked down at the terraces, with below them again the river, dammed off to make a small lake and cascade. On the far side, over a humped stone bridge, woodland covered the hillside. The roof of a half-hidden summerhouse could just be seen above the trees.

'It's so pretty!'

'Well, it will be eventually. Jack wanted me just to rebuild the wall and turf the bottom terrace, and leave it at that, but Mr Hobbs said to carry on as before until you arrived and decided what you wanted to do.'

We went down to the second terrace, where he began to wax lyrical about the uniqueness of the restoration at Winter's End and, as I listened to him, I began to appreciate truly that the completion of the gardens was something he wanted passionately, not only as a monument to both his father and my grandfather, but for his own satisfaction.

Strangely, he seemed unable to see that leaving the lovely old house at its heart to rot would leave a hole in the fabric of his beautiful landscape, but I suddenly found this blinkered viewpoint rather endearing. He'd entirely forgotten who he was with and was talking with a single-minded passion about what was evidently the love of his life. Strands of blue-black hair blew around his strong face and his eyes glowed an otherworldly green as he regarded his handiwork.

I shivered suddenly, but it wasn't the cold.

'The central knot of the middle terrace is in the shape of a rose, as you can see if you look down on it from the Long Room – a very unusual design,' he enthused, 'especially

144

for the time.' Then his eyes slowly refocused on my face and took on a warier but still hopeful expression. 'You can see now how important it is to finish the scheme, can't you, Sophy? We're so close, and there will be absolutely nothing like it in the whole country!'

He didn't wait for my answer, but took my elbow and steered me down another flight of stone steps to the lowest level, which was, quite frankly, a muddy mess.

'So far we've started rebuilding the footings of the retaining wall – all the stones are numbered and charted as we remove them. And we've taken out the late Victorian lily pond, which had a ghastly fountain totally out of keeping with the rest of the garden.'

'Oh? What have you done with it?' I asked. 'Even if you didn't like it, it's probably valuable.'

'It's in one of the stables. Some kind of water nymph, I think, with a big bird.'

'Leda?'

'Possibly, though it looks more like a duck than a swan.'

I looked around the stretch of mangled turf, heaps of stones and muddy holes. 'So, had you and Grandfather come to any decision about what to have here?'

His eyes lost that creature-from-another-planet glow and he grinned, making him look all at once younger and more approachable – *and* worryingly attractive too.

'No, we couldn't agree on it at all. Sir William wanted to repeat the design of the top terrace, but I thought it would be better to create a different sixteenth-century knot, this time using the sort of edging plants they would have used before box became so popular, like winter savory, hyssop, thyme and rosemary.'

The otherworldly glimmer again lit his eyes as he turned back to me. 'It might be harder work to maintain, but it would be an interesting variation and could be infilled with plants available at the time too, perhaps repeated in borders at the back near the wall. But not at the front of the terrace, because the view over the lake and river below is enough.'

'Yes, it's lovely,' I agreed, walking over to the low stone balustrade, the frozen grass crunching beneath my feet, and looking down at the waterfall below.

'Planting anything there would simply be gilding the lily,' he said, following me, 'and— *Don't lean on it!*' he yelled suddenly. Flinging his arms around me, he hauled me backwards with a jerk that made my teeth rattle and I found myself, feet dangling above the ground, crushed against a broad expanse of unravelling Aran jumper.

'I – I think mending that might be a priority?' I said weakly, clutching at him as the stone I had been leaning on wobbled a bit and then settled back into place.

'Yes, straight after we've rebuilt the retaining wall,' he agreed, setting me back on my feet and releasing me, then added grimly, 'providing you don't let your aunt take my gardeners away to clean out hens and dig vegetable beds whenever she pleases.'

'I don't think an hour or two here and there is going to make that much of a difference,' I said, still slightly shakily. Then I gazed up at the shabby house with its dull, dirty windows and it seemed to be looking back at me with the hopeful expectancy of an overgrown puppy. 'The tourists come to see the terraces on open days, don't they?'

'Yes, though obviously they are not allowed down to this level yet. We rope it off. When they've seen the Great Hall and minstrels' gallery, they come out through the cross-passage door onto the top terrace and down to the second. Then they usually go back up to the tearoom.'

'Mmm. It all seems pretty amateur at the moment, but higher visitor numbers would increase the Winter's End revenue, especially if we charged a lot more for entrance.'

'You sound as if you've done this before?' he asked curiously. 'I thought you were just some kind of New-Age traveller.'

'I haven't *lived* on the road for years,' I said patiently. 'My mother and I settled in a commune and ever since I left school I've worked in stately homes, doing everything from cleaning the floors to running guided tours. So I know that to entice more visitors, we need to enhance the attractions, and one obvious thing we could do is promote the possible Shakespeare connection more vigorously, both in the house and out. After all, that would fit in with the date of the knot gardens, wouldn't it?'

He nodded, looking cautious. 'I've read the theories that he spent the Lost Years in Lancashire – but he would have been just a teenager for most of them.'

'Well, we don't have to *prove* he was here, just suggest it. I saw a garden once that was entirely planted with things Shakespeare had mentioned in his plays,' I mused. 'Is there any reason why we couldn't do that on the lower terrace?'

'There *are* Shakespeare gardens,' Seth conceded, obviously turning the idea over in his head. 'It probably wouldn't be much different to my original suggestion of keeping the planting on this level purely late sixteenth century.'

'No, as long as the shrubs and plants were mentioned in one of the plays, you could have what you liked.'

'Easy then,' he said drily.

'Well, Hebe did tell me you did your degree dissertation on garden history, so it shouldn't be too hard. You probably know it all already.'

'I'll think about it,' he said, but the embers of that glow were sparking up again in his eyes.

'Is Jack interested in the garden?' I asked suddenly.

'Not particularly. Jack's only interested in Jack and money.'

'That's a bit harsh. Don't you get on?'

He shrugged. 'We don't have a lot in common these days, and I'm not too keen on some of his business methods either, but we used to get on OK in the holidays when he was home from his posh school – I went to the local grammar. But we didn't see much of each other once we left university, until I came back after my father died, to finish what he started. Jack was against the whole restoration scheme and he wanted me to stop once Sir William died, even though we are so close to finishing.'

'Well, you can hardly blame him, when it has been draining the estate for years,' I said, and, seeing his face set into obstinate thundercloud mode added quickly, 'Mr Yatton told me about your working arrangement with my grandfather.'

'It suits me at the moment. I can still run my own business, while keeping an eye on Winter's End.'

'You design knot gardens, don't you?'

'Yes – "Greenwood's Knots. Topiary, Parterres and Knot Gardens a Speciality".'

'That doesn't exactly roll off the tongue, does it? You could have called yourself something more exciting, like "Get Knotted",' I suggested.

His brow knitted, so he looked quite Neanderthal. 'No, I couldn't. No one would have taken me seriously.'

I don't think anyone had ever teased him before, but if he was going to be so serious then he had better get used to it, because I was finding the temptation to wind him up irresistible.

He looked at me for a minute in a slightly baffled way, then said challengingly, 'So, are *you* going to let me finish what my father and Sir William started?'

'Oh, yes. I think my grandfather would come back and haunt me if didn't! But you may as well resign yourself to it taking longer than you anticipated, because getting the house and its finances back in good order again has to be the priority now.'

'No, it's the gardens that attract the visitors, so they need to be completed first,' he insisted stubbornly.

I glared at him. 'Haven't you been listening to *anything* I've been saying? The house is *equally* important – or will be when it is restored. And I intend to see that it is.' I turned and started up the steps, while he followed behind me in brooding silence.

'That box hedge looks pretty ratty,' I said critically as we reached the top again, just to wind him up.

'It's foxes,' he said shortly.

'*Foxes?*'

'A fox, anyway. It seemed to like the scent. Sir William saw it from the windows rubbing itself against the hedges until they wore away. But it's not a problem any longer.'

I turned and stared at him. 'You *killed* it?'

'No, we found it dead on the tennis court. Natural causes, nothing to do with us – unless it overdosed on box, of course.' Before I could decide if that was a joke, he added abruptly, 'I've got things to do.' And off he strode as though he was wearing seven-league boots.

I stared after him, thinking some extremely random thoughts about the way that his silky black hair was just a bit too long at the back and how the width of his shoulders made him seem incredibly slim-hipped . . . And I was pretty sure the bottom layer of his holey, ratty jumpers was a pink T-shirt with some kind of slogan on it.

Then I came to with a start and went in through the unlocked cross-passage door.

Security seemed just a little lax at Winter's End.

Chapter Thirteen: Grave Affairs

Joan says that in her last hours my mother foretold that I would remain a Blezzard and my child after mee; but my children's children would be Wynters. I do not see how this can be, but it is true that I continue to think myself Alys Blezzard and not Alys Wynter.
From the journal of Alys Blezzard, 1581

There was something I couldn't put off any longer, even though, with the light fading and the temperature dropping, it wasn't the best time for what I had in mind.

I collected Charlie from the kitchen as company, first inserting him into his garish tartan coat, then drove off in the VW down the back drive, which would lead me, I knew, into the village by the churchyard. I parked in the lane and went in through the unlocked mossy lych-gate, though I felt doubtful about taking Charlie into a churchyard. But there was no one about, so I decided to risk it.

'Don't do anything you shouldn't,' I warned him, and he wagged his tail amiably.

The family plot was easy to find – or perhaps that should be *plots*, since centuries of Winters had filled the original enclosure with weathered stone figures of knights reclining comfortably on top of their tombs amid plainer, lichen-encrusted stones, and spawned whole new enclaves around it. Space had been made for William in one of these, his name and dates added to the splendid, polished slate obelisk at the back. It was topped with the same family emblem that I'd already noticed on the arch over the drive, which really *couldn't* be a whippet with a black pudding in its mouth . . . could it?

My mother's grave was nearby – a simple rectangle edged with clipped rosemary for remembrance, with a small marble angel at its head that reminded me very much of my mother: it was standing on tiptoe in a whirl of curls and draperies, seemingly about to take wing, while casually dropping a half-furled inscribed scroll.

'Well, Mum,' I said, 'here we are, back at Winter's End.' The angel regarded me with blank eyes and a slightly spaced-out smile. Either the sculptor knew my mother or had been shown photographs. 'Did you *believe* all those stories you told me when we ran away?'

She'd certainly been the Scheherazade of the family, though of course no one had been trying to kill her, apart from Fate. And diamonds had literally been a girl's best friend, since she must have been selling them one by one to be permanently stoned for so many years.

'*And* you wrenched me out of my setting too, did you know that?' I told her, slightly bitterly, though maybe I had not been so much a diamond as a rather dark, uncut garnet. 'Winter's End is where I belong – where I should have stayed.'

But then, in her casually affectionate way she *had* loved me, even if she had been happy to let Aunt Hebe and Mrs Lark take over most of the childcare. Perhaps she simply couldn't bear to leave me behind, just as I could never have even contemplated a separation from Lucy? Or maybe she feared that if she left me behind Grandfather would have had me taken into care?

From what I have learned of him since my return, I am very sure he would not – just as I am also sure that Grandfather loved Mum, in his own way. It was just that with typical male obtuseness he had expected more of her than she was capable of giving.

If she *had* left me behind at Winter's End, I wondered what it would have been like, once Jack had arrived. The new fledgeling would certainly have pushed me out of being the main focus of Hebe's affections, even if not entirely out of the nest . . .

I remained lost in thought for ages, until I slowly became aware of voices somewhere nearby, coming from behind the little church, I thought. Charlie heard them too: he got up from the slab he'd been irreverently sitting on and trotted purposefully off, like a small round tartan bagpipe on legs.

'Charlie!' I hissed, chasing after him. 'Come here!'

I managed to snatch him up just as he was about to round the corner of the church, then cautiously stuck my head around, to see who else had chosen this god-forsaken hour to visit the dearly departed.

It was lucky I was partially hidden by a rose bush, for there, not fifteen feet away, were Seth Greenwood and Sticklepond's answer to Helen of Troy, Melinda Christopher.

Seth was staring down at the ground as if he found it really, really interesting and she was gazing at him with those strange, caramel-coloured eyes as if she'd like to eat him, boots and all.

Considering he was looking like a cross between Mr Rochester and Heathcliff in their gloomier moments, I suppose this was hardly surprising.

'Yes, you *have* been avoiding me lately, Seth, and I'd like to know why!' she snapped.

'Actually, I haven't. I didn't even know you were looking for me.'

'I keep coming up to Winter's End, doesn't anyone ever tell you?'

He shrugged. 'I thought you were looking for Jack. I don't know why you two fell out just before Sir William died, but don't expect me to fill in the gap until it's kiss-and-make-up time.'

'Don't be silly, there's nothing going on between Jack and me – and you weren't so unwelcoming when I first moved back here, darling, were you?' she said silkily. 'In fact, I got the distinct impression you were pleased to see me.'

'That was before Jack turned up again and I realised where your real interests lay,' he said coolly. '*Lay* being the operative word.'

'Come on, Seth, you know very well Jack and I are just in partnership to knock down that hideous house Clive left me and redevelop the land, though getting planning permission is taking *for ever*.' She lowered her voice to a seductive purr, so that I had to strain my ears to hear what she said, and added, 'But you and I are old friends too – and much *more* than old friends – aren't we?'

'I don't think we were ever friends, Mel. And, as I told you when you got me down to Surrey on the pretext of designing a garden while you were still married to Seldon, my price is way out of your league.'

She flicked his ragamuffin clothes a disdainful glance. 'You can't be that expensive – and anyway, I've got money. I'm a *very* rich widow.'

'Congratulations, then you've got everything you ever wanted. I hope you and your money are very happy together.'

She moved towards him and laid a hand on his arm, a wistful smile on her lovely face. 'Yes, I've got everything – except *you*. When I married Clive I was just so tired of scrimping and saving, trying to keep up with the crowd and look well dressed on a pittance – it seemed so important then. But I missed you so much and you wouldn't even *look* at me after I got married, just like you're not looking at me *now*,' she snapped pettishly.

He cast her a brooding look and said flatly, 'Look, Mel, twenty years ago you played me and Jack off against each other, then you suddenly chose to marry a man nearly old enough to be your grandfather. Perhaps you thought you could have your cake and eat it, but I never fancied playing Mellors to your Lady Chatterley then – or,' he added bluntly, '*now*, if you marry Jack.'

'Oh – Jack!' she said, with a little laugh. 'Forget Jack. Perhaps I did flirt with him a bit when I first came back, but he's not the marrying kind, though you were – once.' She laid a hand on his sleeve and looked up at him appealingly. 'Do you remember proposing to me?'

'I remember a lot of things I'd much rather not – like begging you to marry me instead of Seldon, before it finally dawned on me that you would never marry a gardener's son with no position or money. I was fine for a bit of a fling, wasn't I? But you wanted more.'

'Don't be bitter, darling, that's all water under the bridge. Now I'm widowed, there's no reason why I can't have my cake *and* eat it too, is there? In fact, I could eat you up right now,' she said huskily, sliding her hands up his arms and looping them around his neck.

In the half-light she looked ethereally fair and lovely and I didn't see that he could possibly resist her. My head was whirling with revelations and speculation – and, it has to be said, with a feeling of relief that my handsome cousin didn't seem to have fallen for her all over again.

Seth was the one she had really set her sights on, and if she flirted a bit with Jack, then . . . well, I expect *femmes fatales* just do it automatically when an attractive man comes within reach; that, or it was intended to make Seth jealous, though I didn't think he had the kind of temper that would take very well to that kind of tactic.

'Woof!' said Charlie, as if agreeing with my thoughts, and I quickly clamped a hand around his muzzle and dodged back behind the church. Then I ran back to my mother's grave and set him down, holding on to his collar.

'Ssh!' I warned him, and he waved his tail.

I sat down on a tabletop tomb half-hidden in the grass and waited. A few moments later the throaty roar of a sports car came from somewhere in the village, which I thought was probably Melinda leaving. I was just thinking that Seth must have gone out by the other gate too, when I heard a heavy tread approaching.

A large pair of boots entered my pensively downcast view and I looked up with (I hope) an expression of innocent surprise. And actually, he *had* still startled me, because from my position he looked about seven feet tall and rather forbidding, with his eyebrows knitted above suspicious jade eyes and the chilly breeze flipping his silky black hair about: the Demon Lover in person.

'Oh, it's you, Seth! What are you doing here?'

'Visiting my father's grave – it's the anniversary of his death,' he said shortly, looking surprisingly grim considering he had just had the most beautiful woman I have ever seen in my life practically fling herself at him. 'I like to come and update him on what's happening to his garden – or is *likely* to happen to his garden.'

'Isn't the conversation a bit one-sided?'

'Not necessarily. He was never much of a conversationalist even when he was alive. Anyway, don't *you* feel the channels of communication between the past and the present never quite close?' he asked, to my surprise, because I hadn't had him down as any kind of fey.

'Maybe . . .' I admitted, 'and a definite yes when it comes

to Alys Blezzard. But wherever my mother is, she isn't communicating with me in any meaningful way, any more than she did when she was alive, though I can *feel* her close by sometimes, since I got here . . . and I understand her a bit more, I think.'

'She wasn't a good mother? I thought the story was that she snatched you and ran because she was afraid of losing you.'

'Oh, she loved me in her way. I suppose that's why she took me with her. But she was also light-hearted, good-natured, restless, easily bored, and permanently stoned – *and* she was convinced she was a white witch and could do spells and read the crystal ball, which she couldn't.'

I smiled ruefully. 'She was like a will-of-the-wisp – you just couldn't take hold of her at all, because she was always off after some new craze. That's what she was doing in America when she died, going off with a new man to a new place. Only that time I'd had enough and stayed put in the commune in northern Scotland where we'd been staying, though right up to the moment she got on the plane, I didn't believe that she would really leave me . . . and I don't know *why* I'm telling you this!' I added, surprised.

'Oh, graveyards at dusk,' he said, shrugging broad shoulders. 'And at least you knew your mother. I barely remember mine; she died when I was four. Then my father married Ottie, possibly the least maternal woman in the world. Or maybe it was the other way round – Ottie decided to marry my father.'

'But she is fond of you, I could tell.'

'Oh, yes, and I'm fond of her. When Jack and I were children and got into trouble for pranks, he always looked so angelic that he would have got off scot free if she hadn't weighed in on my side. Of course, Hebe always insisted it was me leading her blue-eyed boy astray, so that never went down well. But it was later that we fell out.'

I could imagine *who* they had fallen out over too, but thought I had better change the subject. 'I don't even know who *my* father is,' I confessed. 'Mum always said he was a gypsy she met at a fairground – but then, she said a lot of things, and most of them weren't true.' I sighed. 'But I loved her anyway.'

Seth looked down at the small angel guarding the grave. 'There are snowdrops and crocus and those little tête-à-tête daffodils in spring.'

'Did you plant them, and the rosemary?'

He nodded. 'I'm not keen on cut flowers on graves, though Sir William insisted on having some sent down every week. I don't know whether you want that continued?'

'No, I don't want cut flowers either. It's fine as it is, thank you. What have you planted on your father's grave?'

'Come and see.' He turned and led the way back round the church, Charlie and I following in his wake.

It was a simple stone carved with spade, fork and watering can, and I liked the wording: 'Rufus Greenwood, perennially bedded here'. The grave was a rectangular knot of low box that must have been trimmed with nail scissors.

It was growing dark and the chilly gloom descended on us like a pall slowly lowered from the sky – not a comfortable thought, even in the nicest of country graveyards.

I shivered. 'I'd better get back home. I've got the van with me – do you want a lift?'

'No, I'll walk back, thanks. I want to think.'

I bet he did. At some point he might want to wipe the pink lipstick off his face too.

Chapter Fourteen: Twisted Wires

Lady Wynter doth question mee closely about the marriage bed and whether I am not yet to bear a child. I too wish it, since I foresee that all my arts will not cause my husband to survive another harsh winter, and a babe would be security for my future here. But I fear there is little likelihood of it coming to pass. When I recall my mother's words on her deathbed – that I would remain a Blezzard, and my child after mee, though my children's children would be Wynters – it puzzles mee much.

From the journal of Alys Blezzard, 1581

Next morning, after a night mostly spent fine-tuning my plans for Winter's End, I had eyes as dark-ringed as a racoon.

After breakfast my very own personal bank accounts manager came to the house with papers for me to sign, which was a novelty in itself. The last time I tried to increase my overdraft by a measly thousand pounds nobody wanted to know me, but now it seemed the world was my oyster. But I wasn't about to use Winter's End either as a cash cow or collateral. It was *my* pearl and I would never risk losing it.

That sorted, I went out to the stables to look for the Victorian fountain Seth had banished there from the lower terrace – and he was right, it *was* truly hideous: a malformed nymph doing something dubious with a long-necked duck.

Mind you, there's a market for everything, so I asked Mr Yatton if it was all right for me to try to sell it.

'Oh, yes, you can do what you like with it,' he agreed, 'with any of your property, in fact, now probate has been granted.'

'Oh, good. I thought I'd phone up one or two architectural salvage places and get them to come out and give me an estimate. Although it's revolting, I might still get enough to send Lucy the money for a ticket home *and* do one or two other things. I'd like to have Alys Blezzard's portrait cleaned, for a start, and I've also promised to have the Larks' rooms redecorated.'

'Lucy is sending me several emails a day with *suggestions*,' Mr Yatton said, 'and lots of very intelligent questions. Though actually I think our today is tomorrow in Japan, isn't it? Oh dear, I do find these time differences quite confusing.'

'So do I, but I think Japan *is* several hours ahead. Lucy isn't trying to tell you how to run the place yet, is she?'

His eyes twinkled. 'Not quite, but she does sound very much like Sir William – straight to the point.'

'Oh, I *do* wish she was here, even if she often drives me mad,' I sighed. 'And I'm sure she's still being pestered by that man. I told you one of her mature students had a fixation about her, didn't I? He keeps following her about and trying to get her to go out with him.'

'Yes indeed, very worrying,' he agreed. 'I'll warn her to be careful when I next email, but I am sure she is sensible enough not to take any risks – and let us hope we will soon have her home again.'

'Perhaps even in time for Christmas! That would be so good, because we've never had one apart,' I agreed, feeling happier.

159

'If you like, I will phone up suitable architectural salvage firms about the fountain,' he offered. 'In fact, I could go out first and take photographs, then email them together with the dimensions. They might even make you an offer without coming out to see it.'

'That would be a great help, if you would,' I said, then settled down to discuss with him just what I was planning to say at the meeting tomorrow. The thought of giving my maiden speech was giving me acute cold feet . . . as was the idea of facing Jack, though in his case there was also a flutter of excitement in my stomach.

'I don't know if Jack will arrive in time for it, because I haven't managed to get him on the phone yet and he hasn't got back to my messages. He doesn't even know that I'm definitely *not* going to sell Winter's End to him and I do feel bad about that, because I led him to believe I might.'

'I'm sure everyone else will be happy with your decision, since the main worry was that if Jack inherited the property he might decide to develop it and sell it off piecemeal, as he did to the home of the widow of one of Sir William's old friends. I don't know the ins and outs of it, but it caused quite a rift between them and I suspect was the crucial factor in Sir William's decision to leave Winter's End and all his property outright to you.'

'You don't really think he would do that to Winter's End, do you?' I asked bluntly. 'Mr Hobbs does, I know – he as much as said so when he came to see me in Northumberland – but I am sure Jack loves the place and has no intention of doing any such thing!'

'He has certainly never shown much interest in running the estate. His life is in London, so that he tends to use Winter's End as a weekend retreat, frequently bringing friends,' Mr Yatton said cautiously. 'Sir William often said he seemed to think Winter's End was a country hotel.'

160

'Well, not any longer,' I said firmly. 'This is Jack's home and he will always be welcome here, but any future visitors will have to earn their keep. I can't afford freeloaders and there's lots to do.'

Then I got Mr Yatton to help me surf the internet and find out what sort of plants and shrubs appeared in Shakespeare's works, so I could impress Seth with my knowledge at our next encounter. And actually, it was really fascinating. The Bard had to have been interested in gardening to have mentioned so many. I had no idea what some of them were, but they sounded lovely – bachelor's-buttons, columbine and gillyflowers. But there were lots of more familiar flowers too, like daffodils, pansies and honeysuckle.

When he had printed it all out for me I asked him what state the Royal Purse was in before ringing up Stately Solutions and placing my order for the specialist cleaning materials, and then dispatching Jonah to the nearest ironmongers with a list of more everyday stuff.

After that I went to the library and looked for the book about treasure that Aunt Hebe had mentioned, which proved to be a slim and well-thumbed paperback called *Hidden Treasure Hoards of North-West Lancashire*, shoved in with a lot of local history books near the door.

It was all very interesting, though oral tradition is like Chinese whispers, so what you end up with probably bears little resemblance to the original tale. But Winter's End and its immediate environs seemed to have attracted more than one legend, so it was only surprising that Seth wasn't constantly repelling a positive Klondike of metal-detector enthusiasts.

The vicar called after lunch, which was something I thought only happened within the pages of Agatha Christie novels. She was a brisk, pleasant woman of about fifty and we had

161

a ladylike chat over tea and biscuits in the drawing room, during which I found myself agreeing that next year's annual village fête could be held, as usual, on the car-parking field.

The rest of the afternoon I enjoyably spent cleaning out the corner cupboard in Lady Anne's parlour, first carefully laying the contents out on a side table covered with an old picnic rug.

But apart from the Elizabethan chest there wasn't much else in there of any value – just the display of wax flowers under a glass dome, a couple of dead spiders, the almost-certainly fake ushabti figures, and a cheap and hideous Japanese teaset messily painted with dragons.

Once the cupboard was clean inside and out, I dusted off the little wooden coffer with a new hogshair brush I had borrowed from Ottie. It still looked dull and homely, but I decided to wait for the specialist (and expensive) Renaissance wax I had ordered to arrive, rather than use Aunt Hebe's beeswax polish on it.

Then I washed and dried the glass dome and teaset before gingerly replacing everything, so that when I finally stepped back to admire my handiwork, the china sent out subtle gleams of red and gold from the dark depths of the cupboard and the wax flowers glimmered palely like spectral coral.

I was so unbelievably filthy after just doing that one corner that I had to go and take a long shower before dinner. It was obviously going to take me hours to clean the whole room to the point where I could start making my patch-work cushions in there, but I was dying to get on with the rest of it.

Call me a sad person if you like, but cleaning is such *fun*!

Before I went down for dinner I tried ringing Jack's mobile yet again, not expecting him to actually answer – so that when he did the sound of his warm, caressing voice imme-diately threw me into a panic.

We'd barely exchanged civilised greetings before I was confessing, in a rush, 'Jack, there's something I *have* to tell you! I'm terribly, terribly sorry – but the instant I arrived back at Winter's End, I realised I couldn't possibly ever sell it, even to you.'

There was a small silence and then he said, reasonably, 'But, darling, you wouldn't be so much selling it as helping to keep it in the family. It will cost a small fortune to put the place right and even the everyday expenditure just to keep the place running is huge – way beyond your means. You have no idea!'

'Well actually, Jack, I *do*. The costs *will* be huge, you are right, but I've worked out a plan, and I think if we all pull together as a team we can do it, even if it is a bit of a gamble. I'm going to sell the Herring horse portrait, but instead of paying off that horrible bank loan with the money, I'm going to use it to upgrade the visitor facilities, with the aim of greatly increasing revenue from opening the house. I'm having a staff meeting tomorrow morning, to tell them about it and get them on board – and I really hope *you* will be there too, to support me, Jack.'

'Hebe mentioned something about a staff meeting, and I've no objection to you taking control of the housekeeping and putting the place to rights, Sophy, because goodness knows it needs it! And it *is* your home too, after all,' he said magnanimously. 'I hope it always will be.'

'Gee, thanks,' I said, the sarcasm just slipping out. Hadn't he been listening to me? 'Look Jack, you don't understand! I'm going to—'

'Don't worry your head about revenue or selling things, darling, just mobilise the troops for a spring clean and leave the rest to me. We'll work something out. See you tomorrow!' he added, and was gone.

163

I was so unnerved by this exchange that I immediately rang Anya and told her all about it.

'Jack sounds to me like the sort of spoiled brat who hasn't grown out of thinking that he can have whatever he wants,' she said thoughtfully. 'It will never enter his head that he can't charm you into seeing things his way – and maybe he can, because you're a sucker for that kind of man.'

'He could charm the birds down from the trees,' I agreed ruefully, 'but really, Anya, I'm not such a soft touch – or not where Winter's End is concerned, anyway.'

'Well, watch out. That kind of man can turn quite nasty if you cross them.'

'Jack's not "that kind of man", he's really warm and lovely and interesting,' I said, with more assurance than I actually felt. I mean, he was a bit scary that time he turned up at the caravan, until he realised I hadn't persuaded Grandfather into leaving Winter's End to me, though I suppose that was perfectly understandable. I might have added that he was also cloth-eared and obtuse – but affectionate . . . 'It's only that he does seem to feel that Winter's End is his by right – only now, unfortunately, so do I!'

'Sounds to me like he hasn't grasped that at all, Sophy. He just thinks he's got a gullible free housekeeper,' she commented bluntly.

'Well, he hasn't, as he will find out tomorrow if he arrives in time for the meeting! But don't think the idea of selling it to him and just being the housekeeper didn't sound tempting. I mean, I could stay here always, looking after Winter's End, without any of the responsibilities and financial worries!'

'You're not serious?'

'No, it was only a moment's weakness when I was feeling overwhelmed by it all. Oh, and about Seth – you know, the head gardener? He's having a fling with the local beauty, a rich and very beautiful widow!' I told her what I'd heard and seen in the graveyard.

'Pity. He sounded like he had more possibilities than Jack.'

'He has no possibilities – what gave you that idea?'

'Oh, I don't know. Maybe it was when you described him as very tall, dark, green-eyed and bad-tempered. But if this local beauty has got her claws into him, obviously that's that.' Then she told me the good news – that Guy had got a job near Manchester, so she was going to come down this way, once he was settled.

I was dying to see her and show her Winter's End – *and* see Seth's face when she rolled up in her converted ambulance. I wouldn't warn him she's coming, because that would spoil the element of surprise.

I wondered if there would be any fireworks from Seth at the meeting tomorrow . . . but perhaps not, because he should have picked up some idea of my intentions from our conversation while he was showing me the gardens. But then again, like with Jack, I was not sure he was really taking in what I was saying.

But if they didn't take me seriously, that was their problem . . . And whatever Aunt Hebe, Anya, or anyone else thought, there was no way Jack could charm Winter's End out of me: it was mine, all mine. Though if he actually *did* feel about it the way I did, then I was sorry for him and I'd be more than happy if he wanted to spend lots of time here, helping me get the place up and running.

What with the thought of all the morrow's ordeals – giving a speech of sorts, trying to second-guess everyone's reactions and convincing Jack that I meant what I said – I tossed and turned restlessly for the second night in a row and only fell asleep with the dawn, waking very much later than I ought to have.

Downstairs Jonah brought me fresh coffee and informed me that Aunt Hebe had breakfasted early and was now rearranging the seating in the Great Hall. 'This bacon's dried out – shall I get Mrs Lark to cook you up some fresh?'

'Oh, no thanks, Jonah. There isn't time. You can clear that away now, if you want to.' I just gulped down my coffee and then ran back up the solar stairs for my notes and to take a few deep breaths, before going stealthily along to the minstrels' gallery and peering over the rail.

Aunt Hebe had evidently grouped the chairs by the fire to her satisfaction, and was now sitting there, together with Ottie, Mr Yatton, and Mrs Lark, who was crocheting something lacy.

Seth, a finger of wintry sunshine haloing his very un-angelic dark head, was seated on one of the ancient cast-iron radiators, morosely whittling something. I hoped it was up to his weight, but since the radiators never seemed to rise to much above lukewarm at least he was unlikely to burn his extremities.

That Mel Christopher might, though.

The rest of the staff and several total strangers were standing about talking, but went silent when I came slowly down the stairs, pausing at the bottom. To my relief I noticed that the stag now had two eyes, even if he was hung aslant, so that he seemed to be looking at me with sideways suspicion – but then, so were half the people present.

In fact, there seemed to be an awful lot of staring eyes in the room, but I soon realised that the occasion had become an extended family outing, with an impromptu mother and toddler group set up in one corner and a senior citizens' day centre on the window seats.

There was no sign of Jack: I didn't know whether to feel disappointed or relieved.

'Here she is,' Ottie remarked loudly. 'I'd stand two steps

up and talk from there, Sophy, otherwise we won't be able to see you, let alone hear you. This lot are the Friends of Winter's, by the way.' She gestured to a dozen or so elderly strangers, who all nodded at me and then sat down in two rows on the benches behind the chairs, like a jury.

I did as Ottie suggested, looking down into a circle of expectant faces and feeling hideously self-conscious. 'I've called you all together,' I began – then stopped, horrified to find my voice coming out in a much higher pitch than usual. I coughed and started again: 'I've called you together today to explain to you how things stand. I'm sure you must all be anxious to know what my future plans are for Winter's End.'

Seth raised his head and I looked away from his direction hastily. 'What I would *like* to do is make my home here at Winter's End, as my grandfather intended, and for it to go on as before so that you all keep your jobs. But if this is to happen, then the estate *must* start to pay its way.'

'That's right,' Jonah agreed with absent heartiness: he was cleaning his fingernails out with a pocketknife, which was something I wished he'd done before serving breakfast.

'The house has been allowed to fall into a state of neglect and disrepair over the last few years – through no fault of the staff, I hasten to add. For too long, the money that should have gone into its upkeep has been entirely diverted into restoring the gardens, an imbalance that must now be redressed.'

Out of the corner of my eye I could see the three gardeners, Derek, Bob and Hal, turn as one man and look nervously at Seth, whose green eyes were fixed on me in a way I was coming to recognise meant trouble.

I looked down at my notes quickly. 'The garden is nearing completion in any case, and so now the first priority must be to refurbish the house. Additional funding for this will be raised by increased visitor numbers, with an extended season, a larger entrance fee, improved refreshment facilities and the sale of Winter's End-related merchandise.'

'You mean a *shop*?' Aunt Hebe said after a minute, in a very Lady Bracknell way.

'Yes, the existing tearooms could be turned into a sort of giftshop-cum-café area. I've seen it work very well elsewhere, because when visitors are sitting having tea surrounded by things to buy, they very often *do*. The temptation is too much for them. We could even sell a range of your rose-based products, if you wanted to, Aunt Hebe,' I added with low cunning. 'With a cut going to Winter's End, of course.'

She sat up a bit straighter. 'What percentage?'

'My sister was always mercenary at heart,' Ottie commented to the room at large.

'That's easy for someone to say who only has to slap a bit of wet clay onto twisted wire to rake in a fortune,' Hebe snapped.

'We can discuss percentages later.' I turned back to the rest of the room. 'So, the situation at the moment is that there's a huge amount of work to be done in the house, where we have very little assistance, but much less in the garden, where we have a larger staff. Clearly that needs addressing and, while I certainly don't want to *lose* any gardeners, you all need to be aware that you'll have to become multitaskers, helping with any jobs around the house as and when asked – such as cleaning all the outside windows, for a start. That will take two of you, and I'd like it done on Monday, please, weather permitting. Perhaps you could decide among yourselves who will do that?'

'I'm up for it,' Bob said, the pink daisy in his hat bobbing. 'Make a change from all the eternal tree clipping! I'm cutting box spirals in my sleep, these days.'

'Do they lean sideways like the ones you do when you're awake, Bob?' asked Hal, and they all laughed.

'Thanks, Bob,' I said. 'After that, I'd like a start made on rubbing down the front gates by the lodge, ready for repainting. Rusting gates aren't exactly the image we want to give our visitors when they first arrive, are they?'

I looked around at the sea of faces. 'Well, that's about it, really. The goalpost we're all aiming for is a grand, pre-season opening day to get publicity going before the season starts in earnest at Easter – say Valentine's Day, February the fourteenth. Given the amount of work that needs doing, that doesn't leave us a lot of time.'

Seth stood up suddenly. 'No, it doesn't – and it's the gardens that bring in most of the visitors, so you can't just take the men away and tell them to clean windows, or anything else that isn't their job, whenever you feel like it!'

'Yes I can,' I said mildly, 'and clearly *they* understand why.'

'But the restoration is so near completion – it would be madness to stop now!'

'We're *not* stopping,' I said patiently. 'Weren't you listening? I'm not taking the gardeners away entirely, just asking them to help with things they wouldn't normally do, when necessary, especially in the run-up to the visitor season. If we don't all pull together as a team my plans won't work, I'll have to sell Winter's End – and that will be an end of it.'

'What about Jack?' Hebe asked doubtfully. 'Have you discussed all this with him?'

'Well, I've certainly told him all my plans,' I said with perfect truth. I swept a glance over the rest of the room. 'So, what do you all say?'

'Hear, hear,' Mrs Lark called. 'You're a sensible lass and your grandfather would be proud of you.'

'He wouldn't be too happy about delaying the garden scheme,' Seth snapped, 'especially rebuilding the retaining wall of the lower terrace. I think you're making a big mistake. Old manor houses are two a penny, but the garden scheme is *unique*.'

'William may have been as blinkered on the subject as you, Seth,' Ottie informed him crisply, 'but it's more than just an old manor house to Sophy, and I think you've met your match. She's as passionate about it as you are about the garden. It won't hurt for you to lend a hand and *I'll* certainly do what I can to help.'

'Like what?' Seth demanded sarcastically. 'Don't tell me you're going to start cleaning the windows or polishing the furniture?'

'No, I'm going to make a sculpture for the garden,' she said simply.

'Oh, *that'll* get the crowds in!'

'It'll certainly get a different crowd in from the usual visitors,' she agreed, '*and* help with publicity about Winter's End. And if times get really hard, Sophy can flog it.'

'Thank you very much, Ottie,' I said, grateful for the thought even if unsure how one of her very modern sculptures would fit into the garden. From the look on Seth's face, the same thought had just struck him too.

'A mixture of verdigris green and shining copper, I think . . .' she mused, her eyes going distant.

'Regarding the lower terrace, Seth,' I said boldly, encouraged by Ottie's stance, 'and our discussion about it, since we're going to create a Shakespeare garden, I thought it would be an interesting idea to have some of the stones in the rebuilt retaining wall inscribed with short quotations from the bard.'

This was a brilliant idea that had come to me in the unsleeping night watches, probably due to looking up all those Shakespearean plants.

I was about to add a joke about a bard in the hand, but after a glance at Seth's face, thought better of it.

There was a horribly silent pause vibrating with tension and leashed energy, of the kind that you get before a thunderstorm. Then one of the toddlers burst into noisy tears, shattering the silence, and Seth raised his voice above the yelling and said shortly, 'Sir William didn't want anything out of keeping with the sixteenth-century design of the other terraces. I think that would look incredibly naff, anyway.'

'Not if they're carved into the original stones that you're rebuilding the wall with,' Ottie put in thoughtfully. 'I didn't know you were having a Shakespeare garden, Sophy? I've visited one in the States – Boston, I think.'

'Now, just hold on a second! Nothing has been definitely decided yet about that and—' began Seth.

Ottie talked over him. 'I think it's a great idea and the inscriptions are too: and I know a young stonemason who could do them. We'll all have to think of our favourite quotes.'

'"The truth is out there somewhere",' suggested Jonah.

'I'm not entirely sure that's Shakespeare,' I said doubtfully.

'"Abandon hope, all ye who enter here"!' Grace piped up suddenly from the darkest corner.

'That's more like it,' Seth remarked gloomily.

The rest of the gardeners, who had been in a huddle talking in low voices, now said they were agreeable to lending a hand with anything needed, especially if it was that or Winter's End having to be sold up and their jobs going, and also if there was a possibility of any overtime, they were up for a bit of extra money.

'I don't think I could do much more cleaning than I'm doing now, love,' Grace said. 'Five mornings and a bit of extra help when visitors come round.'

'No, that's fine, Grace, I wasn't expecting you to do more. So, what do you all say?' I waited expectantly.

'They say yes, of course,' Aunt Hebe said feudally, giving them the cold blue eye. Agree with my plans or not, she certainly wasn't having any dissension in the ranks. And maybe the thought of cashing in by selling her potions and lotions in the shop might have helped swing the balance, too – that and my having deviously given her to believe that Jack knew all about my plans. (And if he didn't, it was his own fault.)

A chorus of ragged 'that's rights' came from most throats, except Seth's. He turned on his heel and walked out.

As if this was some kind of signal, Mrs Lark folded up her crocheting and rose to her feet, then she, Jonah and Grace began serving tea and three sorts of cake from a trestle at the back of the hall, while Charlie walked around hoovering up dropped crumbs. The children, released from their corner, ran about shrieking. A good time seemed to be being had by all and I was so relieved it was over that I'd eaten two giant rum truffle cakes before I realised it.

'I'll have to put my whole stillroom operation on a more professional basis,' Hebe said, appearing at my side.

'What?' I said, swallowing a mouthful of truffle.

'I'll need to produce a line of basic products with nice jars and labels – have to put my prices up too, because of the bigger overheads. Shall we say two per cent of the profit goes to Winter's End?'

'Shall we say twenty?' I countered, which I thought was moderate considering she was growing most of the ingredients in *my* garden, and producing it, rent free, on the premises.

In the end we settled on ten. I thought I'd been done.

Then the Friends of Winter's, who also seemed to be

friends of Hebe, surrounded me and promised their support.

'We will discuss it among ourselves at our regular meetings – we're a historical re-enactment society too, you know – and then talk it over with you at the Christmas gathering,' said Mr Yatton's sister, Effie, who looked just like him.

'*Which* Christmas gathering?' I asked blankly.

'Have you forgotten?' Aunt Hebe asked. 'The staff, tenants, Friends and all their families – *anyone* connected with Winter's End – come here on the morning of Christmas Eve.'

Into my head came a sudden memory of Father Christmas sitting by the fire handing out presents . . . the smell of fir trees, mulled wine and mince pies in the air. 'Yes . . . I think I *do* remember.' And come to think of it, Christmas now wasn't that far away – weeks, rather than months – and I really hadn't given it a thought until now.

Soon people started to drift away home, though some stayed to give Mrs Lark and Jonah a hand to clear the plates and urns back to the kitchen. Ottie returned to her studio and when Hebe vanished in the direction of her stillroom, I picked up the last of the piles of crockery and followed her towards the kitchen door.

I'd barely nudged it an inch open with my shoulder when the sound of voices in discussion stopped me in my tracks, even though I know that eavesdroppers rarely hear any good of themselves.

One of the gardeners – it sounded like Derek, the morose one – was saying: 'But Jack said he would either overturn the will or buy out the new owner, and when he did all our jobs would be safe.'

'Ah, but he says a lot of things, does Jack, and it's mostly hot air,' Hal said. 'Who knows what would happen? I heard him trying to order Seth to just shore up the wall on the bottom terrace and leave it at that – not that Seth took any notice. But it doesn't sound to me like he means to finish what Sir William started. No, I reckon Sophy's ideas are worth a go, at any rate.'

'Seth isn't going to like it. He's like a bear with a sore head.'

'Looks like Seth will have to lump it, then.'

'Sophy's got some odd ideas in *her* head,' Mrs Lark said, 'like wanting me to cook less food. But her heart's in the right place. She's letting me have a kitten, which is something Sir William didn't hold with.'

'And she said she didn't expect me to work more hours than I do now,' fluted Grace.

'That's right,' Jonah agreed. 'I think we should wait and see. And she didn't say she *wasn't* going to let Seth finish the garden, just that it would be slower than he wanted, so I expect he'll come round. And if it all works out, things at Winter's will go on pretty much as they always have, it seems to me, only better.'

'You're not going to do less baking, are you, Mrs Lark?' said another voice, which was probably Bob's, though it was hard to tell because he sounded as if he had his mouth full.

'No, don't be daft! There'll always be a scone or a bite of cake for anyone who wants it in *my* kitchen, and Sophy's got as hearty an appetite as any of you.'

I felt myself blushing hotly and vowed to stop being such a pig. If I carried on eating at this rate they would be able to roll me down the hill on pace-egg day.

'Haven't any of you lot got homes to go to?' said Aunt Hebe's voice suddenly – she must have opened the still-room door.

'Just giving Mrs Lark a hand with the crockery, Miss Hebe,' Derek said, 'but we'll be on our way now.'

I took a couple of quick backwards steps into the passage, so it looked like I was just coming round the screen as they came out, wished them goodbye, and went into the kitchen thoughtfully.

Jonah had begun to stack things into the dishwasher in a slapdash sort of way.

'It's only plain stuff. I don't put the fancy china in there,' Mrs Lark explained, 'or the good glasses. Jonah or Grace do those by hand.'

'I think that went quite well, don't you?' I said, suddenly filled with the euphoria of having got something tricky over with and, after all, what I had just overheard had been *mostly* positive. 'I'm going up to change, then show by example and start cleaning again, but first I'll just take Charlie for a quick walk round the wilderness, or he'll be getting too fat now he's got his appetite back.' I could do with some fresh air too – what with the crowd of people and the roaring fire, the Great Hall had become overheated and stuffy.

'All those things you sent Jonah to the shops for, he put in the cleaning room,' Mrs Lark said.

'Great. Everything else should come by delivery van next week, and can be put in there for me to sort out. I'll explain it all to Grace later. Come on, Charlie!' I added, dangling the lead before his little black nose.

Charlie would much rather have slept off his cake in front of the kitchen fire, so it was more of a quick drag than a walk until he gave in and condescended to trot by my side.

In the orchard a chilly, woodsmoke-scented wind was tossing the piles of dead brown leaves about like an invisible hand, though the bare-branched apple trees were covered with the surprisingly fresh spring green of mistletoe.

It was too cold to linger. Cutting back to the house

through the courtyard I came across a spectacular red sports car, which could only be Jack's. My heart did a quick little hop, skip and jump.

Chapter Fifteen: Boxing

There is a priest in the house. They do not yet trust mee with such secrets, despite my father having entertained these dangerous guests. But I have observed their comings and goings and know it to be near where I often sit in the solar.

From the journal of Alys Blezzard, 1581

After leaving Charlie in the kitchen I went through the West Wing looking for Jack, but finding no sign of him, climbed the steep, winding solar stairs to my bedroom.

I had my hand on the doorknob when the floorboards suddenly creaked heavily overhead, and my first thought was that it was Grace – until I remembered that it was Saturday and she would have gone straight home after the meeting, not upstairs for a sneaky smoke. I ran up the narrow stairs and reached the upper landing just as the door to the attics opened and Jack stepped out, a canvas bag in one hand.

He stopped dead, looking totally taken aback and guiltily thrusting the holdall behind him, but he made a quick recovery, dropping it on the worn cord drugget so he could take me into a warm embrace and kiss first my cheek and then my lips before smiling warmly down at me. 'Hi, Sophy, how great to see you again – and even prettier than I remembered!'

'There you are,' I said inanely, thinking dazedly that he

was twice as handsome as I remembered – if that was possible. My lips had gone all tingly and my knees weak just from one fleeting kiss . . . but with an effort, I managed to get a grip. 'I just saw your car, Jack. Did you arrive while I was talking to everyone in the hall?'

'Yes, and I didn't want to disturb you so I came up the backstairs and listened from the gallery long enough to get the "all hands to the pumps or the ship will sink" message, then popped up to the attic. I've still got some stuff stored up here,' he explained, closing the door behind him and leading the way back down the stairs. 'Must sort it out some-time, because I don't suppose you want my childhood junk cluttering up the place if you are having a big clear-out.'

'I don't mind,' I replied, wondering what he had kept up there that was so embarrassing his first impulse had been to hide the bag behind his back. Old girlie mags, maybe? 'Some of my and Lucy's things are up there too, because it's where Jonah put them when I sent them down. You'll have to point out to me what's yours eventually, but it'll take ages to get the rest of the house in order before I even *think* about sorting out the attic floor and—'

'I can see you want to clean the place up, Sophy,' he interrupted me, 'and as I've said, I'm all for that – but I did suggest you ought to defer any major plans until we've had the roof and timbers looked at, got some estimates, and discussed it all.'

I noted the 'we' with a sinking heart and turned to face him squarely as we reached the corridor outside my room. 'Jack, I did mean it when I said on the phone to you that I couldn't bear to give up Winter's End, you know. I simply *can't* sell it, even to you.'

'But, darling,' he said in his lovely, mesmerising voice, his blue eyes hurt, 'I know it's early days yet, but I thought you felt the same as me and – well, that you wouldn't so much be *selling* Winter's End as *transferring* it back to its rightful owner, before we settle down here for ever – the perfect partnership! I want this always to be your home, too.' He put his arm around me and looked down into my bemused face. 'You know it's the only thing to do, Sophy – the right thing to do?'

One little part of my brain – the everyday, sane, Sophy bit – was jaw-droppingly stunned, wondering what exactly he'd meant by a 'partnership'; the rest of me was drowning in the deep, sincere, cerulean depths of his eyes. His soft voice lapped over me like warm waves, my heart was thumping away like mad and I was starting to go dizzy.

Then suddenly it felt as though someone had poured a bucket of iced ectoplasm down my back and Alys's translucent face materialised, palely glimmering, from the darkness behind Jack.

'I *wish* you wouldn't do that!' I said, with a gasp.

Alys shook her head, more in sorrow than in anger, before fading away, leaving me shivering violently.

The spell was well and truly broken, but Jack had clearly felt nothing, for he was still looking down at me expectantly. 'Do what?'

I pulled back gently. 'Jack, it's so wonderful to find family I never knew I had, and you know you'll always be welcome here, because it's just as much your home as mine. But I didn't realise how deeply I cared about Winter's End until I came back, and now I feel that control of it simply *has* to stay in my hands. It's what my grandfather wanted, what I want – and what the *house* wants too.'

I might have added that it also seemed to be what Alys Blezzard wanted, but thought that might be an assertion too far for him to take in at present.

'I know just how you feel,' he said, though going by his confident smile, I still didn't really think he'd grasped what I was saying in the least. In fact, he looked like a man who'd always known he could have anything he wanted, when-ever he wanted it – including me. 'But you couldn't possibly take it on alone, with no resources, because it needs an awful lot of money spending on it. I'll show you later. There's woodworm up in the attics for a start – and probably worse.'

'*Worse?* What do you mean?'

He shrugged. 'Wet rot, dry rot . . . maybe even deathwatch beetle . . .'

I stared at him with horror. 'Surely not?'

'It may not be as bad as it looks,' he assured me.

'Oh God! Look, just let me change into my jeans and you can show me now.'

'Sorry, didn't I say? I'm going out to lunch.'

'*Out?* But you've only just got here!'

'I've got lots of friends locally, and we like to catch up when I'm here,' he explained, and I immediately felt like Billy-no-mates, especially since he didn't invite me to go with him. 'I thought I'd get it out of the way, so we can spend the rest of the weekend together.'

'Of course,' I agreed, wondering if the friends included the luscious Melinda. 'And actually, I'd decided to make a proper start on the cleaning today anyway. I'd better get on with it.'

He raised a quizzical eyebrow. 'Not on your own, surely? Aren't you going to get people in to help?'

'No, rough cleaning has already done too much damage and I want to conserve what's left. I'll do it one inch at a time and get there in the end – you'll see. I've got industrial-sized amounts of cleaning materials arriving early next week and Hebe has given me beeswax polish and bushels of rose potpourri.'

He looked at me strangely. 'You look excited about *cleaning* the place!'

'Oh, I am, I'm dying to see what a bit of TLC and elbow grease can do. Another pair of hands would be really useful, though, and there are one or two things you could help me

180

with while you're here if—' I had begun enthusiastically, when he glanced at his Rolex and exclaimed at the time.

'Must dash!' He kissed my cheek in a cloud of that delicious aftershave and dashed off, tossing gaily over his shoulder, 'See you at dinner.'

Dinner? Was he going to be out to lunch all afternoon? Only after he'd removed his effulgent presence from before my dazzled eyes did I start to wonder how he'd got into the locked attic in the first place. At least, I was pretty sure I'd locked it . . . hadn't I? I went back up and, opening the door, switched on the light. In the first room my and Lucy's boxes and bags and sticks of furniture were stacked up, and I noticed that the top cartons were untaped.

Had they been like that before? I couldn't remember – but maybe Aunt Hebe had been curious enough to come up here and rummage round when they arrived. Or perhaps neither she nor Jack had believed that I hadn't got Alys's book and one or both of them had searched my possessions for it?

It was not a comfortable thought. I could imagine Aunt Hebe thinking she had the right to do it, but I found it hard to believe that Jack would poke and pry into my personal possessions. He seemed such a sincere person, whatever everyone else said about him, though I suppose there must be a touch of ruthlessness about him where business is concerned, as both Mr Hobbs and Mr Yatton had implied, or he wouldn't be a successful entrepreneur.

Alys didn't seem to trust him either – did she know something about him I didn't? Maybe I should buy a Ouija board and ask her.

I had a quick early lunch alone in the kitchen, helping myself from a vat of cockieleekie soup pushed to the back of the Aga, and then decided to start on Lady Anne's parlour in earnest. I felt drawn to the room, but also I wanted to start

181

making my patchwork cushions in there in the evenings. They're not just a lucrative sideline, they're an addiction.

It was lucky I hadn't advertised for a while, and so had completed what orders I had had before I moved here. Now I could start making a stock of cushions to sell in the brand-new gift shop-cum-tearoom instead, perhaps with the family crest embroidered on each one.

But first things first. I removed the grubby chintz covers from the furniture, revealing a rather nice bergère suite with faded red velvet cushions, a ladylike pair of small Victorian armchairs in a dull, mossy green and a padded tapestry rocking chair. I took the huge armful of dusty-smelling fabric through to the utility room and loaded the first batch into the washing machine on a cool cycle, hoping they wouldn't shrink, before collecting a stepladder and cleaning materials.

'I'll be glad when everything else I ordered arrives,' I said, finding Mrs Lark in the kitchen as I was on the way back, loaded down and shadowed by Charlie. 'I need the proper solutions – *and* Renaissance wax.'

She popped a piece of rather chewy Dundee cake in my mouth, as though she were feeding a baby bird. 'Grace'd love a Dyson. She says that old Hoover's more blow than suck.'

I chewed and swallowed. 'Good idea – and ideally we should have one upstairs and one down. I'll put them on my list when I've got my hands free.'

I'd taken to wearing my little embroidered bag with the notebook, pen and big bunch of keys, permanently slung across my ample chest, messenger style, and the list was now assuming the proportions of a short novel. As soon as I crossed one thing off, ten others took its place.

A few hours later I stepped back and looked at the parlour, brushing strands of hair from my face with one grimy hand, hot despite having opened one of the windows to let in the chilly breeze.

What had looked like a century's worth of cobwebs were gone from the ceiling and light fittings, and I had taken the worst of the dust off everything, though careful washing and polishing remained to be done.

Using the stepladders I'd managed to unhook all but one of the heavy curtains, which now lay bundled on the floor, ready to be sent to the cleaners. I only hoped they would survive the experience. I was just struggling with the last one when Seth's dark head suddenly popped in at the open window.

You know that bit in *Jurassic Park* where the velociraptors are chasing the children round the kitchens? Well, it felt just like that. My heart stopped dead and I nearly fell off the ladder.

He shot out one large hand and steadied it as I wobbled precariously, then regarded first me, and then the room, with mild surprise. '"And beauty making beautiful . . ."' he quoted unexpectedly, adding complacently, 'Shakespeare – one of the sonnets. I forget which.'

I blushed even though I wasn't sure if he was being sarcastic or offering an olive branch, in his own fashion. 'I'm in a beautiful state of filth, that's for sure! And the room still has a long way to go.'

'A bit of dirt never hurt anyone. *I* revel in dirt,' he said amiably.

I looked at him cautiously, wondering what had brought on this sudden friendliness. He must have seen my surprise, because he explained. 'Ottie's given me a rocket. As she pointed out, it would have been even worse if Jack inherited Winter's End because there's a good chance he'd sell it. That's probably why he's been urging me to turf the bottom terrace and leave the garden restoration at that, since Sir William died – he doesn't want any more money spent on it.'

183

'I know you don't think a lot of Jack, but this is his family home and he wouldn't sell it. You are quite wrong about that,' I said hotly.

'You really don't know him that well yet, do you? No, Ottie's probably right, so now I'm not allowed to be anything other than complaisant and helpful ... even if I *do* still think that taking my gardeners off their own work, when we're so near completing the lower terrace, is a bit arbitrary, to say the least.'

'I haven't entirely, they just have to help out with the house now too,' I said patiently. 'You must see that I need help and I can't afford to employ more people in the house, so unless you want to lose a gardener or two entirely, this is the only solution.'

He looked around at my handiwork and had to agree. 'I suppose you're at least putting your money where your mouth is – you've already single-handedly transformed this room.'

I grinned. 'Actually, I *adore* cleaning and have been dying to make a start. It's my one skill. I've spent all my life mucking out minor stately homes. It's something I know all about – that, and doing the tour guide thing.' I turned on the stepladder and began to try to unjam the stiff brass curtain hooks again, and he pushed the window further open and climbed in over the sill.

'Come down from there!' he ordered. 'Those curtains are too heavy. You should have got someone to help you.'

'I managed fine, it's just this last one that's stiff.'

But I was glad to let him wrest the hooks into submission, and when the last curtain was down, asked, 'Would you mind helping me to bundle them up for the cleaners, too?'

'Will they survive it?' he said doubtfully.

'They've got two chances – but they're heavy William Morris fabric, so probably. But if not, I know you can still get the same pattern, at a price. I rather like it, don't you? It's Victorian, of course, but the furnishings and décor at Winter's End are such an eclectic hotchpotch of ages and styles that they somehow blend together and I want to keep it that way.'

Charlie had been sneezing at the dust and getting in our way while we were folding curtains, but as the door swung open he turned and barked wheezily at Jack, not stopping until I picked him up.

'That animal hates me,' Jack said disgustedly. 'It has no discrimination. Hi, Seth, how's the trug and trowel trade?'

Seth sighed deeply, so I guessed he'd heard that line a million times before. 'Fine,' he said, putting the bundle of folded curtain down on the floor with the others. 'See you later,' he added, turning on his heel and going out by the terrace door, but whether he was talking to Jack or me I wasn't sure. The room felt suddenly chilly and full of portents, and I was shivering.

Alys has a cold way of expressing her feelings.

'What on earth are you doing?' Jack asked, surveying me with amusement, and I felt suddenly aware of my dishevelled and filthy appearance. Unlike Seth, Jack clearly didn't revel in dirt.

'Making a start on the cleaning, like I said. I'm just about to do the windows, if you'd like to give me a hand?'

I knew it was a silly thing to say even before he glanced down at his immaculate pale blue cashmere sweater and said, 'There isn't time – or not if you want to wash and change for dinner.'

'It's not *that* late, is it?' I looked at my watch. 'Oh God, it is. I'd better dash.'

I left all the cleaning stuff where it was, but I did close the door, the window and then all the shutters, leaving Alys ensconced in slightly cleaner darkness.

Chapter Sixteen: Polite Expressions

It being Mary Wynter's birthday and she a connection of theirs, tonight the Hoghtons sent over some of their company to entertain us with music and poetry and such like amusements. One of them, they say, came north to escape punishment for the writing of scurrilous verse. He was a very comely youth, perhaps a year older than myself, dark-eyed and with a smile that melted my heart. I could not help myself . . . I gave my husband a draught to sleep deep that night, and had Joan bring Master S to mee . . . For good or ill, this was meant to happen – it was my destiny, I know it.

From the journal of Alys Blezzard, 1581

Quickly I showered off the patina of filth, then brushed my wet hair as flat as possible, even though I knew it wouldn't last. Water just seems to encourage it to curl even more dementedly.

Then I changed into my favourite outfit of midnight-blue velvet jeans and a pretty top in the same colour, sprinkled with tiny silver stars, blasted myself with Elisabethan Rose, slung my embroidered bag over my shoulder and was ready.

And yes, all this effort *was* entirely for Jack's benefit, though I completely forgot about makeup until I was halfway downstairs and it was too late to go back.

There was no sign of Charlie, who had headed off deter-minedly in the direction of the kitchen earlier, but Hebe and Jack were already in the drawing room and Ottie wandered in just after me. She was wearing a knitted striped wrap over a knee-length caftan and silk harem pants, with lots of clunky amber jewellery – you could hear her coming five minutes before she arrived.

Jack pressed us to try some strange cocktail of his own invention, and though I knew by now that Hebe was a sherry drinker, she accepted a glass of the strange absinthe-and-God-knew-what concoction without more than a half-hearted protest, then sipped it gingerly.

Me too. I'm not much of a drinker at all, but I was power-less to resist that bad-boy smile on his handsome face.

Only Ottie was immune to his charm and, firmly declining, poured herself a whisky. I soon wished I'd had her willpower, because the cocktail not only made my head spin, but also scoured my sinuses like caustic soda. (Not that I have ever put caustic soda or anything else up my nose, you understand, but if I had, I would have expected the effect to be much the same.)

'I hope poor Mrs Lark hasn't done something that will not divide into four, like soufflés,' Hebe observed as the gong rang out, looking sideways at her sister.

'If Mrs Lark has cooked something that won't divide, I'll eat my hat – or bread and cheese,' Ottie replied calmly. 'I come over most nights when I'm up here, so why wouldn't she expect me? Sophy doesn't mind my coming over for dinner any more than William did, do you, Sophy?'

'Not at all, you're very welcome. I noticed there's always an extra place set for you anyway,' I said, as I followed her into the breakfast parlour where Jonah was clattering the serving dishes. Then a thought struck me. 'Does Seth . . . ?'

'Mostly caters for himself, or goes down to the pub,

though he's generally here for Sunday lunch. William liked the whole family together, and it's served early, so Mrs Lark can have the afternoon and evening off.'

'That's right – we go to church and visit the family,' Jonah said. 'Now come and get sat down, before your dinner goes cold!' He placed a platter of salmon and dishes of vegetables in the centre of the table, amid a flotilla of crisply folded paper napkin swans (which seemed to be purely for decoration, since we all had linen ones at our places, as usual), and then went out.

'Not that Seth is really *family*,' Hebe said, seating herself, but carrying on the previous conversation. 'Unlike dear Jack.'

Jack grinned and blew her a kiss.

'He's my stepson, which is family enough – and anyway, William was fond of him,' Ottie said. 'So am I, come to that. He's never been the least trouble, even as a child. Always off doing his own thing. Still is.'

I thought of the lonely, motherless little boy, suddenly presented with a brilliant but totally unmaternal stepmother. It was perhaps not surprising that Seth seemed defensive, verging on surly, though today he *had* shown an unexpected charm. And when he smiled, he looked so totally transformed that suddenly it had been all too easy to see why Melinda had been trying to reel him back in . . .

'Penny for them,' Jack said to me, and I went so pink that I'm sure he thought I'd been daydreaming over him.

'Oh, I was just thinking about family relationships – you and Seth growing up here together,' I said hastily.

'I wasn't actually here much except in the school holidays. I went to Rugby, Seth went to the grammar school.'

'I thought he might like to go to boarding school too,' Ottie explained, 'but he just refused. Said he wasn't going to leave his friends and he was happy where he was. Always had his own mind, did Seth . . .'

Jack shrugged. 'We've always got on well enough, but we've got our own friends and interests.'

'You didn't get on when Seth found you digging holes in the garden with that metal detector,' Ottie said. 'Treasure-hunting – and William not dead a week!'

'A slight disagreement,' Jack said, smiling at me. 'I'd just got it, and wanted to try it out, but I only dug where the earth was already disturbed. Seth is a bit hasty, sometimes, where the garden is concerned.'

'I've heard all about your treasure-hunting – in fact, I've read that hidden treasures book in the library,' I told him. '*And* I saw all the Enid Blyton adventure books in the nursery, so I think maybe she has a lot to do with this mania of yours too.'

He flushed. 'Hardly a mania, Sophy – just a little hobby. Don't you think it is exciting that there might be something valuable hidden here at Winter's?'

Before I could reply, Ottie chipped in, going back to what we had been previously discussing with an air of spurious innocence, though her eyes were sparkling maliciously. 'Actually, Jack, you and Seth do have *one* friend in common – Mel Christopher.'

'Now, Ottie,' Jack said with easy good humour, 'you know very well we were all children together, so of course I saw a lot of Mel when she first moved back here – and *before* she moved back here too, for I was the first person she called when she was deciding what to do with that ghastly house Seldon left her. But if she and Seth have something more going on between them now, that's their business and good luck to them.'

He smiled at me across the table and added, 'I've got other interests.'

'Sophy, *you* used to play with Melinda occasionally, when you were a little girl,' put in Aunt Hebe, 'but she was a year or two younger.'

'I *did*?' I cast my mind back and said, doubtfully, 'I do remember a little girl, but I'm sure she wasn't called Melinda. She was a complete pain, always worried about getting her clothes in a mess.'

'Yes, that was her – her mother called her Lindy.'

'And little Lindy was stringing both Jack and Seth along before she upped and married Clive Seldon,' Ottie explained helpfully to me. 'And you can't tell me she married a man old enough to be her grandfather for any reason except money.'

'I am afraid she was always a trifle mercenary,' Hebe agreed, shaking her head sadly, 'though I hate to say so, since her mother is one of my oldest friends. The Christophers are poor as church mice, of course, but Mel is a wealthy widow now, so I suppose she can afford to marry anyone she wants to. I'm glad you can see that she's not the girl for you, Jack. I knew William was quite wrong about that – and it's just as well, as things turned out.' She smiled meaningfully at me and I felt myself go scarlet.

Jack's veneer of affability was showing signs of cracking. 'Mel's just an old friend – don't listen to these two being catty about her, Sophy! Just because she's beautiful and married an older man—'

'More than thirty years older,' interjected Ottie, with relish. 'Even her stepchildren were older than she was.'

'– *doesn't* make her mercenary,' Jack finished determinedly. 'And I can't think how we got onto the subject anyway, because I'm sure we weren't discussing Mel, but Seth, whose horticultural obsessions I find quite boring, to be totally frank.'

Actually, I'd found Seth's enthusiasm and passion worryingly attractive . . .

'You find anything not concerned with making instant money boring,' Ottie said.

'That's not fair,' Hebe defended her ewe lamb hotly. 'Jack

190

loves Winter's End and cares deeply about all of it, including the gardens!'

'Or does he just care for anything that enhances the *value* of Winter's End?' Ottie said, and Jack smiled sweetly at her from across the table, his good humour seemingly regained.

'No, I just want – as Sophy wants – to see my home restored to the beautiful place it used to be.'

'*My* home', I noted, not 'our' or even 'the family home' . . . and I was feeling increasingly Gollum-like in my obsession with Winter's End. It was *my* Precious, and no one else's! A potent combination of irritation and the absinthe cocktail made me decide to throw a conversational spanner into the works.

'By the way, I actually *do* have Alys Blezzard's household book,' I said recklessly, helping myself to more salmon and cucumber.

Hebe dropped her fish fork with a clatter.

Jack's was suspended somewhere between his plate and his lips, while his bright blue eyes were fixed keenly on me. 'The real one, not a copy?'

'Yes, the original. Mum did have it, but she entrusted it to me before she left for America. She said Alys appeared to her in a dream and told her to. So now it's returned to its rightful place.'

'I thought you must have it,' Ottie said, but she looked relieved all the same. 'I hope you have locked it back in the box?'

'Oh, yes. And the box itself is now locked into the corner cupboard in the parlour, for extra security.'

Hebe was staring at me indignantly. 'But you told Jack you didn't *have* the book!'

'Of course I did, because according to what Mum had always told me, Jack shouldn't have known anything about it in the first place. I needed time to think and to see what the situation was like when I got here.'

191

'Ottie always had charge of the key and the book until Susan took them,' Hebe said, 'and although she didn't look after the key very well, I suppose she should have it back again.'

'No, I think Sophy should keep it now,' Ottie said, unconcernedly carrying on with her dinner. 'What she does with it is entirely up to her. I'm passing on my responsibility.'

'I'm so relieved to know the book is safe,' Jack said, 'and I don't mind admitting I'd *love* to see it! Since it isn't a secret any more, won't you show it to me, Sophy?'

He gave me the sort of intense, butter-rich smile that makes you quiver from head to foot like a plucked violin string, but I hardened my heart – with an effort. 'No, I won't. And I know why you want to see it, Jack. You're cherishing the mad idea that Alys wrote down a clue to the whereabouts of treasure. But she didn't and you'll have to take my word for it that the only treasures are the recipes. If you think about it sensibly, you'll see that she hadn't anything else to leave – how could she have? She wasn't an heiress and could have had nothing to conceal of any value.'

'You don't know that!' began Jack eagerly. 'It's rumoured that the family was hiding a priest in the house around the time she was imprisoned, and he had gold plate with him that he was taking to the Continent for—'

'Just an old legend with no proof,' I interrupted firmly, 'and Mum said she was sure the house had been searched from attic to cellar several times over the centuries on the strength of it.'

'I expect you're right, but if I could just *look* . . .' he wheedled.

'No way, it stays under lock and key – and *I* have the key. And what's more,' I stated firmly, 'I won't stand for you, or anyone else, going on any more half-arsed treasure hunts in or out of the house!'

Hebe said primly, 'That is hardly a polite expression to use, Sophy!'

'Don't be such an old spinster. And the girl is quite right, the place must have been searched so many times over the centuries that if there was anything to find, they would have,' Ottie said. 'And *didn't* Sophy sound just like William!'

'Yes, she did,' Jack said, eyeing me thoughtfully. 'Look, Sophy, I admit I'd like to find something valuable, and I'm still convinced there is something to find. But my only motive is to help keep Winter's End in the family. It will take much more money to return it to its former glory and pay for its upkeep than you have any conception of.'

'Yes I have, and I've got a plan,' I said indignantly. 'I keep telling you!'

'A few extra visitors?' He shook his head. 'That isn't going to make a significant difference.'

'Perhaps not, but a vastly increased number of visitors over a longer opening season, all paying more to come in, and spending money while they're here – that *will* make a difference. But first we need to enhance the attractions within the house, like working the Shakespeare and witchcraft angles more, and upgrading the café, so that the gardens aren't the only draw.'

'Using *what* for money?' put in Jack smoothly, hitting the nail on the head because I knew spending the Herring money on upgrading the facilities in order to attract greater numbers of visitors was, to continue the fishy analogy, using a sprat to catch a mackerel.

'Oh, I think we are all going to be very surprised by what Sophy will achieve,' Ottie told him. 'Just wait and see.'

I hoped she was right – and I also hoped that, before too long, *she* would surprise *me* with whatever part of the family secret my mother hadn't been able to tell me.

Chapter Seventeen: Pressed

Today a messenger came for Sir Ralph and later privily gave mee a small packet. Inside were some lines of verse to my dark beauty, though ye mirror tells mee that Master S is more than generous in his praise . . . I sent no reply, nor if he come again will I see him, but make some excuse of illness, for that way danger lies. I am like a butterfly that hath had her one day of dancing and pleasure and must now pay with death . . . though not yet mine. The shadows have left mee to gather around Thomas, who daily weakens before mine eyes, despite all my endevors.

From the journal of Alys Blezzard, 1581

After dinner we all went into the library, where Hebe watched fondly as Jack thrashed me at billiards, and then not so fondly as Ottie wiped the floor with him.

Jack was not, I noticed, a very good loser, which was a bit worrying. I mean, if he went all tight-lipped and threw his cue about just because he lost a game of billiards, what was he going to be like when it finally dawned on him that he wasn't going to get possession of Winter's End? And, whatever he meant by a 'partnership' between us, was that likely to be one of equals?

Somehow, I had begun to suspect not.

Ottie went back to the coach house after Jonah brought the coffee in, and Aunt Hebe got up and started to gather her knitting and garden magazines together.

'I am rather tired, Jack, so I think I will retire and leave you to amuse Sophy – and I expect you have arranged to meet your friends later anyway, haven't you?'

Since he'd already met up with them at lunchtime *and* said he was going to devote the rest of the weekend to me, I confidently expected him to deny any such intention. So I felt a bit stunned and, if truth be told, somewhat chagrined, when he agreed. 'Yes, I did think I'd pop down to the pub for an hour or so and see who's about. If only you hadn't exhausted yourself with all that cleaning, Sophy, I would have suggested you come too, but I can see you're all in.'

'Oh, I'm not *that* tired,' I protested, then gave the words the lie by yawning hugely, though that was probably just the power of suggestion.

He laughed. 'You need an early night – and then tomorrow morning, right after breakfast, we can have a good discussion about everything,' he promised. 'There should be plenty of time before I go.'

'*Go?*'

'Yes, of course.' He looked surprised. 'I'm just closing a deal on a property in Shropshire. But don't worry, I'm not leaving until after lunch.'

I was starting to see what Grandfather had meant about Jack using Winter's End like a hotel. The disappointment must have shown on my face, for Aunt Hebe said kindly, 'Jack is terribly busy, you know, Sophy. It was kind of him to take the time to come this weekend especially to give you the benefit of his advice – and of course he knows *all* about renovating old properties.'

'I'm just sorry I wasn't able to be here when Sophy arrived,' Jack said, smiling warmly at me.

'That's all right – you did send me the lovely bouquet, after all,' I said grudgingly, though still feeling annoyed and short-changed.

'I *am* exceptionally busy at the moment, darling, but *you* can get me any time you like on my mobile,' he assured me. 'And be prepared to see a lot more of me in the future too, because I'm used to popping in and out without warning.'

'We're always happy to see you, when you can get away,' Aunt Hebe said fondly.

'I'm told you often bring friends to stay for the weekend too?' I said, still feeling ratty.

'Yes, of course, in the summer. William never minded who I invited.'

'Neither do I. In fact, the more the merrier, since from now on, all my visitors will have to come prepared to work hard for their keep,' I said firmly, deciding to make my position plain from the outset. I wasn't running a country house hotel and there was no slack in my budget for freeloaders – except Jack, I suppose, who had so far proved to be ornamental rather than useful.

'*Work?*' he said, as though it was an alien concept.

'Cleaning, polishing, painting and decorating – helping to get the place straight again. And if they're here when the house is open to the public, they might even find themselves selling tickets or helping in the tearoom.'

'One doesn't generally expect to work when invited for a country house weekend visit, dear,' Aunt Hebe pointed out. 'You go for walks and play tennis and that kind of thing.'

'Things change, Aunt Hebe.'

Like the tennis court, soon to be transformed into a croquet lawn . . . I'd noticed that Seth had taken down the netting already, though apparently no one else had.

'Right . . .' Jack said, looking thoughtfully at me. 'But you know, I always hated the idea of my home being open to anyone with the price of a ticket, so I really hope you will think better of that idea. It's not going to bring in the kind of income you need to keep a place of this size running.' He rose to his feet. 'But we can discuss it tomorrow – and perhaps, if you are really not too tired, you wouldn't mind running me down to the pub before you go to bed? I'll probably get a lift back.'

He would need to. While I had drunk only one (fairly lethal) cocktail and a lot of water, he had also demolished most of a bottle of wine, and then chased his coffee down with a stiff whisky.

'Yes of course, and I'll come in for a quick drink too, Jack. It's early, after all. But after that, I'll leave you to it and come home.'

For a moment I thought Jack looked almost disconcerted, but I must have imagined it because he said warmly, 'That's even better, Sophy!' and Aunt Hebe beamed on us.

The Green Man was large, full, warm and noisy, though when I walked in with Jack right behind me, there was a sudden lull and every head turned in our direction, as though the film had stuck in one of those old Westerns when the hero enters the saloon. But before I had time to feel paranoid they all looked away again and the babble resumed.

There were familiar faces – Seth and a group including a couple of the gardeners were playing darts at the far end of the L-shaped room, and Grace was perched on a tall stool in front of the mahogany bar, her little strapped shoes dangling way above the brass foot rail. She flapped her hand at me in greeting.

A voice from behind us, very loud and county, bellowed, 'Over here, Jack – and bring your new filly with you!'

197

'This filly, Freddie, is my lovely cousin Sophy,' Jack said, putting a proprietorial arm around my waist. 'Be nice!'

Freddie had a red face, straw-coloured hair and a tendency to talk to my breasts. He was sitting with several other people, who Jack introduced me to in dizzyingly quick succession. I didn't really take in their names, except to notice that the women's included a China and an India – and, for all I knew, a Tasmania and an Outer Mongolia.

They were all eyeing me appraisingly, but I suppose, being Jack's friends, they *would* be interested in the usurper – and *I* was equally interested in seeing the crowd Jack would rather hang out with than be with me. After all, that had been the main reason I'd suggested coming in for a drink in the first place – sheer curiosity.

There was a curious similarity about the women, who were all skinny and wearing skimpy tops and jeans that they hadn't picked up at a supermarket with the weekly shop. Some of them were probably as old as me, but it was impossible to tell because they had all Botoxed, Pilated and face-lifted their way to the same toned and smooth-skinned blankness.

I immediately felt fat, overdressed and cheap – but then, as one of the gardeners at Blackwalls used to say, a weed is just a flower growing in the wrong place. The dartboard end of the room, where Seth seemed to hang out, was *much* more my kind of ambience, and Seth, who had exchanged his usual layers of ratty jumpers for a black fleece and jeans, much more my usual kind of man . . .

Well, apart from the instant antipathy and his bad temper, that is.

Some of the women reluctantly shifted up and made room for me to sit on the curved bench seat, by moving their enormous, baggy leather handbags onto the shelf behind; but the body language was making it very clear

198

that never in a month of Sundays would I be accepted as one of *this* crowd.

Jack went to the bar to get drinks and the group, ignoring me, resumed a desultory conversation about things and people I didn't know that seemed designed to show me just how much of a fish-out-of-water I was. I mean, as far as I'm concerned Polo means a mint with a hole in it, and my one experience of London life was a weekend trip with the WI to see *Miss Saigon* and the wonders of Harrods (mostly the perfume department – they had to prise me out, laden with sample cards).

I thought it would be better when Jack came back, but apart from putting his arm around me again and giving me one of his dazzling smiles, he joined right in. I sat there sipping a Coke and contemplating my exit strategies.

Ten minutes seemed plenty long enough – in fact, if I hadn't been checking the clock over the bar I would have thought it was more like an hour. I was just about to plead exhaustion and make my escape, when a hush fell on the room for the second time that evening.

Thankfully, this time it wasn't me but Melinda Christopher who had provoked the silence, and for a minute or two she just stood there smiling like the Snow Queen in all her shimmering, icy beauty, and let them look at her. The smile brightened when she spotted our group . . . Then her light brown eyes rested on Jack sitting close to me, and narrowed, though I don't know why because she turned on her stiletto heels and made for Seth like an arrow flying to its target.

He didn't seem noticeably welcoming, but he certainly got the full treatment – the kiss on the cheek, the hand on the arm, the earnest gaze up into his face as she stood close to him – all performed with little glances over his shoulder to where we were sitting so that I started to wonder if this was for Jack's benefit?

And if so, was Jack aware of it? Was that the reason why he suddenly remembered my existence and began to flirt with me, or did I have a nasty, suspicious mind? His technique was just as good as Melinda's: his head close to mine, his voice low and intimate . . . The aftershave alone was enough to render me semi-conscious.

Whatever his motives were I was, I have to admit, starting to enjoy it, when a crisp voice said, right behind me, 'Aren't you going to introduce me to your new *friend*, Jack?'

The Ice Queen cometh.

'Budge up, everyone, and let Mel sit on the other side of Jack,' Freddie shouted gaily. 'Make it a clean fight, girls!'

'Shut up, Freddie,' Jack said, looking embarrassed, but he didn't object when Mel squeezed in on his other side. In fact, he made room for her, which left me practically hanging off the end of the bench seat. 'This is Sophy, Mel – a cousin of sorts. I told you about her.'

I leaned forward, so it didn't look as if I was hiding behind Jack. 'Actually, we've already met, in a manner of speaking. Your horse tried to sit on my van, the day I arrived here.'

'Oh?' She gave me a blank, bored stare, though I had the feeling she knew exactly who I was. 'I don't remember – but hi, anyway.' Then she added something in a low voice, so *I* couldn't hear, but everyone else did, because they all laughed.

'Your mother used to bring you over to play with me sometimes when we were little girls too,' I said more loudly. 'Aunt Hebe reminded me. I'd forgotten, but it's all come back to me now.'

'Oh, I don't think so. I can't have been more than a baby when you were last at Winter's End,' she said icily.

'Come off it, *Lindy* – you're only a year younger than me. Don't you remember how I used to call you toffee-eyes, and you would start crying?' I said helpfully.

'You're thinking of someone else.' She glared at me, then

turned her thin back and started to tell the others some terribly long and involved story, which they all seemed to find highly amusing. She kept drawing Jack in for corroboration and after a while he withdrew his arm from behind me and half-turned away, so I would say that Mel had won that round – and probably any other round she decided to engage in. But I came to the conclusion this was merely a demonstration of power that was also intended to make Seth, her real target, jealous, because she was constantly checking the effect her flirting was having on him.

It didn't seem to be putting him off his darts, so she can't have got much satisfaction from that. But then, I have a feeling that sort of tactic simply wouldn't work with a man like Seth.

I decided it was time to go.

The plump, curly-haired woman behind the bar caught my eye and waved at me, smiling. I got up, murmuring, 'Excuse me, Jack, I think I see an old friend,' but I'm not sure he, or any of the others, registered I'd gone. I wasn't out of sight, but I was certainly already out of mind.

But before I could make a hasty exit from the pub, the woman who had waved beckoned me over. 'It's Sophy, isn't it? I thought you'd remember me! Val? We were in the infants' school together.'

She looked vaguely familiar . . . and then it all came back to me. 'Hi, Val! Of *course* I remember you – and especially the day that horrible little boy put frogspawn down the back of your neck!'

She shuddered. 'It's given me frog phobia for life.'

'Wasn't he vile! What was his name?'

'Josh Priestly.'

'I wonder what happened to him? No good, I expect!'

'Well, actually, I'm married to him – he's the landlord, the man at the other end of the bar.'

'Oh,' I said weakly, 'how lovely!' I managed to smile when he waved at me. I hoped he had grown out of practical jokes and nasty surprises.

Val gave me a drink on the house, which I couldn't very well refuse, so I slid onto a vacant barstool. I glanced over my shoulder at the table in the corner, but there was no sign anyone had noticed my absence.

'Cheers!' said the small, rotund man on the stool next to me, catching my eye and lifting his glass in salute. 'And welcome back to Winter's End.'

Thanks,' I said, deciding that he looked harmless. He was middle-aged, yet had an air of puckish boyishness about him that owed a lot to the bright curiosity in his eyes.

'You won't know me – George Turnbull. I only moved into the area a few years ago, but I've heard all about you, of course. The whole place was buzzing after news of the will got out. I heard your cousin's nose was right out of joint.' The grin that went with this remark took away any offence.

'He's not really a cousin – well, I suppose he is, but a very, very distant one, and he's taking it very well,' I assured him, which was no more than the truth, even if I had a strong feeling that the reason for that was because Jack was still convinced he would get Winter's End back, one way or another.

'Someone told me you'd been working as a cleaner, just a single mother trying to scrape a living. Then – *wham* – heiress of Winter's End! It's romantic, that, just like a fairy story.'

I wondered who he'd been talking to, but agreed that yes, it *was* like a fairy story. He was both sympathetic and funny, asking me whether things had changed much since I'd lived here as a little girl, and telling me quite scurrilous gossip about some of the new people who had moved into Sticklepond since I left.

We'd been chatting for several minutes when Seth's dark head suddenly came between us and he said quietly, 'So, has your new friend told you he's a newspaper reporter?'

'*What?*' I said, turning startled eyes on my companion.

George grinned unrepentantly. 'Even a reporter is entitled to his evening off, Seth, though the whole rags-to-riches thing might make a good story. I've heard you've got ambitious plans for extending the visitor facilities at Winter's End, Miss Winter, so you never know when you might need a bit of publicity.'

'I suppose not,' I agreed, sliding off the stool into the small area of floor space next to it not already occupied by Seth's big boots, 'but the right kind of publicity! I'd really hate to see my private life in the newspapers, George.'

'You might change your mind – here's my card. But you'll usually find me here in the evenings, if you want me.'

'I'll bear it in mind,' I said, 'but now I must go – it's been a long day. Excuse me, Seth, I can't get past you.'

But Seth, frowning, was gazing beyond me to where Mel and Jack were now deep in a serious, heads-together discussion of some passion – though of what kind I wasn't sure, except that it didn't seem entirely amicable.

Suddenly I felt amazingly annoyed with Seth for being stupid enough to fall for that kind of woman *and* angry with myself for minding about the way she flirted with Jack.

I certainly didn't feel I needed to say goodbye to either of them and nudged Seth sharply in the ribs.

'You're blocking my way – I want to go. If you're leaving too I could give you a lift?'

The green eyes suddenly refocused on me. 'Why not? There's nothing to stay for.'

He didn't say much on the journey back, except to remark

203

morosely that now I'd told my life story to George I could expect to see it splashed all over the *Sticklepond and District Gazette*.

'I didn't have to tell him my life story because he already knew most of it. I can't imagine who gave him all the details.'

'Well, it wasn't me . . . though it might have been Grace. She was in earlier and they were talking when I arrived.' He shook his head. 'A half of Guinness and she's anybody's.'

'You don't really think he'd use it, do you? I don't think my story is *that* interesting.'

'Depends how short of news they are. But the circulation's very small, there is that,' he said, and lapsed into silence again until I dropped him off.

That was gratitude, considering I'd gone all the way round to take him to the lodge. I should have made him walk from the house.

Chapter Eighteen: Friendly Relations

My poor husband is no more. Last night he could not get his breath and though I tried everything in my power, he left this life at midnight. At the last, to ease his passing, I whispered to him my good news and he squeezed my hand and smiled.

From the journal of Alys Blezzard, 1581

When I got home I didn't feel sleepy any more – too full of confused emotions and edgy irritation. So, with reckless extravagance, I rang Lucy from the telephone extension in my room, which made me feel terribly guilty, even if settling the phone bills was now entirely my responsibility. I didn't stop to calculate the time difference between Winter's End and Japan either (which I usually get wrong anyway), but luckily she picked up.

'Lucy, I wish you were here. Can't you come home?'

'Maybe . . .' she said, showing slight signs of weakening for the very first time, 'though I'd have to pay for my own ticket if I left before the end of my contract.'

'I can find the money for that, somehow. I really do need you here to help me.'

'That's true – goodness knows what you've been doing without me to keep an eye on you!'

'Nothing really, except getting organised for Operation

Save Winter's End,' I said, and updated her on the meeting and how my plans had gone down.

She gave gracious approval. 'But don't *totally* alienate that gardener. He's free, for one thing; and for another, he's sort of family.'

'Only by marriage to your great-aunt Ottie . . . or is that great-great?'

'Whatever. Seth sounds interesting, though, and you still need him to sort out the bottom terrace, don't you?'

'I suppose so,' I conceded. 'And he did sort of apologise later . . . or at least, I think it was meant as an apology – he quoted Shakespeare at me, then helped me take down the parlour curtains. Tomorrow we'll both have to be polite, because apparently all the family, including Seth, gathers round the table for the Sunday roast. Considering Ottie and Hebe are barely on speaking terms, that must be a riot.'

'Why aren't they speaking?'

'It's to do with Alys Blezzard's book.' I had lowered my voice despite the several inches of solid oak between any eavesdropper and me.

'Our witchy ancestor? How can they fall out over a book? Anyway, you've got it.'

'Yes, but Hebe's read it and remembered enough of what Alys said in the foreword to blab to Jack, and now he seems to think there's a hidden treasure at Winter's End!'

'And is there?' she asked, interested. 'I thought that bit in the flyleaf was about the recipes, especially the rose ones?'

I had brought Lucy up to know about Alys, as my mother had done with me, making the book an exciting secret between us. I suppose, through the centuries, that was always how it was . . .

'Reputedly there are at least *three* treasures hidden at Winter's End, including a Saxon hoard somewhere in the grounds. But all old houses have these stories, and generations of Winters have probably sifted every inch – when they weren't busy rebuilding, panelling or stuccoing. The place is a total architectural hotchpotch.'

'I noticed that when I visited. Maybe Alys did hide something, though I don't think it would be any kind of valuable thing in the money sense, would you, Mum? Perhaps just her more incriminatingly witchy recipes, and a few scraps of parchment or paper would be easy to conceal.'

'Yes, that's quite possible. Your grandmother always thought there was something else that only Ottie knew about.' I spared her the information that her great-aunt also thought she was Buffy the Vampire Slayer.

'Or it might be some scandalous titbit of family history,' suggested Lucy, still turning over the possibilities. 'Perhaps the King popped in and showed Alys a right royal good time?'

'I think it was Queen Elizabeth then, and she didn't seem to be inclined that way,' I said doubtfully, because my grasp on history is not brilliant. 'Still, whatever it is, I expect Ottie will tell me in her own good time.'

'Oh, I *do* want to come back and search now, Mum, just in case. It's all so Famous Five! And if either of the great-aunts has any secrets, I bet *I* could winkle them out. You know I can twist little old ladies round my fingers.'

'It's your golden curls and blue eyes that get them every time. But not these two old ladies,' I assured her. 'Anyway, Jack has the same advantages, plus that of being male, and Hebe adores him. He's here at the moment, though he missed most of my speech.'

'Have you told him you're not selling Winter's End yet?'

'I've certainly *tried*, but he just doesn't seem to take it in. I'm sure he's convinced I'm just playing Lady of the Manor and will be sweet-talked into selling eventually. He says he has the money to maintain it, but I could still make Winter's End my home, so I'd be in a win/win situation.'

'Big of him,' Lucy commented.

'Yes . . .' I added after a pause, because I still wasn't entirely sure on exactly what terms Jack envisaged us both living at Winter's End. 'I went to the local pub with him tonight and met some of his friends.'

'Oh? Did you have a nice time? I'm not sure being wined and dined by Jack is a good idea. You're so susceptible to that kind of man.'

'I had an *interesting* time – and I'm not susceptible to *any* kind of man,' I said with dignity, 'I've learned my lesson. If it makes you feel better, Jack didn't wine and dine me, either, just bought me a Coke, let his rich friends snub me, then lost interest in me entirely once one of his old flames came in.'

'Oh, Mum, it sounds horrible!'

'It was. I left early and came back with Seth Greenwood instead.'

'That's more like it. I do like the sound of *him*.'

'I can't imagine why. He's rude, overbearing and obsessed with finishing the garden to the point where he doesn't see anything else. And don't get your hopes up, because he just wanted a lift. Jack's old flame is Seth's, too. I think they fell out over her years ago. But now she's back, she seems to have a thing going with Seth and the flirting with Jack was just intended to whip him back into line. She played the field before she married and, so far as I can see, she's reverted to type now she's widowed.' I sighed. 'She's called Melinda Christopher and she is *stunningly* beautiful in an unusual way – silvery blonde hair and these strange, very light brown eyes.'

'You're beautiful too,' she assured me, loyally but inaccurately, 'and just think of the money you would save by marrying the head gardener!'

'Lucy, apart from the fact that he's having a second-time-round torrid fling with Melinda, I don't even *like* him,'

I said patiently, 'and he doesn't like me, especially since I told him completing the garden didn't have priority any more. The only reason he's being even marginally polite to me is because Ottie's insisting on it. And we aren't actually paying him any wages.'

'Oh, no, I'd forgotten that. Still, at least he is useful, which is more than Jack seems to be.'

'Well, not so far, but he is going to take me round the house tomorrow morning and show me some of the more major things that want fixing, which will be really helpful. He was even hinting at deathwatch beetle earlier, though I think he's exaggerating a bit, because I had a look around myself, and apart from all the superficial neglect, structurally it doesn't look bad at all.'

'I'd trust your gut instinct then, Mum, rather than what Jack says.'

'I don't know why you say that. You haven't even met Jack yet! He's genuinely glad to have me back in the family circle, and he's very sincere, open and affectionate and—'

'Wants Winter's End, one way or another? Yeah, I've got the message.' She sighed. 'I wish I was there to judge for myself. And you will need someone full time to manage the business side, especially when Winter's End is open again. I could do that as well as learning about running the estate from Laurence.'

'Laurence?'

'Mr Yatton. He's *so* sweet.'

It appeared that Lucy and Mr Yatton were such kindred spirits that they were now emailing each other constantly. I thought they were in love. I only hoped they were both in love with the same thing, i.e., Winter's End, computers and the joy of numbers, otherwise their romance was doomed to be short-lived, since he must have about a fifty-year start on her.

*   *   *

209

At breakfast Hebe was clad in shades of white from head to foot, presumably in deference to it being Sunday.

I hadn't taken Jack for an early riser, but there he was with his nose in the trough already. Mrs Lark, unleashed from weekday economy, had outdone herself, and the side table and hotplates looked like a lavish, blow-the-budget page from Mrs Beeton.

They both looked up from their loaded plates long enough to wish me good morning, though my reply to Jack was naturally a bit on the chilly side. Arctic, even.

He seemed to be a black pudding and devilled kidney man, though I wouldn't have eaten either if you'd paid me, especially at breakfast. But I couldn't resist bacon, sausage, eggs, tomatoes, mushrooms and hash browns.

When I sat down at the table I discovered a late, deep crimson rose by my place. Jack, sitting opposite, bestowed his most ravishing smile on me, just as if he hadn't entirely forgotten my existence the night before at the pub once Melinda got a grip on him.

'If Seth sees that rose, you're a dead man,' Jonah told Jack, coming in with fresh toast. 'Protective about the new rose garden, he is.'

'Well, he won't see it, will he? Anyway, I think the family are entitled to cut their own roses, if they want to,' Jack said good-humouredly. 'A rose for a rose!'

'Did you pick it this morning?' I fingered a red damask petal, wondering if it was meant to be some kind of apology.

'Yes, while the dew was still on it. It's a sure charm for softening the heart of a loved one, isn't it, Hebe?'

'Get on with you!' she said fondly. 'I'm sure Sophy's very fond of you already. Her heart doesn't need softening.'

'That's not dew anyway, it's frost melting.' Jonah was determined to be grumpy. 'It's probably full of earwigs, too. Shall I take it away?'

210

'You could ask Mrs Lark if she can find a bud vase for it,' I suggested, and he went out holding it at arm's length, as if it might blow up.

Aunt Hebe and I are not chatty early morning types and had quickly fallen into the habit of eating our breakfast for the most part in amicable silence. Jack was quite the opposite, and I soon found his cheery bounciness, plus the way he talked through enormous mouthfuls of food, rather trying.

Finding me unresponsive, he started to give me hurt glances and, once Aunt Hebe had ordered Jonah to bring her little white Mini car round to the front of the house and gone off to get ready for church, Jack said tentatively, 'You seem very quiet this morning, Sophy?'

'I'm quiet every morning. It's just the way I am,' I said shortly, draining the last of my coffee.

'Oh, good. I thought you might be cross because I didn't see you home last night. You did say you would slip off early, but one minute you were there, and the next you'd vanished.'

'I'm not surprised you didn't notice. You and Mel Christopher seemed to have a lot to discuss,' I said pointedly.

'Just business – nothing personal, darling,' he assured me. 'We've been trying to get planning permission to knock down her house in Surrey, and it's been dragging on for months. It's a dreadful place, like a cross between a hacienda and the Parthenon: you'd think they would be *begging* me to demolish it and put something better in its place.'

He pushed back his chair and got up. 'Come on – let's go and inspect the stately pile! And you'd better get your coat, because I thought we would start with the outside.'

We walked down the drive in the crisp autumnal sunshine, our breath hanging in white clouds on the icy air, then stopped and turned to face the house at the point where it divided to circle the knot garden in front of the porch.

'There,' Jack said, standing behind me with one hand on

211

my shoulder and the other pointing at an area of the roof, 'if you look carefully, you can see all the lead flashing needs replacing. That's enormously expensive, for a start. *And* the chimneys are all in danger of coming down, so they need repointing at the very least, and possibly rebuilding. And see that damp area on the wall over there? That's where a gutter is blocked.'

Seth suddenly popped up in the middle of the round knot garden with all the speed and surprise of a pantomime demon through a trapdoor. He must have been grubbing about bent double behind the fountain, because there was nothing else big enough to hide him.

'You're probably right about the gutter, Jack, but not the rest. Remember, Sir William had the whole roof surveyed and repaired the year before last, after that big storm,' he said mildly. 'Said he didn't want the place falling down about his ears.'

Jack looked disconcerted. 'Yes, but he wouldn't have spent any more money than he could help on the house, so it was probably just patched and it's deteriorated since then.' He gave Seth a dirty look, then took my hand in his and headed back towards the porch. 'Come on, Sophy, I've got something else to show you.'

When the something turned out to be in his bedroom I had a moment of doubt, because Jack was clearly a fast worker, but it proved to be just an old book in a plastic bag. 'You know I brought some of my things down out of the attic yesterday? Well, when I started looking through them I found –' he took the ancient tome out of the bag and flipped it open dramatically – '*this*!'

Inside, neatly snuggled into a tunnel chewed from the book's pages, lay a revolting, fat white grub.

'Oh, *yuk*!' I said, recoiling. 'What is it?'

'Deathwatch beetle.'

'Oh my God – are you sure? I thought they ate wood.' I leaned forward for a better look.

'Books *are* made of wood, Sophy. Probably just the thing for a light snack. But you do see, don't you, that if they're in the *contents* of the attic, they'll already be in the timbers and would cost a fortune to eradicate. This is *really* serious.'

He carefully placed the book back into its polythene bag and we went up to the attics so he could show me where he found it. Then he pointed out what he said were spots of rot or loose tiles letting in damp, and more evidence of beetle infestation – fresh-looking holes and wood dust.

But it all smelled perfectly dry, if dusty; and, as someone who used to go up into the attics at Lady Betty's every time it rained, to adjust all the receptacles under the various leaks in the roof, I couldn't in truth see anything much amiss with it. It was quiet too: aren't deathwatch beetles supposed to make a ticking noise?

It occurred to me, not for the first time, that in his eagerness to get the house Jack might be over-egging the pudding . . . and was what Seth had just said in the garden intended as a sort of warning, meant to put me on my guard?

But then, there was that horrible grub. There was no getting away from *that* bit of evidence.

'You may think you can afford to renovate the place and make it pay its way, just by getting a few extra visitors to Winter's End,' Jack was saying when I broke out of my trance. 'But you have no idea what sort of problems can arise in houses of this age. The sheer daily running costs alone would horrify you.'

'Actually I *do* know, Jack,' I said patiently. 'I mean, apart from having had a few sessions with Mr Yatton, you're forgetting I've worked in historic buildings before, and on a much larger scale than this.'

His eyes widened. 'But I thought you were just a cleaner,'

he said, unintentionally making it sound only one step above prostitution. 'Didn't you tell me that? Or maybe it was Hebe.'

'Yes, I *started out* as a cleaner in a castle in Scotland when I left school, but often had to double up and show visitors round at weekends during the season, or sell the tickets. My last job was at a fortified manor house, Blackwalls, in Northumberland, and I did anything and everything – cleaning, tour guide, ticket seller, housekeeping, passing orders on to the gardeners, cutting and arranging flowers, acting as Lady Betty's PA – you name it, I did it. I may not be terribly good at the accounting and number-crunching side of things, but everything else I'm pretty clued up on.'

'Oh,' he said, rather blankly.

'So you see, I do know what I'm doing, and I'm determined to make it work, whatever problems Winter's End has – even deathwatch beetle. I'm sorry if I led you to believe I might sell it at first, but I had no idea how I would feel when I got back.' I looked at him nervously. 'You've been so kind, Jack, and I hate to disappoint you, but there's simply no way I could do it.'

'But, Sophy,' he said softly, sliding an arm around my waist and looking down at me with a tender, teasing smile, 'it really doesn't matter which of us inherits in the end, does it? Don't you see that by leaving Winter's End to you, William was just trying to bring us two together?'

'*What?*'

'Yes, I'm sure he thought you would be a steadying influence on me, and that leaving you the place would bring you back here – and the rest would follow as the night the day. As it has . . . as it *will*.' He bent his golden head and brushed my mouth lingeringly with his.

At first sheer surprise held me still under the gentle pressure of his lips. But as he gathered me closer to his broad chest I decided to go with the moment, closed my eyes, and kissed him back, even though a little imp of common sense was telling me I'd regret it.

If there had been any windows where we were standing, they would have steamed up.

'I see you and me and Winter's End going on into the future *together*,' he murmured, raising his head at last, 'don't you, Sophy?'

'I – I don't know,' I said breathlessly, hardly taking in what he was saying, since he was still punctuating his words with little kisses. I'd never played with fire before but – my God! – I could get to like it. This couldn't be me, Sophy Winter . . . I felt as though I had stepped into the central role in a chick-flick, but I didn't know the part.

Jack, at least, knew his role perfectly. 'Yes, you do! You, me, Winter's End – it was *meant* to be.' He abruptly stopped kissing me and held me slightly away from him. 'But William wasn't as clever as he thought he was, because he left one vital thing out of the reckoning.'

'What was that?' I asked, dazedly opening my eyes and blinking.

'Pride. *I* should have inherited Winter's End and instead all I've got is the title. One day I'd like to invite the woman I love to share *my* home with *me*, not the other way around . . . and that's why I'd really like you to sell the house to me now, or sign it over at least, Sophy,' he said earnestly. 'That's not unreasonable, is it? Then we can turn it into a true family home.'

He tried to kiss me again, but as his words slowly sank in, my state of boneless bliss began to dissipate slightly and I pulled back.

He looked tall, gloriously handsome and rather hurt. 'Darling! I don't want to rush things, but you *do* feel the same way too, don't you? That we have a future here, together, once this is sorted out?'

'But I hardly know you yet, Jack,' I began, feeling rushed, flushed and confused.

He laid one finger over my lips. (His other hand was running lightly up and down my spine in a rather distracting way.) 'Come on, Sophy, you know you feel just the way I do, admit it! And you said yourself that William should have left Winter's End to me.'

'Did I?' I couldn't remember saying that, but I suppose I might have done – *before* I came back and fell under the house's spell again.

'Yes you did, and all you have to do to make things right is sign the place over to me. All your problems will then be mine to resolve, with no need to turn the place into some kind of Shakespearean theme park. In fact, we won't need to open to the public at all, this can just be our home.'

My legs might have gone a bit weak while he was kissing me, but my brain, such as it was, hadn't entirely turned to mush. Sign over my inheritance? Cancel all my lovely, exciting plans?

At this not entirely inopportune moment the air stirred icily around me in a now-familiar way, and I heard a thready whisper: '*Don't do it – Winter's End belongs to you and only you.*'

I stared around wildly, but there was no sign of Alys.

'What's the matter, darling?' Jack asked tenderly. 'Are you shivering?' He took off his jacket and slung it around my shoulders, the silk lining still warm from his body.

'It's nothing,' I said, wondering if this time I had only imagined those words of warning, that chilly presence? I shivered, but this time not from the thrill of Jack's nearness. In fact, I discovered to my astonishment that although I found him very attractive, the idea of marrying him held no charm whatsoever – if that was what he (and not just Hebe) had in mind. I mean, even if I had been as mad about him as he evidently thought I was, did I want to spend my life watching him forget my existence every time Mel Christopher, or any other beautiful woman, walked into the room? Or spend even another minute with his boring, hideous friends? I don't *think* so.

Anyway, I was getting really excited about *my* plans for the estate!

I stole a glance at him: he was looking as icily angry as he had the first time we'd met, like an irate Lucifer who turned out to be my guardian angel instead, though actually Alys's shade seems to have taken on that role now.

'Jack, can't you see that your solution would put *me* in the position you say you find unbearable?' I pointed out gently.

Letting me go abruptly, he turned to stare out of the window.

'I'm sorry, Jack,' I said, miserably aware that I had led him on a bit . . . or maybe that should be a *lot*, 'but that's how I feel. I'm just being *honest* with you.'

Sophy Winter, now eligible for Slut of the Year.

To my relief, when he turned he was smiling again, albeit ruefully. 'I'll just have to change your mind then, won't I? I expect people have been telling stories, prejudicing you against me, that's what's making you so cautious. But you *can* trust me – and once you really get to know me you'll realise we both want the same thing for Winter's End, and I hope we want each other too. Now, are you going to come and see me off?'

'*Off*? I thought you were staying for lunch?' I said, following him downstairs.

'Afraid I can't after all. I'm already packed and Jonah should have brought the car round to the front and put my bags into it by now. You'll have to say goodbye to old Hebe for me.'

I fetched my duffel coat and gave him back his jacket

before we went outside, where the long, lean shape of his sports car was indeed sitting in front of the porch. Beyond it, Seth was leaning over with one large hand braced against a spouting dolphin, picking dead leaves out of the fountain.

There was no escaping Jack's final, lingering kiss, though this time it did absolutely nothing for me, not even a slight tremble around the kneecaps. This might have had something to do with the fact that Seth watched our embrace rather sardonically – which I know because I kept my eyes open this time.

Still, Jack seemed satisfied enough with my wooden response and drove off, tooting his horn triumphantly. Maybe Obtuse and Optimist are his middle names – but then, he is warm, affectionate, tall, rich, handsome, charming and right out of my league, so why should it ever enter his head that I could refuse him anything he asked?

Chapter Nineteen: Suitable for Bedding

The baby is darker than the Wynters . . . but so am I, taking after my mother in such things. It was beyond disappointment to them that it was a female child, but already they are planning one day to marry her to her cousin and so the line will go on . . .

Another Wynter – I think often of my mother's words and am comforted in my grief and guilt, for surely these things are ordained and the pattern cannot be changed?

From the journal of Alys Blezzard, 1581

Seth had gone back to his leaf picking, but I walked round the knot until I was facing him. 'Was any of that true, what Jack said about the roof?'

He straightened and rubbed his straight nose reflectively. 'I don't think so. The house is structurally sound, just shabby and neglected – a fact I seem not to have noticed until you came along. So maybe Ottie's right about my being blinkered about the garden, after all – only it is so frustratingly close to completion!'

It was a partial capitulation, but I had more important things on my mind at the moment. 'The house is in a worse state than you think: Jack just showed me a deathwatch beetle grub he found in an old book in the attic and he says it's rife up there, plus wet rot, dry rot and goodness knows what else.'

'Does he?' Seth said sceptically. 'Strange – I could count the number of times I've ever seen Jack voluntarily open a book on the fingers of one hand.'

'He *said* he found the grub while he was collecting some of his belongings from the attic.'

'You can take it from me, books weren't part of them. Look, Sophy, perhaps I'm being a bit unfair to Jack, but I would tend to take anything he says with a pinch of salt. I know he can be very persuasive.'

'I'm not so easily taken in,' I said defensively, though I knew I had blushed. Maybe he would think it was the cold air making me pink-cheeked?

'I'm glad to hear it.' Seth had turned and was looking thoughtfully at the neglected façade. 'Sir William told me he wanted *you* to have the place, and Lucy after you. The house may be down at heel, grubby and shabby, but he wouldn't have let it fall into total disrepair, because he loved it – he just loved the garden more.'

'As you do.'

'Yes,' he said simply.

I frowned. 'So, are you implying Jack brought the grub with him? But surely he wouldn't do something like that just to scare me into selling Winter's End to him, especially if he seems to think he can get it for nothing, just by—' I stopped dead and this time went totally scarlet.

Seth raised one eyebrow. 'Jonah tells me Jack took one of the Danse du Feu roses to give to you this morning – very romantic.'

'The snitch.'

'Come with me to the rose garden,' he said abruptly. 'I've been thinking about the Shakespeare angle and I think we could follow it through a bit there . . . It's still a work in progress, as you can see. Once William had put in all those beds of shrub roses along the drive, he thought we might as well go the whole hog and have a rose garden proper. This space wasn't really doing anything.'

It wasn't doing much now, either. It still looked rather bare and forlorn. 'If it makes you feel any happier, I would much rather Jack had left the rose on the bush,' I said. 'It must have been the last flower left in the garden.'

'Just about, though I've known the old moss roses to have the odd bud even at Christmas.' He shrugged. 'Anyway, I just got some new rose catalogues and when I was flicking through I found a very attractive crimson William Shakespeare *and* there's a Dark Lady, an Ophelia, a Thisbe, a Falstaff – lots of roses with Shakespeare connotations. And a Sophy's Rose, too – described as suitable for bedding,' he added gravely, though I was pretty sure he was laughing at me.

I looked at him suspiciously. 'There aren't any Sophys in Shakespeare, are there?'

'Perhaps not, I can't think of any – but it would look good in this back border.'

'A Shakespeare rose garden would be lovely,' I said thoughtfully. 'He mentions musk roses too – we ought to have some of those.'

'Yes, and now would be a good time to order new roses, ready for bare root planting.'

And mean yet more expense. Winter's End seemed to need constant drip-feeding with money. 'If you let me have a list of what you want to order, I'll see what I can do,' I conceded.

'I've got some short Shakespeare quotes for the wall too. Ottie and I had a brainstorming session,' he said. 'Ottie says to tell you she will have them carved as a gift to you and Winter's End.'

'That's very generous of her!'

'Oh, you can't fault her generosity and *she* seems to think it's a good idea. But as soon as the engraving is done, I'll need *all* the gardeners back to get that wall rebuilt,' he added firmly. 'We can't start on the last knot and the beds properly until then.'

'I expect they'll have finished most of the major tasks I wanted done by then anyway,' I said. 'After that I'll just need them for odd jobs as they crop up.'

He was about to say something – and probably a fairly *terse* something – when a tall, stringy man with a camera in one hand walked through the arch.

'Hello! I thought I heard voices. Would you by any chance be Sophy Winter?' he asked me.

'Yes, I am. But who—'

He whipped up the camera and took several shots in quick succession and then, as Seth started towards him, took to his heels and ran. A motorbike roared into life on the drive a second later.

'Gone. He must have wheeled it up here, or we'd have heard him,' Seth said, coming back. 'You do realise what this means, don't you?'

'That you have pathetically desperate paparazzi in Lancashire?'

'No, that it's a slow news week in the *Sticklepond and District Gazette*, and you're about to make the centre spread.'

After that, I made Seth go up to the attics with me to see the evidence of rot and infestation that Jack had pointed out, even though he protested that he was no expert at anything except knots.

'*And* I was going to go back and change for lunch. Your aunt Hebe will give me the fishy eye if I turn up like this.'

He had a point. He was wearing the usual layers of jumpers that looked as if they had been ravaged by a giant moth and the outermost one was unravelling at the hem. But I dragged him up there anyway.

He walked after me through the attics in silence but, when I pressed him, said that it was odd the way all the places that showed signs of infestation were near a working light bulb. 'And the woodworm holes are regular, almost as if they've been drilled. They're all new too – there don't seem to be any old ones nearby – and this powdering of sawdust underneath looks fresh.'

'Jack said he came up here to get some of his old things, but everything is covered in thick, undisturbed dust, except for my belongings in the first room,' I said reluctantly. It's not that I *wanted* galloping woodworm, wet rot and death-watch beetle in the attics, it's more that I didn't want Jack to be proved to be so devious as to plant the evidence of them. 'He was carrying a holdall when he came out too.'

'To bring out the book in, naturally,' Seth said drily. 'I can't see anything up here that looks as if it belongs to Jack, and if there are any more books, they're packed away in boxes, not lying about.'

'Yes, OK,' I snapped. 'I think I've got the message loud and clear! He *does* want me to sell Winter's End to him, but you are wrong about his motives because he sees us running it together as a family home.'

'I see,' Seth said. 'But there was no need to bite my nose off for pointing out the obvious. You made me come up here, after all!'

I knew it was unfair of me, but after all, he had made me wonder just how devious Jack was. I didn't want to believe he was using his considerable amatory technique simply to get me to part with Winter's End, even though I knew a man like him could have pretty well anyone he wanted . . . and probably had. No, I was sure Jack was sincere – but that wouldn't stop the businessman in him trying to get it for less!

It hadn't worked anyway – the merest suggestion that I

signed over Winter's End and I went all Gollum, even without Alys putting her oar in. I thought we had reached an impasse in our relationship . . .

Seth and I were still glaring at each other when the gong rang, so that we arrived for Sunday lunch late, cross and cobwebby.

'What a pity Jack had to rush off like that, Sophy, just when you were getting on so well,' Aunt Hebe said, anointing her roast beef with a generous libation of horseradish sauce. 'I am so glad, it will be the perfect solution.'

'What will?' Ottie asked, looking up from her plate. 'Solution to what?'

Hebe ignored her. 'Poor Jack was terribly hurt that William didn't leave Winter's End to him, and he hates the idea of it being commercialised and spoiled when there is no need for it. It should be his – and, of course, if he and Sophy make a match of it, then it *will* be!'

I nearly choked on my roast parsnip.

'We're not going to make a match of it, Aunt Hebe,' I said firmly. 'Fond though I am of him, of course, we won't be traipsing together down the aisle together any time soon.'

'Yes, aren't you going a bit fast?' Ottie demanded crisply. 'Sophy hardly knows the man! And she hasn't so far struck me as being *entirely* stupid either, even if Jack has been turning on the charm.'

'I expect you are worried that Melinda is still around such a lot, Sophy,' Aunt Hebe said kindly, 'since she is so terribly attractive *and* wealthy. But Jack has assured me that it isn't *him* she comes to Winter's End to see, but Seth, so there is no need to be jealous.'

'I'm not jealous,' I said flatly and rather untruthfully.

Seth, who had been quietly but methodically demolishing roast beef and Yorkshire pudding, looked up. 'Mel loves the thrill of the chase, so I expect she's trying to use me to make Jack fall back into line with the rest of her numerous admirers.'

Going by what I had seen and heard in the graveyard, I thought Seth was seriously underestimating her interest in him.

'Oh, no, Seth,' Aunt Hebe said, 'Jack isn't interested in Melinda in the least, he told me so. *You* were the one who was devastated when she married Seldon. I remember William saying that you had sworn never to marry anyone else. And you haven't, have you?'

He coloured slightly under his tan. 'That was an awfully long time ago!'

'Yes, and even though he hasn't married, he hasn't exactly lived like a monk for the last twenty years, pining for his lost love,' Ottie pointed out. 'Far from it!'

'Thanks, Ottie,' he said, deadpan.

'And when she came back and the unattainable became the opposite, I expect you quickly got her out of your system,' she said kindly.

'Look, could we leave my personal life out of this? Mel was just a youthful folly and I think we're all entitled to at least one of those,' he said, looking as embarrassed as any teenager being quizzed by his elders about his love life.

'I'd agree with that,' I said, thinking of my brief marriage, 'and I'm not about to commit any more, youthful or otherwise. I'm sorry, Aunt Hebe, but though I'm already very fond of Jack, it's just in a sisterly sort of way.'

Ottie nodded agreement, but Seth was looking so sceptical that I would have thrown my dinner at him, had I not somehow managed to clear the plate while we were talking.

It was clear from Aunt Hebe's expression that she didn't really believe I could resist Jack's charms either, however much I protested.

And unfortunately, I feared, neither did Jack.

* * *

I tossed and turned all night, going over and over everything, so I was bleary-eyed by the time I reached the estate office that morning. You'd think I would fall into a stupor of exhaustion every time I climbed into my gorgeous antique bed – but no, I am Sleepless in Sticklepond, which doesn't sound quite as romantic as Seattle . . .

Mr Yatton, who had enough energy for both of us, had already made more appointments for me with the accountant and Mr Hobbs.

By mid-morning, after some lively bargaining in the stables, he had also closed the deal on the fountain for more money than I thought anyone would be prepared to pay for a limp stone girl with a deformed duck, and started looking into the price of airline tickets back from Japan on the internet, just in case.

I did some calculations with what was left of the money and decided to have Alys Blezzard's portrait sent away for cleaning, buy Grace the Dysons of her dreams, Seth his rose bushes (as a sweetener to his temper), and have the Larks' rooms redecorated and a shower installed . . . And that would probably be it, apart from a small contingency fund.

'The next step is to sell the Herring painting,' Mr Yatton said, 'which should fetch enough for you to begin upgrading the visitor facilities. Would you like me to contact the auction house?'

I'd brought the painting down to the office that morning, and it was really rather nice . . . but the house was nicer, so it would have to be sacrificed for the greater good. 'Yes, please.'

Jonah popped his head in and said, 'Sophy, there's a delivery van just been from an outfit called Stately Solutions. Where do you want all the boxes put?'

'In the cleaning room. I'll come in a minute and sort it out. Thanks, Jonah.'

Mr Yatton supplied me with sticky labels and a marker pen, and Mrs Lark some large empty jam jars, and I went off to unpack everything. When it was labelled and stowed away, I called Grace in for a little chat.

She looked around the room curiously. 'Well, you have been busy!'

'Yes, as you see, Grace, I'm making one or two changes, though it shouldn't affect you too much. I'm very happy with your work and I don't want to change your routine. I still want you to change the beds and do the bathrooms on your regular days, sort out the laundry, and clean all the floors. But you won't need to worry about any further cleaning, dusting, or polishing, because I intend doing the rest of it myself.'

'You mean I'll have *less* to do?' she asked doubtfully. 'Do you want me to come in fewer days, then?'

'No, exactly the same as you do now.'

She knitted her brows. 'So you want me to do less work in the same hours?'

'Yes, that's right.'

'For the same money?' She clearly thought I was quite mad.

'Yes. Now, there are just a couple of things I'd like to change about the way you clean. First, I'm going to buy two Dyson cleaners, one to be kept upstairs in the housemaid's cupboard, and one down here.'

Her eyes lit up. 'That'll make a difference!'

'I hope so. Now, see these little foam rubber cylinders? They fit onto the end of vacuum cleaner hoses, so that when you're cleaning around furniture and into corners with the nozzle, things don't get banged and scratched.'

I demonstrated with the end of the old Hoover. 'Could you remember to start doing that right away?'

'All right,' she said absently. I think her mind was full of Dyson dreams.

'The other major change is that all floor washing is to be done with this special solution.' I showed her the container. 'You need only this capful in your bucket; a little goes a long way.'

'Can I put a bit of bleach in with that?' she asked doubtfully.

'Absolutely not. You need only this stuff, nothing else.'

'I always put a bit of bleach in,' she said stubbornly, 'especially in the bathrooms.'

'It will be best if you clean everything with the solution from now on, including the bathroom floors, otherwise you would have to keep a separate bucket and mop for bleach because you couldn't use the same one for both. Now, do you think you could do those things for me?'

'If you like. When will I be getting the Dysons, then? Mrs Lark's got an Argos catalogue in the kitchen; they've got them in that.'

'Perhaps you could get the catalogue and show it to Mr Yatton? We might be able to order them this week, but in the meantime, don't forget to put the foam on the end of the old Hoover, will you?'

'All right,' she agreed, obviously humouring me. She glanced over the room again. 'It looks different in here – what're all these little brushes in the jars for, and the white cotton gloves and stuff?'

'I want to try and preserve everything in the house, and the best way is to keep special brushes, dusters and cotton gloves for cleaning and handling specific things. See,' I said, showing her a label on the shelf, 'this is the Silver Dip, and the brushes, dusters and cotton gloves are only for that purpose. The brass and copper have their own. Over here are cobweb brushes, and this is a banister brush – you might want to use this when you do the stairs, but nowhere else. Don't mix things up or use anything for other than its real purpose.'

'You've put tape and foam around everything, even the metal bits on the paintbrushes?'

'Yes, to stop any scratching. I'm not aiming for perfect conservation, because I'm no expert. Besides, Winter's End is a family home rather than a stately pile, so I'll just do my best. I'll still use feather dusters and window wipes, when it suits me! Oh, and this is my own hand-held vacuum cleaner – it will be handy for cleaning fixed furnishing fabrics.'

'I saw the parlour curtains all bundled up in the laundry room,' she said, 'and the chair covers hanging on the drying rack. Do you want me to put another load of them in, and then iron the dry ones?'

'That would be great, if you have time, Grace. I'll put them back on myself later, when I've cleaned the chairs – unless there's a set of winter covers?'

'There is for the drawing room, I think,' Grace said. 'Maybe I've seen them in the linen cupboard.'

'I'll have a look later, but now I must phone up and get the parlour curtains collected. They are old, they'll have to go to a specialist cleaner.'

'Right, I'll get on with me floors, then.'

I handed her one of the foam tubes. 'Thanks, Grace – and there's your bucket over there, with a new mop. You do understand why I'm doing all this, don't you?'

'Yes,' she said, 'and I'll whiz through everything, once I've got me Dyson!'

When I went back later to see how Mr Yatton was getting on, Grace had already taken him the catalogue with a big cross next to her preferred model.

He was arranging the packing and collection of the Herring and the portrait of Alys, but I phoned up about the curtains myself, using a firm Lady Betty had favoured, who collected and delivered.

The rest of the day passed happily or, in my case, bliss-fully. Upstairs, Grace sang as she cleaned and Mrs Lark, rosy with excitement, had made her arrangements and was planning an afternoon visit to a cat rescue home to look for a kitten.

I'd set Jonah the task of soaking the rag rug from the Great Hall in an old tin bath of mild soap solution, and on my way to and from the cleaning room I heard him singing to rival Grace, only more discordantly. I put my head round the laundry-room door and discovered he was walking up and down on the rug in the bath in his bare feet, trousers rolled, as though he were treading grapes. Going by the colour of the water, the method seemed to be working.

Bob and Hal were outside cleaning the windows, rattling the long ladders as they extended them, with lots of shouting and many breaks for cups of tea and cake in the kitchen.

And I – well, I was in my element, cleaning and polishing the parlour until the panelling and furniture softly gleamed and the windows lost their soupy murk.

Chapter Twenty: Having Kittens

The baby thrives in Joan's care, and she is such a simple creature seemingly that they have accepted her into the household as they never have myself. Sir Ralph dotes on the child, but I can see my Lady wishes mee gone . . .

From the journal of Alys Blezzard, 1582

Seth obviously believed in striking while the iron was hot, because he came up after dinner with some rose catalogues.

Since Hebe was dispensing her dark arts in the stillroom, he found me alone in the parlour carefully cleaning the chairs with the little hand-held vacuum, through a net cover to protect the fabric.

Charlie was keeping me company, mostly by lying on my feet whenever I stopped moving, and sighing deeply. His nose was well and truly out of joint because of the fuss being made over the new kitten in the kitchens, but I expected he would get used to it.

I didn't hear Seth come in, what with the noise of the vacuum cleaner and having the radio on, so my heart gave a great *thump* when I looked up and caught sight of him. Mind you, it seems to do that anyway whenever I see him unexpectedly.

He took in the room with an expression of astonishment. 'It looks so different in here – what a transformation!'

'It's getting there, and it'll look even better when the curtains come back. Now I just have to do the same to the rest of the house!'

'Without the full-time assistance of Hal and Bob, I hope. I presume they *have* finished cleaning the windows? I haven't seen them all day.'

'Yes, they finished and they worked really hard.' I didn't mention the frequent refreshment breaks. I seemed to have fallen over one or other of them every time I passed through the kitchen.

'So I can have them back again tomorrow, then?'

'Well, yes . . . though I do want the front gates rubbed down and repainted while the weather is dry. But I suppose they could do that as overtime,' I conceded.

'That would be much better, because this mild weather is good for working on the lower terrace too.'

'I *have* asked Bob to come tomorrow morning and help Jonah to clean all the inside windows,' I confessed quickly, feeling strangely guilty. 'It'll be much quicker than doing the outside, so you should have him back by afternoon. I don't want Jonah climbing any ladders, at his age.'

Seeing his expression grow a little thunderous, I suggested hastily, 'Let's move into the drawing room – there's a fire there, and we can have a drink.'

He gloomily and silently followed me, but mellowed once he had a glass of good single-malt whisky in his hands and we were poring over the lovely catalogues and deciding what roses to order.

Charlie sat between us on the sofa, and nudged the catalogues from underneath from time to time whenever I stopped stroking him to write something down. This was quite often, actually, because I'd never seen so many lovely roses. It would have been so easy to get carried away, except that I knew my budget would only stretch so far.

After a while Mrs Lark sent Jonah in with a three-tiered orange Bakelite cake stand laden with cheese puffs and ratafia biscuits, plus news of what the kitten was up to. I could see that the Adventures of Gingernut were likely to become hourly bulletins.

'She's taken it upstairs now and she's going to pop a hot-water bottle wrapped in a blanket in the basket with it, in case it's missing its mother.'

'Mrs Lark's got a kitten,' I explained, handing the cake stand to Seth. 'Have a ratafia biscuit? They were my last employer's favourites. I took her some last time I saw her.'

'You were fond of her?' he asked, taking one.

'Yes, Lady Betty was always very kind. In fact, she gave me this little brooch that I always wear, when she was in hospital after a fall. She had a premonition she would never see her home again, though I told her she was wrong, and I'd give the brooch back the day she returned to Blackwalls . . . Only she never did, she went to a nursing home instead. I've rung to see how she is a couple of times, but they won't tell me.'

'Couldn't you phone up the family?'

'No, there's only the nephew, and he's a toad,' I said shortly. 'But I've written to the cook, so I should get some news soon, I hope.'

I brought my mind back to the present. 'Well, I think those are all the roses we can afford at the moment, Seth.'

'There will be enough to make a difference, and we can list the varieties in the Winter's End guidebook, which I suppose you will want to update anyway?'

'Yes . . . I've been thinking about that, and I'd like it to be more a glossy brochure than a pamphlet, and with more emphasis on Alys the witch and the Shakespeare-was-here angle.'

'Ottie seems to be having second thoughts about using Shakespeare to reel in the tourists, for some reason,' Seth commented, 'maybe because it's so apocryphal? Mind you, we don't have a lot of concrete evidence about Alys the supposed witch, either.'

'But that's why she was imprisoned, wasn't it? And she was born, got married and died, so those dates must be recorded.'

'Oh, yes, I made a few discoveries when I was researching for the pamphlet. That's how we came to find the original plan for the planting on the terraces, while Sir William and I were turning out the Spanish chest in the estate office in search of Alys's records. Alys Blezzard's maternal grandmother was quite lowborn, from a family that became notorious a century or two later for witchcraft, the Nutters. But her grandfather was a scholar, so she married above her station. And then Alys's mother married a Blezzard, who were minor gentry.'

'I'd heard about the Nutter connection. And I suppose when Alys married Thomas Winter, that was a step up again?'

'Yes, though she seems to have come here in the first place because she had been well versed in healing by her mother. She nursed the heir to Winter's End back to health, then he insisted on marrying her. She had one child, a daughter, was arrested for witchcraft fairly soon after that and died while in custody.'

'That's all so terribly sad!'

'It's even sadder when you think that she was only about seventeen when she died.'

'Good heavens! How old can she have been when she married?'

'Perhaps fifteen – it wasn't unusual then.'

'So young? Poor Alys . . . and no wonder she's still here!'

He gave me an odd look and I said hastily, 'I didn't see her grave in the churchyard – where is she buried?'

'Since they thought she was a witch and her mysteriously

sudden death might be suicide, they wouldn't have put her in hallowed ground. Legend has it she's buried somewhere on the estate – and when I was cutting back some of the undergrowth last year, not far from the pets' graveyard, I found a large plain slab of dressed local stone. I *suspect* that might be it, but I'm not going to disturb it and find out.'

'Definitely not! But I know she loved Winter's End, so she will be happy to be buried in the grounds.'

He didn't ask me *how* I knew.

'I'd better have another look at the pamphlet, Seth. I haven't really read it properly yet.'

'You won't find anything very sensational in there – more facts than legend.'

'We'll have to change that – spice it up! Then it'll sell like hot cakes.'

'You seem very mercenary and cynical for the child of a hippie,' he said, looking at me curiously.

'*Because* I'm the child of a hippie – one of us had to be practical. But I'm prepared to do anything to keep Winter's End going – *anything*!'

'Then marrying Jack might be counterproductive,' he commented drily. 'At best you'd find yourself living in one wing, with the rest of the estate divided up and sold off piecemeal as swanky country homes.'

'Who's cynical now?' I said tartly. 'Couldn't he just love the place like I do, and only want it so that he can preserve it? And anyway, as I said earlier, I have absolutely no intention of marrying him, whatever wishful thinking Hebe's indulging in.'

'From what she was saying at dinner, Jack's indulging in it too – but then, he's always been prepared to go the extra mile to get his way.'

'So, you're implying that he would only want to marry

235

me to get Winter's End?' I said indignantly. 'Thanks a bunch!'

I don't know why it made me so cross, since the same suspicious thought had already entered my own head. That Jack was falling for me was something that seemed believable only when he was there in person, telling me so . . .

'Look, that's not what I meant,' Seth began to protest. 'I just wanted to warn you that—'

'Yes it was,' I broke in hotly, 'but whatever his reasons were, it wouldn't work out anyway. I've already told him how I feel.'

I suppose, since he had seen Jack kiss me before he drove off, I couldn't blame Seth for looking sceptical – or for abruptly changing the subject to something less fraught with pitfalls.

'Ottie and I found a few good Shakespeare quotes that seemed relevant when we had our brainstorming session,' he said, handing me a list, 'or relevant to gardening, anyway.'

'"This knot intrinsicate of life . . ." *Antony and Cleopatra*,' I read out. 'That's good.'

'"And Adam was a gardener", from *Henry VI* – we must have that,' he said. 'And I like the *Othello* one: "O thou weed!"'

'I raided the book of quotations in the library before dinner myself, and found one or two of my own. A bit more general than yours, like "Alas! poor ghost."'

He looked at me, one eyebrow raised. 'Any particular ghost?'

'Yes, Alys, of course. Aunt Hebe was right about her walking,' I confessed. 'Though so far she's proved more of a guardian angel than a ghost.'

He seemed unsurprised by my revelation. 'In what way?'

'Oh, just turning up and . . . well, never mind, you'll think I'm mad – which brings me nicely to my next quote, also from *Hamlet*, "O my prophetic soul!"'

236

'Well, I suppose they don't all have to be about gardening. Would your ghost approve of "What's past is prologue"?'

'Probably. Where's it from?'

'*The Tempest*. That's my favourite Shakespeare play, because, as it says in *Macbeth*, it's like much of life, "full of sound and fury, signifying nothing".'

I think he must have meant his love-life.

I went and fetched the book of quotations from the library and we added a few more, then we started discussing what plants to have in the Shakespeare garden on the lower terrace, and turned to the 'I know a bank' speech from *A Midsummer Night's Dream*.

'Musk roses again, of course,' I suggested.

'Yes, and for the rest, we have lots of shrubs and plants to choose from: the list is endless, from thyme, balm and bay, to carnations, columbine, daisies and daffodils.'

'And bilberries, burdock, bay and burnet,' I said, throwing in a few I remembered from my research. 'I Googled it.'

Seth looked unimpressed. 'Shakespeare mentions so many plants that he must have been interested in gardening.'

'Maybe that's what he was doing in Lancashire during the Lost Years, working as a gardener,' I said flippantly, and he gave me a withering look.

Out in the passageway the grandfather clock started to chime and didn't look like stopping any time soon. The evening had simply flown by and the cake stand was empty, though I had no recollection of eating anything. There wasn't even a crumb left, except those caught in Charlie's whiskers.

The central chandelier was suddenly switched on, flooding the room with dazzlingly bright light.

'Are you still up?' Hebe said, then she caught sight of Seth sitting next to me on the sofa and looked at us with acute disapproval.

'We were discussing the planting scheme for the Shakespeare garden, Aunt Hebe,' I explained, feeling like a guilty teenager, 'and the quotations for the wall. I didn't realise it was getting late.'

Seth drained the last of his whisky and got up. 'Yes, I think we have enough ideas to be going on with, for now at any rate.'

Aunt Hebe lingered behind in the study while I escorted Seth to the front door and locked it behind him. She re-emerged just as I'd washed up our glasses and the cake stand, and settled Charlie in his basket in the kitchen, then followed me upstairs, as though she suspected I might double back and let Seth in again if she didn't. She would probably have liked to lock me into my bedroom, but had to content herself with frostily wishing me good night.

I'd left my mobile phone in my room again, and found I'd missed three calls from Jack, but nothing from Anya or Lucy. I missed another one from Jack while I was in the bathroom, going through the motions of cleaning my teeth in a haze of sudden exhaustion. Then, just as I got into bed, he rang me *again*.

'Hello? Sophy?' he said, in a warm, intimate voice. 'At last – don't you *ever* carry your phone around with you?'

I propped myself up against the pillows sleepily. 'Yes, but sometimes I forget. But I've been in the house most of the day, except for walking Charlie, so you could have got me on the house phone if it was urgent.'

'Well, I've got you now, darling. Sorry I had to dash off like that yesterday, but business is business and I've got three properties I want to complete on, before Christmas.'

'Oh? I thought you did them up one at a time,' I said sleepily. 'You've already bought Melinda's old house, haven't you? That'll make four.'

'Mel's house is so ugly that I bought it just for the land

it's standing on. She gets a percentage when I sell it on for a housing development, but I'm still waiting for permission to knock the main building down. It's taking ten times longer than I bargained for.'

'So it isn't a nice house?'

'No, it's a ghastly sixties concrete monstrosity, by some Dutch architect who only built a couple of them over here. But never mind that. I hope you've been thinking about me and what I said to you?'

The truth was, that apart from that brisk exchange with Seth on the subject, before we settled down to the exciting task of choosing roses, the day had gone by in such a flash that I'd hardly thought of him at all for hours. Before I could stop myself, my blunt tongue had said so.

There was a hurt pause. 'You seem to have been making a late night of it. Hebe just called me, quite upset because you spent the evening with Seth. I hope you aren't harbouring any hopes in that direction, because he's involved with Mel.'

That must have been what Hebe was doing while I was letting Seth out. The devious old witch!

'Look, he brought some catalogues up so we could choose roses for the garden,' I snapped. 'I don't even *like* the man, but he *is* my head gardener, in case you'd forgotten! And anyway, I'm not accountable for how I spend my time – to you or to anyone else.'

'Of course not,' he said quickly. 'I just wished it was me you'd spent the evening with, that's all.'

'Jack, you had every opportunity of spending an evening with me when you were here at the weekend,' I pointed out. 'You decided to go to the pub instead, to be with your friends.'

'Oh, I see!' he said, with an air of discovery. 'This is all still because of Mel. You're jealous of her, aren't you? But really, there's no need to be – she's *very* old news as far as *I'm* concerned – just a friend.'

'I am *not* in the least jealous of Melinda and I don't care what sort of news she is,' I snapped and he laughed infuriatingly.

'Good night, darling, sweet dreams – of me!'

I said something unprintable but he'd already gone, cocooned in smug delusion. Paradoxically, the more I saw how irresistibly gorgeous *he* thought he was, the less attractive I seemed to find him.

And as for Seth, if he was stupid enough to fall for someone like Mel, and let her give him the run-around all over again, then he deserved all he got!

Chapter Twenty-one: Ghost Lace

There has been another priest hidden in the house these three days, but he is to leave as soon as it is dark tonight – the house has been searched once and it is feared they mean to search again. Joan says there is a rumour abroad that he is carrying gold from Lord R. back to France with him, but I do not know the truth of this.

Sir Ralph is much scolded by his wife for putting them in such danger and I overheard him promise that they should no more profess the Catholic faith but instead throw in their lot with the new religion, though he is in fear for his immortal soul.

From the journal of Alys Blezzard, 1582

Ottie retired to her house and studio in Cornwall until Christmas, though I couldn't imagine anywhere more inspiring than Winter's End.

Each morning the view across the valley from my bedroom window changed quite magically as autumn firmly advanced towards winter, stripping the last of the bronze leaves from the trees and picking out the knots and bushes on the terraces below with frost.

Indoors, Jonah kept roaring fires going in the Great Hall, helping to dispel the chilly dankness of the rest of the house, and I embarked on an exhausting but enjoyable flurry of frenzied cleaning.

The days flew by as Winter's End began to emerge like a butterfly from a rather dingy chrysalis. I was happy as a pig in clover and so, it seemed, was just about everyone else.

Grace swooped about the house with her new vacuum cleaners, singing shrilly. Whenever I had the gardeners into the house to help, Jonah followed them around, telling them how *he* would have done everything had he been twenty years younger, which seemed to give him great satisfaction. And as for Mrs Lark, she was so grateful at being allowed to have the kitten that she seemed to feel the need to stuff food into me at every turn.

'If I wasn't burning off so many calories with the cleaning, I'd simply have burst out of my clothes like the Incredible Hulk by now,' I told Anya on the phone. 'I might have burst altogether. I wonder if our *insides* are green?'

'I shouldn't think they're a pretty sight, whatever colour they are, so let's not go there. Tell me everything that's been happening instead, because it's like *Upstairs, Downstairs* from both viewpoints at once.'

'Nothing terribly exciting,' I said doubtfully. 'I've met my accountant and one or two other people Mr Yatton thought I ought to, and signed loads of papers that gave me acute headaches to get my head around . . . I've removed yards of cobwebs and dispossessed some of the biggest spiders I've ever seen in my life, and I've polished so much panelling I'm doing it in my sleep.'

'Go on, what else?' she prompted.

'Two of the gardeners have been helping me to move heavy furniture and roll rugs, and luckily one of them, Hal, is a dab hand with the paste pot and brushes, so I've arranged for him to redecorate the Larks' rooms. The other one, Bob, is concentrating on repainting the front gates.'

'And how is the Gorgeous Gardener taking that?' she enquired with interest.

'He's not so much gorgeous as grumpy. He tends to go off the deep end even if I just borrow one of them for an hour and it took me *ages* to get it through his thick skull that Hal and Bob were going to do most of the extra work as overtime. He's *obsessed* with finishing the lower terrace – but even when we had a cold snap and the ground was too frozen, he was up in the woodland, chopping down dead trees.'

'So, does your aunt Hebe still think you two have got a thing going on?'

'No, not now she's seen the way we argue all the time, and I'm sure Jack never believed it at all; he's too confident of his own attractions. He's taken to phoning me up late every night, schmoozing me.' I sighed. 'You know, it's only a few weeks since I would have thought that was wonderful, but now I just wish he wouldn't, because I'm shattered by bedtime. But I have to answer it, in case it's Lucy.'

'At least you don't seem to be besotted with him any more, that's one good thing. You had me quite worried there.'

'I was never besotted,' I replied with dignity, 'just dazzled. You wait until you see him, then you'll understand why I found it hard to think straight when he was there! And I am growing fond of him – just not in any relationship kind of way any more, and certainly not handing over Winter's End fond!'

'I expect he'll get the message eventually.'

'I hope so, but Aunt Hebe's also driving me crackers by constantly telling me how wonderful he is and what a great husband he would make – which perhaps he might, but not mine, even if he asked me – which he hasn't, directly, just hinted. It'll be difficult when it does finally dawn on both of them that I really *am* here to stay, and Winter's

End is going to open to the public with a bang next year, whether Jack likes it or not.'

'I'm looking forward to seeing it, at last,' Anya said, for now that Guy had got the job near Manchester she was working her way down, via a string of autumn craft fairs, to visit him and then drop in on me.

I wasn't sure what Aunt Hebe would make of my best friend, with her red dreadlocks and nose ring . . .

'How are you and your aunt getting on, apart from the campaigning on Jack's behalf?' Anya asked, as if reading my mind.

'Oh, we're settling down into a routine. She has her own preoccupations and I have mine, so we live pretty separate lives; probably much as she did with Grandfather. Neither of us is a great talker at breakfast, thank God. That was the worst thing about Jack: he was too damned cheerful at dawn! And we aren't often in the kitchen at the same time for lunch. But we have a genteel chat about our respective days over a glass of sherry every evening, before dining together, followed by coffee in the drawing room while she knits.'

'Very civilised. What's she knitting?'

'I think it may be some sort of jumper or cardigan,' I said dubiously. 'It's snotty green and quite big, so I hope whatever it is, it's meant for Jack.'

'And what do you do? You must be tired with all the cleaning by the evening.'

'I sit in the parlour with Charlie, listening to Radio 4 and sewing my cushions.'

With a glowing wealth of bright silk and satin scraps scattered across the polished top of the needlework table, a fake but cheerful electric coal-effect fire in the grate, and Charlie at my feet (or even *on* my feet), I was perfectly happy.

And if sometimes the presence of Alys Blezzard in the

room was so real that I spoke aloud to her – well, there was no one else there to hear me and think me mad.

Apart from Charlie, of course, and *he* was aware of her too.

I was still awaiting the return of the parlour curtains (preferably in one piece), and though the windows had wooden shutters, that night I had left them open because the terraces looked so pretty with the knot gardens frosted and palely gleaming under a full moon.

I was engrossed in embroidering a rose onto an ivory silk patch, when a sudden sharp rapping at the terrace door nearly gave me a heart attack – and all I could see was this hulking great shape lurking outside, a pallid face pressed to the glass.

But it was the sheer size of the monster that gave its identity away, after one long, ghastly moment when I remembered every horror story I'd ever read – especially one particularly scary one where a drowned man was summoned back from the sea . . .

I let my breath out in a great sigh and nudged Charlie off my feet so I could get up. He was still snoring – some guard dog.

'Did you *have* to knock suddenly like that?' I demanded, turning the key and letting Seth in, along with a chilly breeze. 'My heart's still racing!'

'Sorry, I didn't think. I often walk around this way when I'm going to the pub, then take the short cut through the shrubbery, and I saw you through the window looking very domestic and cosy. In fact, the whole house is starting to look different, and I can see all the hard work you've put into it,' he said, which I think was as close to an apology for his grumpiness as he could get.

He walked over to the table and examined my sewing. 'What are you making?'

'Crazy patchwork cushions. I used to make them as a

little business, but I thought I would get some ready for our gift shop before I advertise again. My friend Anya makes jewellery, and Aunt Hebe is going into production on a line of rose-based creams and lotions, so it's going to be a very upmarket little shop. But we will still stock all the usual bits and pieces visitors like too – pens, pencils, rubbers, teatowels, mugs . . . all kinds of things.'

'So you still intend combining it with the teashop?'

'I think so, but I need to give that whole area more thought, because it could be a real moneyspinner.'

'You could stock my book too. It will be out by then,' he suggested.

'Which book? I mean, I knew you'd written one or two, but no one told me you had a new one coming out.'

'Yes, *The Artful Knot*. It's a short history of the knot garden in this country.'

'That sounds perfect for the shop. You'll have to give me the details so we can order some in – and sign them too.'

'I'll do that,' he said, and bestowed one of his rare – and, if truth be told, devastating – smiles on me. He wasn't wearing his layers of jumpers tonight, just one the colour of butterscotch under a soft, natural leather jacket and his shoes were beautiful. His silky black hair was brushed straight back from his forehead . . .

I was just thinking that when he scrubbed up he made a *very* good job of it, when he said, 'Well, I'd better be off – but why don't you come with me?'

'To the pub – tonight – me?' I began, then stopped, because actually, there was no real reason why I shouldn't, and suddenly I *wanted* to. 'I'm a bit tired but it would be lovely to get out,' I agreed. 'OK – just let me get a coat and put Charlie in the kitchen. I'll leave a note on the table for Jonah too, for when he comes downstairs to lock up.'

* * *

It was so bitterly cold that the breath hung in front of our faces like white clouds and I was glad I'd brought my warm scarf and gloves, but the sky overhead was a magical dark velvety blue sprinkled with stars.

Seth was silent until we'd crossed the top terrace and rounded the corner of the house, where he switched on a torch to light our way. Then he said:

'The stone mason has started lettering the first stones for the retaining wall. He's going to bring them back in batches as he does them, so I can start on rebuilding it at the end of this week.'

'That's fast!'

'Yes, but I suppose it makes a change from gravestones.'

'Is that what he does, memorial carving? I thought he was a sculptor and that's how Ottie knew him.'

'He's that too, he just makes his living from doing the other stuff. So,' Seth added, giving me one of his more minatory sideways glances, 'we'll have the wall rebuilt quite quickly – if you leave my gardeners alone.'

'I always leave you Derek,' I pointed out, 'your right-hand man.'

'Just as well, since he's the only one of us with the skills and experience to rebuild the wall and he'll be in charge of it. But he can't do it alone.'

'He won't have to. Bob's going to finish off the front gates at weekends and Hal's redecorating the Larks' apartment as overtime too. So unless I suddenly think of something else they can help me with, you can have them,' I added provocatively.

'You're just trying to wind me up,' he said gloomily.

'Yes,' I admitted, 'and actually, I'm really starting to look forward to seeing the wall finished and a start made on landscaping the terrace, because that wooden shuttering looks really ugly and it's such a muddy mess down there. Have you decided on the design for the central knot yet?'

'Yes,' he said, but didn't offer to show it to me, so I assumed he was sulking.

I'd been half afraid that Jack's friends would be in the pub, but it was much quieter than last time, with no sign of them or of Mel Christopher, so I expect most of them live in London and only come home for weekends – that, or they usually meet at a more upmarket pub somewhere. I couldn't tell if Seth was disappointed by Mel's absence or not, but then, I don't suppose he would have invited me to go with him if he had had an assignation there with his lady-love.

Grace waggled her fingers at me from the fireplace corner where she was sitting with the journalist, George. I only hoped she wasn't telling him any more of my life history – if there was any left to tell – but since nothing about me had appeared in the local paper, not even the photograph, I expect he had given up on me as way too boring.

I drank Guinness and played darts with Seth, Bob, Hal and the community policeman, Mike, who was a displaced Liverpudlian. After a bit Val came out from behind the bar and took a turn too.

I felt relaxed and happy when I walked back later with Seth, in companionable silence, our footsteps sounding loud in the cold darkness.

As we passed the graveyard I could see the glimmering whiteness of my mother's angel in a swirl of movement – but whether landing or taking off I wasn't sure.

Chapter Twenty-two: On the Rails

*Last night my Lady told mee to put on a dark cloak
and lead the priest from the house by the woodland
path beyond the walled garden, to set him on his way
to a safer house. This I did, but I feared for the poor
old man, though he was calm and resolute enough. He
blessed mee before he left, though he will have heard
the rumours of witchcraft that Mary Wynter hath put
about so assiduously.*

From the journal of Alys Blezzard, 1582

The local newspaper came out again, thankfully without
any mention of me in it, so I decided I could stop worrying.
Even in Sticklepond and the surrounding villages, there had
to be a lot more exciting stories than 'Mrs Mop inherits
manor house'.

Life was fast becoming a near rural idyll – that is, if I
managed not to think about running costs, income tax
demands, the costs of accountancy firms, solicitors, public
liability insurance and the like, fortunately all the things
that Lucy and Mr Yatton seemed to find both comprehen-
sible *and* exciting.

My financial troubles might now be on a truly magnificent scale, but they didn't seem to feel as insurmountable,
probably because I was not struggling alone any more. And

with my best friend now making her leisurely way down from Scotland in her converted ambulance, I just needed to gather Lucy back into the fold to feel totally happy. All I ever really wanted from life was a settled home and a family around me – could that really now be within my grasp?

Slowly I settled into a pleasant routine, the whole house starting to glow and come alive as the reek of dust, damp and neglect was replaced by the mingled scents of beeswax, lavender, rose potpourri and love. Aunt Hebe had taken to saying approvingly that one day I would make Winter's End an excellent mistress, so I didn't know what she thought I was doing now – playing house?

In the early afternoons I generally took a break and walked with Charlie down the terraces and over the little bridge, climbing up through the woods on the other side of the valley to the summerhouse perched among the trees, which gave me a whole new perspective on Winter's End.

It was weathered and half-rotted, as Seth had pointed out to me when I started using it, but the wooden pillars holding up the lintel and roof seemed firm enough and the bench seat inside was dry. From there, I could see the gardeners all toiling away on the lower terrace, with Seth easy to spot, since he was much taller than the rest. The wall was coming along in leaps and bounds, since, as Seth pointed out, I wasn't hijacking his workforce quite so much, even if they were all tired out from doing other jobs around the house in their free time.

Seth was a hard taskmaster. If they were not working on the terrace or in the woodland, then they were kept busy elsewhere in the garden and greenhouses.

He'd taken to dropping into the parlour most evenings, though, via the terrace, so we could discuss progress – or rather, if I were honest, bicker in comfort. We seemed perfectly capable of arguing over *anything*, fighting our way to each truce.

Currently, he was reluctantly incorporating some sensational material I had written into the Winter's End guidebook, but in return I was letting him design a separate garden guide, though I did stipulate that he should include a Shakespeare Trail.

The lower terrace wouldn't be finished until the guidebook went to print but at least Seth seemed perfectly happy about the design now. I was sure that, with typical male forgetfulness, he had entirely forgotten that the best suggestions were mine.

Seth and I also managed to disagree over what was to go on the revamped display boards in the Great Hall, whether the 'William Shakeshafte' mentioned in local documents was actually William Shakespeare, practically all my ideas for Winter's End merchandise – and anything and everything else. In fact, a few times we argued our way down to the Green Man, all through a game of darts and a couple of drinks (with Hal and Bob grinning behind their beer mugs, and Mike the policeman cheerfully refereeing), and back again.

I never saw Jack's friends there, so I concluded they only came to meet up with him . . . and maybe Mel did too, for there was no sign of her either. When I asked Val, she said she rarely came in, so if she and Seth *were* having an affair (and how could he resist her?), then they met up elsewhere.

I wouldn't know – he never mentioned her at all.

One morning after breakfast, when I was up in the minstrels' gallery polishing the wooden balustrade, something came over me – second childhood, unfortunately.

Putting down my soft cloth and jar of beeswax polish, I swung myself astride the wooden banister, my fingers automatically slipping into the groove that ran down beneath, as if carved for the purpose. I hesitated for barely one second, looking over my shoulder down into the depths of the hall, then let go.

It was fast – far faster than I remembered – *scarily* fast. My fingers, slippery with polish, were not slowing me down and I realised my back was going to hit the carved post at the bottom with a thump likely to break one or both of us . . .

They say your life passes before your eyes at moments like this, but all that passed before mine was a brief recollection of the last time I'd slid down the rails like this . . . when, as now, two large, strong hands stopped my progress just in the nick of time.

Eyes still tight shut with terror, I was hauled off and held upright on trembling legs that wouldn't take my weight. For a moment I was eight again and, when I opened my eyes and looked upward with fearful reluctance, I half-expected to see my grandfather's angry face.

Instead, it was Seth, who held me in a grip of iron, white-faced and furious.

'What on earth were you doing?' he demanded, giving me a shake. 'You could have seriously injured yourself if you'd slammed into the post!'

My knees gave and the room whirled dizzyingly around but his arms closed around me, holding me upright. It felt wonderfully comforting.

'Oh, Seth!' I whispered, clinging to him like a drowning woman to a rock, and we stared into each other's eyes from a couple of inches away, united in the horror of what might have happened, had he not been there. His eyes were like a green sea you could drown in . . .

Then the stag's head fell with a clatter onto the stone flags and broke the spell. *Déjà vu*. I took a deep breath. 'Th-thanks for catching me! I used to slide down the banisters all the time when I was a child, but this time it seemed so much faster. I had beeswax on my hands so perhaps I just didn't have the same grip.'

'It certainly wouldn't help,' he agreed, but at least he wasn't looking angry any more. In any case, I'd quickly realised that the anger had been because I might have hurt myself . . . and looking back, I'm sure that was why Grandfather had been so furious with me too.

'Last time I did it, Grandfather caught me just like you did,' I told him. 'In fact, that's the last time I saw him, and for ages I thought it was all my fault we had to go away, because I'd been naughty.'

'You were only eight, weren't you? So nothing was your fault, Sophy. And your colour's coming back – you looked white as a ghost,' he added with relief.

'I'm all right,' I assured him, though my hands were still clutching the outer layers of his ratty wool jumpers – and come to that, his arms were still around me. I felt safe like that . . .

'Good, I wouldn't want anything to happen to you, Sophy,' he said seriously.

'Only because you know that Jack inheriting the place would be even worse. He'd be digging treasure-hunting pits all over the garden, for a start,' I said, rallying, and he grinned.

'No, because your *daughter* would inherit, and she sounds like hell on wheels.'

I began to say indignantly, 'Lucy is *not*—' when a cool voice broke in.

'Am I interrupting something, Sophy? Only the front door was unlocked, so I just walked in – but I'll go away again if you want to get all hands-on with the help. I suppose like calls to like.'

Mel was standing by the carved screen, immaculate in a quilted jacket and tight cream jodhpurs, her light brown eyes cold and furious.

I loosed my grip on Seth's jumper and his arms slowly released me, his face going all shuttered.

'I fell off the – the chair,' I explained quickly, not wanting to mention that I was doing something as childish as sliding down the banisters. 'Luckily, Seth caught me.'

'Oh?' She looked at the nearest chair, which was a knobbly triangular neo-Gothic affair some feet away, and raised a thin brow. 'Jack suggested I should call in and see if I could give you any advice – new kid on the block and all that – but it doesn't look to me as if you need it. I'd certainly recommend Seth for emergencies, though – and if you can get him away from his knots, he's brilliant at all kinds of bedding too, aren't you, Seth?'

She took out a packet of cigarettes and started to root about in her pockets, presumably for a lighter.

'Thanks for the recommendation,' Seth said evenly, though he was white-lipped and clearly furious, 'but I agree that no advice *you* could give her would do Sophy any good.'

Her manner changed in an instant and she smiled at him, a full beam job a bit like Jack's best efforts, exerting a force field of personal attraction. 'I was going to come and look for you afterwards, Seth,' she said caressingly. She spared me a casual, dismissive glance. 'If you've quite finished with him, you don't mind if I borrow him for an hour or so, do you? There's a little something he can help me with.'

I thought the old-fashioned seduction technique was dated, but I didn't bother looking at Seth to see how it was going down: I could guess. 'His time is his own,' I said shortly. 'And by the way, you can't smoke in my house.'

She'd found her lighter and stuck the cigarette in her mouth, but now paused. 'Oh, well, we'll go out then. Coming, Seth?'

But Seth's gaze had gone to the window and hardened into a lethal glare. 'Only to see you off the premises. You've tied your bloody horse to one of the topiary trees, and it's practically got it up by the roots!'

I watched from the porch while Mel ran to retrieve her

horse. It was tossing its head and jerking at the tree, which was trimmed into three balls of box in decreasing size. Before she could grab the reins her velvet hat, which was perched on the topmost one, was suddenly catapulted off and landed in the basin of the fountain, where it floated upside down.

Seth stamped the tree back down into the ground, then retrieved her hat, shaking the water off it. I couldn't hear what they were saying, but I could see Mel was trying to get round him, with one hand laid on his sleeve, smiling that surely irresistible smile up at him – but she was impeded by her horse, who had had enough of standing about in the cold.

It seemed to like going backwards and after a moment Seth took the reins from her and turned and walked off down the drive and, after looking briefly over her shoulder in my direction in what was surely triumph, Mel hurried to catch up.

That was a very neat demonstration of 'this is my property, so hands off' – so it *must* be Seth she was really interested in, not Jack. Presumably that night at the pub she just automatically swung into her usual routine to show me that she could also have Jack – or any other man – any time she wanted to. At least, for Seth's sake, if he was keen on the woman, I *hoped* so.

Climbing the steps back up to the gallery, I wondered what Seth had come to find me for, but I didn't see him again for the rest of that afternoon to ask him – I was just grateful he had been there at the right time.

I polished like a Fury, though. Every surface in the gallery was like glass by the time I'd finished with it.

Then afterwards, feeling strangely unsettled and needing to be alone, I took Charlie and drove to the sea near Southport in the Volkswagen and we had a walk along a cold, blowy beach, followed by a brew-up on the stove – and except for Lucy not being there, it was just like old times.

Chapter Twenty-three: Lost Treasures

*I was seen, returning to the house – or at any rate, the
cloaked figure of a woman – and they suspect us of aiding
a priest to escape so come to question us tomorrow . . .
I have made such preparations as I can, if it go ill with
mee, charging Joan with the care of my child, that she
may know my secrets when she is old enough.*

From the journal of Alys Blezzard, 1582

Aunt Hebe told me over dinner that the bare-root roses we
had ordered had arrived. She'd seen Derek unloading them
while Seth checked them over, so it seemed that he hadn't
spent the entire afternoon helping Mel with her bedding,
after all.

Not that it was any of my business anyway, unless it
affected his work – but I couldn't imagine any woman ever
becoming more important than the garden, even one as
beautiful as Mel.

By a strange coincidence, that evening Jonah had removed
the flotilla of paper-napkin swans and replaced them with
red ones folded into roses. He'd laid a separate one, with
a stem of green florist's wire, by my plate.

'Thanks, Jonah,' I said. 'The roses are really pretty – you
are clever!'

'Seth won't mind about that one, and no earwigs neither,'

Jonah said, grinning. 'The kitten ate one that dropped on the floor and it went through the poor little thing like a dose of salts. If I hadn't caught him with the last bit of red paper, I'd have been that worried, because the litter tray—'

'Jonah,' Aunt Hebe interrupted firmly, 'I can see lamb chops, but are we to have no mint sauce?'

Later, as I sát sewing in the parlour, I reflected that roses seemed to be a recurring theme at Winter's End for, once I started to notice them, I discovered they were everywhere. Briar roses were carved on pillars and panelling, and the ancient rose of Lancaster cut into stone corbels. They appeared in tapestries and embroideries, formed the design of the knot garden on the middle terrace and even featured (along with the family whippet-and-black-pudding crest) in the stained-glass quarries set among the plain diamonds of the Long Room windows.

According to Mr Yatton, the crest is a hound holding a black gauntlet, rather than a black pudding, though I am not convinced. But it's quite jolly, so I intend having it printed on lots of things for the gift shop, from pencils to tote bags. There will be two or three different ranges of items, something to suit all tastes, I hope, from roses and Shakespeare to witchcraft. I just keep jotting ideas down as they come to me.

Jack said (and keeps saying in his phone calls, *ad nauseam*) that he hates the idea of Winter's End being 'commercialised' and I should forget about opening the house and just concentrate on getting it back in order again. But if sharing such a beautiful place with other people generates enough income to keep it running, why not? Luckily Seth seems to feel the same way about the gardens as I do, and actually *wants* lots of people to see them, because we don't want a glowering gardener among the vegetation.

But above all, I was quite sure that Alys approved of all the changes I was making. In fact, that evening she felt especially close, so I actually *asked* her if she would mind if I copied out one or two charms from her household book and had them printed on postcards to make money for Winter's End? Call me mad, but I got the distinct impression that she didn't in the least. She might not have lived here long, but I knew she loved it as much as I did.

Still does, come to that.

Tonight Hebe was occupied with her furtive customers in the stillroom and anyway, rarely came into the parlour, which she didn't seem to like. It was too late for Seth to call (not that I ever *expected* him, because he was probably frequently otherwise engaged), and the Larks were settled in for the evening upstairs in their quarters, with Gingernut the kitten and the telly, until it was time for Jonah to do his last rounds of the house.

So I fetched Alys's book from its hiding place and, using a pair of clean white cotton gloves, even though centuries of sweaty Winter fingers had turned the pages already, mine included, I opened it at the front, where there were inscriptions in two different hands – for, of course, this had originally been her mother's book, passed on to Alys at her death.

Alys's writing was still clearly legible, firm and bold, if a little over embellished with loops and curls for current tastes, and hard to decipher:

Herein are many household receipts and hints, which I had from my mother, for the use of simples to cure divers ailments, some that the superstitious would call witchcraft in these sorry times. I have continued to add to the book, as I hope my daughter, Anne, will do after mee, and onward down the generations in the

258

female line for we women know better how to value such things and keep them safe. The treasures within are both my mother's legacy and my own, and the rose lies at their heart. I charge you to use them well.

Alys Blezzard, 1582

Well, that was clear enough – the treasures were the recipes in the book, especially the rose-based ones. I don't think even the Famous Five could conjure a mystery out of that, so Lucy would be disappointed.

And perhaps my mother thought she should have been the keeper of the secret, rather than Ottie, and took the book away with her so she could pass it on to me, her only legacy – apart from the camper van, of course.

But it should never have left Winter's End – even my dotty, spaced-out mother must have known that!

I copied out a couple of recipes that I thought would be suitable for postcards without poisoning anyone who tried them, one for rose tea and another for a sort of universal salve. Aunt Hebe was probably already using them, and Mrs Lark seemed to think she hadn't managed to dose anyone to death yet.

I flicked through the rest of the book, thinking that despite Alys's defence, some of her mother's potions sounded very Dark Arts to me. And so did some of Alys's own additions at the end of the book, interspersed among innocent instructions about which herbs to use to sweeten wooden floors, and how to make sops-in-wine.

Unfortunately, there weren't any recipes for discouraging a persistent lover, and Jack continued his schmoozy evening phone calls to ask how my day had gone, and whether I missed him – which, though fond of him, I hadn't really. It was hard to pinpoint the moment when I had passed from a state of dazzled infatuation to a sisterly – if slightly exasperated – affection, but it wasn't his fault that I'd recovered from the fever so quickly.

He apologised for not being able to get to Winter's End more often. 'I'll make up for it at Christmas, and I'll try to get down for lunch one day soon – I'll let you know when. Just concentrate on getting the house looking wonderful. We'll work out our future plans at Christmas, darling.'

'I've already worked mine out. You should have listened to *all* my speech to the staff,' I said drily, and though he laughed, I thought I had started to detect a note of impatience in his voice.

Perhaps it was at last dawning on him that I hadn't so much got a toehold on Winter's End, as captured the castle.

I finally received an answer to the letter I wrote ages ago to Mrs Dukes, the Blackwalls cook, asking if she knew how Lady Betty was.

It had taken some time for my letter to be passed on because she resigned after she, too, was denied permission to visit her mistress in the nursing home. She said she thought Conor had treated his aunt disgracefully, especially in isolating her from her friends and staff.

I had no other way of finding out what was happening, but by a strange coincidence I received an official missive from a solicitor only a day or two later, giving me the sad but not unexpected news that Lady Betty had died.

Conor hadn't thought fit to inform me of it, but I would have travelled up for the funeral, had I known.

Mind you, I didn't leave him a forwarding address, though Tanya at the caravan site was kindly sending on my mail, which is how I got the solicitor's letter. But Conor did have my mobile phone number, from when I worked there.

I admit that I had a little weep for Lady Betty, so it was a few minutes before I read on and discovered that under the terms of her will, all the permanent household staff would receive a keepsake, which she had personally chosen. Picking them out must have given her hours of pleasure!

Mine was an Egyptian artefact, and the author of the letter enquired if I would I like the solicitor to arrange to have it packed and delivered to me. I wondered which item, from Lady Betty's mainly bogus Egyptian collection, she had left to me. I only hoped it was not the stone sarcophagus, though when I told Seth while I was helping him plant the new rose bushes, he said that it would make quite a good display, planted up – so long as the mummy wasn't still in it.

I knew him well enough now to recognise when he was joking, even though he kept his face straight. It was a good sign, because he'd been a bit gloomy and preoccupied since the day Mel found us in that unfortunately compromising-looking clinch in the Great Hall. And though he still dropped into the parlour sometimes in the evening, his heart didn't always seem to be in our arguments any more.

I didn't think Mel was good news as far as Seth was concerned. Can you have your heart broken twice by the same person? He could be infuriating, but I found I didn't want him to be deeply unhappy, which I suspected was because I was starting to think of him as family, too.

Mr Yatton was to write to the solicitor to arrange delivery of my Mystery Parcel from Lady Betty. I'd treasure it, whatever it was. Lucy said she hoped it was a mummified cat, a ghoulishly strange desire that would gain no endorsement from Mrs Lark, that's for sure, and Gingernut, who seemed to have no respect for other people's property, let alone his own ancient ancestors, would probably eat it.

I wouldn't like to see the mess *that* would make in his litter tray.

*   *   *

261

Apart from the sad but not entirely unexpected news of my former employer, there were no flies in my balm of bliss until the end of the week.

Then the local rag came out again – and to my horror there I was, after all this time, headlined in the *Sticklepond and District Gazette*.

'WINTER'S END FOR MRS MOP!' it said in huge capitals, followed in slightly smaller type by 'MYSTERY HEIRESS FOUND'.

The meagre and unexciting facts of my inheritance had been used to support a huge edifice of speculation and possibility . . . a bit like what I was doing with the guidebook and display boards, come to think of it. Maybe I should have been a journalist.

It was all very sensational, and accompanied by the photo of Seth and me that had been taken in the new rose garden. I looked startled and fat, as did Charlie – but then, he usually does. Underneath it they'd put, 'To the manor born – the new Lady Winter with one of her gardeners at Winter's End,' and then quoted Seth as saying, 'The new mistress doesn't know her a** from her antirrhinum,' which I imagine he might well have done in the first flush of fury after I arrived, though he says not. (And I'm *not* Lady Winter. Unless I married Jack, I would never be Lady *anything*.)

Seth was furious, but I think it was mostly wounded male vanity, because he said the article and picture made him sound and look like a bucolic half-wit. Mind you, it was true that I didn't know what an antirrhinum was, so I asked him and he said it was like a snapdragon.

That should be his middle name – Seth Snapdragon Greenwood.

The day after the horrible article appeared, Jack called in for lunch on his way somewhere. Though he'd let us know he was coming, he arrived much earlier than I expected, so that I was down on the lower terrace getting some air after a morning spent cleaning the furniture in the Chinese bedroom.

Also, the footings for the retaining wall were in, and a couple of plain courses laid, and Seth insisted I put the first of the engraved stones into place.

The stone was a lot heavier than it looked so he had to help, standing right behind me with my hands over his as he carefully manoeuvred 'I like of each thing that in season grows' into place.

I turned in his encircling arms and smiled up at him as the other three gardeners clapped, probably more to restore some circulation to their cold hands than for any other reason, but his answering smile was surprisingly short-lived – then he moved away as if I was suddenly contagious.

A familiar voice hailed me peremptorily from above. 'Sophy!'

It was Jack, standing at the top of the steps looking like an advert for smart men's dressing. Then he ran quickly down, took a couple of strides and kissed me, though I turned my head at the last minute so that it landed on my cheek rather than my lips. It was instinctive, but I felt ungrateful. It wasn't that long since any signs of affection from a dazzlingly handsome man, with no obvious defects or hang-ups, would have been received with loud cries of joy – and now here I was taking evasive action.

'There you are, Sophy – and how nice to see you and Seth getting so *close*,' he said lightly, but with an undercurrent of such unmistakable anger in his voice that it made me flush guiltily even though he'd misread the situation. 'I've been looking all over for you. What's so engrossing about a wall that made you forget *I* was coming?'

'I hadn't forgotten, Jack. You're early. And this isn't any

old wall – some of the stones have got quotations from Shakespeare carved on them, to add to the whole theme of the garden,' I explained enthusiastically. 'I've just officially laid the first one.'

'Isn't that an unnecessary expense?'

'Ma's paying,' Seth said briefly, looking up from sorting the next stones ready to hand to Derek, when he had finished fiddling with his plumb line.

'Oh? I didn't think Ottie was interested in gardens, any more than Sophy was.'

'I *love* the garden,' I protested, as Jack put a familiar and rather possessive arm around my waist and gave me a squeeze. 'I just love the house more, even though I know they complement each other.'

'Well, you can see them any time, but *I'm* only here for an hour, so come on, Sophy – I'm famished and it seems ages since I saw you.'

To my relief he dropped his arm, so we wouldn't have to make our way awkwardly back up the steps like conjoined twins, and instead took my hand.

In the Great Hall the fire burned brightly, casting a rosy glow onto the subtle, faded colours of the newly washed rag rug and gleaming off the polished wooden furniture.

Jonah was sitting on one of the settles in front of the fire, buffing up a pair of halberds, like small axe heads on very long shafts, with Renaissance wax. I'd found them and their wooden mount in the attic, and the battered stag was about to be banished up there instead. The kitten, a ball of fluff the colour of a gingernut biscuit (hence his name), was curled up on a cushion at his side and Charlie was stretched out on the rug. I hoped this meant he was getting used to the usurper at last. At the sound of our footsteps on the stone floor he lifted his head high enough to see Jack, then emitted an indignant bark or two of disapproval without bothering to get up.

'The place looks different,' Jack said, 'I noticed as soon as I came in. And it smells different too!'

'I think it just smells clean and well-aired rather than musty, that's what it is,' I shrugged. 'Come on, let's go and find that lunch, if you're hungry and in a hurry.'

We were eating lunch of minestrone soup, accompanied by garlic bread and the cheeseboard in the breakfast parlour, rather than the kitchen, in Jack's honour. Aunt Hebe was already there, ready to fall on her blue-eyed boy with all kinds of questions and anxious enquiries.

Aunt Hebe indignantly told Jack all about the newspaper article, but he thought no one would take any notice of such a little local rag. He was bright and cheerful, especially on the subject of his wonderful self, telling us about some major property killing he had just made.

But when I started telling him all about what *I'd* been doing at Winter's End, he just shook his head sadly. 'Cosmetic changes are all very well, Sophy, and you've worked wonders, but the place needs the sort of overhaul only money can buy.'

The inference was clear: he had the money and I had the enthusiasm, so that together we would make a beautiful partnership. Aunt Hebe beamed on us benevolently.

'Oh, I don't think there's much wrong with the house, Jack, and anything expensive will just have to wait until funds start to come in and the place pays its own way. And I'm sure that will be quite soon, once we get the visitor numbers rising steadily,' I said with more optimism than I felt, because it was all going to be a huge gamble. 'I'm going to open Winter's End four days a week, from Easter until the end of September.'

'Yes, and I will have much to do if my range of products is going to be ready to sell in the shop by then,' Hebe said.

He frowned. 'I thought we'd agreed that we would discuss our plans for Winter's End at Christmas? You know how I feel about opening it to the public, Sophy. I'd much rather just keep it as our family home and—'

His phone, which he had laid next to his plate on the table, buzzed like a dying fly with an incoming text and he snatched it up, though it didn't seem to be the message he wanted.

'Where was I?' he asked.

'Eating cheese,' I said diplomatically, passing him the board – my favourite one, with a china mouse attached to the cheese wire. 'Your phone's buzzing again.'

'It doesn't matter,' he said, and ignored it after that, even though it went off about every ten minutes.

When lunch was over he accepted, with every sign of delight, the completed snot-green knitted garment that an excited Hebe presented to him.

It wasn't just good manners – his acting was *superb*, which was quite an eye-opener and really made me think. I mean, he is caressing and affectionate and had given every appearance of falling in love with me – but frankly I am not *that* gorgeous; more of a penny plain than a tuppence coloured.

When Hebe, with monumental tact and immense self-sacrifice, reluctantly tore herself away on some pretext, leaving us to have coffee together, he gave me his wonderful smile and said persuasively, 'You really *won't* make any more plans to open Winter's End until we can discuss it properly at Christmas, will you, Sophy?'

'I think I've probably already made most of them, actually, Jack. And you exaggerated the problems with Winter's End, especially the deathwatch beetle, so I would sell it to you at a low price, didn't you?'

He actually laughed, as though he had done something clever. 'Of course I did, darling, though it really *could* do with a bucket of money poured into it. But you don't have to sell it to me if you don't want to, because I meant it when I said I wanted us to live here together, happy ever after – and I suspect you're a traditionalist, so we'll get married eventually, if only to keep Aunt Hebe sweet. So, what's mine will be yours and vice versa, won't it?'

I closed my eyes, but when I opened them again he was still there with that confident smile on his handsome face.

'But, Jack, that's *never* going to happen. I'm not going to sell Winter's End, enter into any kind of partnership, or sign it over to you – and I'm certainly not going to marry you! I've quickly grown very fond of you, but I'm not in love with you and I don't think I ever will be,' I said frankly. 'But I *am* growing to love you like a brother.'

He looked absolutely flabbergasted, but that may have been the unintentionally Victorian sentiment of my last sentence, which just slipped out. Or perhaps he'd never even seriously considered it was possible that I could, in the end, refuse him anything. How could I resist him?

Indeed, I thought, looking at him again – tall, athletically built, golden-haired, blue-eyed and reeking with charm and subtly expensive aftershave – how *had* I managed to fall for him and then un-fall, so quickly? I mean, what exactly was I *looking* for in a man?

He still couldn't take what I'd said seriously, but he was shaken a bit, I think, though he rallied. 'I've rushed you, that's what it is, and I think you're still jealous of Mel, even though it's Seth she's got her claws into, not me, as I keep telling you. She just flirts the way other people breathe.'

I wished she would stop doing both – but maybe that was a bit mean.

I told him that I was not at all jealous of Mel, which unfortunately seemed to encourage him to think I just needed a little more time and persuasion. I was glad when

267

he and his buzzing phone departed, though this time he managed to plant a kiss full on my mouth before dashing off in his sports car.

After he'd gone I felt a bit restless and irritable, so I collected Charlie and went out into the crisp autumnal air, and we were just walking through the wilderness towards the rear drive when I heard a female voice, pitched rather high – Mel.

Charlie and I seemed to have an unerring nose for her assignations and, like last time, I scooped him up and clamped his muzzle shut before he could emit any of his wheezy little barks. His tail flapped – he would much rather be carried than walk, any day.

I supposed it would be Seth she was meeting, but instead of turning away I crept forward until I could see her big grey horse, tied to one of the posts of the stone shelter where the milk churns were once left.

She was standing in the little clearing behind it, talking to Jack. I could see the bright red paintwork of his car further on through the trees, pulled off the drive. Was this a fortuitous meeting, or had they arranged it?

'Did you have to keep texting me all through lunch, Mel? You knew where I was,' I heard him say testily.

'Just reminding you of my existence, in case other distractions made you forget me and our little business arrangements.'

'That's not very likely is it?' he said bitterly. 'And you shouldn't keep coming up here. It could make it awkward. I don't want Sophy to think there's something between us.'

'Why should she think that? There are other attractions at Winter's End, you know. Seth is always glad to see me, even if you're not.'

'Look, Mel,' Jack began angrily, 'I don't know—'

She stopped his words with a kiss, one that went on and

on, with her brown eyes wide open, looking in my direction. I don't know if she saw me or not.

Jack didn't seem to be putting up much resistance. But then, I expect few men would. Did it mean anything? It didn't really matter to me now, but it would, I was sure, to Seth . . .

Then Jack suddenly pushed her away and stood there glaring at her and breathing heavily, so maybe he, at least, wasn't entirely putty in her hands.

I backed away slowly until I couldn't see them any more, not bothering too much about the noise.

I circled the maze aimlessly for quite a while with Charlie, before going back to the house. There was no sign of Seth on the terrace, or in the kitchen, where Mrs Lark said she hadn't seen him that day, so I wondered if he too had slipped away to meet Mel. If so, she might be a little late . . .

But he knew what sort of woman she was; it was his own stupid fault if he had fallen for her all over again!

To Mrs Lark's delight I ate four chocolate brownies, then played with the kitten before finally going off to finish cleaning the Chinese bedroom.

At dinner Hebe remarked that she had seen Mel's horse tethered behind the lodge that afternoon, when she was looking for fungi in the dark trees that surrounded it. (No, don't ask what she wanted them for.)

'So you see, it *is* Seth that she comes to visit. Ottie was quite wrong about things. Jack and Mel are simply friends now.'

'I'm sure they are. She seems a *very* friendly type,' I agreed, and something in my voice made her give me a sharp look.

'You and Jack haven't fallen out, have you? I thought you were getting on really well at lunch.'

'We were, Aunt Hebe, and I love him like a brother, warts and all.'

'Jack hasn't got warts!' she said indignantly. 'There isn't a blemish on his body!'

'Just a turn of phrase. I can see he is perfection personified.'

I sat and sewed in the parlour that evening, as usual, but there was no sign of Seth. He probably had other fish to fry.

But I wasn't entirely alone, because apart from Charlie snoring on my feet, I once or twice looked up to glimpse Alys in the convex mirror on the opposite wall. It made her appear all nose – not a good look.

Chapter Twenty-four: Stunned

Mary Wynter hath told the officers that they were true churchgoers and would not harbour a priest, but that it was well known that I was tainted by witchcraft and would leave the house stealthily by night to attend blasphemous sabbats ... Her face was filled with spite and I saw her true intentions written there. Yet I could not say the truth, for that would condemn mee equally – perhaps more so, and be greatly detrimental to the family and so also to my sweet babe.

From the journal of Alys Blezzard, 1582

'You're famous, our Sophy,' Jonah said, putting a national tabloid down in front of me at breakfast the following Tuesday, folded to reveal a grainy blow-up of the *Sticklepond Gazette* photograph and an embellished rehash of the article.

'Bloody hell!' I exclaimed. I mean, I hadn't thought my story exciting enough to make even the local paper, let alone be syndicated to a daily.

Aunt Hebe, her attention wrested away from the less sensational pages of *The Times*, said disapprovingly, 'Language!' Then she twitched the newspaper from my trembling hands and read it herself, her silvery eyebrows going up and down and her lips moving with silent outrage.

'This is beyond a joke!' she said at last. 'And half of it is not true anyway – sheer sensationalism! They are just trying to make a rags-to-riches story out of it.'

'But it *is* a rags-to-relative-riches story, I suppose, Aunt Hebe, and I don't think they've actually said anything blatantly untrue, just implied things.' I scanned the article again and noticed something I'd missed the first time under the subtitle 'BARONET BUMPED OUT OF INHERITANCE'.

'This quote from Jack wasn't in the last article – listen to this! "Jack Lewis, now Sir Jack, said today, 'Of course it was a shock, but Sophy and I have become very close and I couldn't be happier for her.' But he wouldn't be drawn about rumours of an engagement between them."'

'I'm sure Jack wouldn't talk to the press,' Aunt Hebe said positively. 'Though he might well put an announcement of your engagement in *The Times*.'

'There is no engagement, Aunt Hebe,' I said wearily, 'there never will be. It's simply a figment of the journalist's imagination.'

And maybe Jack's.

Mr Yatton commiserated with me over the article, though he said nothing could be done about it. But I was still so steaming with anger that I went down to the terraces to look for someone else to pick a fight with, preferably Seth, who could be almost guaranteed to give back as good as he got.

Derek and Hal were sorting out the next layer of stones for the retaining wall, which was rising with amazing speed, while Seth and Bob were removing what remained of the turf and digging over the ground.

It was a chilly, dank sort of day, perfumed with the scent of wet woodsmoke, but it must have been hot work because both men had stripped down to their T-shirts. Bob's was yellow with a smiley sun on it, but Seth's was the pink one I had occasionally glimpsed through the strata of holey jumpers. Now I could see that it had 'Gardeners like to get down and dirty' printed across the front.

'Nice T-shirt,' I said, momentarily distracted.

'Present from Ma,' he said, stopping digging and leaning on his spade. Then he added shortly, with a glance at the newspaper in my hand, 'Congratulations on the engagement. When's the happy day?'

I supposed everyone within ten miles had seen the newspaper.

'Oh, don't be daft,' I said crisply. 'You know very well that there isn't going to be one. The journalist was just trying to add a bit of romance to a boring story. And I'm sure Jack never said anything to imply that we were going to get married.'

'Are you?'

'No, of course he wouldn't, or say all this other stuff about my sad life of drudgery. It makes me sound like a half-witted Mrs Mop,' I said, perhaps more positively than I felt. 'Do you think that's it now, and interest will die down?'

'I expect so, unless you do something newsworthy to keep it going – but we could turn the publicity to your advantage when we have the grand reopening of Winter's End,' he suggested. 'Angled to suit ourselves this time, of course.'

Somehow, when Seth used the royal 'we', it didn't annoy me half as much as when Jack did it. I supposed it was because I felt that, despite our battles, Seth and I were working towards the same end, while I had begun to have a sneaky feeling that Jack had an agenda of his own.

I turned Seth's suggestion over in my mind, though. 'You mean something like, "Heiress saves family home from disintegrating into dust. Hanging Gardens of Sticklepond the Eighth Wonder of the World"? Yes, I see what you mean.'

He grinned, and his sudden smiles are possibly the *ninth*

wonder of the world, because it was amazing how they took the forbidding aspect away from his rather formidable face.

I found I was smiling back and feeling better about things. 'And the hanging gardens are coming along well, aren't they? The front gates look almost finished too, Bob – well done.'

'Yes, we're getting there. It was fiddly work, but I spent all last weekend on them, so now there's only the gold highlights to put on.' Bob stopped digging and looked at me hopefully, fanning his hot, ruddy face with his hat so that the pink plastic tulip in the band nodded up and down. 'Would you like me to go and do it now?'

Seth's relatively benign expression swiftly switched to thundercloud mode, so I said hastily, 'No, there's too much dampness in the air. It's not a good day for painting.'

'I'll finish it off on Saturday as overtime then, shall I?'

'Yes, if the weather's right. Thanks, Bob.'

With all the extra expenses of things like overtime, I was going to need a sudden rush of money to the bank account fast. But Christie's would be putting my Herring painting up for auction before Christmas, and since Mr Yatton managed to find some provenance for it among the family papers, showing that it was commissioned by the baronet of that time to portray his favourite hunter, I hoped it would fetch a very good price. Even so, I needed to keep enough in reserve to repay the instalments on the bank loan until the gate money started to roll in.

There wasn't a single day when I didn't feel thankful for Mr Yatton: what on earth would I have done without him?

Seth hadn't called by the parlour since the day Jack came to lunch, and I'd missed the cut and thrust of our often lively discussions, so I was actually quite pleased when he turned up that evening, even though he seemed rather gloomy. I expect that was the Mel effect. I often glimpsed her horse or her distinctive low, silver car, near the lodge house. I could have banned her from the estate, of course – and don't think I wouldn't have loved to do it. But of course, it was impossible without a better reason than simply disliking her.

Seth tersely informed me that he was going away for a few days. 'I've got a commission to design a small knot garden for a manor house in Devon. I'll be off tomorrow.'

'That's a bit short notice! What about the wall and the lower terrace you were so determined to finish?'

'Derek's the expert where the wall is concerned, he'll be in charge until I get back.'

Derek seemed to be a very hard worker, so I didn't suppose the rebuilding would slow down much, even without Seth's eagle eye on it, but I felt unaccountably cross anyway.

'I haven't seen much of you lately and there are a few things we need to discuss.'

'I've been busy,' he said shortly.

I could imagine what, or maybe that should be *who*, with.

He spotted the huge vase of roses on a side table and, since they were a flagrantly passionate scarlet, it would be a bit hard to miss them, and said jokingly (I hoped), 'From your fiancé?'

'They *are* from Jack, and they must have cost a fortune. I wish I knew a tactful way of telling him that if he *must* send me something, I'd much rather have a rosebush.'

'But I suppose sending a bare-rooted bush wouldn't rank as quite the same flamboyantly romantic gesture?'

'I don't want romantic gestures,' I said curtly, which I didn't – or not from Jack, anyway. 'I'd much rather fill the gaps in the rose garden.'

Somehow it was odd without unexpected glimpses of Seth about the place; not to see him striding about in the distance, up a ladder clipping something, snatching lunch in the kitchen, or the top of his dark head on the terrace below . . .

And I had no one to argue with either except, occasionally, Lucy. She now seemed to have stopped wavering and decided to work right to the end of her contract anyway, even though I knew she was dying to come back and get to grips properly with the business side of Winter's End. She was so stubborn!

To my relief the man following her turned out to be a harmless computer nerd half her size, who simply wanted private English lessons. 'I told him I would, but only in a café near where I'm living – so no need to worry about it any more, Mum.'

But I *did* still worry – illogically, I suppose, since harm could come to her anywhere, including here . . . and I had a worrying awareness of some dark shadows coming, gathering on the edge of my consciousness again . . .

I hoped that whatever danger they foretold, it threatened me and not my child.

A couple of days after Seth left for Devon I took what had become my usual afternoon walk up to the summerhouse in the woods with Charlie, since it was one of those sad, dead-leaf-scented, end-of-autumn days when you want to consider life, the universe and everything. Up in my ramshackle eyrie was as good a place as anywhere.

I paused before going in, to see what was making Charlie lag behind. But of course, as soon as I turned he sat down on the path – never stand when you can sit is his motto. 'Come on, you wimp! I'm not picking you up, we're there,' I told him, and going up the steps strode into the shadowy interior.

As the wooden floor bounced under my feet, making the whole thing tremble like a stage set, I noticed a strange but not entirely unfamiliar scent on the air. Then something caught sharply at my legs and the whole world caved in on me as I went flying headlong into dark oblivion.

I awoke in my bed at Winter's End, with a pounding head and a doctor asking me if I could see double. And for a minute I could – there seemed to be two Charlies, who had somehow got upstairs and onto the bed. Then my vision cleared and we were back to just one.

'Charlie is my darling,' I said idiotically, and he thumped his tail.

'She's delirious,' Aunt Hebe's voice said.

'No I'm not,' I assured her. 'I've got a headache though. What happened?' I frowned. 'Wasn't I up at the summerhouse in the woods?'

The doctor, who had been holding my wrist, let it go. 'I'm afraid you had a bit of an accident, Miss Winter. The building collapsed on top of you, and your head took a glancing blow. But it could have been much worse. It was a lucky escape.'

'I didn't think the building was in that poor a condition,' I said, trying in vain to remember what had happened, 'though Seth did warn me that he thought it was getting to the point of collapse. But I loved sitting up there. I wonder if he can repair it?'

'It's probably beyond it, but don't worry about that now,' Aunt Hebe said, laying a lavender-scented flannel on my forehead. 'You know, I do believe that you are going to have a black eye.'

'Great,' I said morosely. 'How did you find me?'

'The gardeners on the terrace heard Charlie barking and noticed that the summerhouse roof was at an odd angle, so they went to investigate and found you out cold. Charlie was sitting faithfully next to you in the rubble, still barking, and he has refused to leave your side ever since,' Aunt Hebe said. 'He is quite the hero of the hour!'

'Just as well for you,' the doctor said, packing things back into his bag again, 'or you could have been lying there in the cold for hours.'

'Well, dinnertime, at least,' I agreed. 'Everyone would have known it wasn't like me to miss a meal. Good dog, Charlie!'

'I'll leave you some painkillers for the headache, and I'd like you to stay in bed for a couple of days. If you have any other symptoms, including double vision, phone me immediately.' He must have seen my mutinous expression, because he added, 'If you don't stay in bed and rest, you won't recover as quickly. The bang on the head was nasty.'

So I had to stay in bed like an invalid, black eye and all.

Seth was still away, so I suppose he wouldn't hear a thing about it until he got back, but as soon as Jack got the news from Hebe he paid me a flying visit, bringing a little hamper of Fortnum and Mason goodies and a big box of Godiva chocolates, just as if my strength needed building up, which it certainly doesn't.

Mrs Lark was rather miffed about the foodstuffs, since she said there was nothing in there that she couldn't do better, though I felt that producing caviar from the virgin sturgeon might be a feat even beyond her capabilities. Mind you, I found it so weird that I gave most of it to Charlie, thinking the fishiness might do something for what brain cells he possessed.

But it was thoughtful of Jack, and he was so concerned, quiet and kind, that I let him hold my hand and waffle on about our future together in his lovely, mesmerising voice, which just about sent me to sleep.

This time I simply wasn't up to arguing, just glad *someone* seemed to care.

Chapter Twenty-five: Follies

I am imprisoned, though Sir Ralph has seen to it that I am housed separately, in a chamber near the gaoler's lodging. I am afraid – I fear the Wynters wish to be rid of mee, and are taking this opportunity of doing so. Yet punishments for such wrongdoings are seldom harsh – my mother's distant connections, the Nutters, have frequently been accused of witchcraft and escaped with little more than imprisonment or a ducking . . . but others they have hanged, it is true. I have written to my father, to beg his aid, for I have a very great fear of hanging . . .

From the journal of Alys Blezzard, 1582

As soon as I was allowed up and about, Mr Hobbs reminded me that I hadn't yet made a will – a suggestion that cheered me up no end, as you can imagine.

But actually, once the headache vanished I felt totally rejuvenated, so perhaps a couple of days' enforced rest did me good. I threw myself back into the cleaning, sorting, polishing and rearranging with renewed vigour.

Since Seth wasn't there to complain, I had Bob and Hal move the two glass-topped curio tables from the Long Room into the gallery, either side of a column sprouting yet another of those strange light fittings in the form of a naked arm holding an ice-cream cone.

I thought the odd collection of curios would interest the visitors, though I would have to identify and label some of the stranger ones. I was still up there writing a list, with descriptions and little drawings, when my mobile phone rang. For once I hadn't left it in my bedroom.

'Sophy?' a familiar, high-pitched voice said. 'This is Conor Darfield.'

'Hello, Conor!' I said, surprised that he had actually had the grace to phone me about his aunt, rather late in the day though it was. 'I had the solicitor's letter a few days ago and I can't tell you how sorry I was to hear of Lady Betty's death. It must—'

'Never mind that,' he interrupted rudely. 'That isn't why I called. It might interest you to know that I have been going through the will and checking the insurance inventory.'

'I bet you have.' That sounded much more like the Conor I knew and loathed.

He ignored my comment. 'I have been checking items off, and there are two pieces of my aunt's jewellery missing, one of them a brooch. In the form of a *bee*,' he added meaningfully, and my fingers unconsciously curled protectively around it.

'*Then* my attention was called to a picture of you in the tabloids – and what do I see?' He paused dramatically.

'Well, you didn't see a bee – and you're starting to sound like a Dr Seuss book,' I said shortly.

'Your coat is open in the photograph and I am positive that you are wearing—'

'Look, Conor,' I broke in, 'if I was wearing the crown jewels, you couldn't tell from that photograph. But if you *really* want to know, there's no secret about it: Lady Betty *gave* me her little crystal and enamel bee brooch, and I treasure it.'

'I knew it! But when? *When* did she give it to you?' he

demanded. 'There is no record of it, and I'm told she was wearing it the day she had her fall and went into hospital – and the necklace.'

'Of course she was, she always wore them – they were her favourites. But when I went to visit her in hospital, with Mrs Dukes, she suddenly decided to give them away and wouldn't be swayed.'

'Mrs Dukes? Who is Mrs Dukes?'

'The cook who worked for your aunt for thirty years, remember? You know, the one you fired recently?' I didn't mention that Lady Betty had given *her* the string of lapis lazuli beads. Neither item was of any great value, except to us for sentiment's sake; and in any case it was none of Conor's business.

'The cook was impertinent,' he said stiffly. 'So, are you alleging that my aunt gave you the jewellery while she was in hospital? In that case, it may interest you to learn that the receptionist at the nursing home is certain she saw Lady Betty wearing both items when she arrived there! She also noticed that *you* were wearing that very distinctive brooch on a later occasion, so perhaps you took them when you managed, despite my instructions, to get in to see her?'

'I'm not alleging anything,' I snapped. 'The receptionist is either vindictive or a fantasist, and it happened as I said. Lady Betty said she felt that it was time to hand the pieces on, and I was deeply touched.'

'So you say, but I intend to investigate the matter further so, if you wish to escape prosecution, I suggest you immediately return the missing items to me. My aunt was clearly in no fit state to give away her property and, in any case, could not do so because *I* had the power of attorney. Do you und—'

'Conor,' I said, cutting him off again in mid-diatribe, 'what I understand is that you are a greedy little windbag and I wouldn't give you the time of day, let alone something of such huge sentimental value to myself! Good*bye*!'

I was trembling with anger, even though I was sure his accusations had been all hot air.

Afterwards I wondered if I should write and tell Mrs Dukes of Conor's threats? But then, it would only upset her and there was no way Conor could claim back either the brooch or the necklace. It was just pure greed that had led him to try.

Since I'd recovered from my accident (apart from the black eye, which was only just starting to fade), Charlie and I had been redirecting our walks down the drive, just as far as the lodge and then back through the parterres and the yew maze. This gentle amble suited both of us at the moment, though at some point I would have to go up and look at the sad remains of the summerhouse.

That afternoon, as we rounded the bend through the trees, I could see that the lights were on in the large windows at the back of the lodge where the building had been extended.

Seth was back.

It felt oddly right to have him home again, but I couldn't stand like a stalker among the dark trees indefinitely, so after a while I nudged Charlie off my feet and we turned back for home.

Winter's End had been a Mel-free zone since his departure. I wondered how long it would take her to learn he was back?

Someone must have told Seth about my accident, because he inspected the remains of the summerhouse very early next morning, and then after breakfast came to find me and insisted I go back up there with him.

'I haven't had the heart to look at it since the accident.'

'You'd better come now, if only to assess the damage. Nice black eye,' he added.

'Thanks. I'm getting to quite like the yellow and blue shades myself.'

I was panting by the time I got up there, partly because I found it hard to keep up with Seth's long, impatient strides, and partly because Charlie went on strike and I had to carry him most of the way.

What was left of the summerhouse looked even more desolate than I thought it would, for it was not only wrecked, but also slightly charred. 'What happened?' I asked, puzzled. 'Did lightning strike it?'

'No, I think someone tried to set fire to the place, only of course it's all too damp to catch at the moment. Do you remember how it came to fall on you?'

'Not really, only walking up here.' I looked sadly at the wreckage. 'You were quite right when you said it was getting unsafe, Seth. If I'd listened to you, it would still be standing.'

'It would probably have fallen down eventually, but I think it fell on you because it was booby-trapped. Hal thought he spotted a bit of broken twine tied to one of the doorposts, but by the time they had got you back to the house and he came back to look for it, it was gone.'

'He never mentioned that to me!'

'He wasn't sure about it, so he waited until I got back. And I think he was probably right. Look at this.'

He showed me one of the wooden posts that had held up the lintel, which had a groove cut into the soft, powdery wood halfway up. 'I'd say that had had something thin, like baler twine, tied round it and across the doorway to the other one. The two posts already moved when you walked on the boards between them, didn't they? So it wouldn't take much to bring them down.'

'You mean – someone did it on purpose? To hurt me?'

'I don't suppose whoever did it expected the building to collapse, just that you would have a nasty fall.'

'But who do you think could have done it?'

He stopped prowling around the debris and turned his green eyes on me. He looked angry, but that was probably because the summerhouse was now ruined beyond repair. 'Perhaps it was aimed at you personally? You're a creature of habit; you came up here most afternoons with Charlie.'

He turned away and contemplated the ruins again, adding gruffly, 'That lintel is heavy – it could have killed you.'

'Are you implying someone at *Winter's End* rigged it up?'

He shrugged. 'Not necessarily, but maybe someone with connections here – and perhaps a grudge. Though probably it was meant as a malicious trick, not a serious attempt to injure you.'

'Well, that's OK then,' I said drily. 'I can't imagine who would want to hurt me anyway, so you're probably wrong.'

'Can't you?' he said, looking searchingly at me.

'You aren't thinking it was *Jack*, are you?' I asked incredulously. 'I'm sure he wouldn't – and in any case, why should he?'

'No, I wasn't thinking of Jack. He's only ruthless in business – and I don't think he's quite that stupid either, because if anything happened to you, I suppose Winter's End would go straight to Lucy, wouldn't it?'

I nodded. 'According to Mr Hobbs, but he's drawing up a will for me anyway; says it makes things easier.'

'Of course, he might have thought that with Lucy being so young, it would be much easier to persuade her into selling the place,' he said thoughtfully

'He hasn't met Lucy yet,' I added fairly, 'so he wouldn't know she's far from a sweet, malleable young thing.'

'But as I said, violence is very much *not* Jack's thing.'

'Of course it isn't. He was so kind and concerned when he visited me after the accident.'

'Maybe you should tell the police? You could just have a quiet word with Mike.'

'No, I really don't want to do that,' I said quickly. 'I'm sure it must have been local youths larking around, not personal at all. We'll have to keep a closer eye on the grounds.'

'It's your property – and your head.'

I surveyed the wreckage with a sigh. 'It was very pretty . . . do you think we could rebuild it to the same design?'

'I expect so. There are photographs of it. But it will have to wait its turn. I'll get the boys up here later, though, and we'll salvage what we can of the original and stack it in one of the empty stables.'

We descended the woodland path, slippery with a mulch of slimy dead leaves, then crossed the bridge to the lower terrace. Bob and Hal suddenly started working with renewed energy, though Derek seemed capable of carrying steadily on at the same pace for ever, like an android.

'It's coming along really fast,' I said admiringly. 'Just as well, if it is going to be finished by Valentine's Day. You know, it occurred to me the other day that I don't even know where they sell the tickets from on open days! There's so much still to find out.'

'The ticket office is the lodge on the other side of the arch from mine,' said Seth. 'The side window has been turned into a stable door, so they open just the top of that. Do you want to see it? We could walk down and look now, if you like.'

'All right,' I agreed, though Charlie made it clear when we passed the house that he wanted to stay behind, and I had to detour and let him in. I came back out with chunks of warm ginger parkin, which we ate while cutting through the rose garden. It looked a lot less bare now, even though the new bushes were just sitting in the wintry soil not doing much.

It was odd that I hadn't noticed the little stable door in the side of the lodge before, but then it was usually dark and shadowy under the archway.

'Believe it or not, a whole family lived in each lodge once, even though the buildings were tiny. Mine was extended out at the back when I moved in, but this side is still the basic model.'

Seth had a key to the door and flicked on a light switch, revealing a small square room with a flagged floor and a fireplace. A wooden counter top had been fixed to the wall at one side.

'There's the cash box – they need a float at the start of the day, so they have change, like at the tearoom. The tickets will be in the estate office, but you'll need to have new ones done anyway, if you are changing the prices. They have guidebooks here – and they can sell the garden leaflets too, if we get them done in time.'

'We will,' I said firmly, 'if not on Valentine's Day, then for the Easter opening. I think the maze and the Shakespeare Trail will rope them in in droves.'

'One of the Friends in the Great Hall checks the tickets again when they go in,' he said. 'The visitors can't get to the terraces any other way, because the paths at the side of the house are roped off. We can't entirely stop people sneaking in up the back drive, or over the wall, but we can stop them coming into the house unless they've paid.'

'What about the coach parties, do they all have tickets?'

'Yes, a special colour. They have to book in advance, because we can't fit more than one party into the house or tearoom at a time.'

'What puzzles me is how on earth the coaches get up the little lane into the car park,' I confessed.

'They don't. There's a bottom gate on to the main road and they park down there. It's just cars at the top. Hal and Bob take it in turns to check up on the car park, to see everything is OK.'

'I haven't noticed any facilities for disabled visitors.'

'I think Sir William said that since it's a private house, you don't have to have them, and in any case it would be almost impossible to adapt a house of this age. He allowed pushchairs and wheelchairs through the house, but not those enormous baby buggies or electric scooters. And of course they have to get up and down the steps at either end to get in and out.'

'Perhaps we can put wooden ramps at the front and back doors when we are open. And you know the golf buggy Grandfather used in his last months to get around the gardens, the one that's still in the stables?'

He nodded.

'It's a big one, so I thought someone could go up and down the drive on open days picking up and dropping off any visitors who have trouble walking.'

'Why do I have the feeling there goes another gardener?' he groaned.

'Oh, I don't know. I think one of the Friends might enjoy driving it. I'll discuss it with them at this Christmas party I'm supposed to be organising.'

He locked the ticket-office door behind us and then invited me into his side for a cup of coffee and, since I was desperately curious to see his home, I agreed.

We went straight into a comfortable small sitting room and through into a large, untidy, light and airy studio at the back. There was no evidence of Mel's presence here, not even a photograph or a lingering trace of the mingled fragrance of horse and Arpège that was particularly her own. But there were shelves and shelves of books, a workbench

287

and a drawing board with a half-completed diagram of a knot on it. There was also a leather sofa that I arranged myself on, trying to look as if I hadn't been nosily poking about, before Seth came back with the coffee.

While we drank the coffee he told me all about the knot he had been designing down in Devon and I told him about all the weird things in the curio cabinets that I hadn't yet identified. He was just promising to come and have a look at them, when we heard a vehicle pull up outside and the sound of voices, and went out to investigate.

There, with its nose under the arch, was a large, elderly ambulance, painted a fetching sky blue with fluffy clouds drifting up the sides. Facing it, planted firmly in the centre of the drive with his hand held up, was policeman Mike.

A woman was leaning out of the window, her long red dreadlocks swinging, and neither of them noticed us: she and Mike were too busy staring at each other.

Then suddenly Mike's face split into a great grin and she smiled back.

Beside me, Seth assumed an expression of resignation. 'Don't tell me,' he said, 'it's a friend of yours, isn't it?'

Anya had arrived.

Chapter Twenty-six: First Impressions

*I have received word from my father who says that he knew
I would come to a bad end and that he washes his hands
of mee. No one it seems will say anything in my defence
and several near Wynter's End have now come forward to
say I have cursed them ill . . . Mary Wynter will not let my
baby come to mee, but Joan is to bring mee any necessities.
My chamber is damp and dark and my cough worsens.*

From the journal of Alys Blezzard, 1582

'Oh, Anya, it's so good to see you!' I said, as I sat beside
her in the van. Looking in the wing mirror I could see the
two men standing on the drive gazing after us. Mike, looking
dazed, raised one hand and flapped it.

'I think Mike's waving at you.'

'Is that what he's called? He's not your run-of-the mill
fuzz, is he? And he's cheeky, too. When I stopped he said,
"Stand and deliver – your money or your life." I'm sure
that's not in the policeman's handbook.'

'He's from Liverpool, he can't help it,' I explained.
'Scousers are all like that. Did he say anything else?'

'Yes, he asked me if I had a ring on my finger as well as
through my nose. Then he said he didn't think he could
arrest me for anything just yet, but he would work on it,
and was I a friend of yours?'

'You certainly seemed to make an impression on him *and* on Seth too, though since I think he was half expecting a whole convoy of New-Age travellers to turn up, he wasn't as horrified as I expected.'

'Seth being the handsome gardener?'

'Oh, Seth's not really handsome, or not the way Jack is. He's stunning!'

'Attractive, then, if you want to nit-pick. He looked pretty good to me.'

'He *is* attractive when he's all glowing and enthusiastic about his knot gardens,' I conceded.

'And Mike's not bad either. In fact, you seem to be entirely surrounded by tasty men. Are there any more lurking in the undergrowth?'

'Wait until you see Jonah, he's the best of the bunch,' I promised her. 'Carry on left here at the front of the house. You can leave the van in the courtyard at the back and we'll bring the rest of your things in later.'

'Not if that's the house.' She had come almost to a stop and was staring at Winter's End aghast. 'I'd much, much rather stay in the van.'

'Don't be such an inverted snob! If *I* can live in Winter's End, my friends can too. It isn't that grand.'

'This from someone who lived in a two up, two down, tied cottage with an outside toilet – or even in a static caravan for a short while? No, thanks, and I'll hide the van out of the way somewhere. What's through that arch over the other side?'

'The pigsty and the rear drive. You can get back into the village that way.'

'The pigsty sounds much more my scene.'

She drove through and parked neatly behind the coach house, half-hidden by bushes, then gave me a little tissue-wrapped parcel. 'It's a sorry-you-got-banged-on-the-head present,' she explained. 'Though the black eye is a bit of a disappointment – it's practically gone.'

'It was a cracker while it lasted.' I eagerly unwrapped the paper to reveal a pair of earrings that she had made herself, from snipped tin and appliquéd chocolate bar wrappers.

'Oooh, wonderful! Let me put them on.' I admired myself in the rear-view mirror. 'You are clever! Come on, let's take your bags and I'll show you round the house. I'm sure you'll change your mind about not wanting to stay there. I've got the Chinese bedroom ready for you, and you'll love it.'

She looked doubtful, but I took her in by way of the kitchen and introduced her to the Larks first, before springing the rest of the house on her. She immediately endeared herself to them by playing with the kitten and eating four large, sugar-sifted warm doughnuts, one after the other, which was two more than even I could manage.

Mrs Lark admired my earrings. 'I don't think I've ever seen anything quite like them. Are those KitKat wrappers?'

'Yes – Anya made them. She makes jewellery from things people throw away, like tin cans and chocolate wrappers. Just like a Womble.'

'I'll make you a pair of earrings too, Mrs Lark,' promised Anya.

'I'm hoping to sell Anya's jewellery in our shop,' I said, getting up and wiping jam and sugar off my chin. 'Well, come on and I'll show you round the rest of the house.'

'You were right, Jonah *is* a dish,' she said when we were in the Great Hall with the heavy kitchen door shut behind us. 'It's the mutton-chop whiskers that do it for me.'

'If elderly men float your boat, I also have a vintage but *very* handsome estate manager – my steward, Mr Yatton. But he's only here weekday mornings and you might have to compete with Lucy when she gets home.'

'Has she said when she's coming back?'

'Not yet. I thought she was on the point of giving in her notice, but now she's gone back to saying she must see out her contract to the end.' I sighed. 'Well, never mind. Do you want to do the guided tour now?'

'Love it!' she said promptly.

Charlie had followed us out of the kitchen and now lay stretched out on the rag rug in front of the fire, instantly asleep. We left Anya's bags at the bottom of the stairs and I took her all over Winter's End, telling her my plans, until we ended up, ages later, in the dismal excuse for a tearoom.

'I haven't really started on this area yet, except for deciding what sort of basic stock we should have – you know, mementoes of Winter's End. I want it to be a craft shop and gallery as well as a tearoom. I've already got Aunt Hebe on my side about opening the house by offering to sell her lotions and potions in the shop.'

Anya looked around assessingly. 'You have two very good-sized rooms here, plus that little conservatory thing – you can probably seat as many as forty people.' She flung open a door, revealing an empty room with a channel down one side of the stone floor and some metal shelving. 'What's this?'

'I think it might have been the brewery once, and now they use it to store stuff in for the tearoom.'

'I'm sure there are lots of other storage rooms doing nothing, and you could fit this out as a proper shop.' She turned on her heel, and waved a hand at the rest of the place. 'I mean, hang paintings around the café, and have narrow shelves out there filled with things to sell, by all means, but have the till and most of the stock in here.'

'I see what you mean . . .' I said thoughtfully. 'But we'd have to have more lighting in here, and an electric socket or two.'

'I think it would be ideal. What were you thinking of

doing with the tearoom part, Sophy? It looks depressingly dreary at the moment.'

'Paint the walls a warm cream colour, for a start, and then have all the tables and drop-in chair seats covered in the same material . . . something lively.'

'A large gingham check would look good. You can get PVC tablecloth material in that too, which would save laundering,' Anya suggested. 'What kind of food do they serve?'

'Just cakes, scones, sandwiches, with tea or coffee. I suppose they have cold drinks too.'

'Well, that's all right if you don't want to provide full meals, though you could quite easily have hot soup and rolls and maybe salads? Plus, there's plenty of room for a freezer for lollies and ice cream, plus a tall chiller cabinet over there by the wall, so people could collect their cold drinks first and put them on their trays while queuing for food.'

'That sounds a lot more practical – and professional,' I agreed. 'But the teashop is manned by my volunteers, and I'm not too sure yet how they will take to change.'

'I've worked in both teashops and craft centres, don't forget,' she said. 'I could help you set it all up and get it running.'

'I did think of asking you, but would you actually *like* a permanent job? I know you said you'd like to settle down near Guy, but I wasn't sure if you were serious. And the salary wouldn't be very high, especially at first.'

'Yes, I'm serious, though I'm pretty sure I'd still want to travel in the van every winter for a month or two, and sell my jewellery at craft fairs. I don't need much money and I'll be selling my jewellery in the shop too, won't I? I could even set up a workshop area at the back and make it there when it is quiet, so people can watch me.'

I smiled at her ideas. 'Oh, Anya, it would be even more fun if you were here too!'

'Yes, I think it *would* be fun, with the bonus of being

able to see more of Guy – though not too much, because he won't want his mother popping in every five minutes.'

'How is he settling in?' I asked, because she had been to see him before coming here.

'Fine. He's renting a flat and enjoying his job, but he finished with his girlfriend just a couple of weeks ago, so he's a bit down about that. Maybe he'll find someone new where he's working – it's some sort of research lab, not much more than thirty miles from here. It's odd how conveniently things have worked out.'

'I wish Lucy were only thirty miles away too, and maybe I wouldn't worry quite so much.'

'Lucy's the most sensible, capable, kick-ass girl I've ever met in my life, so don't worry, Sophy.'

'I can't help it. Mr Yatton hatched a cunning plan to lure her back home again by getting her involved in running the estate. He emails her all the time with figures and spreadsheets and stuff, but although she's fascinated, it hasn't worked yet.'

'It probably will with a bit more time, because she loves number-crunching and paperwork, doesn't she? And she's a born manager.'

'She's a bossy-boots,' I agreed.

'Well, just don't let her rule your life again when she does get back. Guy sends both of you his love, by the way.'

'I'll tell her. She keeps asking after him.' I had a sudden idea. 'Look, why don't you and Guy come here for Christmas? It would be lovely to have you, and we could make a start on sorting the shop and café out then, too.'

'Sounds good.'

It was getting late, so I persuaded her into taking her bags up to the newly cleaned and polished Chinese bedroom, which Grace had made ready for her. 'The bathroom's across the hall. When you hear the gong, dinner's ready.'

'You'll come and get me before you go down, won't you?' she asked nervously. 'Your great-aunt sounds scary!'

'She isn't . . . really. But we'll go down together and it will just be the three of us tonight. My other aunt is in Cornwall and Jack's not likely to drop in.'

'Pity,' she said, 'I'd like to have a look at *him*.'

'He's not your type, Anya.'

'I don't think he sounds like *anyone's* type. He's probably in love with his own reflection,' she said unkindly.

Once Aunt Hebe had got over the surprise of Anya's large nose ring and red dreadlocks they got on surprisingly well.

When I told her that Anya was to reorganise the shop and tearoom she informed her that her range of rose-based products *must* have the best position.

'Of course,' Anya said tactfully. 'I'm sure they'll be our best-sellers.'

She admired the central table display of paper napkins, which tonight featured both roses as well as the flotilla of paper swans, which seemed to be appearing as a centrepiece to every meal now.

'Nice swans,' she said, picking one up to examine it closer.

Aunt Hebe gave a sniff and, shaking out her linen napkin, spread it across her lap.

'Jonah makes them. He's learning how to do it at evening class. The paper ones are just for decoration but he does it with the linen ones too, sometimes.'

'I'll make you a special one, if you like them,' Jonah promised, overhearing from the side table where he was clattering dishes. She thanked him and said she, in turn, would show him how to make a decent duck later.

Speaking of which, we had savoury ducks for dinner, a delicacy I had forgotten about while up in the frozen far north, and which had absolutely nothing to do with ducks or, in fact, any kind of fowl. In some areas they were called faggots, which was just as puzzling.

I'm not sure Anya had ever even seen a savoury duck before, but after staring at it suspiciously for a moment, she ate it, along with the accompanying onion gravy, colcannon and caramelised carrots.

'It's Guy Fawkes night tomorrow, Aunt Hebe, and we're going over to the bonfire at Middlemoss. Seth says he'll drive us in the estate car – would you like to come?'

'Oh, no, thank you, dear. It's the omnibus of *Cotton Common* tomorrow on the TV and I want to catch up, but you go and have a nice time. What a pity poor Jack is so busy just now. He would have gone with you.'

'Yes, he does seem to be frantically trying to close deals on several properties at once, doesn't he?' I said. 'And all before the New Year, for some reason.'

'I hope he isn't overstretching himself,' Aunt Hebe said worriedly. 'I know he still hasn't got planning permission to knock down that house of Melinda's yet, to sell the land for building. Apparently it's a Kinkerhoogen.'

'Kinkerhoogen?'

'He was an architect in the sixties and this is one of the few houses he designed over here. Although it is very ugly, Jack says they might try and put a preservation order on it, so I hope he doesn't do anything hasty.'

'I'm sure he won't,' I said soothingly, though I had no idea what she meant. I mean, what *could* he do – kneecap the council until they gave him planning permission?

We had coffee after dinner in the drawing room as usual, and then Aunt Hebe flitted off to flog potions to the desperate.

Anya and I then walked down to the Green Man, where she beat a clearly smitten Mike at dominoes, whilst I told

Seth all about our plans and that Anya would soon be a permanent fixture about the place. I thought he took it remarkably well.

Walking back through the crisp, cold darkness, I teased Anya about Mike and she retaliated by saying she thought Seth and I made a perfect couple.

'Perfectly mismatched,' I said, astounded. 'Are you quite mad? He's the exact opposite of my kind of man, and we're always arguing. In any case, I'm sure he's still having a torrid affair with this Mel Christopher I told you about, and she's absolutely gorgeous.'

'She sounds more like a match for the equally beautiful Jack, then,' she pointed out.

'Yes . . . and sometimes I've wondered which of them she really wants. Maybe it's both. She's certainly *had* both. But no . . . really, I'm sure Seth is her main target. Not that it matters to me, of course,' I added quickly.

'Of course not,' Anya agreed, 'or not now you've come to your senses about Jack, anyway.'

'You just wait until you see him, at Christmas! You'll fall for him and poor Mike will never get a look-in again.'

'Not me. My guardian angel has warned me about him already.'

'Did she say anything about tall, dark policemen?'

'Mind your own business,' she said with a grin.

Chapter Twenty-seven: Infernal Knots

Joan brought mee a lock of my baby's hair – but also some-thing of my mother's brewing that she entrusted to her, saying that one day I would be in dire straits and need it. I think she foresaw this moment, for now they talk of putting mee to trial, which I may not be able to bear. I have given her my keepsake and must soon give her this book, for though I conceal it, yet its discovery would go ill for mee.

From the journal of Alys Blezzard, 1582

Next morning we were turning out the cupboard that was once the escape route from the priest's hole, when Jonah appeared, bearing the tray holding the remains of Mr Yatton's breakfast.

'There you are then, Sophy. There's a call from a man who says he's your husband. Mr Yatton told him you hadn't got one, but he's pretty insistent, so he says, do you want it putting through, or will he get rid of him?'

'Must be some crank who's spotted that stupid news-paper article,' I said, carefully putting a Sèvres teacup down on the seventies marbled Formica hostess trolley, which we were using to transfer what was left of the delicate china to the kitchens for washing.

'Mr Yatton says he's got a slight Scottish accent,' Jonah said helpfully. 'Name of Lang.'

Startled, Anya and I stared at each other.

'OK, Jonah, tell Mr Yatton to switch it through to the parlour,' I said, feeling as if someone had punched me in the solar plexus, and he went back off down the corridor, rattling crockery.

'Come on, Anya – whoever it is, ex-husband or some crank, I may need moral support. But it *can't* be Rory, can it?'

As I nervously picked up the phone Mr Yatton said, 'Putting it through.' Then there was a click as he replaced the receiver at the other end.

Into the slightly crackling silence a ghost from the past, in the form of a rather posh voice with the faintest hint of a Scottish lilt, demanded, 'Sophy, is that you? Sophy, are you there?'

'*Rory?*'

'It *is* Rory?' Anya whispered, her eyes wide. 'Are you sure?'

I nodded, my heart racing. It might have been over twenty years since I last heard it, but it's hard to forget your only husband's voice. For a brief moment I was transported back to feeling like the naïve young girl, desperate for a home and family of her own, who had been agonisingly in love with a handsome, charming older man . . .

'Sophy, *darling,*' he said, his voice going all furry and warm, 'I've found you at last! I can hardly believe it!'

He couldn't believe it? My heart stopped pounding and the power of speech returned with a rush.

'What on earth do you mean, Rory Lang, you've *found* me at last? You could have done that any time you wanted to these last twenty-two years. Where the hell have you been?'

'I had a bit of a breakdown—'

'So did our marriage!' I snapped.

'I couldn't help it,' he said in an aggrieved tone. 'I was actually quite ill – hardly knew what I was doing. And afterwards I went abroad. I've been running a diving school in the Caribbean, but please believe me when I say that every time I came home, I searched for you.'

'Lying bastard!' muttered Anya, who now had her dreadlocked head pressed to the other side of the phone and was scowling horribly.

'You can't have searched very hard, because your cousin at the castle would have told you where I was. I wrote to her after Lucy was born.'

'Lucy?' he echoed.

'You haven't forgotten I was expecting a baby when you did a runner?'

'Of course not, I just didn't know that you'd had a girl or what you'd called her – and my cousin never told me she knew where you were. And I truly *did* search for you every time I came back, but with no success at all until I happened to see your picture in the paper recently.'

Anya, who had known him during our whirlwind courtship and the few brief weeks of our married life afterwards, couldn't contain herself any longer and snatched the phone from my hand.

'You lying louse! You abandoned Sophy and the baby totally, and *never* tried to find them until now. If you'd really wanted to, you know very well that all you had to do was go to the commune and my mother would have told you where she was. You're only getting in touch now because you think there's something in it for you.'

'Who is that?' he demanded sharply. 'Put Sophy back on the line.'

'It's Anya. Remember me? I remember *you* all right.'

I removed the phone from her grasp. 'Look, Rory, Anya's right, you could have found me and Lucy any time you wanted to. I don't know why you've decided to contact me now, but we're divorced, nothing to do with each other.'

300

'*I* never agreed to a divorce.'

'You weren't there to ask, were you? And you didn't have to agree, because I divorced you for desertion. So we've nothing to say to each other and—'

'My daughter! I have a right to see my daughter,' he said hastily.

'Then you'll have to travel a long way. She's in Japan,' I snapped, and put the phone down, my legs going trembly. His voice had all the persuasive charm I remembered – much like Jack's, which made me think that maybe Anya was right and I have a history of falling for smooth-tongued snakes . . . though actually, Jack hadn't done anything *terribly* dreadful other than try to trick me into selling Winter's End at a reduced price.

I dialled Mr Yatton. 'That *was* my ex-husband, but if he phones again, I'm not home.'

'Very well,' he agreed, obviously bursting with curiosity but too well-mannered to say anything. But neither Anya nor I thought that Rory would phone again now that he had opportunistically dipped his toe in the water and found it too hot for comfort.

By the time we'd talked it out and then spent another hour or two finishing cleaning the cupboard, and carefully washing and drying the remains of several very pretty old dinner services, I was quite calm again.

We both had to go and shower off the filth afterwards – it's a wonder I haven't washed myself away since I came here. But then, I suppose if it weren't for all the activity, the good food would have made me the size of a hippo by now.

I did mention salads to Mrs Lark once, but she pointed out that they were not in season, in a very final way, so I expect they will make their appearance in spring when it is too late to save my figure.

* * *

301

After dinner Seth drove me, Anya and (not altogether to my surprise) Mike over to the village of Middlemoss, where they always have a large bonfire, though they have the strange tradition of burning Oliver Cromwell instead of Guy Fawkes.

In fact, from what Seth was telling us on the way over, they have their own rather odd way of doing *everything* in Middlemoss, including performing a weird-sounding mystery play every New Year.

There would be a charity snack stall and, as our contribution, Mrs Lark had made two trays of black treacle toffee, which Jonah smashed to bits with a little metal hammer and put in greaseproof paper cones, though we all sneakily ate some of it on the way over. I suspect we had black teeth afterwards, but luckily it was too dark to tell.

When we got there we handed over what was left of it and then all got hot punch or coffee and roast chestnuts. Anya and Mike wandered off together after a while but, knowing no one else, I stuck to Seth's side.

He seemed to know lots of people there, especially women . . . or maybe they were just smiling at him because he looked devilishly impressive in the firelight, all tall, dark and brooding? But he had competition – there was another tall, dark man there who was pretty tasty too.

He knew Seth and came over to speak to us, and it turned out he was Nick Pharamond, one of the family from the local big house. He told Seth that his wife hadn't come because she had gone right off fireworks after a nasty incident.

A few minutes later I knew just how she felt, because a particularly loud bang seemed to set off a sort of chain reaction in my head and I grabbed Seth's arm excitedly. 'I've just remembered something about the day I had the accident. As I went into the summerhouse I could smell perfume and—'

302

I stopped dead, because there was only one woman I knew who wore that particular combination of hot horse and Arpège.

Seth was looking down at me, frowning. 'Are you sure?'

'Yes . . . or at least, I think I am. But perhaps I imagined it, and it doesn't get us any further anyway, does it?' I said hastily. 'Forget it!'

I found I was still holding on to his arm and he'd put one of his large hands over mine in a very comforting sort of way. 'If I knew who did it . . .' he began menacingly, but the rest was perhaps fortunately drowned out by a series of loud flashes and bangs.

'I think that was the grand finale,' Anya said, appearing out of the darkness with her knitted hat jammed down right over her dreadlocks and her coat collar turned up, Mike right behind her. 'We're a bit sticky because we've been eating candyfloss – that's not something you usually get at bonfire parties, is it?'

'It is in Middlemoss,' Seth said, and then suggested we all call in at the Green Man on the way home. He entirely forgot to let go of my hand until we got back to the car, but I expect his mind was on something else, like one of his infernal knots.

It occurred to me suddenly, right out of the blue, that I'd had more fun since I got to Winter's End than I had done in the last twenty years, precious moments with Lucy excepted.

We were late getting back to Winter's End. The fire in the Great Hall was banked down, with the guard in front of it, Charlie was snoozing in his basket in the kitchen and Aunt Hebe and the Larks long gone to bed.

I'd left my phone behind again and missed three calls from Jack. I hoped he'd given up for the evening, but no, he called again just as I was climbing into bed, which was really annoying because I'd plugged the mobile into the charger on the other side of the room.

'Sophy? Where've you been?' he demanded.

'Out celebrating Bonfire Night. My friend Anya's staying here for a couple of days and we drove over to Middlemoss with Seth and Mike – do you know Mike? He's the local bobby.'

'No,' he said shortly.

'We had a great time. But funnily enough, it seemed to kick-start my memory, and I remembered something I'd noticed, just before my accident in the summerhouse.'

'Oh? Well, it wasn't *me* lurking about in the undergrowth, darling.'

'I know that, it was nothing to do with you – unless you've started wearing Arpège perfume, that is?'

He sighed. 'Mel? Actually, I suspected as much, though I'm sure she didn't mean you any real harm.'

'But why would she want to hurt me at all?' I asked, trying to imagine the elegant Mel being that vindictive . . . which actually wasn't hard.

'Because she's jealous of you, of course.'

'Jealous of *me*?'

'Yes, because of Seth. She's crazy about him, and not only did she find him in a clinch with you in the Great Hall that time, he also seems to be spending more and more time with you. Like tonight, for instance,' he added smoothly.

'Me and two other people! And Seth's not interested in me that way, so she has no reason to feel jealous.'

'Perhaps if you weren't seen out and about with him so much . . . ?' he suggested.

'He's my head gardener – of course I'm going to be seen with him! *And* he's family. But the point is, she could have killed me, and she might have hurt Charlie too. It was sheer luck he was OK!'

'I'm sure she didn't mean anything except to give you a warning scare,' he said easily. 'She thinks you're invading her territory.'

'Oh, yes? And this would be the woman I saw snogging you in the shrubbery when you came here for lunch recently?'

There was a small pause. 'Oh, come on, darling, that was nothing! Mel still likes to think she could get me back if she wanted to, though I've made it clear that I'm only interested in you. That's annoyed her, but not half as much as thinking you're moving in on Seth too.'

'Well, I'm not,' I said shortly.

'I'm glad to hear that,' he said softly. 'It seems ages since I saw you, but I'll be down for Christmas, of course, and I'm looking forward to spending lots of time with you then – *and* afterwards, because I have an invitation to pass on to you.'

'An invitation? For me?'

'Yes, I always go out to Barbados to stay with friends the day after Boxing Day, and when I told them about you, they said they would love to have you too.'

'What, *me*? The Caribbean?' I exclaimed, all tiredness suddenly dispelled by thoughts of coral beaches and palm trees.

'Yes, you!' He sounded amused. 'I assume you've got a passport?'

'Well, yes, I won a weekend in Paris a few years ago. But—'

'We'll have a great time, Sophy, and really have a chance to get to know one another – three weeks in paradise. They have a lovely house with a pool, and we'll go snorkelling and water ski. And they throw wonderful parties – everyone comes, you'll love it. It'll be romantic, too . . . imagine you and me in the evenings, walking along a coral beach.'

'But, Jack, I can't possibly go away after Christmas,' I said blankly, 'there's too much to do organising everything in time for the Valentine's Day opening, for a start!'

'Oh, come on, Sophy, it'll be much more fun than playing Lady of the Manor! It's time you scrapped these mad ideas and let me take care of all your worries. I promise you, you'll feel totally differently by the time we get back from Barbados.'

'I'm not the one with mad ideas, *you* are!' I snapped, now wide-awake but exhausted enough after an eventful day to be ratty. 'I won't feel differently because I'm not going to Barbados – I'm enjoying planning everything here at Winter's End and there's loads to do.'

'Check your passport is still current, darling,' he said, blithely ignoring most of what I'd just said, 'because I'm very sure I can change your mind over Christmas!'

I said something so rude that Aunt Hebe would have been scrubbing my mouth out with disinfectant, but it was too late – he'd gone. I had to content myself with waking Anya up and pouring what he'd said, word for word, into her reluctant ears.

I was *so* going to miss her when she left next day – and I was already missing Alys, who hadn't seemed to have been around lately. Perhaps she'd return when I was alone?

Heading back down the dimly lit corridor to my bedroom, I whispered experimentally: 'And where was my guardian angel when the summerhouse fell on me, Alys?' but there was no reply, not even a chill breeze round the extremities.

Chapter Twenty-eight: Vixens

Sir Ralph came to mee and said his conscience was sore troubled, as well it might be, but begged mee not to tell the truth in the matter of his hiding the priest, since it would bring disaster upon the house. I told him I would not, for my child's sake, but nor would I admit to practising the dark arts for the same reason. Then I began to cough and could not stop, to his alarm, for I have the same malady that affected my husband and the days of my life would soon run through my fingers like sand even were I not imprisoned here.

From the journal of Alys Blezzard, 1582

I awoke one morning to find a fluffy white blanket over the landscape, and after breakfast I went out to the top terrace to admire my very own winter wonderland.

Below, with his broad back to me, stood Seth, brooding over the fact that he would get no work on the terrace done that day.

It was just too much to resist . . .

My first snowball landed with a *flump!* right between his shoulder blades and the second skimmed the top of his dark head. Then I dodged down behind the balustrade, but too late – he'd seen me.

'Come out, Sophy! I know it's you,' he called up.

I should have had better sense than to stand up, because I was instantly almost knocked off my feet by his return shot. Snow got in my hood and melted, trickling icily down my back.

He was grinned triumphantly.

'I'll get you for that, Seth Greenwood!' I yelled, and for the next few minutes we pelted each other, though since I was higher up I think I had the advantage . . . though maybe he was the better shot.

Anyway, honours were about even by the time Aunt Hebe popped her head out of the door and demanded to know what on earth I was doing.

'Nothing,' I replied innocently, just as a parting shot from below almost propelled me into her arms.

I just hoped Seth was as cold and wet as I was.

'Your voice sounds odd,' Anya said, ringing me from somewhere near Coventry, where she was doing a Christmas craft fair. 'Where are you?'

'I *was* inside a packing crate,' I said, picking bits of straw and polystyrene beads out of my hair. 'Lady Betty's legacy has arrived, and it's rather large, to say the least.'

'What's she left you?'

'It looks like a stone statue of a hippopotamus.' I glanced at the head, which was the only bit unwrapped, and it looked back in a fairly amiable way. 'There were at least two Egyptian gods who sometimes appeared in that form, but if it looks pregnant when I've unpacked it, then it's Tawaret. I don't know if it's really old or not. It looks pretty authentic, but a lot of her collection was fake. She had no eye for antiquities at all.'

'Have you decided where you're going to put it?'

'Yes, there's an empty alcove in the Long Room and I've already moved two ushabti from the parlour up there, so

I can have an Egyptian antiquities corner. It's so big that it's going to take all the gardeners, including Seth, to carry it upstairs. But it shouldn't take long, so I don't think he'll mind *very* much.'

'Oh, the Gorgeous Gardener might protest a lot, but I suspect he's really putty in your hands, Sophy.'

'Don't be daft,' I said, amazed. 'I have to fight him over every little thing. He might be putty in *someone's* hands, but they're certainly not mine. Are you doing well at the craft fairs?'

'Fine. I'm hoping to be sold out by Christmas. How are things your end?'

'We've had a cold snap and it snowed. The garden looks so magical that Mr Yatton's taken lots of photographs and we're going to use one or two for postcards. He and Lucy are currently sourcing stock for the shop on the internet – you know, the sort of place who will print what we want on everything. When I told Lucy you and Guy were going to be here for Christmas I could tell she was dying to come home – but no, she has to be Little Miss Honourable and stick it out to the end of her contract.'

'That's Lucy for you,' Anya commiserated, 'though it would have been lovely to see her again, of course. Have you had time to do any more to the shop and tearoom?'

'Yes, Grace helped me to clean the place out and I've bought the material for the curtains and chair cushions – bright red gingham in a big check – which someone in the village is going to make up. Mr Yatton found me a supplier of a matching PVC table covering by the metre on the internet, but we can cut that to fit the tables ourselves. I'll get the electrician in to install a couple more electric sockets and better lighting later, when the Herring painting is sold and I've got a bit of money. I simply daren't do anything expensive at the moment.'

'Well, that's a start,' she agreed. 'You've been pretty busy!'

'I don't think I'm going to do much more to it before the New Year, except hijack Bob and Hal to paint the rooms when Seth isn't looking – not that there's a huge amount to do in a garden at this time of year anyway. But I need to keep him sweet because he's designing the new garden guide and helping me put the last touches to the guidebook. They're almost ready to go to press.'

'He's worth his weight in visitor tickets, that man. You need to hang on to him,' Anya said. 'And you're not even paying him anything!'

'Actually, I'd arrived at much the same conclusion myself,' I confessed, 'though if he comes with Mel permanently attached, the price of having him around might be too high.'

'Perhaps he's got over her now, like a fever?' she suggested optimistically. 'I mean, you said you'd never seen them out together?'

'No, but I see her car, or her horse, near the lodge and in the grounds often enough. She haunts the place when he's here.'

'Maybe, but could you see her living in the lodge, a gardener's wife?'

'No . . . actually, I couldn't.'

'Or Seth wanting to live anywhere except Winter's End?'

'Not really, but it would depend how mad about her he was, wouldn't it? He might be prepared to make the ultimate sacrifice, but we will just have to wait and see.'

'Mike's been keeping in touch,' Anya said casually. 'He phones me for a chat every now and then. His parents originally came from Antigua in the Caribbean and he's hoping to go there on holiday next year. It sounds like paradise!'

Although she deserved to be teased after her comments about Seth, I nobly restrained myself. Mike is very nice, and if something comes of their obvious attraction to each other, it will be another anchor to keep her living near me, which would be lovely.

In fact, everything seemed to be coming together in a very fortuitous way, like a preordained pattern, even if Jack did so far seem incapable of understanding that I was no longer even remotely romantically interested in him.

It's a pity I was all over him like a rash that time he kissed me, or he might have been easier to convince.

But luckily he was still too preoccupied with business to do more than drop by occasionally, and even his late-night phone calls had a rushed air, as if he was always about to dash off and clinch another deal.

Perhaps, if he ever was really attracted to me, I was losing my charm.

It took all four gardeners to get the heavy statue upstairs, with Jonah supervising the operation, though luckily that didn't impede them much.

'What did you say it was?' Seth asked, panting, when it was finally manoeuvred into place.

'It's an Egyptian goddess, Tawaret – she's often depicted as a pregnant hippo standing upright. But maybe it's just fat, in which case it could be *you*.'

'*Me?*' He looked at me as if I had run mad. 'You think I look like a hippo? And I'm *not* fat,' he added with wounded male pride, casting a glance down at his torso, as if he feared his six-pack had suddenly turned into a beer barrel.

'I never said you were, and you don't look anything like a hippo. But the evil brother of Osiris was called Seth or Set, so this could have been your namesake.'

He patted Tawaret on the head. 'I think this one is female, all right.'

'Careful – she's a bit of a fertility symbol,' I warned.

'I think I'm unlikely to get pregnant, Sophy,' he said mildly.

Bob and Hal were grinning and nudging each other until he said, 'Come on, we've wasted enough time – back to work. There's plenty to do.'

'Mrs Lark's been making Chelsea buns this morning; they should be out of the oven by now,' Jonah hinted.

'Go out by way of the kitchen and ask for some to take with you,' I said hastily, seeing Seth's face darkening.

In his own way, he is as driven as Jack. Or me, come to that. I'm pretty single-minded in my determination to make the house beautiful again and paying its way.

Ottie returned from Cornwall via London, where according to Seth she was arranging for a major retrospective exhibition next year and catching up with her friends.

She was preceded a couple of days earlier by a van bearing the unfinished model for *The Spirit of the Garden* sculpture she is making for Winter's End, wrapped in damp sacking.

It was good to have her back again, though once she had admired the changes I had made to the house and seen the progress of the Shakespeare garden, she retired to her studio to work on the sculpture. I could see her at all hours of the day and night when I was passing through the courtyard, working away in one of her oversized, checked lumberjack shirts.

I think I am starting to feel much as Grandfather did about having all the family around me, and though some of them are more annoying than others, I have grown to love them anyway.

Another strand in the fabric of Winter's End was strengthened when the cleaned painting of Alys came back, too. It wasn't a good painting – in fact, it was a very bad one – but without the dark coating of dirt and old varnish I could see that the artist had managed to catch something sad and secretive about her eyes – though I would love to know what Alys thought of the pursed rosebud lips, which she had never possessed, and the simper. But apart from that bit of artistic licence, it was a fairly faithful, if un-inspired, catalogue of her features. Dark curls lay on the young girl's long white neck, and her neat nose had the hint of a tilt at the end, just like mine. For the first time I could see that I looked very like her – or how she would have looked, had she lived to my age. After being for so long the atypical dark Winter, I suddenly felt a renewed sense of belonging. Alys's blood ran in my veins and the two opposing strains of Blezzard and Winter were forever united there.

Maybe *I* should wear a pentacle and a cross, like Aunt Hebe, to symbolise this strange union?

One afternoon in December I was sitting contentedly on the bottom step of the flight of stairs down to the lower terrace, watching Derek and Hal lay a herringbone path in Tudor bricks along the new border in front of the rebuilt wall. The weather had taken a slightly milder turn, but it was still chilly. The freshly dug beds were dotted with pots of shrubs ready to plant out and larger, container-grown trees stood about as if simply dropped from the skies. But I knew there was method in this seeming randomness, because I'd seen Seth's planting scheme.

He'd already marked out the central knot before I got there and was now measuring and laying out the designs for two smaller ones at either end, using some kind of red spray. From where I was sitting it looked a bit like a sten-cilled, boxy Christmas cracker.

When he'd finished Seth came and sat on the step next to me. 'You'll get piles, sitting on cold stone,' he said mildly.

'That's an old wives' tale, like the one that says eating

too much sugar gives you worms. Yuk! Anyway, *you're* doing it too.'

We sat there in amicable silence for a moment or two, contemplating the terrace. 'It's odd how suddenly it's all starting to come together,' I mused. 'Now I can imagine what it will be like once it has all settled and grown a bit – but I suppose you could see that in your head right from the start?'

'Yes, though it's changed a bit as we go along. Using that pile of weathered old bricks from behind the pigsties for the path will give it a settled look instantly and then when we put the gravel down, the pattern of the knots will be more defined until the edging shrubs grow together.'

'Didn't you tell me they used several different colours of gravel in the late sixteenth century?'

'Yes, but I'm sticking to one throughout here, because we've already got the contrast between the bricks and the wall, and it all has to blend together. We'll plant up the compartments inside the knots later with flowering plants popular at the time.'

Now I was starting to see it coming to life and colour too. 'Where are you putting the big topiary trees?'

'The pyramid yews are for either end of the terrace and the holly balls for the corners of the central knot. I've got a large spiral for the middle that I've been nurturing for years – but then, topiary takes time. It's the wrong time of year to do all this, but to be ready by next year, we have to push on when we can.'

'It should look pretty good by Valentine's Day, and absolutely *amazing* by the time we open for the season at Easter,' I said optimistically.

'The major work will certainly be finished by February, so when Derek takes over as head gardener he should be able to keep the place up with just Hal and Bob's help.'

Startled, I turned to look at him, but he was gazing off across the valley. 'Why, where are *you* going?'

'Well, you won't want me once it's finished, will you?' he said diffidently. 'I know you're just letting me stay on to complete the scheme.'

I stared at him, astonished – until I remembered that that was pretty much what I *had* thought at first . . . It seemed a long time ago. 'But Seth, I don't want you to leave!' I exclaimed. 'You're family, for one thing, and you *belong* here.'

'I'm only family by marriage, not related at all, really.'

'You *feel* like family.'

'Do I?' He gave me one of his more unfathomable looks.

'Yes, and you have a stake in the garden too. You know you love it.'

'Yes, of course, but—'

'Look, Seth, do you *want* to go?'

'Well, no . . . but—'

'If it suits you to stay here as before, then that's fine by me. I *really* don't want to lose you.' I found I was gripping his arm as if I could hold him at Winter's End by force, and snatched it away, going a bit pink. 'Free gardeners don't grow on trees,' I finished lightly.

'That's what Ottie says, and that the arrangement seems to suit both of us. Have you seen that sculpture yet, the one we're suppose to fit into the garden? I don't know where she thinks we're going to put it!'

'I thought we'd decided on the rose garden. And do you think I should go and look at it? I thought she might not want me to see it until it's finished.'

'She won't mind. In fact, she may not even notice you're there.'

'She *does* seem pretty engrossed – Jonah takes her dinner across to the studio to her every night. The lights seem to

315

be on in the studio day and night, so she must have a very extreme work ethic – or maybe a work addiction.'

'Yes, you can't say she isn't focused.'

'Every time I pass, there she is working away – wearing one of those enormous lumberjack shirts too. She's so elegant, they seem an odd choice of overall.'

'They were my father's,' Seth said shortly. 'I think she's practically worn them to death.'

'Really? I think that's very touching.'

'I suppose it is. They were pretty wrapped up in each other, though my father's passion was the garden and Ottie's her sculpture. I suppose it equalised out.'

'So where did you fit into the scheme of things?'

'Around the edges, mostly. Ottie was always kind to me, and my father loved me in his own way, but neither of them was very good with children. Things got better once I was older.'

'I always longed to be part of a large family,' I confessed, 'or at least to get back to the feeling of family I'd had when I lived here. Of course there was the commune in Scotland, but that felt more like belonging to a tribe. And then, when I did come back here, I found Jack had taken over the place I once had and I was *horribly* jealous.'

'Natural.'

'I suppose so and now I know Jack I don't really mind quite so much, because I'm fond of him too.'

He got to his feet and looked inscrutably down at me. 'Yes, you are, aren't you?'

'It was lovely to find I had a relative I didn't know about,' I explained. 'Oh, well, I'd better go and get on. Mr Yatton has drawn up a list of all the children who will be coming to the party on Christmas Eve, so I'm going to go and buy presents for Father Christmas to hand out. I suppose I'd better get some spares, too.'

'And I'd better get back to work.'

'Yes . . . Seth, there aren't any box trees down here, are there?' I asked tentatively, because something had been puzzling me.

'I was moving a couple of container box spirals on the top terrace earlier – do I reek of it?'

'Yes, you do rather,' I said with a grin. 'It's not the nicest of smells, though you may attract the odd vixen.'

'You can say that again,' he said obscurely, then went off to admire Derek's bricklaying while I took my frozen and numb bottom back to the house.

Later, I did what I had been longing to do and went over to the studio. I could see Ottie standing in her usual contemplative pose in front of the sculpture, back towards me, so I tapped gently on the glass door before opening it.

'Hi, can I come in? I don't want to disturb you,' I said cautiously, though my eyes were irresistibly drawn to the large shape beyond her

'That's all right,' she said, turning and refocusing her bright blue eyes on me with, it seemed, an effort. 'I was just about to make a cup of tea. Want one?'

'Yes, please, but really I wanted to see how the garden sculpture was coming on, if you don't mind?'

'Look all you like – and there's the maquette; that will give you more idea of how the finished thing will look.' She pointed out a small model on the work surface, then plugged in a clay-smeared kettle and got out a battered tin tea caddy decorated with a portrait of Charles and Di on their wedding day.

I looked from the sculpture to the model . . . and back again. There seemed to be a face, half-animal, half-human, at the heart of it, amid a whirlwind of spiky wings – the Spirit of the Garden, presumably? It was masculine and vaguely familiar . . .

317

Then I got it.

'It's Seth – and he looks like a lion exploding out of a spiky horse chestnut casing!' I said without thinking, but Ottie just grinned and said that that was it in a nutshell.

The tea was Earl Grey, just as it came out of the pot, but after some rummaging about she produced a box of gingernut biscuits, and proceeded to dunk hers.

'I'll be sending *The Spirit* away to be cast soon. Have you decided where to put it, yet?'

'Yes, I thought it might make a good focal point in the rose garden,' I said, following suit and dunking my biscuit. Ginger and Earl Grey make an interesting combination. 'What do you think?'

'That should brighten it up a bit. I find roses so boring. They stand about looking hostile and thorny for months and then suddenly decide to have masses of flowers.'

'I think Hebe would find that idea practically heresy.'

'So would my husband have done too. You know, I thought Seth would want to hide the sculpture away in the wilderness or in the trees on the other side of the valley: he's such a traditionalist.'

'But the rose garden is new; there's no reason why it shouldn't fit there very well. We've planted lots more roses too and winter-flowering hellebores – Christmas roses – so it won't look quite as bare as you remembered.'

'Speaking of hellebores,' she said obscurely, 'are you still managing to resist Jack's untrustworthy but not inconsiderable charms? You had me quite worried at first and Seth is *still* convinced you're in love with him.'

'Then Seth's wrong!' I snapped, nettled. 'I admit I *did* fall for Jack, and I'm still very fond of him, but in a sisterly sort of way. I've tried to tell him, but he's very . . .'

'Vain? Overconfident? Won't take no for an answer?'

I laughed. 'Well, yes – all of those! I keep thinking that

318

I've finally got through to him how I feel, and also convince him that I'm here to stay at Winter's End, and then the next minute he bounces right back again.'

'So you're not even going to share it with him, married, partnership, or otherwise? Good,' she said with satisfaction, 'because although he's a charming rogue and I'm quite fond of him, he's not good for Winter's End – or you.'

'Seth should stop worrying about *my* love life and think about his own,' I said darkly, his remark still rankling. 'I wouldn't trust Mel as far as I could throw her!'

'Ah, yes – Mel. From what I hear she does seem to have been at Winter's End rather a lot while I've been away.'

'She has, but not up at the house,' I said pointedly, not mentioning the one occasion when she had called in and found Seth and me in a slightly compromising-looking position. 'But she's so beautiful it is hardly surprising if he's fallen for her all over again – and she's a rich widow now, so I suppose that's an added attraction.'

'Not to Seth. He's never been interested in money. Jack's the one who ought to find that irresistibly attractive.'

'But Jack says it's Seth she's mad about . . . though actually, I did see Jack and Mel kissing in the shrubbery once, which made me wonder if he was being entirely truthful.'

'Hmm . . . well, I heard some odd rumours when I was in London and I don't think Mel's husband *did* leave her as well off as everyone assumes. It would make sense, because we were all surprised when she moved back to live with her mother. She picked up with Seth again, then when Jack turned up made a dead set at him, probably because she knew he had money and thought he was William's heir. But then suddenly it was all off and she was all over Seth again.' She shook her head. 'But I'm sure he's got her measure. He knows she'll only marry someone rich, however fascinated by him she is.'

'She seems pretty cold-blooded. I hope Seth knows what he's doing.'

'He hasn't been pining away for love of her all these years, you know. I'm sure he quickly realised he already had everything he wanted right here at Winter's End, just as his father did.'

'So have I,' I said, absently gazing at the sculpture.

'I think it's time I told you the last family secret,' Ottie said abruptly – and did so.

When she'd finished I stared at her. 'You can't be serious!' I said, and broke into a peal of laughter. Hyenas had nothing on me. I think Ottie was a bit put out.

Chapter Twenty-nine: Battle Positions

Sir Ralph came again. I see he now believes that his wife's jealous imaginings were no more than the truth, and is afraid of mee. I told him he must swear that my carved oak chest and all it contains should go to my daughter, and none other should have it. If he did not do this, I would curse him through eternity. He said it would be done.

From the journal of Alys Blezzard, 1582

Once I'd turned the family secret over in my head for a while, it occurred to me that, true or not (and how could it *possibly* be true?) it would make for absolutely marvellous publicity!

Releasing a story like this just before the opening season would hugely increase visitor numbers and could make all the difference between financial success and simply making ends meet.

And even if the story *is* apocryphal – well, lots of families have their legends, don't they? It's only when people start researching their family history and discover that actually Uncle Bernard had never even set foot in a rowing boat, let alone gone down with the *Titanic* while playing 'Nearer, my God, to Thee', that the boring truth is revealed.

Unfortunately, Ottie was adamant that the secret be kept

clutched fast to our bosoms for ever, and a fat lot of good it would do Winter's End like that.

It was frustrating not being able to talk it through with anyone else, but Hebe couldn't be trusted not to tell Jack and I didn't like to discuss it with Lucy over the phone.

I still think the revelation was the funniest thing I'd heard for ages, and somehow the person I most wanted to share it with was Seth, who unfortunately, being a mere man, was forever to be excluded from knowing about our dramatic little skeleton in the family cupboard.

I was still mulling it all over a few days later, but a worrying feeling that something threatening was about to happen had started to distract me from it a bit.

I hoped Mel wasn't planning any more little booby traps – even though Jack assured me he had had it out with her and she had contritely said that she couldn't believe she could have done anything so spiteful and potentially dangerous.

Neither could I – an apology might have been nice.

But it turned out that the gathering shadows threatened Lucy, and when she phoned me up I knew something was wrong the moment I heard her voice.

'Mum, I'm coming home, and so is Kate,' she said abruptly. Kate is the girl she had been sharing a room with, and they had become good friends.

'What, straight away? But has something happened? Are you both all right?'

'Yes, we're fine, Mum – calm down,' she said, though sounding strained. 'We've just had a bit of a scare, that's all, and it's really spooked Kate. She wants to get the first plane out and I don't fancy staying here without her.'

'You'd better tell me what's happened.'

'You know I said the geek following me was just shy, and really he only wanted me to give him extra English conversation lessons? Well, his friend asked Kate too, and since they seemed harmless she persuaded me we should do it together, for some extra money.'

'Oh, Lucy!'

'Come on, Mum, we weren't mad enough to agree to go to a house or anything like that, just meet after work at a nearby café. And at first it was OK, they bought us coffee and said they wanted to chat to improve their English conversation. But then, when Kate went to the loo, I saw the other man put something in her drink, so when she came back I just made some excuse and got us out of there, fast. They followed us out, so we ran all the way back to our digs.'

'But that's terrible! Lucy, what if you hadn't noticed, or you'd both gone to the loo or—'

'Well, we wouldn't,' she said bluntly. 'We always watch each other's drinks or take them with us, and that would have seemed odd with a cup of coffee.'

'Did you report them to the police?'

'No. I mean, how could we? It would be just my word against theirs. I'd no proof. And we are fine, just a bit shaken, especially since they trailed us back and hung around outside for ages. Kate got hysterical and phoned home, and her father told her to get on the next plane, which was easier said than done. I managed to get us two seats eventually, but it's so near Christmas it was a miracle.'

'Thank God,' I said devoutly. 'So, when do you get here?'

'The early hours of the day before Christmas Eve. Kate's family will pick her up in London, but I've booked a connecting flight to Liverpool. Do you think you could meet me, or will you be too busy? It's the Winter's End staff Christmas party the next day, isn't it? I can get a taxi.'

'I *should* really be here . . . but I'd much, much rather come and meet you. Look, leave it with me and I'll sort something out. But I'm so glad you're both coming home. I think it's the sensible thing to do. You will be careful before then, won't you?'

'Kate's such a nervous wreck she doesn't even want to leave the building, but we're going out later with a whole bunch of friends to do some Christmas shopping and have a leaving party – but we're all staying together, don't worry.'

Of course I was worried, but so glad she was coming back! And when I found Seth wolfishly devouring roast beef and horseradish sandwiches in the kitchen later, he offered to drive me to the airport to collect her. This was really kind of him, because I didn't know the way there and was likely to be too nervous and excited to concentrate.

'I think I'll turn my mum's old room into Lucy's. Did you know it hasn't been touched since she ran away, all those years ago? Grandfather wouldn't have it changed in any way, which is quite touching, but now it's time the ghosts were banished and maybe all the rosebuds too. Lucy isn't a terribly *girly* girl, if you know what I mean.'

'I'm starting to get some idea,' he agreed.

'Only there isn't much time between now and Christmas, and I'd like to paint the walls and perhaps move the furniture . . .' I looked hopefully at him.

'*I'll* come in and help you – you leave Hal and Bob alone!'

And he did too. I packed one small trunk of Mum's things for the attic and the rest I sent to a charity shop. We flung open the windows to let out the last ghost of patchouli and let in the chilly, cleansing air, while obliterating trellised rosebuds with two shades of light mulberry emulsion paint.

I had a shopping expedition to St Helens and bought some new fixtures and fittings for the room, then we carried down her boxes of belongings from the attic, so she could unpack and rearrange as she wanted.

When we'd finished it looked lovely and my excitement

must have been contagious, because I even caught Aunt Hebe putting two Coalport potpourri holders full of dried rose petals on the bedroom mantelpiece, as her contribution to the welcome.

Luckily, Lucy had asked me not to send her Christmas presents out there, but save them for when she came home. Now I would be able to make her a Christmas stocking too . . . and maybe one for Guy. Is anyone ever too old for a Christmas stocking?

Ghosts banished, the room remembered only the happy hours and, having had a memory like a particularly happy and spaced-out goldfish, I expect my mother had had a lot of those.

It was a bumper mistletoe harvest this year, and for a few days it was all hands to the packing station in one of the big greenhouses, while Mrs Lark came in and out with sandwiches and hot soup.

Jonah, as was apparently the tradition, spent a day down at the lodge selling bunches of it at the gate, and some of it went to local suppliers, but most was dispatched down to London where it would fetch the best price.

It was odd to think that Winter's End mistletoe would be adorning houses all over the south of England this Christmas – and, since it is lucrative, be helping to support the estate too!

There was still plenty left growing wild up in the woods for decorating the house, and also plenty of holly with bright red berries – the sign, usually, of a hard winter, though we'd only had a couple of cold snaps so far.

'Thank you for the Christmas present, Anya,' I said. 'What possessed you, you idiot?'

She giggled down the phone. 'I know someone who

breeds peacocks and they seemed just the thing for Winter's End. Did they get there OK?'

'Yes, your friend brought them in a crate on the back of a pick-up, just after Sunday lunch and when Jonah told us there was a delivery of birds we all went out to look. I was just grateful they weren't flamingos or macaws or something! It's lucky I like that sort of plaintive scream they make!'

'What did Seth think?'

'He wasn't too pleased at first, because he said they would make a mess in the garden, but Hebe was surprisingly keen. She had the gardeners wheel the crate round to an empty run in the walled garden until they settle down, and says she will feed them with the hens. She's named them, too.'

'What?'

'Fanny and Johnnie after the Cradocks who used to do cookery shows on TV. Apparently the inspiration was Ottie saying that the male peacock looked henpecked.'

'Nice. I look forward to meeting Fanny and Johnnie at Christmas.'

'Which is practically here. And guess what, Lucy is coming home, after all!' I said, and told her all about it.

Of course she thought it was all arranged by our guardian angels, which I suppose Lucy's might have done, but I'm pretty sure that mine has not left the building, let alone jetted off to Japan. In fact, ever since Ottie did her Last Revelation thing, I have the distinct feeling that whenever I'm in the parlour in the evenings, Alys is trying to tell me something.

Whatever it is, I hope it doesn't take her as long as it took Ottie.

I woke up the day before Christmas Eve more excited than any child on Christmas Day, and all because Lucy was coming home! I just hope she loves Winter's End as much as I do. At least it was now looking its best – warm, clean, inviting and smelling of rich foods and spices because Mrs Lark was cooking up a storm in the kitchen, both for the party tomorrow and Christmas itself.

There was still lots to sort out for the party, but Seth and I had to set out for the airport right after breakfast. I was so glad he was driving, because not only were the roads icy but I was a bundle of nerves, even though I knew everything would be fine once I saw her.

Lucy, looking pale, and with her red-gold hair dishevelled, staggered out onto the airport concourse laden with twice as much baggage as she went with.

She dropped everything and gave me a huge hug. 'Hi, Mum! I'm *sooo* glad to be back – and I'm shattered, haven't slept a wink on the plane. Where have you put the camper?'

'I've brought the estate car instead, and Seth drove me. He's waiting for us in the short-stay car park – come on.'

The cold air woke her enough to give Seth a very serious once-over followed, I was relieved to see, by one of her more delightful smiles.

'Mum's told me all about you, and you're just the way I imagined, only *more* so!'

'Has she? I mean – *am* I?' he replied, startled, and gave me a dubious look. 'Well, you look exactly the way I imagined you would too!'

She nodded. 'I know, apparently I'm a typical Winter and once you've seen one, you've seen them all. Mum, you sit next to Seth,' she ordered, climbing into the back seat. 'Oh – there's a dog in here,' she added, as Charlie woke up and then greeted her like a long-lost friend, all wet tongue and cold nose.

'It's just Charlie. I'd forgotten he'd decided to come with us. Do you want me to have him in the front?'

'No, he's fine,' she said, and next time I turned around they were both curled up together fast asleep.

Seth and I comfortably bickered in low voices all the way home, merely because I'd had the audacity to ask Hal to go into the woods and cut me plenty of holly and mistletoe to decorate the Great Hall, without consulting him first.

I felt unspeakably happy.

When we got back, the Great Hall was half transformed ready for the party. I'd left my CD player up in the minstrels' gallery ready for carols, but Mr Yatton must have put one of his own on, for Handel's 'The Arrival of the Queen of Sheba' was majestically unscrolling itself into the spiced air.

It was strangely appropriate, for as we entered, everyone stopped and formed into a smaller, indoor version of the greeting line I had faced on my arrival: Grace, the Larks – even Ottie, who suddenly appeared as if she had divined by a sixth sense that another Winter had returned, gave Lucy a back-thumping embrace and a muttered, 'Chip off the old block!' before vanishing back to her studio again.

I hoped she would remember to come for dinner, though I might have to send Jonah over to fetch her.

As 'The Queen of Sheba' came to a halt, Aunt Hebe, all in spectral white, drifted silently down the dark stairs. After staring at Lucy intently for a moment, a gaze that Lucy returned in full measure, she embraced her and welcomed her home with much more enthusiasm than she had shown me.

But then, they were as alike as two peas in a pod, except that Aunt Hebe's hair was now white instead of red-gold. Somehow, I got the feeling that Lucy's being a despised female wasn't going to enter into the equation any more . . .

'Well, we'd have known you for a Winter anywhere, young Lucy!' Mrs Lark said, stating the obvious.

'That's right,' agreed Jonah. 'Ho, ho, ho!' he added, in a surprisingly deep bass and Lucy cast me a wide-eyed look.

'Don't worry, he's practising his Father Christmas act for tomorrow's party,' I explained. 'Now, I've told you all about everyone, so you only have to put faces to names. This is Mrs Lark and her husband, Jonah, of course – and this is Grace . . . and here come two of the gardeners, Hal and Bob, with some holly.'

'So I see,' Seth said, and the two gardeners edged behind me.

'Don't be a grump, Seth. I only want them to help Jonah put the holly and mistletoe up, and then they can go back and do whatever it is they're supposed to be doing.'

'Raking the gravel, and Bob's chopping the logs,' Hal said, without noticeable enthusiasm. I'm sure they would much rather be inside because it was literally freezing out there.

'Well, make sure Jonah doesn't go up the ladder. You know what you're like, Jonah, trying to do it all yourself.'

When I turned back, Hebe and my daughter were arm in arm. 'Oh, it's so good to be home!' Lucy said, her eyes shining. She smiled, the mirror image of every Winter I'd ever met, except the one in my mirror – and Alys, of course. 'I'm so happy to be here – home at Winter's End at last.'

The magic seemed to have worked its trick and another piece of the pattern of Winter's End seamlessly fitted into place.

After a while I showed Lucy to her room, which she loved – especially since it had once been her grandmother's – and then gave her a quick tour of the house to get her bearings, finishing by introducing her to Mr Yatton, who was busily doing something or other in the solar.

In fact, I left them there together in the end as they seemed to have so much to discuss, and went back to the Great Hall to help. Seth and Derek had brought in a huge

Christmas tree while Jonah and Bob had gone up to the attics to bring down the boxes of decorations that were stored there.

By the end of the afternoon, when the sky outside was darkening, the hall looked lovely, and Lucy had slotted so seamlessly into place that I'm sure everyone had already forgotten that she hadn't always been there.

But I wasn't jealous, as I had been with Jack, for one day Winter's End would belong to Lucy and I wanted her to love it too.

The Great Hall looked wonderfully festive, festooned with holly, mistletoe and swags of greenery tied with big bows of wide red ribbon, and the tree sparkling in the corner, which we all helped to decorate.

The trestles, covered with festive tablecloths, stood ready to receive the mounds of food already prepared by Mrs Lark. Portmeirion Christmas serving bowls and dishes were lined up the middle for nuts, sweets and nibbles, and a stack of plates and scarlet paper napkins were at one end.

Charlie lay in the centre of the revived rag rug in front of the fire like a dead dog, exhausted by watching all this activity.

A large, hooded porter's chair was dragged forward nearer to the fire and garlanded, ready for Father Christmas, and the presents for the children arranged in piles on the table behind him.

Then it was ready. I felt an air of toe-tingling excitement and expectation that I hadn't felt for . . . well, *ever*, really.

Jack arrived late. I heard the peal of his rather noisy horn while I was showering after having helped Lucy unpack some of her stuff. He was last down in the drawing room too, not excepting Ottie, who had remembered to come only because she had finally completed the sculpture.

Seth wasn't there. I'd invited him, but he'd said he had something else to do, and I had a pretty good idea what *that* meant.

When Jack walked into the drawing room, with his usual air of expecting to see a fatted calf laid on for him, the first thing that met his eyes was Lucy, seated on the sofa with a great-aunt on either side, like triplets. His face was stunned. I had quite forgotten to tell him that Lucy was coming home, and Aunt Hebe mustn't have mentioned it either.

For once she didn't spring to her feet with loud cries of joy at the sight of her beloved boy, just smiled and said, 'Oh, there you are at last, Jack – and here's Lucy!'

He recovered quickly. I think I was the only one to notice that his nose had been put out of joint, just as mine had when I first returned to Winter's End and found him cock of the walk.

'Well, this *is* a surprise,' he said, coming forward to shake hands and then kiss Lucy's cheek.

Lucy summed him up, and then a smile that I knew from experience to mistrust appeared on her lips. 'It's not a surprise to me. Mum's told me all about you and I knew you were coming for Christmas.'

Watching them, it occurred to me that, next to Lucy, Jack didn't look quite as splendid. His hair was just gold, not the precious fine red-gold that hers was, and his blue eyes seemed to lack the true azure depth of Lucy's. They both had the typical Winter high-bridged nose, but in Lucy's case her features were delicately drawn and her skin so translucently white she looked like porcelain.

'How lovely to have the family all together,' Aunt Hebe said as the gong went. 'Oh, no time for a drink first I'm afraid, Jack. We'd better go through.'

He changed course from the drinks cabinet. 'Of course.'

He smiled delightfully. 'And I hope I will be able to sit next to my newest cousin and get to know her better.'

'Actually, you're so much older than me that I think of you more as an uncle,' Lucy said sweetly. 'A great-uncle.'

Battle seemed to have commenced, but I wasn't quite sure that Jack had yet grasped the nature of his adversary. But by the time we'd eaten our way through potted shrimps with French toast and Jonah had brought in the Beef Wellington and glazed carrots, he was starting to get a glimmer of understanding.

Jonah had excelled himself in the paper napkin department tonight: there was a huge central display of red paper roses nestling in green crepe paper holly leaves. I complimented him on it.

'It's very festive. You are clever, Jonah, thank you.'

'There's nothing to roses, I could make them in me sleep. Of course, since that time the kitten ate one and it went through the poor mite's system like a dose of salts—' he began, but Hebe, who had been staring with vague disapproval at the bright scarlet roses, interrupted him.

'Of course!' she exclaimed. '*Roses! That's* what it said in Alys's foreword to her mother's household book – that the secret was at the heart of the rose . . .' She frowned. 'Or maybe the heart of the rose was the secret?' she added doubtfully.

'Hebe!' Ottie snapped. 'Button it!' But the warning had come too late. Jack was staring intently at his aunt, his knife and fork suspended.

'Oh, sorry, Ottie, I didn't mean to just blurt that out,' began Hebe, flustered. 'It's just – well, forget what I said, everyone, it's nothing.'

'Is that what it says – roses?' Jack said eagerly. I saw his eyes dart from the flowers carved along the top of the panelling to those embroidered on the firescreen, and feared

332

he was about to embark on a whole new treasure hunt, fruitless though I knew it would be.

'She only meant the use of roses in the recipes, Jack – don't get excited,' I said soothingly. 'Now, could I help anyone to some more of this lovely beef?'

After dinner we all retired to the drawing room but Lucy's long journey was catching up on her, Ottie was in a state of exhausted euphoria due to having completed the sculpture, and Hebe and I were shattered after the preparations for the party, so we all decided on an early night.

Jack was the only exception. Suspiciously bright-eyed and bushy-tailed, he said he would watch TV in the library for a bit, though as I was going out he kissed me good night and suggested I stay for a little while. 'I've hardly seen anything of you, darling. We haven't had a minute to ourselves since I got here.'

'Sorry, I'm just too tired, Jack – and if I know Lucy, she'll be waiting for me to come up. We've still got a lot of catching up to do.'

'So have *we*,' he said, 'but I suppose we can make up for it tomorrow.'

'Perhaps, but it's going to be even more hectic than today. My friend Anya is arriving early in time for the Friends meeting, and her son, Guy, is coming later. They're both staying for Christmas – did I say?'

'No, you don't seem to have told me anything!'

'Oh, didn't I? I thought I had. Well, anyway, they're staying, and then there's the meeting and the party, and clearing up afterwards – so tomorrow is going to be busy. I'll be really glad of your help, Jack.'

'I don't know why you decided to carry on with these feudal traditions, Sophy. I told William often enough that it was a waste of time and money.'

'I think it's a lovely thing to do, to thank everyone for all their help over the year,' I said. 'Good night!' and I dodged when he would have kissed me again.

Some instinct – or maybe it was Alys's chilly presence making herself felt in the passageway – made me go and lock the door to the parlour before I went upstairs, which is not a thing I normally do.

'You reek of horrible aftershave,' Lucy said disapprovingly when I walked into my room to find her sitting on the bed.

'Actually, it's lovely, but you probably associate it with Lady Betty's repulsive nephew Conor. It's the same one he always wore and it was *entirely* wasted on him. In fact, it seemed to wear Conor, rather than the other way round, while Jack's made it entirely his own – a part of the whole handsome and expensive package.'

'Yeah, right,' she said, sounding unconvinced.

I sniffed the air. 'Have you been at my Elisabethan Rose?'

'No, it's something Aunt Hebe brewed up, but it does smell similar, I admit. She just gave it to me on the way to bed, as an early Christmas present.'

'You're honoured. Now come on,' I said, climbing onto the bed next to her and giving her a hug, 'you tell me your secrets and I'll tell you mine!'

Chapter Thirty: Rival Attractions

Now it is clear that my relatives will not intercede for mee, they have subjected mee to the indignities of searching my person for such places as might suckle an imp or devil and threaten sterner measures should I not confess my wrongdoing and name my accomplices.
From the journal of Alys Blezzard, 1582

Jack was conspicuously *not* his usual bright-eyed and bushy-tailed self at breakfast. In fact, he looked a little wan, which I expect was entirely due to his having spent a large part of the night up and about – as evidenced by his fingerprints all over every carved, engraved, embossed or stuccoed rose in the house.

He can hardly have had time for much sleep after that either, because when Hebe went out this morning she discovered that he must have been in the walled garden at first light with his metal detector, digging holes among the apothecary roses.

She was furious, though when she tore him off a strip, he tried to laugh it off. 'But all I found was a silver threepenny bit and a few bent nails, Hebe. I hardly touched the garden.'

'There are holes all over the place,' she said crossly.

'I'll come and help you fill them in right after breakfast, Aunt Hebe,' Lucy offered, and Jack gave her a dirty look.

Clearly he was out of favour at the moment, though I was sure it wouldn't last very long.

'Don't forget the Friends are coming at ten thirty for the meeting before the party,' I reminded them. 'Anya should be arriving any minute too. I asked her to try and get here in time for it, since she'll be running the tearoom and gift shop end of things.'

'You aren't *still* determined to turn the place into a Shakespeare theme park, are you?' Jack said. 'We agreed you would wait and discuss it with me at Christmas before finalising anything.'

'*Not* a theme park, Jack,' Aunt Hebe said disapprovingly. 'Just opening as we have done for many years now, only with a very tasteful little shop too.'

'Of course Mum is going to open the house to the public next year. It's the best way of generating income to keep the place going,' Lucy said combatively. 'And I'm sure your products will be our best-sellers, Aunt Hebe.'

'Thank you, dear.'

'But it all needs organising *now*; she can't hang about waiting for your input, Jack,' Lucy went on. 'Anyway, I'm sure she's got a lot more experience at running this kind of thing than you have. She did everything at Blackwalls!'

Battle *had* commenced, and I knew who my money was on to win. 'Everything *is* pretty well finalised already,' I agreed. 'It has to be, though the February open day is a sort of dry run, to see how it all goes. Then we can fine-tune it ready for the start of the season at Easter.'

'Mum's got some brilliant ideas to increase visitor numbers.'

'Why don't you come to the Friends meeting, Jack?' I suggested, but he said tersely that he had other things to do and sloped off to his bedroom, probably to catch up on his sleep and sulk.

Hebe and Lucy headed for the walled garden and I helped

Jonah clear away the breakfast things before dashing upstairs to change into a festive red tunic and jingle-bell earrings, because I didn't think I'd have time between the Friends meeting and the party.

I hadn't seen Seth that morning, but when I looked out of my bedroom window he was standing on the middle terrace, looking down at his new knot. I only hoped he wouldn't forget about the party and start messing about with the design, because he wasn't wearing his gardening clothes and also – well, it wouldn't be the same without him looming about the place.

Anya arrived with just enough time to dump her bags in her room and then have a cup of coffee and a slice of pudding cake in the kitchen with the Larks and me. Then Lucy and Aunt Hebe came in, slightly earthy, and joined us.

'We'll have a good catch-up later, Lucy,' Anya said, having given her a rib-crushing hug. 'And Guy is coming shortly too, if he can get that terrible old car of his to start.'

I looked at my watch. 'Come on, it's almost time for the meeting and everyone will be arriving shortly. We'll go into the breakfast parlour, out of Mrs Lark's way.'

'Jonah had better take Gingernut up to our rooms. He keeps getting under my feet and he'll be safer up there,' Mrs Lark said as the kitten made a dive for the hem of her apron. 'And I'll keep Charlie in here when the party starts, so he doesn't get trodden on.'

I was worried about how the Friends would react to my plans, because asking them to voluntarily staff and steward Winter's End for more than twice the number of days next year, and over a longer opening season, was a big ask.

They all came in together and took their seats around the table, which Jonah had extended again by inserting a couple of the leaves. None of the group was young, and some of them already looked familiar, like Mr Yatton's sister, Effie, a spare, wiry woman wearing a tweed skirt and a lilac jumper sewn with pearls, and a pair of elderly men who were so alike they had to be twins. They all cast curious looks at Anya, with her red dreadlocks and nose ring, but Lucy's presence seemed to be not unexpected.

'Welcome to the meeting,' I said nervously. 'I'm afraid I don't know all your names yet, though I hope I soon will. First of all, I'm going to outline my plans for Winter's End and see what you think of them – I'm sure there will be a lot to discuss. But before we start, I'd like you to meet my daughter, Lucy.'

'Hi,' Lucy said, from her seat beside me.

'And my friend, Anya. I've asked Anya to be here because she is going to create a gift shop in part of the tearoom area and will be in overall charge of both operations.'

'You mean, she would run the tearoom too, and be in charge of the money and everything?' Effie asked, and I braced myself for resentment.

'Well, yes, that's the idea. You would be doing the actual catering, of course, but Anya would cash up for you and get change, order stock . . . all that kind of thing.'

'How *wonderful*! That will take a great deal of pressure off you serving wenches, won't it, Pam?' Effie exclaimed, and the others murmured agreement.

Pam, who was a buxom woman with a high colour in her apple cheeks, beamed. 'Oh yes, Effie! I mean, we can take the money and serve the food all right, but when it comes to even adding up the float for next day, we get stuck, let alone totting up the takings!'

This was a good start and they listened to the rest of my plans with interest, seeming fairly enthusiastic about it all – and not terribly surprised. But since they all seemed to be friends of Aunt Hebe, I am sure she had kept them updated on things.

'I intend opening four afternoons a week, so we would be closed from Sunday to Tuesday. I know Sunday would be a good day for visitors, but since so many of the people involved with Winter's End attend church that day, it wouldn't be practical or right. But we *will* open on Bank Holiday Mondays.'

Effie seemed to be the one in charge of the group, arranging the rotas for who did what on which day. It appeared that the Friends liked to do everything in twos, from manning the gatehouse to stewarding the minstrels' gallery. They all like to stick to their particular areas too, though when I said that I proposed having a sort of taxi service from the car park to the front door by golf buggy, for those who had difficulty walking so far, four elderly gentlemen fought a battle over who got to drive it.

'If Winter's End is going to be open four days a week you can take it in turns,' Effie pointed out firmly. 'We always have a few Friends free too,' she said to me, 'so someone can fill in as and when necessary if it is busy, or during tea breaks.'

'Yes – tea breaks,' I said, looking down at my notes. 'From now on, you will all be entitled to a free pastry or sandwich during your break. If the teashop is busy, Mrs Lark doesn't object to your taking it through into the kitchen, though I hope before the end of our first season of working together to make a little Friends staffroom out of one of the disused rooms in the East Wing.'

That idea seemed to go down well.

'Lucy and I will be sort of floating personnel, filling in where needed, so if any of you can't get to the house for a break you can radio for what you want, and one of us will bring it.'

'Meals on wheels,' Pam said.

'Meals by golf buggy, anyway,' I agreed. 'Now, two other changes that I hope will also make your jobs easier are that you will all have radios, so you can contact each other if necessary; and all Friends will be paid travelling expenses.'

'By radios, do you mean walkie-talkies?' asked one elderly man, whose head had been going up and down like a nodding dog throughout the whole meeting.

'Yes – little ones. We had them where I worked before, and they are very useful.'

An excited buzz of conversation broke out. Effie held her hand up. 'I think I can speak for all of us when I say that that is all very acceptable and shows you value our input into preserving Winter's future.'

'I certainly do. I don't think Winter's End would *have* a future, without you,' I said sincerely. 'None of my plans would work without your help.'

Pam, the buxom lady, nudged Effie and said something in a low voice. 'Ah yes,' Effie said. 'There is just one thing that I wished to ask, on behalf of us all.'

'Ask away,' I said lightly, though my heart sank, wondering whether it would be something that would scupper my whole plan.

'It is this: the Friends originally started as a re-enactment society, which we still are, really.'

'Effie and I started it up,' Aunt Hebe put in, 'though these days I have so many other commitments that I can't always attend the meetings.'

'Oh?' I said, interested. 'What historical period do you re-enact?'

'Elizabethan England,' Effie said.

'Well, that's very interesting,' I began, not quite seeing where the question lay.

'The thing is,' Effie added in a rush, 'that what we would all really like is to be in costume when we are working at Winter's End.'

'You *would*? All of you?' I looked around the ring of faces, astonished.

'Oh yes,' they all chorused.

'Cool,' Lucy said. I could see she was wondering how she would look in a farthingale and ruff.

'Each of us has our own preferences. We take on parts from all walks of life,' Pam said, 'but we serving wenches prefer working in the teashop, appropriately enough!'

'And we're yeomen,' said one of the twin brothers. 'We collect the entrance money at the gatehouse.'

'Well, I think that would be a lovely idea,' I said, 'if that's what you really want to do. And it would certainly fit in with the increased emphasis on the Shakespearean connections of Winter's End and the late sixteenth-century knot gardens. But won't the costumes be uncomfortable, especially in summer?'

'Oh, no, we're used to them,' Effie said, 'and we would welcome the opportunity to wear them more often.'

'I did ask William once,' Aunt Hebe put in, 'but he didn't like the idea.'

'What part do you play?' I asked her.

'Queen Elizabeth, of course,' she replied, as if I should have known. And I suppose I should have guessed, since apart from her hair being no longer red, she bore a striking resemblance to portraits of the Virgin Queen.

'I also would have no objection to donning my costume for an hour or so on visitor days, and walking about the house and grounds with my courtiers.' She bestowed a regal smile on Mr Yatton. 'But I won't have time for more than that – there is much too much to do in my garden and stillroom.'

'That would certainly be an added attraction. Thanks, Aunt Hebe.'

'You must be guest of honour at our next meeting, which will be in the New Year,' Effie suggested. 'Costume optional.'

'Thank you, that would be lovely.' I looked around the table. 'Well, that was certainly a surprise – but a nice one.

I was already thinking of having quiet sixteenth- and early seventeenth-century music playing in the Great Hall, so to have everyone in period dress too will really add to the whole experience.'

'If you don't mind, *I'll* stay as I am,' Anya said.

'Oh, yes, we don't all need to dress up,' I agreed. And it was just as well, because Seth in a doublet and hose could be an attraction to rival Aunt Hebe's Gloriana – I mean, visitors could be killed in the rush.

We had thrashed out lots of details by the time Jonah popped his head around the door.

'People are gathering on the drive, Sophy,' he announced, 'so I'm off to put me Father Christmas suit on.'

'We'd better adjourn the meeting, then,' Aunt Hebe said, getting up. 'Have you mixed the punch, Jonah? Not too strong, I hope.'

'Ottie's doing it now – the usual mixture, that wouldn't hurt a lamb.'

'It had better not,' she said. 'Several of them are driving.'

We all went through to the Great Hall, which smelled of pine and looked magical, with the decorations, sparkling tree and the leaping flames from the fire in the enormous hearth. Anya and Lucy went to help with the food, and Seth came out of the kitchen door backwards, carrying an enormous punch bowl hung with little cups, followed by Ottie bearing a tray full of glasses and cloudy lemonade in a huge glass jug.

There were already big bottles of dandelion and burdock and Vimto at one end of the table, next to a stack of festive paper cups. I helped peel the cling film off the plates of sandwiches, party pies and sausage rolls, helping myself to one or two as I did so. It felt like a long time since breakfast.

'Where's Jack?' Hebe asked. 'He should be here!'

'Perhaps he's still asleep. Maybe someone should go and knock on his door?' I suggested. 'He'll miss all the fun.'

'No, I won't – I'm here,' he called from above, and ran lightly down the stairs, a vision in a silky, open-necked shirt, his golden hair attractively ruffled. 'All ready to hand out alcohol and good cheer to the masses, as usual.'

Clearly his batteries were now fully recharged, which was just as well, for Aunt Hebe sent him straight back upstairs to switch on the CD player.

Good humour unabated, he returned to the sound of 'Good King Wenceslas' and started filling cups with punch for the Friends. Then Jonah appeared from the kitchen, unrecognisable in a totally bogus cotton-wool beard, red suit and black wellies. He arranged himself in the hooded chair while Grace, who had flitted in after him like a wizened Tinkerbell in silver stilettos and a spangly handkerchief-hem dress, prepared to assist in finding the right presents.

'Ready, Miss Hebe,' he said.

'I can hear people crunching about on the gravel outside, Aunt Hebe,' I said nervously, as we took up our positions in front of the door, ready to regally receive our visitors. 'Why haven't any of them knocked?'

'They are waiting for the door to be opened, of course. Seth – could you do the honours?'

Seth, who had been leaning on the fireplace with one booted foot up on the fender, looking rather broodingly into the fire like a mislaid extra from a romantic drama, said, 'Of course.'

Then he cast a handful of pine cones onto the flames, which changed colour like a magic trick. 'Let the festivities commence!'

Chapter Thirty-one: Lord of Misrule

They have not let mee sleep these three days, so that I grow dizzy, and have little time alone in which to think – which I must suppose is their intention. I have ink and paper for letters, so may still write, but it becomes harder to conceal my book. I must ask them to send Joan to mee soon, and let her take it away.

From the journal of Alys Blezzard, 1582

By the time Aunt Hebe finally let me relinquish my place at the door, my hand had been shaken so many times it felt twice the size it usually did, and slightly numb.

The Great Hall was full, hot and noisy, and I didn't remember seeing half the people there come in. Many of them were total strangers, but there were lots of familiar faces too, like Mike, off duty and in jeans and sweatshirt, talking to Anya, Milly from the mobile dog parlour, the tenant farmer, the gardeners, the Friends . . . *and* all their families right down to grandchildren and, for all I knew, great-grandchildren.

No wonder my Christmas gift list had been a long one!

And thank goodness I had wrapped up a few extra presents too, because an excited queue of children still waited for their turn with Santa. The adults had found their own (mainly food and drink) gifts on one of the trestles, and they also seemed to have found the punch bowl . . .

In fact, there must have been a run on it, because it looked as though Jack was mixing a fresh batch. As if feeling my gaze he looked up and smiled at me, then abandoned his post and brought me a glass over.

'Drink this – you look as though you need it!' he said, slipping a friendly arm around me and giving me a squeeze. 'Enjoying your first Winter's End party?'

'Actually, I don't think it *is* my first,' I said, sipping the spicy mixture cautiously. Lady Betty had always mixed a mean bowl of punch, but although it caught at the back of my throat in a familiar way, this tasted nothing like it. 'I vaguely remember them from when I was a small child, especially Santa. It's odd how things keep coming back to me that I'd totally forgotten about.'

'Ho, ho, ho!' bellowed Santa suddenly, his eyes glittering and his cheeks flushed above the white beard. A small child burst into tears, snatched her present and scuttled off, and Jonah took a long drink out of a small tankard. I hoped it contained lemonade or something else entirely innocuous, but rather doubted it.

'There's hardly any alcohol in this punch, is there, Jack? Only Jonah looks a bit flushed and . . . well, lots of people seem to be getting very noisy and a bit excited.'

He shrugged. 'That's parties for you, darling – the punch is harmless, about one part brandy to a hundred of the other stuff.'

'*Wassail!*' yelled Bob in my ear, almost unrecognisable without his hat, clinked glasses with me and then ambled off, grinning. Someone had stuck a 'this way up' sticker on his back that I remembered from the hippo crate.

I took another, more suspicious, sip of my drink and rolled it around my tongue. My eyes watered. 'Jack, I'm sure this—' I began, when to my astonishment I spotted Mel Christopher making her way into the hall, supporting a small, silver-haired woman with black eyebrows and red lipstick.

'What's *she* doing here?' I exclaimed.

Jack turned and looked where I pointed. 'Mel's mother's an old friend of Hebe's but her health isn't good, so I haven't seen her about for quite a while.'

'I think Mel's got a damned cheek, showing her face here after booby-trapping my summerhouse!'

'Well, even so, I don't think you can very well throw her out without causing a scene, if Hebe invited her mother. But let's not worry about *her*,' he added, and I realised he had been quietly edging me into the darkest corner, near the pushed-back screens, without my noticing. 'Now, darling, let's talk about you and me and Barbados—'

'Jack Lewis!' said a voice pitched to shatter glass. 'I've got a bone to pick with you!'

'Er – hi, Mel,' he said weakly, letting go of me suddenly. 'Happy Christmas!'

Her eyes flashed with fury. 'Balls to that! I've just discovered you've knocked my house down without even bothering to mention it to me – *and* without permission from the council either.'

He looked taken aback. 'I told the boys to do it after Christmas when I was away! And I was *going* to tell you, Mel. We're partners, remember?'

'But there'll be a swingeing fine for knocking it down without permission. I didn't expect to be partners in *that*,' she snapped.

'The fine's nothing, when you think how much we will make from selling the land for development,' he assured her. 'They can't make us rebuild the house so we're bound to get the planning permission eventually.'

'And you were going to tell me this *when*, precisely?'

'Before it happened, obviously, Mel.' He tried out a

charming, placatory smile, but it didn't seem to be having much effect.

Her cold brown eyes fell on me. 'Something else seems to have slipped your mind too – like telling me you were off to Barbados with Ben's crowd by private jet right after Christmas – and taking *her* with you.'

'A private jet?' I squeaked.

'Of course. How else do you think I could get you on a flight at a moment's notice?' he said, glancing at me impatiently. 'Now, look, Mel—'

'Look nothing! I found out when I ran into Ben in London and he asked me too. He said I could take anyone I wanted with me.' She looked around and gave a ravishing smile at Seth, who was standing nearby, his clouded jade eyes fixed sombrely on her lovely face. 'Seth's coming – so that's going to be cosy, isn't it? Love Island!'

I suddenly felt unbearably sad, which was probably due to having inadvertently drained the whole large glass of punch. I could feel it burning its way down into my innards. Innocuous, my foot!

'Actually, it won't be that cosy, Mel, because I won't be going. I've got too much to do here,' I said, 'but I hope you three have a lovely time.'

Jack stopped being placatory and shot daggers at Mel. 'Sophy, darling—' he began, but I quickly put as many people between us as possible, though I hadn't realised that Seth had followed me until he said, practically in my ear, 'I wouldn't have any more punch, if I were you. I think Jack's spiked it.'

'I thought as much and there's practically none left now. But there's loads of lemonade and other soft drinks, so perhaps they'll drink that instead and it will dilute it.' I looked up at him. 'Shouldn't you be at home, packing your Bermuda shorts and sun lotion?'

'Shouldn't you be restringing your bikini?' he countered.

'I haven't got a bikini, and you must have heard me say I'm not going. I'd already told Jack when he first invited me, but nothing seems to get through his thick skull once he's got an idea lodged in there. It didn't sound like my idea of fun even if I hadn't got too much to do here already – and I've only just got Lucy back again, so I couldn't possibly go off right now.'

'Neither could I,' he agreed. 'It's not my scene either.'

'Mel seems to think—'

'Mel thinks I'm a dog that can be whistled up any time she likes. She hasn't even asked me – that was the first I'd heard of it.'

'Oh,' I said, suddenly feeling a bit happier – but that was probably the effect of the glass of punch. Just as well I'd only had the one.

A strange figure emerged from behind the huge carved screen and did a bit of languid cavorting in a very take-it-or-leave-it way. 'Is that Derek? Why is he wearing antlers and greenery?'

'Because he's the Lord of Misrule.'

'The *what*?'

He shrugged. 'Lord of Misrule. There's always one and nowadays it's usually Derek.'

He took the empty punchbowl back to the kitchen, while I sipped cold lemonade and watched Derek's antics. They consisted mainly of jogging half-heartedly across the room from time to time and holding what looked like a mistletoe-draped bladder on a stick over the heads of some unlikely couple, until they kissed.

I found this quite amusing until Jack resurfaced, having managed to shed Mel, and Derek shambled across and held his stick over our heads. Jack grabbed me and tried to comply a little too enthusiastically, his aftershave almost

348

entirely extinguished by the smell of brandy – so not *all* of it had gone in the punch.

I was just thinking that it didn't so much feel like being kissed as attacked by a leech, when a grave voice in my ear said, 'Hello, Sophy.'

'Guy!' I exclaimed, repulsing Jack with more force than politeness, and hugged Guy warmly. 'How lovely to see you.'

It was several months since I'd last set eyes on him and he was even more handsome than before – dark auburn hair and the same dark-ringed grey eyes as Anya.

He returned the hug. 'There are six Morris dancers outside, Sophy, and they say you have to go and officially invite them in.'

'Lucy is going to be *so* pleased to see you! How long is it since you last met – about two years? She had such a bad time in Japan, but now she's back—'

'The Morris dancers,' he reminded me patiently. 'It's brass monkeys out there. Don't bother about me, because I'll sort out who's who after the party. And there *is* Lucy . . .' He trailed off, staring across the room at her. She was handing round mince pies, wearing a crown of twisted silver tinsel on her head and a pair of white fairy wings.

Lucy glanced in our direction, caught Guy's eye, did a double take and stared at him incredulously, though she'd known he was coming. But then, he had changed a bit in the last couple of years . . .

Guy was staring back, his face serious, then they began to move slowly towards each other through the throng, like sleepwalkers.

'Funny, I thought they'd be pleased to see each other,' I muttered.

Just as Lucy came to a halt a bare couple of inches from Guy, Derek capered up and practically beat them over the head with the mistletoe stick.

They were still kissing when Seth came to remind me about the group of now shivering Morris men and we had to take the poor things into the kitchen to thaw out. But after a drink or two they warmed up with a brisk measure in the middle of the Great Hall.

Then the fiddler with the Morris men started playing a catchy tune and suddenly everyone was dancing, including me and Seth, and it didn't matter that I didn't know how, because the fiddler called instructions out as he played. We all circled and hopped and swung around until we were hot and breathless.

I tell you, I'm not used to going it like that in the *evening*, let alone late morning.

I didn't see Mel or Jack dancing, though Santa got up and danced with Mrs Lark, and Anya and Mike, Lucy and Guy and most of the Friends joined in. I saw Ottie sweep past with Bob, and Aunt Hebe tripped a very stately measure with Mr Yatton. In the end there were so many dancing that you could do little more than jig up and down, which I found myself doing, nose to nose with Seth. Or maybe, since he is a lot taller than me, that should be nose to chest.

When the music stopped he grabbed me and kissed me right on the lips, so Derek must have popped up even though I didn't see him that time. Then he looked down gravely and said, 'Happy Christmas, Sophy.'

I stared up into his green eyes. 'Happy Christmas, Seth.'

His arms tightened around me. 'Sophy—'

'I'd put her down, you don't know where she's been,' Melinda slurred, grabbing his arm – but more to stop herself falling over than possessiveness this time, I think, so maybe Jack had been keeping her quiet with his brandy stash.

'This one's mine,' she said to me. 'You might as well make do with Jack, if you can get him.'

'I think perhaps it's time you left, Lindy,' I said coldly.

'In fact, you've got a nerve even coming here, after rigging that accident up for me in the summerhouse!'

Her lovely face went blank, so clearly she'd entirely forgotten about it. 'That was ages ago . . . and it was just a *joke*,' she muttered, looking away.

'You told me that you had nothing to do with it,' Seth said, turning to look at her with a frown.

'Well, it's over, let's not rake it up,' she slurred. 'And I don't see why I shouldn't be here, because Jack and I are old friends and anyway, Seth wanted me to come, didn't you, Seth?'

'No,' he said uncompromisingly.

'Liar.' The smile was supposed to captivate him, but was lopsidedly tipsy. She looked back at me and said spitefully, 'Do you think Jack would want you if you didn't have Winter's End? You don't even know who your father is – but he was probably some gypsy from the look of you.'

'I do know, actually – and you're quite right, he was a gypsy.'

'No, he wasn't,' Ottie said unexpectedly from behind me, where she was standing with Hebe and Mr Yatton. 'Is that what Susan told you?'

'Well, it was *one* of the versions,' I confessed, 'but it seemed the most likely one. Do you mean it wasn't true?'

'Certainly not, it was one of the Pharamonds, from over at Middlemoss.'

'That's what William thought,' Hebe chipped in doubtfully, 'but apart from the dark colouring, she doesn't really look like them, does she?'

'No, but I saw them together once and Susan admitted it to me – but I'm not saying which one, because he was married then, and he's dead now. Sophy, we'll talk about it later, OK?'

'OK,' I said a bit numbly, having found and lost my real

351

father inside a couple of minutes. I thought about Nick Pharamond at the Middlemoss bonfire, who presumably was some kind of relation to me ...

'It doesn't really matter who her father was anyway – Sophy's a Winter, *that's* the important thing,' Aunt Hebe declared.

Lucy broke through the interested circle that had formed around us and linked her arm in mine. 'What's going on?'

'Nothing, darling – and here comes the coffee, everyone!' I called, as Mrs Lark and Grace trundled a trolley in.

Mel looked as if it would take more than a cup of coffee to revive her. She was now in a state of almost total collapse, supported only by Seth, whose face was inscrutable.

'Chloe!' called Aunt Hebe in her crystal-clear tones, head and shoulders above most of the crowd. 'Melinda has had too much to drink – you'd better take her home!'

Between us we loaded Mel into the passenger seat of their car, though we had to pry her fingers off Seth first. Then Chloe drove gingerly off, sitting bolt upright behind the steering wheel.

'Perhaps someone should have taken them home?' I said doubtfully.

'Don't look at me,' Seth said. 'I had some punch too, don't forget.'

'It's Chloe's car, she'll be all right,' Aunt Hebe assured me.

The appearance of the coffee urns had been a signal that the end of the festivities – and the unexpected entertainment – was nigh. Now people began to leave, laden with leftovers because, as Ottie put it, we didn't want to be faced with party pies and limp crackers at every meal for the entire festive season.

'Or even for dinner tonight,' she added.

'It's Lancashire hotpot,' Mrs Lark said, offended. 'It's all ready, it just needs warming up.'

'You must be exhausted, Mrs Lark,' I said, 'after all that.'

'Not me – but I'll put me feet up for a bit after everything's cleared away.'

'You do that now – *we'll* clear up,' Lucy offered, 'won't we, Guy?'

'We'll all help. It won't take long that way,' I suggested, which it didn't, especially since Mike had stayed to help too. Jack seemed to have vanished totally.

Mrs Lark must have let the kitten out, for I found it curled up asleep with Charlie on the rag rug by the fire. From the way Charlie's stomach was distended, he'd been fed at least one mince pie too many by the children when I wasn't looking.

Chapter Thirty-two: Touched

They talk of putting mee to the water next, and the thought of the icy river chills mee to the bone. The gaoler says there is so much evidence against mee now that unless someone in high position speaks for mee, I may yet hang – unless I drown or die of the cold first, I suppose.
From the journal of Alys Blezzard, 1582

When everything was cleared away, Lucy said she was going to help Guy take his things up to his room and then show him the rest of the house – and goodness knows what else, because they had been more or less permanently entwined since setting eyes on each other.

The aunts had gone off on their own affairs and I discovered Jack fast asleep on the drawing-room sofa, with the whisky decanter next to it, snoring with his mouth open. Not a pretty sight.

So that left just me, Seth, Anya and Mike, and since Mike was on duty that night and had to go home, the rest of us decided to walk into the village with him for some air. I made Charlie come, too – he needed to burn off some of those mince pies and other unsuitable titbits. So did I, come to that, but also I needed to clear my head and think about things. It had been an eventful day. Although the snow of a few days earlier had quickly vanished, it was very, very cold, especially after the warmth of the Great Hall. There was still ice on the puddles in places where the sun couldn't reach and leaves crunched crisply under our feet.

At first we weren't very talkative on the way down and Seth looked rather brooding – as well he might, with his lover trying to play him off against Jack. But he revived slightly when I remarked, on passing through the rusted rear gates of Winter's End, that rubbing down and repainting *those* was another important job for the New Year.

'Are you serious? It's *low* priority,' he insisted. 'The visitors aren't going to see them, so they can wait. There are other, more urgent things to do first.'

'They may rust away entirely in the meantime, and they're lovely gates,' I said, noting that he had lost the brooding, abstracted air and that the glint of battle was back in his eyes.

We were still bickering about it when we got to Sticklepond, where Anya elected to stop off at Mike's house for a bit and then make her own way back up to Winter's End.

Seth, Charlie and I carried on through the village and up the lane past the Winter's End car park.

'See how nice the front gates look now they're repainted and gilded,' I pointed out as we came within sight of them. 'And the rear gates are smaller and less fiddly, so it wouldn't take Bob so long to do . . .'

I tailed off as we spotted the familiar shape of Mel's large grey horse tied up behind the lodge house.

Could she possibly have sobered up that quickly? It was only a couple of hours since we'd poured her into the car and seen her off with feelings of profound relief! Pity we hadn't come across her earlier, so Mike could have arrested her for being drunk in charge of a horse.

Seth's face had gone all tight-lipped and brooding again.

'I see you've got company,' I said coolly. 'See you later. Come on, Charlie, nearly home.'

Seth grabbed my arm. 'Sophy, I—'

The lodge door began to open. 'Oh, damn!' he said, letting go of me suddenly and striding off.

I left him to it. I had a call I wanted to make anyway. I needed to ask Ottie one or two questions about what she'd said about my father. I found her in the studio as usual, though she wasn't wearing her working overall of plaid shirt and streaks of clay, but slim black jeans and a cream silk shirt.

'Hi, Sophy. I was expecting you to drop in. Have a glass of champagne?'

'Are you celebrating something?'

'Yes, finishing the sculpture – and one or two other things,' she said, handing me a glass, and though after the glass of punch earlier I'd rather gone off the idea of alcohol, I took it.

'Ottie, was that true what you said earlier – my father *was* one of the Pharamond family?'

'Yes. I assumed Susan had told you.'

'She told me so many different versions, but never the real one. Are you sure?'

'Quite sure. His name was Leo Pharamond and he was married at the time – and he is dead now. He was charming, but he certainly put it about a bit – like Jack, come to think of it.'

'Oh? Well, it's good to know, even though I can't very well make myself known to the family, can I? But I have a family of my own now, so it doesn't really matter any more.'

'Yes, and it is remarkable how like that portrait of Alys you are. It's much more evident now you've had it cleaned.'

'There are one or two dark-haired Winters among the portraits, though perhaps not quite as dark as me, so my colouring isn't entirely due to the Pharamond genes.'

'Mmm . . .' Ottie, the subject explored, seemed to be losing

356

interest and, glass in one hand and cheroot in the other, was regarding her finished sculpture fondly. '*The Spirit of the Garden* can go to be cast right after Christmas.'

'It's very generous of you to give us a sculpture, Ottie. I'm sure lots of people will want to come and see it. Seth showed me that small biography of you they did at the time of your last big exhibition, *Ottilie Winter: Cast Lives*. I thought we could stock copies of that in the shop, and perhaps have postcards done of the sculpture too.'

'You could have postcards made of the sketches for it as well, if you like?' she offered. 'In fact, you can *have* the sketches. You could hang them in the café to give the punters something to look at with their tea.'

'Thanks, Ottie,' I said gratefully, though I thought that even sketches by my celebrated aunt might be too valuable to risk on open display.

'And remember, if push comes to shove and you look like losing the house, you can sell the sculpture.'

I sincerely hoped it wouldn't come to that, but she was right – it did give me a valuable asset. But it also might prove a visitor attraction.

'Seth not come back with you?' she asked. 'And where's that nice friend of yours got to?'

'Anya's gone to Mike's house for tea. He's coming for Christmas dinner. I left Seth at the lodge because he had a . . . visitor.'

'Not Mel? Don't tell me she sobered up *that* quickly,' Ottie said in amazement.

'Perhaps she's come to persuade him to go to Barbados with her after all.'

'Well, he won't,' Ottie said confidently. 'Even if he'd wanted to, which I'm sure he doesn't, he wouldn't leave his beloved knots for that long, would he?'

'Probably not,' I conceded.

'What about you, though? Doesn't the idea of joining the jet set in the sun appeal?'

'No, not in the least. I'd much rather be here, getting Winter's End ready to open.'

'You know, you and Seth have *so* much in common,' she mused.

'Unfortunately, we have even more *not* in common,' I assured her.

I'd left my bag containing my bunch of keys and notebook upstairs in my room that morning, though tucked out of sight at the back of the wardrobe. They were still there, but so too was a familiar, lingering trace of Amouage Gold.

I flew downstairs to the parlour, which was empty apart from more aromatic evidence that Jack had been there. Could he *really* have been so unscrupulous as to take my keys and look for the household book in my absence, or did I have a nasty, suspicious mind? I hated the thought that he might have even touched Alys's coffer . . . though if he had opened it, he would have been disappointed to find only a Victorian book of bible stories inside.

While I was still standing there, undecided, the man himself startled me by sticking his head round the door. 'There you are, darling! I've been looking for you. I hoped you would come back alone.'

'Have you already been in here today?' I asked him sharply.

'Yes, of course – upstairs, downstairs and in my lady's chamber,' he said, smiling innocently.

'Oh,' I said lamely, wondering if I'd misjudged him. 'Why were you looking for me, Jack?'

'To apologise for putting brandy in the punch – but honestly, it was only a smidgen out of my hip flask to liven it up, not much at all. I've already apologised to Aunt Hebe and she's forgiven me,' he said virtuously. 'We've kissed and made up, and I think you and I should kiss and make up too, Sophy, after all those horrid scenes.'

'It doesn't matter,' I said, which was no more than the truth.

'Yes, it does. Mel is such a bitch! She'll say – or do – anything when she's in one of her jealous rages. But just because we had a quick fling years ago, it doesn't mean I can't fall for someone else now, does it? She just can't bear to let any man go.'

'True, I think she's mending her bridges with Seth right now,' I agreed. 'But, Jack—'

'Come and sit here on the sofa with me, Sophy, I want to talk to you,' he said, looking very serious.

I did, but as far away from him as possible, poised for a fast flight if he started to get smoochy. Alys's warning presence was so evident that I was surprised he wasn't aware of the sudden chill in the atmosphere.

'We've got to know each other very well, haven't we? I knew practically from the first minute I saw you that you were the one for me, and I could tell that you felt the same. Maybe I rushed you a bit too much, but—'

'Jack,' I interrupted, 'please don't!'

He shuffled along sideways like a parrot up a perch and took my hand. 'I know I got things wrong at the start, maybe let pride stand in my way, but now – well, now I see things more clearly. I love you, Sophy!'

To my horror he got down on one knee and presented me with a ring, a huge, flashing diamond. 'Marry me, Sophy. You can open the house if you must, do exactly what you like – just say you will marry me. We'll have a long engagement and—'

'No, Jack,' I began, trying to snatch my hand away as he pushed the ring onto my finger. 'I've been telling you for weeks that I don't feel that way about you.'

'Perhaps you still can't quite believe that I love you, but

by the time we get back from the Caribbean you'll be as mad about me as I am about you,' he said confidently. 'I've even sent the notice of our engagement to *The Times* already – *that's* how serious I am.'

I was tugging at the ring, trying to get it off, and starting to feel angry. 'For goodness' sake, Jack! I really don't feel like that about you in the least and I don't want to marry you!'

He attempted to take me in his arms just as Charlie, alarmed by my raised voice, sank his teeth into his ankle.

'Bloody hell!' Jack roared, and letting go of me, kicked him away.

Charlie yelped, and I swept him up into my arms and kissed the top of his silky, indignant head. 'Darling, are you all right?'

Lucy burst in. 'What on earth is happening? It sounded like a massacre in here! Is Charlie hurt?'

Then she noticed the blinding flash of the ring still on my finger. It would be a bit hard to miss – vulgar simply wasn't in it. '*Mum!*'

'It's not how it looks,' I said hastily. 'I just can't get it off. I think it will take soap.'

'Oh, come on, Sophy, we can tell her – we're engaged,' he announced to Lucy.

'No we're not! I keep telling you, Jack, I'm not marrying you. I'm not even going to Barbados with you. Not, not, *not.*'

'She doesn't love you that way,' Lucy explained to him kindly. '*I* could have told you that.'

'And you'd better take that announcement out of the paper again,' I said. 'Honestly, to think you could do that without asking me first!'

'I did ask you, and you said you just needed a bit more time to get to know me,' he protested.

'No, that's what *you* said.'

He'd thought he could sweep me off my feet, but I could see it was finally and belatedly dawning on him that it wasn't going to work.

'Could you leave us alone?' he asked Lucy and she looked at me doubtfully.

I nodded at her.

'OK – but I'm just next door if you want me. Come on, Charlie.'

When she'd gone, he said discontentedly, 'I can't believe you really mean it.'

'I do. Sorry, Jack, I'm not in love with you and I never will be.'

'Is it Seth? Mel thought you were getting too close. But she's determined to have him – and what Mel wants, she gets.'

'No, of course it's not Seth – it isn't anyone. I simply don't want to marry again, and I don't need to. Winter's End will always be your home, too, but you must stop all this.'

'You can't blame me for thinking you were in love with me. You led me on,' he said crossly.

'I know I did at first, and I'm sorry,' I said contritely. 'I soon realised I didn't feel that way about you, though I am very fond of you, Jack.'

'That's not good enough! Winter's End should be mine. That's what William really wanted – for us to get together. That's why I borrowed money on my expectations – and now I'm overstretched and it's all your fault. If you won't marry me, the least you can do is help me out.'

I looked at him, puzzled. 'What do you mean?'

'Increase the loan against Winter's End to bail me out, until my company's back in profit again,' he said sulkily.

'Absolutely not!'

'Look, it's just a temporary fix I'm in – but it's your fault that I need the money. It's not fair!'

'I'm sorry,' I said finally and, looking furious, he slammed out of the room.

Lucy came back in, carrying Charlie. 'Seth is so much nicer than Jack. I don't know what you ever saw in him.'

'Nice Seth is at this moment shacked up in the lodge with Nasty Mel and, for all I know, will be jetting off to Barbados with her after Christmas.'

'I'm sure he won't. Anyway, we need him, there's lots to do.'

'Tell me about it!' I snapped, sinking down onto the sofa.

'There's no need to be ratty with *me*, just because you made a mess of things,' she said, hurt.

'Sorry, darling, it's just been a bit of a day, to say the least.'

'Hebe told me what Ottie said about your father being one of the Pharamonds,' she said, plumping down next to me on the sofa.

'Yes, I've just been to see her and it's true. It's nice to know for sure, but I'm not going to approach the family. They know nothing about it, so there's no point in raking it all up.'

'It doesn't matter to me,' Lucy said. 'Mum,' she added, having gone into a trance for quite five minutes, 'Guy has to go back to work on Tuesday, so I thought I would go back over there with him for a couple of days, if you don't mind. We have a lot of catching up to do.' She sighed. 'I hadn't realised how much he'd changed . . .'

'No, that's fine,' I said, though feeling a bit hurt that she was leaving me so soon.

'He'll probably come back here with me at the weekend, if that's all right?'

'He's always welcome here. We'll keep the old nursery bedroom ready just for him, if you like, then he can come and go as he pleases.'

'Thanks, Mum!' she said, giving me a hug.

'Where is Guy at the moment?'

'In the stillroom with Aunt Hebe. When she found out he was a biochemist, she said she had one or two things he could help her with.'

'Oh?' I wasn't sure if that sounded ominous or not. 'Anya's off to Scotland for the New Year, but she'll be back well before Valentine's Day, though she says she won't stay in the house, she'll live in her van somewhere on the estate.'

'She seems to have got on well with that policeman – Mike, is it?' Lucy said, interested. 'He's nice – maybe she will stay with *him*!'

'Maybe. You can never predict what Anya will do, so we'll have to wait and see.' I made up my mind, since the day had been one of confessions and revelations, to add one more.

'Lucy, there's something I have to talk to you about,' I said, and told her about her father making contact. 'I didn't want anything to do with him, but perhaps I should have asked you how you felt before telling him to get lost?'

'I don't want anything to do with him, either. We've managed fine without him up until now, haven't we? And I don't believe all that stuff about not finding us was true, do you, Mum?'

'No, to be honest. I think he must be hard up and when he spotted the article in the paper thought I'd come into money. I don't suppose we'll hear from him again.'

'Good,' Lucy said. She got up. 'I'll go and make some tea and bring it through. You look as if you need it!'

Jack had slammed his way right out of the house and didn't reappear for dinner, though Mel's mother, Chloe, phoned later to say that he was dining there.

That was another surprise – I thought Seth would be too preoccupied with Mel to turn up, but no, he suddenly appeared in the kitchen while I was trying to get that damned ring off. Mrs Lark had suggested immersing my hand in icy water for ten minutes and then applying soft soap, and I had just succeeded in finally wrenching it over my knuckles when he came into the kitchen. In fact, the ring shot off and landed at his feet, shining with soapy iridescence.

'There, that's off,' Mrs Lark said with satisfaction. 'Jack gave it to her, Seth, only it was too small and her finger was swelling up.'

Seth, expressionless, picked it up and handed it back. 'Should I congratulate you?'

'No,' I said shortly, but felt in no mood for explanations. He wasn't looking in the best of tempers himself, so things mustn't have gone well between him and Mel. But then, it was his own stupid fault for having an affair with her in the first place.

Aunt Hebe was upset that Jack was not at dinner, presuming, correctly, that he and I had had an argument. But apart from that the meal went quite well. Lucy and Guy were in good spirits, Anya was cheery, and even I was reviving with the relief of actually having got it through Jack's thick skull at last that I wasn't going to marry him.

Ottie was in an expansive mood, due to having finished the sculpture, and then downed a bottle or so of champagne. In fact, she insisted on sending Jonah down to the cellars to fetch a couple of bottles up, and got the Larks in to have a glass while toasting many Happy Christmases to come.

Only Seth remained quiet and gloomy.

Chapter Thirty-three: Dodgy Dealings

Joan has brought my household book as I requested, so that I might add some words to it, directed to my precious child. I must be guarded in what I say: she will take it with this, my journal and lock them away.

From the journal of Alys Blezzard, 1582

Jack reappeared at breakfast on Christmas morning, chastened, ingratiating and apologetic, though he tended to avoid my eye and I knew he was still feeling furious and aggrieved.

For the sake of Aunt Hebe we all pretended nothing had happened, even though everyone knew by now that he and I had had a row, and about the ring.

Come to that, my finger was still sore and swollen.

Like me, Anya is not a chatty person early in the day and once Jack had got his normal bounce back again and gone all cheery, I could see her wanting to kill him.

Lucy and Guy were the last to come down, and too wrapped up in each other to notice much at all, so I hoped this was True Love. I know Anya felt exactly the same – we just never thought it would happen.

Lucy was wearing a jewelled crown that had been in her Christmas stocking, and Guy a pirate scarf. Aunt Hebe gave them a slightly puzzled look, but said nothing. She probably thought they were the latest fashions.

We indulged in an orgy of unwrapping in the drawing room, while Charlie disembowelled a doggie stocking of treats on the priceless, if threadbare, rug.

The gifts ranged from the mundane (Jack had bought everyone a box of chocolates, though apparently he and Seth exchange a bottle of whisky every year, in some pointless male ritual), through the unusual (Anya's recycled tin and paper jewellery and my little patchwork lavender hearts), to the bizarre (Ottie gave everyone a decorative hen, made in Africa from strips of old plastic packaging and twisted wire).

Seth's, which he'd delivered to the house earlier in a trug, were all small potted plants – except mine, which was a single moss rosebud tied up with a sprig of greenery.

'He's cut one of his roses – for *me*?' I said, amazed.

'Strictly speaking, he's cut one of *your* roses, for you,' Ottie said with a grin. 'One of the old moss roses does sometimes have a flower or two at Christmas, though it's not like him to sacrifice it.'

'No, it isn't!' I agreed, stroking the closed petals with one finger to check it was real. 'What's this green stuff?'

'Myrtle,' Aunt Hebe said, giving me a strange look. 'Moss roses and myrtle . . .'

I went to fill a bud vase with water for my rose, which I carried up to my bedroom.

Downstairs everyone was still unwrapping and exclaiming, so I took the opportunity to quietly hand the ring back to Jack. 'I hope you can get a refund. It looks valuable,' I whispered, embarrassed. 'I got soap all over it, but I washed it off.'

'Thanks,' he said shortly, pocketing it, then noticing Aunt Hebe's eye upon us, kissed my cheek and said with a falsely bright smile, 'Happy Christmas, Sophy!'

He adjusted the blue cashmere scarf that Aunt Hebe had

given him around his neck with a flourish and announced, 'Now I'm going to take my favourite aunt out for a drive! Come on, Hebe – a bit of fresh air will give us an appetite for dinner.'

'But it's starting to snow,' I pointed out, for though the day had started off clear but freezing, leaden clouds had been gathering and the first flakes had begun to fall.

'Oh, it won't come to anything,' he said confidently, 'the forecast said a light scattering at the most,' and Aunt Hebe allowed herself to be persuaded.

After they had gone, I slipped away and went out to the camper van, checking no one was watching me. It had occurred to me that now Jack had checked Alys's coffer, he wouldn't bother again, so I could safely return her book to its rightful place – which is what I was longing to do. I just felt it was like putting the last piece of the jigsaw together, the vital bit.

And Alys must have felt the same, for as I locked her treasure away I felt her presence and a soft, satisfied sigh echo through the room.

The other book I replaced in the van. It would be a dead giveaway if Jack saw it lying around the house!

Seth arrived with Mike, and I thanked him for his present and said what a lovely gesture I thought it was. 'But you shouldn't have cut one of the roses off, just for me.'

'It was that or dig the whole bush up,' he said obscurely, then smiled. 'But I'm glad you like it.'

Lucy and Anya had found some games in the cupboard next to the drawing-room fireplace, and we'd all been happily playing Cluedo for ages when Jack and Hebe came back and put a damper on things. I could see from Hebe's expression when she saw me that he had been giving her his version of events, but she also looked worried and upset, so he'd probably spilled the beans about his financial problems too.

Actually, I did feel a little guilty about those, even though it wasn't my fault he'd got into such difficulties. But certainly not guilty enough to risk losing Winter's End by bailing him out.

Ottie glanced at her sister with a worried expression and Seth and Jack didn't look at each other at all: suddenly, there weren't so much hidden undercurrents in the room as hidden rip tides. It was quite a relief when Jonah came in to say that dinner was ready.

The table in the morning room had been extended and covered with a crimson cloth, and there were crackers and linen napkins folded into crisp stars by every place setting.

Lucy, Guy and Seth helped to bring the food to the table, and then Jonah and Mrs Lark sat down with us to eat it.

It's amazing how much good humour can be restored with a turkey dinner, a couple of glasses of good wine, crackers and silly hats.

Anya and I offered to clear away the remains afterwards, while the Larks left for their usual visit to relatives, and Mike and Seth gave us a hand.

Afterwards I took coffee and mince pies through to the library, where Hebe and Ottie were watching television in unusual amity and Lucy and Guy had started to lay out the pieces of an enormous jigsaw on the billiard table, but there was no sign of Jack.

'He's gone round to visit friends; he thought it would cheer him up,' Hebe explained, looking at me reproachfully. 'And luckily he was right about the snow – the merest sprinkling.'

'But very pretty, and I'm so stuffed with food I think I need a walk,' I said quickly, before Ottie asked why Jack should need cheering up. I could see the question was hovering on her lips.

'Good idea,' said Anya, and Mike and Seth said they would come too, though I hadn't the heart to wake Charlie up and drag him out with us, he looked so blissfully rotund and replete.

We started off down the drive together, the crystalline snow squeaking beneath our boots, but had soon split into two pairs, since Anya and Mike lagged behind us.

Seth and I were silent for quite a while, but after a bit we did start to talk. Well, I say *talk*, but in fact we were soon embroiled in one of our more animated discussions over my suggestion that Derek could repair the lime mortar between the stone flags of the Great Hall floor.

'Isn't it enough that you keep borrowing two of my gardeners?' he snapped. 'Now you want Derek, too! And I suppose you'll have them doing anything and everything but gardening, when the house opens to the public.'

'Well, actually, I did think they might take it in turns to check up on the car park and perhaps both go down after everyone's gone to pick up any litter and empty the bins. And what do you think about having the sole entrance for cars and coaches on the main road, where just the coaches come in now? It seems silly having separate entrances, don't you think?'

'I suppose so,' he agreed grudgingly. 'But we'd have to change the access details in the guidebook before it goes to press.'

'Ottie's sculpture will be off to be cast soon. We'll have to make a base for it in the rose garden before it comes back, I suppose.'

'Yes – another job for Derek,' he said gloomily, helping me over a stile.

When I turned to see how far back the others were, I noticed that Mike now had his arm around Anya so that looked promising, anyway.

I skidded a bit on a frozen puddle and Seth took hold of my arm. I was starting to feel a bit *Pride and Prejudice* – and just my luck to be stuck with the tall gloomy one, who wasn't about to declare his passion for anything other than knot gardens and was in love with the female version of Mr Wickham.

Jack left for London early on Boxing Day morning, so I presumed that, in financial straits or not, he still intended to take off for Barbados.

Without him, apart from Ottie and Hebe having one of their spats early in the day on an undisclosed subject, we were all a lot happier, including Alys, who made her presence known more often, in a friendly sort of way.

Lucy went back to Guy's flat with him for a couple of days and Anya and I threw ourselves into sorting out the tearoom and gift shop before she left for New Year in the Highlands. I missed her, but she would soon be settling down nearby for good, which was a nice thought. Seth was again coming up most evenings, because we were finalising the arrangements for the opening day, but since it appears that Mel flew off to Barbados after all, I suppose he had nothing better to do. But he does seem remarkably cheerful about it. I don't know if that is a good sign or not?

Jack phoned Hebe up several times from Barbados, and it turned out that he has persuaded her to sell enough of her stocks and shares to get his firm out of trouble. That's what Ottie suspected and what made her so mad – and me too, when I found out about it, though sort of guilty as well.

How could he do that to her? Hebe said she didn't need the money and he would pay her back anyway, so I hoped he would.

* * *

'I'm told by an inside source that Jack will be featuring on a popular TV programme tonight,' Ottie said, popping in as we were finishing breakfast on New Year's Day. 'It's called *Dodgy Dealings* and I think we should all watch it. It's at seven, Sophy. I'll come over.'

'*Dodgy Dealings*?' I stared at her. 'You mean, exposing something he's done, like a rogue traders programme?'

'Something like that, I think.' Ottie, standing by the hotplate, helped herself to a roll and filled it with crisp bacon.

'I'm sure your information is incorrect,' Hebe said with conviction, 'dear Jack wouldn't do anything wrong.'

'Wouldn't he?' said Ottie indistinctly, through a mouthful of food.

'No – I mean, there may have been one or two little tiny misunderstandings in the past, but that is all.'

'We'll see,' said Ottie.

We all foregathered in the library early that evening, including Seth, whom Ottie had insisted come over.

Lucy – now back from Guy's – as though we were about to watch some blockbuster film, had made a huge bowl of popcorn in the kitchen and was passing it around and we each had a glass of sherry or whisky.

The programme started by explaining that they were there to expose people who hadn't, strictly speaking, done anything illegal, but prospered by taking advantage of the elderly and/or desperate.

They had been contacted by someone who had signed over her house to Jack – an elderly lady, frail and pretty in pink cashmere and pearls. Aunt Hebe exchanged a look with her sister.

'That's Clara Cathcart!' she exclaimed.

Clara explained how she had been widowed and found keeping up the family home very difficult on a reduced

371

income, yet she had hated the thought of leaving it. When Jack Lewis came along, offering to buy the property for a good price and promising that, as part of the deal, she would be able to live out her days there rent free, it had seemed the answer to her prayers. She trusted him because he was the nephew of a friend of her late husband . . .

Mrs Cathcart had duly signed, but soon discovered that by not reading the small print of the contract, she was powerless to stop what happened next.

'I was moved into an estate cottage while my house was "repaired", she said. 'But actually, instead it was divided up into luxury apartments. When I understood what was going on and protested, Mr Lewis explained that I *would* eventually be moving back into the house – into a flat on the ground floor, in what had once been the kitchen quarters,' she said indignantly.

'This fulfilled his contract to house me. Most of the contents of the house had gone into storage . . . I now had to sort and sell most of my belongings, which no longer fitted into my much reduced living space.'

'What do you think of your current accommodation, Mrs Cathcart?' asked the interviewer.

'The flat is quite nice, but it is not at all what I bargained for. It would have been better to sell up in the first place and move away, rather than live in a small part of what was once my home, now full of strangers.'

I think the correct term for what happened next is a sting.

The production team had set up an elderly female actress as the supposed owner of a small stately mansion somewhere in Cheshire, who had answered one of Jack's carefully worded advertisements.

We watched film clips of his original visit, where he exuded the sort of charm I already knew he possessed. Then it cut to his second visit, during which he clearly expected to clinch the deal, with the papers all drawn up ready to sign.

But this time the old lady was directed to insist on slowly reading every word of the small print and querying things, and you could see Jack start to get rattled.

'It says here that you will move me out of the house while renovations take place?'

'Of course. We wouldn't want you breathing in all that dust or being disturbed by the noise. But you would return as soon as it was finished,' he assured her.

'That sounds all right,' she said doubtfully.

'You can trust me,' he said, with one of his delightful smiles. 'Now, if you'd just like to sign here and—'

This was the point where the TV team came in and the presenter said, 'I'm Brent Collins of *Dodgy Dealings*, and I think perhaps you forgot to explain to this lady that when she moves back into her home, it will only be to a small flat in part of it.'

Jack looked initially appalled but soon attempted to talk his way out of it, saying he thought the lady understood his proposals and that he had many former customers very happy with their custom-made accommodation, in which they lived rent free. 'And what I am doing is entirely legal!'

'But you *are* misleading vulnerable people into signing documents that they don't understand, with false promises,' said the presenter. 'But this is one property you won't be getting. Perhaps you could explain—'

But Jack had had enough. 'No comment,' he said, pushing roughly past the TV team and the next shot showed him gunning away down the drive in his familiar sports car.

There was a short, stunned silence around the TV. Then Ottie said brightly, 'Well, that *was* interesting, wasn't it? He's going to find it very hard to persuade anyone to sell their house to him after that, and you can kiss your money goodbye, Hebe.'

'I am sure Jack didn't intend to deceive anyone,' Hebe began indignantly. 'It—'

'Oh, come on, Hebe,' Ottie said. 'Of course he did! I've heard he's borrowed on his expectations too. And there are one or two other strange rumours going round – I've asked friends to look into them.'

'I'd heard about Clara Cathcart from Sir William,' Seth admitted, with a worried sideways look at me. 'I told Jack he was sailing a bit close to the wind – we argued about it. And if he's a bit overstretched, then he's going to find it even tougher now, isn't he?'

'This must be why he's been so keen to close all those deals before Christmas. He must have known this programme would be on,' I said. 'He might have warned us – and no wonder he suddenly decamped to Barbados!'

'I think what he did to those elderly people was ethically *totally* evil,' Lucy said. 'I hope he goes bust.'

'Lucy!' said Aunt Hebe, shocked.

'Well, I bet he'd have done the same to Winter's End, if Mum had been spineless enough to sign it over to him.'

'Oh, I'm sure he wouldn't – and Jack is terribly fond of Sophy!'

'It's in much safer hands with Mum, take it from me,' Lucy assured her, but although the programme might have shaken Hebe's faith, she continued to defend him.

Next day the announcement of my engagement to Jack appeared in *The Times* (I had entirely forgotten that he'd said he'd sent it) and I had phone call from a tabloid, though Mr Yatton fielded that one.

I wrested Jack's number in Barbados away from Aunt Hebe and phoned him, telling him we had seen the TV programme and also that he'd forgotten to cancel the engagement announcement.

He sounded relaxed and amused. 'The programme was a big deal about nothing. They can't touch me, I haven't done anything illegal. In fact, I made very nice little apartments for the owners, all mod cons. And I didn't cancel the announcement because I thought it would get my debtors off my back until things are sorted out, if they think I'm about to marry you. Look, just play along with it for a couple of weeks, OK?'

'*Not* OK! Absolutely not!' I said, and slammed down the phone.

I sent an announcement to *The Times*, unengaging myself, despite Hebe's pleadings.

Chapter Thirty-four: Revelations

Joan promises to teach the child well, to give her the key to the coffer when she should be of an age to value its contents and to make known to her the truth.
                    From the journal of Alys Blezzard, 1582

'It's nice to be just us two again, isn't it?' Lucy said a week or so later. She was curled up on the parlour sofa with a book and I was sewing my patchwork. Charlie was lying on my feet, which had gone numb, though I hadn't got the heart to move him.

'Yes, it doesn't often happen now, what with Hebe and Ottie constantly around, not to mention Guy turning up at the weekends. And you spend every morning with Mr Yatton.'

'I'm as likely to find you arguing with Seth in here every evening, or even vanished down to the pub,' she retaliated. 'And at least my mornings with Mr Yatton are productive. The Winter's End visitor website is up and running and we've successfully bid on eBay for a chiller cabinet for the tearoom, and a couple of display cabinets.'

'My arguments with Seth are productive too,' I protested. 'Well, they are if I win them . . . He is so stubborn, sometimes there's just nothing doing with him. But that's head gardeners for you.'

She cast me an unfathomable look. 'Aunt Hebe said that rose he gave you at Christmas was significant.'

'I don't know what she means by that, but it was certainly a surprise. I didn't think I rated one of his precious roses.'

'Oh, I'm sure he thinks you're worth a rose. Mum, while we are alone, do you think I could look at Alys's book again? It's ages since I've seen it.'

'You're not going to start treasure-hunting like Jack, are you?'

'No, I just want to refresh my memory, and I'm curious to see the box too.'

'All right,' I agreed, but I still made sure the shutters were closed over the windows and locked the doors before I opened the corner cabinet.

I lifted Alys's household book onto the table, while Lucy admired the way the inside of the chest was carved, and the compartments and false drawer fronts.

'This is really cute,' she said. 'What are these little stones?'

'Some sort of runes, I think, but I'm not sure. Put these cotton gloves on if you are going to touch the book. I keep some in here specially.'

She sighed, but did as I asked and then opened the book at the flyleaf, thoughtfully reading the inscriptions.

'I'll go and make us some coffee,' I said. 'Do you want gingerbread? Mrs Lark said she was making it earlier.'

'Mmm . . .' she said, engrossed.

When I came back she had gone back to examining the box, and had not only entirely pulled out the little drawers but was carefully studying the interior, her fair head bent low.

'What are you doing?' I said, setting the tray down a safe distance away from the chest. 'I know the inside is interesting, but not *that* interesting!'

Lucy, a look of concentration on her face, removed an

apostle coffee spoon from a saucer and applied the tip of the handle gently downwards . . . There was a small sound: 'There!' she said triumphantly.

'What is it? You haven't damaged it, have you?'

'No, I just had a hunch. There was only one rose carved among all those leaves and flowers, right down inside the central part of the chest where the household book was, so since Alys said the secret lay at the heart of the rose, I wondered if something might happen if I pressed it – and it has. See?'

I leaned over and she demonstrated. 'This bit of wood that looks like part of the carved design slides out at the front and there's a cavity underneath.'

Something lay within. 'It's another book – and hidden right under the first! I wonder what this one is. It's a tight fit,' I added, manoeuvring with the end of the apostle spoon.

'I was thinking the other day, when I read in the new guidebook about how Alys came here in her mother's place to try and heal the heir of Winter's End, that maybe she would have brought some recipes for the remedies she would need, written down. So I bet it's Alys's *own* household book.'

'Let's see if you're right,' I said, opening the slender volume with great care. On the first page was written, in faded ink and a difficult-to-read hand, 'This is Alys Blezzard's book, in her tenth year.'

'You seem to be right – except she began it long before she came to Winter's End.'

Side by side we sat, trying to make out the entries on each page. Most were lists of herbs and plants, with their uses, and recipes, some more esoteric than others. Gently leafing through, eventually we came to an upside-down page. A couple of scraps of loose parchment fell out, one inscribed with the pre-Christian symbol of good fortune called a Chi-rho cross, the other a line or two of verse. I picked it up, read it through, then stared at the scrawled initials on the bottom.

'A poem?' Lucy said, peering at it. 'The ink is more faded than that in the book, isn't it?'

I held it, my heart beating fast, remembering how I had laughed when Ottie had told me the family secret.

But Lucy was more interested in why the middle page of the book was upside down. 'Oh, I see,' she said, turning the whole thing over, 'she wrote something else, starting from the back. It looks like a sort of diary, though there are no dates, just years.'

I tore myself from the scrap of parchment, but not before gently laying it down in the centre of the table, as though it would shiver into dust at the lightest touch.

Lucy was right, it *was* Alys's journal of sorts, her thoughts from the day she was told she was to come to Winter's End in her mother's place and, though the handwriting was difficult to make out, we deciphered most of it.

It took us ages and at some point I heard Jonah try the door on his rounds of locking the house up, pause, and then go on. But we couldn't stop reading until we got to the end, and I know my face was wet with tears when I finished it – it was so sad. Lucy was sniffling, too.

Where it abruptly ended, another hand had added:

Some say they see the ghost of my mother, dressed in grey, beckoning the priest from the house and others say they have seen her shade dance like one abandoned in the oak glade. I feel her presence sometimes when I am in the little parlour where she spent much of her time, or walking in the fine knot garden; and some-times there is a scent of roses where none blooms. She did betray her husband, yet the Wynters in their turn betrayed her. But I feel she is now at peace, believing her actions were preordained and would one day be of use to her descendants here, in the place she loved. Until that day comes, if come it does, her inmost secrets were best concealed from curious eyes. Anne Wynter

'So Anne knew about this book too. But she only passed on Alys's secret orally; she didn't tell anyone else about the existence of a second manuscript . . .' I said slowly. 'Or the little verse.'

'This maid that's mentioned in Alys's journal must have told her how to find it.' Lucy turned a page or two and said, 'Here's where she says that her lover sent her a "line or two of verse, to her dark beauty". Do you think that's the one on the parchment?'

She reached over to pick it up and I said quickly, 'Be careful – I think it may be rather valuable.'

'WS?' she mused, studying the initials.

But I'd spotted another addition on the back of it, in Anne's bolder hand. I read out hollowly, '"These lines were penned by my true father, who was afterwards one of Lord Strange's men and made a name for himself in London with playwriting . . ."'

'Playwriting?' Lucy looked up at my bemused face. 'It's not – it can't be . . . ?'

'Shakespeare? According to Aunt Ottie, yes it is.'

Lucy went off into a peal of laughter, just as I had done when Ottie'd told me.

'No, really, Mum, it can't be true!'

'It all looks pretty authentic to me,' I said soberly. 'You know, it does sound as if Alys expected the truth to come out one day, when it would help Winter's End and her descendants – and there is nothing more likely to put Winter's End on the map than discovering something like this!'

'It certainly would be mega, mega publicity, whether we could prove it was true or not,' Lucy agreed. 'Oh my God – Shakespeare's my ancestor!'

'The only thing is, Ottie was totally against me using our supposed Shakespeare connection even before we found all this, so I am sure she will hate the idea of making it public.'

'We'll have to persuade her,' Lucy said, her eyes shining.

We called Ottie in next day for a secret pow-wow, while Hebe was down in the village for some meeting or other.

When we showed her what we'd found, she was amazed – and, I think, rather miffed that Lucy had been the one to discover the secret of the box, after all her years of custodianship. She was still reluctant to publicise the discovery, yet it was very clear, at least to Lucy and me, that this was the moment that Alys had predicted, when her secret could save Winter's End.

'And we will have to have the finds verified in some way, by experts, I suppose,' she said.

'They mustn't leave the house,' I said quickly. 'Alys wouldn't like that. I suppose we could get the experts to come to us . . . if we swear them to secrecy first.'

'What if they don't authenticate them?' asked Lucy.

'Oh, I should think they will fall out and argue about it for ever,' Ottie said, 'especially if they are not allowed to take them away to London. But that won't matter, will it? That you found them, and what they appear to be, are the two facts that will bring publicity and visitors flocking to Winter's End.'

'I think we are going to have to involve Mr Yatton,' Lucy said. 'We can trust him totally and we'll need his help.'

'And Seth,' I suggested. 'I'll need him to help me word the press release and all kinds of things.' Which was a bit of a turn around from the day when I was so angry to discover that he knew all about Alys's book . . .

'There are other people we could trust to keep it secret too, like Guy and Anya, but perhaps the fewer that know in advance, the better. What are we going to do about Hebe?' Lucy asked. 'She'd tell Jack right away, wouldn't she?'

'Yes, but she will know something is going on,' Ottie said. 'Perhaps we should tell her that we have discovered Alys's secret treasure hidden in the box, and that it is just another, smaller household book that proves irrefutably that she was a witch? Even if she passed that on to Jack, he wouldn't find it very exciting.'

'So,' Lucy said, her eyes sparkling with excitement, 'when do we go public?'

On Tuesday I drove Aunt Hebe, who was attired in the full regalia of Queen Elizabeth I, including farthingale, ruff and red wig, down to the Friends' meeting at the village hall.

When we got there, even familiar faces like Mr Yatton's looked utterly different in Elizabethan dress. In fact, it looked like we had stepped back a few centuries. They wore costumes from every walk of life, but with a preponderance of the gentry, which I suppose is natural; how many of us would choose to be peasants if sent back in time?

After an official welcome I was introduced to one or two Friends who hadn't been at the meeting, including a small, shy man called Mr Glover, a local antiquarian. He had a bald head framed by wisps of hair and large, lustrous brown eyes . . .

I had a brilliant idea. 'Mr Glover, we could really do with someone to walk around on open days in the character of Shakespeare – and you would be perfect!'

He looked horrified and shrank away. 'M-me?'

'Oh, yes,' Effie agreed, 'what a good idea! And Mr Glover is a poet, too, you know – he would fit the part so well.'

'The odd slim volume,' Mr Glover said modestly, trying to edge away.

Aunt Hebe blocked his escape. 'Come along, Terence, we all have to do our bit.'

'What would I have to do?' he enquired nervously.

'Just wander about the place, holding a quill pen and a roll of parchment, looking for inspiration. You don't have to talk to anyone if you don't want to, you can remain mysteriously silent,' I said encouragingly.

'You might be quite inspired by the experience?' suggested Effie and, in the end, he allowed himself to be persuaded.

'Well, that's that sorted,' Aunt Hebe said, 'so gather round and let's get on with the meeting.'

It appeared that much manoeuvring for favourite jobs had been going on, but an equal sharing had been arrived at – probably by my aunt performing some sort of Judgement of Solomon on anyone reluctant to capitulate.

We had tea and biscuits while the Friends' roles were fine tuned, and then I was escorted to a sort of tissue-paper bower (something to do with the Brownies' activities) where I was to sit and watch the Friends trip a few stately measures.

Some of the serving wenches' blouses barely contained their ample bosoms during the livelier passages, which made Mr Yatton look even happier and poor Terence Glover even more petrified.

In the car going home Aunt Hebe said, 'Well, I think that went very well!' Then she took her wig and crown off, because she said her head was hot.

I caught Lucy in the kitchen this afternoon teaching Mrs Lark how to make sushi. She has given her one or two other recipes too, and apparently our starter tonight will be taramasalata with carrot batons. Wonders will never cease.

I am not sure what Aunt Hebe is going to make of that.

Jack returned from Barbados and paid us a flying visit, greeted by Hebe like a repentant prodigal son, though Ottie took him into the library and gave him a tongue-lashing for borrowing Hebe's money that we could hear from every corner of the house.

He emerged looking hurt and misunderstood, but promised he would pay Hebe back, with interest, when planning permission was granted for the site of Mel's house and he could sell it to developers. He also apologised to me for *The Times* announcement – but then he kissed me and said he would marry me tomorrow if I'd changed my mind, so he is quite irrepressible. But I do think he is genuinely starting to grow fond of me, as I am of him, despite all his devious machinations.

Seth, who was passing through the Great Hall at the time, gave us one of his sardonic looks, but since I saw Mel's grey horse tied up outside the lodge earlier that day, he had no need to talk.

He didn't say whether he found her repentant or not, but the visit did not seem to improve his increasingly dodgy temper and she soon took herself off to London.

Two elderly Shakespeare scholars were practically coming to blows in the parlour (under vows of strict secrecy – I told Hebe they were paper conservation experts), and the rest of the house and grounds resembled an ants' nest that had been stirred with a stick, as the weeks shortened before Valentine's Day.

Seth had finished planting out the lower terrace and was now practically manicuring the rest of the garden with his harried assistants, and Guy was here every weekend, allowing Lucy to boss him into doing all kinds of jobs or vanishing into the stillroom, where he was helping Hebe with her production line.

Anya came back – and quickly moved in with Mike! I heard it was the talk of the village, but I expected they would get over it. She was up here every day, setting up the shop and the stands, arranging stock, getting Lucy to chase up late orders, and making jewellery in the little workshop area she had set up.

There was so much to do and so little time – but there was an air of expectancy and excitement building up at Winter's End that united us all – including Alys. She was happy too, I knew.

One night, a few days before the Grand Opening, I went down to the Green Man with Seth.

As I thought, the journalist, George, was sitting in the corner, reading the paper and drinking a pint of bitter. I went and sat down opposite him, uninvited, and he looked at me warily over the top of his paper.

'George,' I said, 'how would you like me to give you a *huge* scoop, a story that the daily papers would fight to publish?'

'A scoop?'

'Yes, a shocking and amazing family secret handed down through the generations.'

He looked at me cautiously. 'What's the catch?'

'No catch – except that I don't want the story to come out until Valentine's Day. So, you would have to promise to keep it to yourself until the very last minute. Are you on?'

Naturally he couldn't resist the bait, but when I told him all, I thought he might have a heart attack before he wrote the story and had to buy him a double brandy before he got his colour back.

I agreed to let him photograph some of the evidence too – well, facsimiles of some of the evidence, to be honest – for while the real things could never leave the house, I intended to put it about that they were safely locked away in a bank vault.

The article duly appeared in a major daily paper on the morning of Valentine's Day:

> *THE WITCH WHO PUT A SPELL ON THE BARD!*
> *Recently found documents suggest that Alys Wynter, the notorious local witch, was Shakespeare's Dark Lady. If so – even more astoundingly – could the present-day Winter family of Winter's End, near Sticklepond, be the playwright's direct descendants?*

George had made quite a sensational job of it, and the phone began to ring and ring from dawn – but all they got was the estate office answering machine, telling them, 'Winter's End will be opened to the public from one p.m. today. If you are calling about the Shakespeare connection, then no further information will be given at present, though press handouts will be released.'

We were all too busy anyway – busy *and* nervous. The stage was set, the players were in place – lights, camera, *action*!

Chapter Thirty-five: Much Ado

I am not yet seventeen – how brief was my day of dancing in the sunlight! Yet there is enough of my mother in mee to foretell that my child will have a happier life and that all that happened to mee was meant to be. I have laid up a treasure for her descendants. That must console mee.

Alys Blezzard, 1582

I was up on Valentine's Day in time to watch the dawn rise, which it did with serene promise. For once the weather reports were right and it was going to be my favourite sort of weather – bright, sunny and cool.

A late-home fox in the woods on the other side of the valley gave a sharp, short cry, and far below I could see the convoluted pattern of the new knot on the lower terrace outlined with baby box trees, like dark running stitch against the lighter gravel.

The butterflies in my stomach that I'd had all the previous day were totally vanished. I examined the future for portents, and found only the vaguest of darkness around the edges, wispy and insubstantial, no great threats. I wore flat boots, a cord skirt and a fitted mock sheepskin jacket with a broad belt around my waist – Anya said I looked faintly Cossack. The bee brooch, my lucky charm, was pinned to the collar.

Aunt Hebe, still somewhat miffed at not being told about the discovery in advance, was trying to pretend that it was just another day, and said that once the opening ceremony was over she intended seeing to her walled garden, the hens and hives, as usual, though she *might* pop in to see if her line of rose-based items was selling later . . . all in full Queen Elizabeth I dress, of course.

The post brought me a big Valentine's card in Jack's unmistakable handwriting, and it occurred to me that he would probably have read the papers by now too . . .

Everyone was in place. The press and at least two TV crews were assembled in a special area near where I would be cutting the ceremonial ribbon across the drive, and behind me were my VIP guests.

Beyond the red ribbon were massing the public, many clutching copies of the glossy guidebook that had been delivered in the nick of time.

The sun was shining weakly and, as the clock in the stable tower chimed the hour, Fanny and Johnnie tried to upstage me by walking to and fro across the gravel emitting the occasional lost-soul cry. But they vanished the instant the first small child ducked under the ribbon and tried to grab them and I launched into my short speech.

'A hearty welcome, all of you, to the first open day of the year at Winter's End Manor. As you know, our unique garden restoration scheme is nearing completion – a fitting memorial both to my grandfather and the previous head gardener, Rufus Greenwood.'

'Hear, hear!' shouted Hal and Bob.

'Rufus Greenwood's son, Seth, is our present head gardener, and has worked wonders to complete the last part of the restoration in time.' I smiled across at Seth, whom I was pleased to see was not wearing his layers of ratty jumpers, though you still couldn't have mistaken him for anything else except a gardener.

'Now, some of you will have seen the papers this morning and read about our exciting discovery. Many old houses and families have secrets, and Winter's End and the Winters have more than their fair share. I'm afraid I'm going to go a bit *Da Vinci Code* here, but there has been a family tradition handed down among the women of the family, that the present day Winters are direct descendants of William Shakespeare, through a sixteenth-century ancestor, Alys – better known locally as Alys Blezzard, the witch.'

There was a buzz of comment, some of it from the press enclosure. I held up my hand.

'When this secret was revealed to me, I thought it was too incredible to be true. However, we recently discovered both Alys Blezzard's original journal and evidence that this legend was, in fact, true – I believe incontrovertibly, though I expect the experts will fight over it for years to come. You will find a small display, including some facsimiles of the documents, in the Great Hall, and you can also follow the Shakespeare Trail round the grounds. Winter's End is still a work in progress, and I hope that when the house reopens at Easter, you will all come back to visit us again.'

I stepped forward and Seth handed me a pair of large scissors. 'I would now like to declare Winter's End open!'

As soon as the ribbon fell to the ground a great stream of people started to rush past me, rather like the start of a marathon.

'How do you think that went?' I asked Seth, as he leaned over to switch off the mike.

'Fine. But brace yourself, here come the press,' he warned, as they converged on me.

* * *

'That went very well, I think,' Mr Hobbs remarked, when most of the assorted reporters and camera crews had rushed off into the house, or were standing about with their phones to their ears. To my embarrassment, I had been interviewed on TV – as had Aunt Hebe, in full farthingale.

'Miss Hebe looked magnificent, didn't she?' he added, but I had spotted a latecomer, a small, frog-faced man, plodding up the drive.

'Excuse me, Mr Hobbs, but I can see a very unwelcome visitor arriving. Do you remember when I consulted you about the phone call from the nephew of my old employer? Don't go away for a moment, will you?'

I stepped forward as he pushed through the VIPs to get at me. 'Conor, what are you doing here? I'm in the middle of opening the house to the public.'

'Brazenly wearing a stolen piece of jewellery to do it!' he said loudly, practically spitting with rage. 'And I had to purchase a ticket before they would let me through the gate!'

Guy, who was right behind him, said apologetically, 'I didn't like to radio ahead to warn you, in case you were still speaking, but I thought he looked a bit deranged so I followed him.'

'Thanks, Guy. And I do know him – unfortunately.'

'Yes – you know me well enough to realise that I meant it when I said that your theft would not go unpunished, if you refused to return my aunt's possessions—'

He broke off, for Aunt Hebe had reappeared, escaped from her own bevy of excited photographers, in time to hear his last sentence. She was a truly magnificent and, it has to be said, slightly scary sight, in full Queen Elizabeth mode, including red-gold wig and a sceptre.

Conor's mouth dropped open.

'Who is this man accusing my great-niece of theft?' she demanded. 'A *Winter*! How dare he!'

I thought that was a bit rich, since family connections had been well and truly tarnished on national TV by Jack's revelations. Unfortunately, Conor had also seen the programme, for he rallied and said, 'Ha! That would be the Winter family related to the Lewises, who defraud elderly widows out of their houses, would it?'

'Well, you should know, Conor,' I said tartly. 'It's just what you did to Lady Betty, only worse – you killed her.'

'He *murdered* her?' Hebe exclaimed.

'Just about. He got her to sign a power of attorney while she was in hospital after a fall, then he had her put into a nursing home and wouldn't let her back. He took over completely.'

'Rubbish!' he blustered. 'My great-aunt lost her mental faculties after a fall. And in any case, it is beside the point. Sophy persuaded her to hand over two items of valuable jewellery – a brooch and a necklace – and I want them back.'

Aunt Hebe turned to me. 'Do you indeed have these items?'

'She's wearing one. That bee brooch there is mine!'

'Lady Betty did give me this brooch, but I don't have the necklace, she gave that to someone else at the same time, while she was first in hospital and fully in possession of her faculties.'

'Rubbish. The receptionist at the nursing home says she had it when she arrived there, and *then* saw you wearing it after your last visit!'

'She's lying.'

'Prove it!'

Mr Hobbs, who had looking on as if watching a puzzling play, said, 'My dear sir, before making this kind of allegation, you should check your facts properly. There is indeed proof that Miss Winter is speaking the truth and I have verified it.'

I dug into my bag and produced a folded sheet of paper. 'I think Lady Betty had already begun to suspect your motivation when she gave me the brooch, and the cook, Mrs Dukes, the necklace. She insisted on signing a statement saying what she had done and had it witnessed by the vicar, who had known her for over thirty years. So you see, you're not going to get them back.'

His mouth opened and closed. 'Forged,' he said at last. 'You've discovered how valuable they are and—'

He yelped as Aunt Hebe smote him across the head with her sceptre. It was only plastic, fortunately, but it still made him stagger about, clutching his ear.

'I'll have the police on you! Assault – theft—'

'Actually, I *am* the police,' said Mike, who must have arrived while I was distracted.

'Then I wish to charge this woman with assault and—' began Conor.

'*I* didn't see any assault,' Mike said. 'Did anyone else?'

'No,' we all chorused.

'And if you attempt to charge my client with the theft of a brooch to which she has a perfect right, we will countersue for defamation of character,' said Mr Hobbs.

Conor glared around impotently at the circle of hostile faces. 'You ought at least to pay me the value of it. The yellow diamonds alone are worth—'

I squinted down at it. 'Diamonds? I thought they were crystals! But whatever it is made of, it doesn't matter. I love it because Lady Betty gave it to me, not for any other reason, and I'm still not giving it up.'

'I am afraid you haven't got a leg to stand on, Mr Darfield,' Mr Hobbs told him with finality. 'I would advise you to leave now, before charges against you are pressed.'

'Yes, perhaps I should escort you to the gate,' suggested Mike. 'It's time I was off, in any case.'

As they vanished down the drive I said, 'Thank you, Mr Hobbs – and Aunt Hebe, you were magnificent.'

'I know how to deal with *his* sort,' she said regally. 'Now, if you will excuse me, I want to see how my products are selling in the shop, and then change and get back to the garden.'

'Why don't you go and have tea with Mr Hobbs first, before the rush starts? I should think most people are still outside yet.'

'I suppose I could,' she agreed.

'And I had better go and do the rounds, see how everything is going on,' I said absently as a tall figure came into view in the distance, a giant among a family of Japanese tourists. Seth seemed to be directing them into the maze, and I just hoped he would rescue them later if they got lost, for I was sure they would not be able to see over the top of the hedges.

Mr Glover, ruffed and carrying his quill and furled parchment, scurried furtively along a distant path, shadowed at a respectful distance by several visitors. He turned his domed bald head in my direction briefly, then was gone.

When it all got too much for him, I had given him directions to hide in the fern grotto, which was out of bounds to the public. I made a mental note to have a tray of refreshments taken down there later. The poor man would have earned it.

It was late afternoon before things started to quieten down, and I managed to snatch a break, sitting on a bench on the top terrace with Ottie and Hebe (now attired in more mundane cord trousers and a padded gilet).

In fact I was feeling exhausted but very happy, when two things happened to make it rain on my parade: Jack suddenly appeared from the house, and then I spotted Mel

393

Christopher and Seth talking together below. She looked up, then headed towards the steps, trailed by Seth.

'Jack, dear boy!' Aunt Hebe said. 'We didn't know you were coming! Didn't you tell me you wouldn't be able to make it?'

'That was before I read the newspaper this morning!' he said, and I could see he was furious. 'Didn't any of you think to share your fascinating little discovery with *me*?'

'I didn't know either until this morning,' Hebe said. 'They kept me in the dark too – but it is quite wonderful, isn't it?'

'You'll certainly be raking the money in now, Sophy. And this poem, or whatever it is, will be worth a fortune!'

'It doesn't matter what it's worth, we won't be selling it,' Ottie said. 'But it certainly won't do visitor numbers any harm!'

'And don't you think you should give *me* a share in all this?' he demanded angrily.

'Share in what?' asked Mel from behind him. 'Jack, I thought you might be here. I want a word with you!'

'Not now, Mel,' he said impatiently.

'It's never now – and things are getting a little *urgent*,' she snapped.

'You know, I had an interesting phone call from an old friend the other day,' Ottie said conversationally, but in carrying tones. 'I'd asked her to check some rumours out for me – and guess what? Jack and Melinda are married.'

'Married?' I gasped, turning to stare at Jack, the man who had been professing love and pressing me to marry him, all this time. 'Are you *sure*? I mean—'

'Yes, they married quietly in London, a short time before William died. Presumably they kept it quiet because he disapproved of Mel.'

Hebe paled. 'Surely there is some error? Jack—'

But he was looking at me, blue eyes earnest. 'We soon realised it was a mistake, Sophy! When I went down to make her an offer for the house . . . well, one thing led to the other. But we're getting divorced.'

'And you owe *me*, for agreeing to keep quiet about it, all this time!' Mel snapped.

'Oh? And does poor old Seth know anything about it – or that he's been replaced by your rich new lover in London?' Jack said nastily.

I was so stunned by all this that I had entirely forgotten that Seth had followed Mel, until he took two hasty strides forward and felled Jack with a single blow. Then he stood back, breathing heavily.

Jack got up slowly and warily. 'I suppose I deserved that.'

Seth frowned and examined his skinned knuckles. 'Actually, I'm not sure you do. Maybe you deserve an apology instead, since I'd no idea Mel was married to you when she came back here or I wouldn't have—'

He broke off and turned on Mel. 'You lied to me.'

'It was always you I loved, Seth,' she said nervously, taking a step back.

'I can't imagine why you and Jack got married in the first place,' Ottie said frankly, 'except that you are both shallow, grasping types. I suppose like called to like.'

'Thanks, Ottie,' Jack said, with a glimmer of humour.

'Jack thought I was a hugely rich widow,' Mel said sweetly, 'but actually, Clive tied all his money up in his children, without telling me, the bastard. All he left *me* was that monstrosity of a house and a small annuity. But then it turned out that Jack wasn't rich either and he didn't even get Winter's End. I always rather fancied living here, a Lady.'

'You'd never be a lady, because you can't make a silk purse out of a sow's ear,' Ottie said frankly. 'So you fell out when you discovered each other's lack of cash?'

Mel nodded sulkily. 'Jack said if I kept quiet about the wedding, he'd pay me off when Sophy signed Winter's End over to him and I could have money *and* you, Seth. I always loved you!'

Seth's arms were folded across his broad chest, probably to stop him hitting anyone again. 'I don't think you know the meaning of the word.'

'Actually, you have made a slight error of judgement, Mel, because Seth is by no means penniless and he will be *very* well off one day,' Ottie said. 'I've been raking in the money for my sculptures for years, plus my investments have done rather better than Hebe's, and I've left everything to him. He's as close to a son as I've got.'

'*What?*' Melinda looked from one to the other. 'I thought you would leave everything to Sophy!'

'I've given her a sculpture – if she gets desperate she can flog it. Mind you, if Seth is daft enough to marry you once you've divorced Jack, I might be tempted to change my will.'

'I won't be,' he said. 'Her new, rich lover in London can have her.' And, turning on his heel, he walked away.

'Seth!' wailed Mel, running after him and catching at his arm, but he shook her off. She looked back at us and then trailed away.

'So everything you said to me was just a sham, Jack?' I said sadly. 'I never really believed you were in love with me, but to find you'd been trying to cheat Winter's End out of me like that . . .' I shook my head, tears welling.

'Sophy darling,' he said, hurt, 'of course I love you! I meant every word, and we'd have been married the minute my divorce came through. We still can be, if—'

'Oh, shut up!' I said shortly, the tears popping right back into my ducts. 'You wouldn't know the truth if it bit you on the ear.'

396

His smile became more genuine. 'I do love you, Sophy – you're so *acerbic*!'

'Well, come to that, I suppose I still love you, in a way – warts and all. But like a brother.'

'I don't know why you keep saying that Jack has warts,' Hebe said, rallying from her state of stunned stupor. 'I am sure everything has been a frightful mistake and if we go back to the house and talk things over . . .'

'I don't think there's very much left to discuss, Aunt Hebe, and I've got things to do – excuse me.'

Suddenly I wanted to be alone and made for the private side of the garden, where I sank down onto a rustic bench in the wilderness and burst into tears.

'Don't, Sophy,' Seth said, behind me. 'I can't bear to see you cry.'

'Well, go away then!' I snapped, fishing out a tissue and blowing my nose.

Instead he came to sit next to me, looking troubled and sad. 'Jack's not worth crying over, you know – but I suppose there's no point in telling you that. I'm so sorry.'

I stopped sniffling and stared at him. 'I'm not crying over him, you idiot. It's just, well, it's all come as such a shock and I don't know what's real and what's not any more. And I know *you* loved Mel, so to hear all that must have been just as bad for you. But maybe Mel does still love you, in her way, so—'

'I don't think she even understands what the word means. Once I realised that, I knew that a beautiful face just wasn't enough any more.'

'But you've been having an affair with her all this time, so you must care for her and—'

'No, I haven't! I'm ashamed to say I *did* succumb briefly – but that was before I met you. She never gave up trying to get me back, even though she could see I was falling for you.'

'For *me*?' I said incredulously.

'Practically from the moment I met you. But it's all right – I've always known you were in love with Jack, even if you couldn't quite bring yourself to trust him completely,' he said gloomily. 'I knew he was an untrustworthy character with a dodgy set of ethics – and that he and Mel had been having an on-off relationship since she was widowed – but I couldn't say so, could I, while you were head over heels in love with him?'

'But I've *never* loved Jack,' I protested.

He looked up. 'Never?'

'Well, admittedly, I was dazzled by him a bit at first, as you were by Mel, though it soon wore off. How could you possibly think I was in love with him?'

'I haven't been able to think properly at all since you arrived and started turning my life and my plans upside down,' he said, sounding more like his old, argumentative self. 'And I was jealous of Jack.'

I met his eyes and discovered that otherworldly glow in them – this time for me. 'I've been jealous of Mel too, and I knew she was still involved with Jack to some extent because I saw them kissing in the shrubbery once. But I just didn't want to admit to myself that I'd fallen for a big, stupid, argumentative—'

He cut my words off by grabbing me and kissing me hard. Being a perfectionist, his kiss was perfectly planted.

Someone in my head was singing 'Sowing the Seeds of Love'.

Later, walking back to the house, his arm around me, he said, 'Did you never notice that I made a true lover's knot for you in the Shakespeare garden? Or that the moss rose I gave you for Christmas meant my heart was yours?' Is there *no* romance in your soul?'

398

I sighed happily. 'No – and this is never going to work, you know. We're like chalk and cheese, we argue all the time.'

'Yes, but I think we'll make a good partnership now we've both come to realise that the house and the gardens are equal in worth – that, like the two of us, the one is nothing without the other.'

'Perhaps you're right, Seth. After all, if *I* love the house best and *you* love the garden, that balances perfectly. The jewel and the setting – that's what Alys said to me once.'

'Alys? You still think she's talking to you?'

'I *know* she is. And she's currently saying the sixteenth-century equivalent of "What took you so long, dimwits?"'

'It's been a comedy of errors,' he agreed, taking me in his arms again. Then he said, punctuating the words with kisses, 'Shall I compare thee to a summer's day? Thou art more lovely . . .'

He broke off as Lucy came through the arch near the maze. She smiled on us benignly.

'There you are, Mum. Ottie just told me what happened with Mel and Jack, and I wondered if you were all right.' She grinned. 'But I see you are *more* than all right.'

'Yes, but you look a bit pale, darling – are you exhausted?'

'No, I'm angry. I just met my father for the first time, at the gate – drunk,' she added in disgust. 'Guy radioed me when he turned up and said who he was, but I wouldn't have known him from that old photo you've got.'

'Your *father*?' Seth said.

'Don't worry, Mum hasn't seen him for over twenty years,' Lucy said to him kindly.

'My ex,' I explained. 'I'm sorry you had to meet him like that, Lucy.'

'He called me his "wee lassie" in a terribly bogus accent and tried to kiss me, but I told him I knew all about him and didn't want anything to do with him, and that you didn't want to see him, either. Then he got angry and said maybe the papers would want to know some of the things he could tell them.'

'I can't imagine what he *could* tell them, unless he makes something up.'

'I told him to get lost. What a sleaze bag!' she said disgustedly. 'Let's hope that's the last time he turns up.'

I looked at my watch. 'Come on, it's nearly time to close up and we've been away for ages.'

'Relax, Mum. Guy and I have sorted everything out and everyone's coped really well – no crises at all, except Charlie got out of the kitchen at one point and some children fed him cake until he threw up. But he's all right now.'

Everything, in fact, seemed to be all right now . . .

Chapter Thirty-six: Endpapers

This proof of what my mother said should lie hidden, for it would go ill if it were discovered, even though she believed it would one day ensure the fortunes of her descendants and their continuance at Wynter's End. I pray it may be so, but do not see how that might ever come to pass.

Anne Wynter, 1602

One of the newspapers paid Rory money for some lurid stories about my past but, as I pointed out to them when they asked me for my version of events, I was too young when I married him to have had one. I told them all about my struggles as a suddenly single mother instead. The paper ran our two stories side by side and apparently Rory left the country soon after that.

Not surprisingly, I didn't hear from Conor again after Hebe hit him on the head with her plastic sceptre.

Hebe grew reconciled to our marriage, and for her sake Seth and Jack declared a truce. He may be a complete rogue, but I couldn't help but still be fond of my handsome cousin . . .

The Shakespeare scholars continue to argue over the evidence and don't look like coming to a conclusion any time soon, but Seth and I kept the story going by judiciously feeding titbits to the press, through the medium of George.

By May, it was clear that Winter's End had become a top visitor attraction, and we were accepting coach bookings months in advance. My gamble had paid off.

Foreign tourists hung around for hours, cameras at the ready, awaiting Hebe's appearances as the Virgin Queen or to take photographs of each other arm-in-arm with the bashful Bard – if they could catch him.

But then, all the Friends, in their colourful costumes, were a big hit – especially the silent young woman with the curly dark hair who seemed to appear practically out of nowhere when visitors were admiring the paintings in the minstrels' gallery, even though she only smiles and shakes her head when they ask her questions . . .

One fine Sunday, a few days before our wedding in May, Seth and I were looking down at the lower terrace, which had begun to grow together and showed promise of being the most beautiful of the three.

The house was closed, but faint shouts were borne on the breeze as Derek, Hal and Bob earned some overtime, helping to install *The Spirit of the Garden* among the roses.

'I never thought everything could turn out this happily,' I sighed, but Seth, who had that familiar faraway look in his eyes, was obviously turning over some knotty garden problem in his head and didn't reply, except to tighten his arm around me a bit.

'Guy and Lucy will move into the lodge together, when we've had it done up a bit . . . Mike is trying to persuade Anya to tie the knot with him, too . . . And it even looks as if Ottie will manage to badger Jack into repaying Hebe's money, now he's sold the site of Mel's property to developers.'

And there would be no conflict in sharing Winter's End

with Seth, because the house is my passion, the garden his. We complement each other in every way . . .

It was Alys who had made all this possible and I knew she approved of what I was about to do.

I gave Seth a dig in the ribs with my elbow and he grunted indignantly. 'What was that for?'

'You're not listening to me, and there's something I want to show you.'

'Oh God – it's not another design for a replacement summerhouse, is it?'

'No, it's a sort of wedding present, from Alys.'

I fished in my by now battered embroidered bag and produced a card folder containing a slip of torn parchment between two pieces of acid-free tissue. 'Here you are. It's another thing we discovered with the hidden cache, but we didn't tell anyone about it.'

He examined it with interest. 'I recognise that symbol. It's an ancient one, the Chi-rho. And while it's nice of Alys to want to share her magical symbols with me, I don't quite see—'

'Turn it over,' I said patiently. 'She reused a bit of some other document.'

He did and suddenly went still and silent.

'It *is* the lost bit of the garden plan, isn't it?' I asked. 'And though it's pretty faded, can you see what's in the middle of the lower terrace?'

He lifted his head, his green eyes glowing in the way that always made me feel oddly breathless. 'Yes – it's a true lovers' knot,' he said softly, then pulled me into his arms and thanked me in the way I'd hoped he would – while safely holding the precious scrap of parchment well out of harm's reach, of course.

You could never take the gardener out of this man and that, luckily enough, turned out to be just the way I liked it.

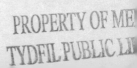

Which season are you?
Take our fun quiz and find out!

1. If you won £5000 on the Lottery what would you spend it on?

A – You would immediately whisk yourself and your loved ones away on a fantastic beach holiday, no expense spared!

B – You would do that home improvement that you've always dreamed of – a swanky new bathroom or an extension to the kitchen.

2. When surfing the net, which are your most visited websites?

A – Your first click is always something that lets you know what's going on in your area – sites like *Time Out* or *Daily Candy*.

B – You are a dedicated Facebooker, and love spending your lunch breaks (or sneaky ten minutes when the boss isn't looking!) catching up with old friends.

3. What kind of food do you most like to cook?

A – You're adventurous in the kitchen, and love to try complicated South-East Asian dishes with unpronounceable ingredients.

B – You're a big fan of comfort food – yummy favourites like mashed potatoes or overflowing bowls of pasta.

4. When it comes to taking time off, what's your ideal way to spend your holiday?

A – Holidays to you mean two weeks of total relaxation, lying on a warm beach with a good book in one hand and a long, cool drink in the other . . .

B – Your ideal break is cultural as well as recreational and you always prefer far-flung destinations to package deals. You're not fulfilled unless you have to get vaccinations before your trip!

MOSTLY A's – Spring/Summer Suzy

Like a lizard, you love the heat and like to be out and about between March and September. You're never happier than when you're lazing on a beach, enjoying an alfresco drink in a pub garden or wielding the tongs at a BBQ!

MOSTLY B's – Autumn/Winter Annie

You love everything about the winter months, whether it's making rib-sticking puddings to insulate you from the cold, wrapping the family's Christmas presents or crunching through piles of autumnal leaves!

Everyone has something to hide . . .

'Trisha at her best' –
Carole Matthews